Undone

Virginia Henley

A SIGNET BOOK

SIGNET
Published by New American Library, a division of
Penguin Group (USA) Inc., 375 Hudson Street,
New York, New York 10014, U.S.A.
Penguin Books Ltd, 80 Strand,
London WC2R 0RL, England
Penguin Books Australia Ltd, 250 Camberwell Road,
Camberwell, Victoria 3124, Australia
Penguin Books Canada Ltd, 10 Alcorn Avenue,
Toronto, Ontario, Canada M4V 3B2
Penguin Books (N.Z.) Ltd, Cnr Rosedale and Airborne Roads,
Albany, Auckland 1310, New Zealand

Penguin Books Ltd, Registered Offices:
80 Strand, London WC2R 0RL, England

First published by Signet, an imprint of New American Library,
a division of Penguin Group (USA) Inc.

ISBN 0-7394-4025-X

This book is dedicated to every woman who has survived a bad marriage, one way or another.

ACKNOWLEDGMENTS

I would like to thank Karen Arasimowicz, a media technician in a school library in Meriden, Connecticut. Karen recognized me while on vacation in Florida and introduced herself. I told her I hoped to write a book about Elizabeth Gunning and was having difficulty finding research sources. Karen had her friend Joanne Pfluger, a retired school librarian, write to offer her research services. I would like to thank Joanne for all her efforts in trying to search out sources for me. I know it was difficult and frustrating because there was so little out there.

I would also like to thank my son, Sean Henley, who is a veritable genius at finding information on the Internet.

Chapter One

County Roscommon,
Ireland—1751

A brilliant beam of sunlight reflecting on the water momentarily blinded him, then, in the blink of an eye, a radiant vision appeared before him. *Is she real, or is she a wood sprite?* he mused. *After all, this is Ireland.*

The girl was slim and delicate, with an ethereal quality about her. As he stared, a sunbeam touched her, forming a glorious halo about her head, and her shining hair, falling in ringlets below her waist, turned the color of pure-spun gold. She stood amidst the tall grasses of the riverbank while dragonflies and tiny insects with transparent wings flitted about her, rising like motes of dust from the myriad wildflowers. He had the distinct impression that if he moved or spoke, he would break the magic spell and she would vanish into thin air.

John Campbell, unable to help himself, couldn't resist quoting *A Midsummer Night's Dream.* "Ill met by moonlight, proud Titania."

The queen of fairies turned her head to gaze at him. "What, jealous Oberon?" She raised a dismissive hand to the dragonflies. "Fairies, skip hence." She lifted a proud chin and glanced away from him with disdain. "I have forsworn his bed and company."

The tall, dark young man took a step toward her and delivered Oberon's line. "Tarry, rash wanton! Am not I thy lord?"

Titania smiled and sank into a curtsy. "Then I must be thy lady."

He closed the distance between them in two strides and, laughing, took her hands and raised her. "What on earth is a beautiful English lady doing unattended in a meadow in the wilds of Ireland?"

He looked compellingly dark and dangerous, but her glance traveled over the fishing basket and the rod slung casually across his back. "I live here. I've come to the River Suck for salmon, just as you have, sir. Come, I'll show you a good spot."

He followed her as if mesmerized to a place where the willows hung low on the riverbank to dip their weeping branches into the water, then sat down beside her and cast his line. The enchanting creature was a mystery he could not fathom. Though barefoot and wearing a threadbare smock that shamelessly revealed her ankles, she spoke in a cultured English voice and was obviously well-read. "You have no trace of Irish dialect in your speech."

Pretending a confidence she did not quite feel, she crossed her legs, cocked her head to one side and launched into a ditty:

"In Dublin's fair city, where the girls are so pretty,
I first set me eyes on sweet Molly Mallone;
Through streets broad an' narrow, she wheeled her
    wheelbarrow,
Cryin' cockles an' muscles, alive, alive-o!"

Her Irish brogue was rich and authentic; her singing sweet and melodious. Her accent changed from Irish to Scots in a heartbeat as she decided to trust him. "I detect a wee burr in yer own speech, laddie. I'd guess ye've spent time in Scotland."

It was an understatement. He'd spent time in Scotland all right. When the Jacobite rebellion broke out to overthrow the king, his father was appointed to command all the troops and garrisons in the west of Scotland. He'd fought alongside his father and the king's son, the Duke of Cumberland, at Inveraray, then at Perth, and finally at the horrific Battle of Culloden where the uprising had been crushed once and for all.

John banished thoughts of war and smiled at her. "My mother is Scottish."

She proceeded to tell him a joke about two Scotsmen concerning what they wore beneath their kilts. The subject matter was quite risqué, and John was almost overwhelmed by a powerful desire to take the delectable morsel in his arms and devour her whole.

She smiled at him; her golden lashes swept to her cheeks then lifted, and he received the full impact of violet eyes. "I've been trained for the stage." When she immersed herself in a role, acting out a part, she was able to hide her acute shyness. "I'm going to be an actress!" she said importantly.

John Campbell's breath came out in a rush of relief. Here was no lady, St. Patrick be praised, but an *actress,* which made her fair game for seduction. "How old are you?"

"I'm sixteen, almost seventeen—quite old enough," she assured him. "How old are you, sir?"

The corners of his mouth lifted in amusement at the inappropriate question, asked so matter-of-factly. "I'm eight-and-twenty and have all my teeth."

"Do you have a name, sir?" The fine English lady was back.

"My name is John." He did not offer his family name. "As you guessed, I am in Ireland to fish . . . and hunt." He stressed the last word, glancing at her breasts, then his gaze returned to her lips.

"How do you do, John? My name is Beth. These parts are renowned for fine game birds. We have snipe, quail, pheasant, goldcrests, and even partridge, though I've never tasted it."

"Really? It just so happens I have a plump roast partridge and a bottle of wine in my basket. Why don't you share them with me?"

"I'm not the least bit hungry, but since it would be impolite to refuse your hospitality, it would be my pleasure to taste the partridge, sir, though not the wine."

"Why not the wine?" he asked, amused.

" 'Tis rumored that it steals the senses. Would you like me to hold your rod, John?"

For a moment her words dizzied him, then he realized that she had stolen his senses—she was innocently offering to hold his fishing rod while he got the food. He handed it to her then opened the basket and extracted a large linen napkin that held the roasted fowl. He unwrapped it and broke the bird into pieces.

"Take it quickly." She handed the rod back. "I believe you have a salmon on your line at this very moment."

He reeled it in and with a swift motion dipped his net into the water and flipped the fish onto the riverbank. *With any luck, I'll lure another to take my bait.* His dark brown eyes studied the lovely golden female at his side. "Tell me, Beth, how do you intend to catch a salmon without a rod?"

She picked up a leg of partridge with the thigh attached and bit down with relish. "A man needs fancy paraphernalia. A maid must manage without!"

John's dark eyes widened. Had this enchantress made a racy observation regarding their anatomy to provoke his male lust? He watched her select a breast with its wing intact and saw her lick her lips in anticipation. She had denied that she was hungry, yet she was making short work of the partridge. When she set down the bones and licked her fingers, he felt his cock stir. He moved the napkin closer to her, and when he saw her look at the remaining pieces with longing, suddenly wished she'd look at him that way.

"You're not hungry, John?"

He shook his head in denial. He was hungry, all right, but not for food. All he wanted at this moment was to watch her eat. With a feminine, feline grace, she quickly bit into the fowl with sharp, white teeth, closed her eyes with untold pleasure when she swallowed a morsel, then licked her fingers to savor the taste. He wondered if she would relish everything in life with such lusty enjoyment, and his imagination took erotic flight.

She devoured the last of the partridge and wiped her hands on the linen. Then she stretched out beside him, prone in the grass, and gazed down into the water's depth. A shadow beneath the surface inched forward. She waited patiently until it edged closer, but the moment she slid her hand into the water, the salmon darted away. "We've been making too much noise," she whispered, placing a finger against red lips that looked berry-stained.

John reclined beside her so that their bodies almost touched. *I'll let you hold my rod, sweetheart.* He didn't say it aloud, though it was what his body craved. He watched her lovely heart-shaped face as she focused fully on her task. Her skin was like translucent porcelain, and this close he could see the tiny blue veins of her eyelids. As her glance followed the shadow of the fish beneath the water, the tip of her pink tongue licked her full lower lip, and he was lost.

He hardened instantly and reached for her. His arms swept about her, holding her captive against his hardness, while his lips took possession of her tantalizing mouth. He drank in her loveliness thirstily, knowing he'd never tasted anything as sweet.

Shocked beyond belief, Beth bit down on his lip and sprang to her feet. He stood too, towering above her, wanting to gentle her to a giving mood. "How dare you try to ravish me, sir?" Her breasts heaved with indignation as she drew back her arm, reached up on her tiptoes, and slapped him full across the face. She turned on her heel and began to run.

"Beth, wait . . ."

Suddenly she stopped, turned around, and strode back to him, violet eyes blazing. She swept him with an accusing glance then bent and snatched up the fish he'd caught. "My salmon, sir!"

On the journey home her thoughts were filled with the dev- astatingly handsome devil she'd encountered by the river. He was tall, with a dark smouldering quality about him that should have warned her he was dangerous—but, truth to tell, she hadn't experienced fear until she'd felt the strength of his well- muscled body when he'd held her against him. Still, she mused, the fear of him was minuscule when pitted against the fear she felt of returning home without a salmon for dinner. It would take far more courage than she possessed to face her mother empty-handed.

Bridget Gunning was an extremely attractive woman, whose red hair only hinted at her sharp tongue and flaming temper. She was the undisputed authority figure in their household, whom none would dream of disobeying, least of all her hus- band. Beth's mother never let them forget that she had sacri- ficed her promising career as an actress on the London stage to marry John Gunning and give him two beautiful daughters. She called her husband feckless, which Beth acknowledged was true enough, but she loved her handsome father, known as Jack to his friends, for his easygoing ways and ready smile.

Jack Gunning's family were well-to-do landowners in St.

Ives, Cambridgeshire, but since he was the youngest son and could hope for neither wealth nor title, he had become an adventurer and a gambler. When he wed an actress, his reputation as the black sheep of the family was sealed, and the arrival of two daughters in rapid succession put an end to Bridget's promising career on the stage. He took them to St. Ives to live off his family's charity, where they were barely tolerated, while he haunted London's gaming clubs.

Then, by a stroke of fortune, or so it had seemed at the time, her father had won Castlecoote in a card game at White's. The couple instantly packed up their daughters and moved to their castle in Ireland. Castlecoote, it turned out, was no castle at all but a rambling old hall in need of repair. It stood, however, on a lovely piece of rolling farmland in County Roscommon, so they made the best of their disappointing situation and stayed. Though they were surrounded by prosperous sheep and cattle farms, Jack Gunning was no farmer and eked out a living by tending a few goats and selling the animals' milk and cheese.

The Gunning daughters, Maria and Elizabeth, were exceptionally beautiful girls, and their mother, focusing her own aspirations on them, decided to train them for the stage, where they would undoubtedly make their fortune once they were old enough. To this end they were taught to sing and dance and were made to practice a scene from a play every night of their lives. Though their mother was a strict taskmaster, Beth knew she was more lenient with Maria who was elder by two years. Because of her exquisite looks, she was her favorite. Beth felt no resentment. It was right and proper that Maria's beauty made her special.

"Elizabeth Gunning, where the devil have you been?" her mother demanded sharply the moment Beth stepped into the kitchen.

Tongue-tied as always in the face of her mother's wrath, she held up the salmon for explanation.

"Is this to be another dumb show, where you practice your mime? Don't think the salmon excuses you from bringing the water from St. Brigid's well. Maria had to wash her face in ordinary well water today because you forgot."

"Don't fuss, Bridget. Water is water." Jack winked at his daughter as he took the salmon.

"Water is not water, Jack Gunning! Your daughters owe their flawless complexions to the water from Holywell House."

"Beth can run there and fetch a jug, while I fillet the fish."

"Do not call her Beth. Her name is Elizabeth. I picked beautiful names for our daughters, names that will benefit them when they are on the stage."

Beth almost made a grab for the jug, but her mother's critical eye stopped her. Instead, she lifted it gracefully from the stone sink and sank into a curtsy. "I shall be pleased to go for the water now, ma'am." She would do anything to please her mother.

"Much better, Elizabeth. Never forget that plainer girls must try harder to please."

"Why didn't you tell her about the letter?" Jack asked when Elizabeth left the house.

"And spoil the surprise for Maria? I shall tell them tonight after they've practiced their parts."

Elizabeth encountered Maria as her sister came out of Holywell House. The two girls fell into step and they walked toward St. Brigid's well. "I'm sorry, Beth. I told Mother it was your turn to fetch the water today. Will you forgive me?"

"Of course. I met a man today—he was fishing by the river."

"Was he a gentleman?" Maria asked avidly.

"Well, he wasn't Irish, if that's what you mean."

Maria laughed at her sister's droll remark. "I mean, was he rich and well-spoken?"

"Yes, English gentry I expect, here for hunting and fishing."

"Oo-la-la, most likely staying at the royal hunting lodge at Ballyclare. Was he handsome?"

"Handsome in the extreme," Beth said with an involuntary sigh.

"Did he try to kiss you?" Maria asked knowingly.

"How on earth did you guess?"

"Oh, Beth, you're so innocent! How could any man resist you?"

"Well, I resisted *him,* I can tell you!"

"Little goose. You shouldn't have resisted. If he fancied you, perhaps he'd take you to England with him. How else will you get out of this godforsaken country? Tomorrow, I'll come with you and try my own luck."

Beth pulled on the rope then tipped water from the wooden bucket into her jug. For all her beauty, Maria had no reticence and said whatever thought came into her head, whether it was appropriate or not. "You'd truly let a man kiss you, Maria?"

"I'd let him do anything that pleased his fancy, if he'd take me to London, Beth. Only if he was rich, of course."

During the course of the afternoon as John Campbell caught half a dozen salmon, his thoughts were filled with the image of the enchanting wood sprite he'd encountered. She was easily the most beautiful female he'd ever seen, but that wasn't the only thing about her that was so arresting. She was direct, without subterfuge, and he found it enchanting. She was also natural and free-spirited, speaking her thoughts without coquetry or calculation, and she was completely unaffected as if she had no notion of her exquisite loveliness.

When he arrived back at the lodge, he saw that his companions, who had been hunting, were there before him. He left his catch with Ballyclare's chef then joined the other men.

His younger brother, Henry, raised his glass of Irish whiskey in a salute. "You missed out on a damned good hunt, old man. I bagged a red deer."

"How was the fishing?" enquired his friend William Cavendish.

"Fresh salmon for dinner," John announced with a grin. "I don't think I missed anything." He pictured Beth in his mind. "Enjoyed myself so much I believe I'll try my luck again tomorrow."

"Speaking of dinner," said Michael Boyle, waggling bushy red eyebrows, "we all need to bathe before we dine, and since the lodge has such amenable maids—thanks to our host, Will Cavendish—what are we waiting for? Let the water games begin."

All the young men present were lords in their own right. Michael Boyle was the nephew of the wealthy Earl of Burlington, Will Cavendish was heir to the Dukedom of Devonshire, and John Campbell was heir to the great Dukedom of Argyll, no less.

"You have my father to thank for the amenable maids. What's a hunting lodge without sport? Still, the randy old devil

is finally past it. His only indulgence these days is drink."
Will's father was the regal Viceroy of Ireland, appointed to this
lucrative post by Robert Walpole, late Prime Minister of England. "He has become such a hard drinker," Will jested, "'tis
rumored he killed two *aides-de-camp* this year who tried to
keep up with him."

John Campbell laughed. "What a waste—I'd rather die on
the upstroke any day."

"By the number of women who throw themselves at you,
brother, I've no doubt you'll get your wish." Henry tossed off
his whiskey and set down the glass. "Well, I'm off for some
splash and tickle. How about the rest of you?"

All the males, save one, drained their glasses and eagerly
headed toward the staircase. "Coming, John?" his brother
asked.

"You go ahead." John poured himself a glass of claret. "If I
came up to the bathing room, what chance would you have?"
The chorus of rude raspberry noises his friends threw at him
didn't perturb him. Truth to tell, his afternoon encounter with
the ethereal golden goddess had quite spoiled his appetite for
coarse Irish bawds with fleshy titties.

At Castlecoote, after an early supper, the goddess pulled on
a pair of britches and one of her father's tie-wigs. Jack brought
two smallswords from the cupboard while Bridget opened the
costume box and handed Maria a paper fan. Tonight's play was
The Rakehell, and they were enacting a scene where two rivals
fight a duel over a ravishingly beautiful, but innocent, damsel.

"Why can't I take the male lead? I long to fight with a rapier.
Elizabeth has all the fun!" Maria threw down her paper fan.

"Absolutely not, Maria. I forbid it. We dare not take the
chance of the guard coming off the sword. If the point of the
rapier touched your face, it would mar your beauty forever!"

"Ah, it's because my beauty is greater than Elizabeth's."

Beth and her father exchanged an amused look. Apparently,
the danger to her younger daughter's face did not constitute a
calamity. Jack said, "No, it's because Elizabeth is an excellent
swordsman. I've taught her everything I know, and I was
trained by a fencing Maestro at Cambridge."

Her mother cajoled, "Maria, you play the beautiful, innocent heroine to perfection. All who see you will fall instantly in love. Some day, you will be the toast of London."

Maria picked up the fan and delivered her lines. It took no acting ability to be beautiful; she simply had to be herself.

Jack played the villain who had lured the titled young beauty to a secret rendezvous with the vile intention of seducing her. Elizabeth played the noble hero who uncovered the plot, challenged the rakehell to a duel, and saved the damsel from ruin. The moment the rivals crossed swords, her father's superior strength and experience were obvious, but what Elizabeth lacked in height and reach, she made up for with speed and agility. She handled the rapier with great flair, relishing the risk of the thrust and parry with flamboyant, practiced moves designed to make an audience gasp.

At first she was careful to make it look like the villain was winning, allowing him to take the offensive as he backed her across the stage and gaining the sympathy of the audience by playing the underdog. Then, the moment they thought all was lost, she ceased to be on the defensive. With obvious enjoyment, she began to lunge and extend, beating back her opponent with daring strokes and reckless courage, skillfully holding the audience in the palm of her sword hand. The *coup de grâce* came when she deliberately caught the button on the tip of her opponent's sword in the intricate basket design of her rapier's hand guard and with a swift twist of the wrist sent it sailing across the stage. Then, holding her weapon close, so the edge of the blade touched her nose, she took her bow.

"Bravo! Well done! Now your mother has a surprise for you."

Both girls turned to Bridget Gunning with expectant faces.

"I've had a letter." She looked like the cat who'd swallowed the cream as she withdrew the envelope from her bosom.

"From Peg?" Maria asked with a squeal of delight, while Beth drew in a ragged breath of hopeful anticipation.

"Yes, from my dear friend, Peg Woffington!" Bridget confirmed.

It was a name that conjured magic in the Gunning household. Peg, now the reigning star and leading actress of Drury Lane Theater in London, had begun her stage career with Bridget when they had taken any bit parts that fell their way. Then, as fate would have it, Bridget found herself pregnant, just as Peg snared a role in *The Beggar's Opera*. The play proved such a favorite that it was performed at Smock Alley Theater in Dublin. Peg stayed on at the theater to do her apprenticeship and became an accomplished actress. She moved to London, acted with the great David Garrick, and the rest was history. When she became Garrick's mistress, he bought Drury Lane Theater and made her its star.

Bridget unfolded the crackling pages of the letter with more reverence than she would accord the Magna Carta. She did not read verbatim but rather paraphrased what was written on the precious parchment. "Peg is in Dublin! She has returned in triumph to play the Smock Alley Theater and insists that we go to see her."

Both girls gasped with delight.

"I wrote to her about you and told her of Maria's exceptional beauty. Peg wants to take a look at you both and promises to see if she can get you parts at Smock Alley!"

The Gunning sisters shared a bedchamber, and that night in bed, the girls whispered long into the night about going to Dublin and finally getting a chance to act on a real stage. Elizabeth's dreams were often filled with the roles she hoped to play and, without fail, she was always adorned in a lovely costume, but tonight when her dreams began, they had nothing to do with the theater. Instead, she dreamed about food.

Spread out before her was an array of delectable dishes that made her mouth water. There were platters of roast fowl, braised lamb, and baked salmon. Meat pies with flaky crusts sat next to dishes of Yorkshire pudding, egg custards, and warm crusty bread. The desserts took her breath away. Fancy cakes and pastries vied with piles of russet apples and bowls of strawberries and cream. The trouble was the food belonged to John, the dark and dangerous man she had met by the river.

He gestured toward the dishes. "Why don't you share them with me?" he invited.

She looked longingly at the food then glanced with hesitation at the dark, attractive male, wondering if she could trust him. Finally, her hunger and the temptation were too great. "It would be my pleasure." And indeed it was. He insisted on feeding her with his own fingers, and she relished every morsel as if it were ambrosia from the gods. As he fed her, Elizabeth's fear of him vanished and she began to enjoy his company as much as his food. She licked her lips, then, with great daring, licked his fingers.

Chapter Two

*T*he following day, while John Campbell lingered along the banks of the salmon-rich River Suck, Elizabeth Gunning was kept busy fetching a bucket of water from St. Bridgid's well at Holywell House, then washing her sister's silvery-blond tresses. They sat in the sun while Elizabeth brushed in the finger-ringlets and formed dozens of tiny tendrils around the perfect, oval face.

Bridget darned the girls' only stockings then began to take down the hems on their cotton dresses. There would be no showing their ankles in Dublin; it would create a scandal.

"I'll walk over to Longacre Farm and see if Tully will buy the goats," Jack said.

His wife gave him a scorching look. "We need transportation to Dublin. Don't come home without it."

When Beth saw her father tethering their six goats with a rope, her heart flew into her mouth. "Where are you taking them?"

"I'll see if Tully will buy them."

She felt a measure of relief. Longacre was a prosperous place, and Tully took good care of the farm's livestock. "I'll help you, Father. I'll carry the baby." She picked up the little black nanny goat and dropped a kiss on its nose. She'd stayed up the entire night with its dam when it had been born to ensure a live birth and named it Eyebright, after the weeds in the meadow.

At Longacre she left the men to their business talk and went into the barn. In a back stall she found a sheepdog with a litter of black-and-white pups. She stroked the bitch and told her what a good mother she was, wishing with all her heart that she could have one of the litter. She knew it was impossible, for the Gunnings had only enough to feed themselves. With a sigh of resignation she pulled herself away from the happy little family and went back to the stable yard.

"I've talked him into a cartload of turnips in exchange for the goats. We'll have to return the mule, of course, but we can sell the turnips once we arrive in Dublin."

"Well, a cart and a mule are certainly what we need, since we can't walk to Dublin . . . and the turnips are a bonus." She hoped and prayed her mother wouldn't rant and rave when they got home.

"Only trouble is," Jack said, running a hand through his thick blond hair, "the turnips are still in the field."

"I'll help you, Dad." She immediately braided her golden hair into a thick plait. "Turnips are big and round—it won't take that many to fill up a cart. You get the mule and wagon, and I'll go to the field and start pulling up the turnips."

As it turned out, it was dirty, backbreaking work. The turnip field was a sea of mud, and Jack didn't dare take the mule-drawn cart close to the crop. So Beth bent over and extracted the turnips from the oozing mud, while her father carried them to the cart at the top end of the field. By the time they had a full load of about two hundred turnips, the sun had begun to set, but there was still plenty of light for Jack to see the state his daughter was in. "You're mud from arse to teakettle. Your mother will throw a bloody fit!"

Beth's knees were already shaking at the reception they'd both get. "Let me off here. I'll bathe in Lough Ree and wash my smock at the same time. You go and convince Mother that you made a good swap for the goats."

She walked along the bank of the river until it opened up into the scenic Lough Ree. She breathed in its beauty with deep appreciation. As the red ball of the sun slowly sailed down the sky to dip beneath the lake, she thought surely there could be no more mystical place on earth. She threw off her smock beneath the sheltering branches of a bay tree and slowly waded into the water until it was breast-high. She shivered as the cool water closed over her sensitive skin, then began to wash off the clinging mud. She spotted what she thought was an otter swimming close by the bank. She'd seen the playful creature there before with his mate. On impulse, she decided to approach and try to swim with him.

Beth filled her lungs with air then slipped under and swam beneath the water to the place where she'd seen his dark head.

She glided up smoothly, without splashing, and stared into a pair of glistening brown eyes. They were not the eyes of an otter.

"My Lord Oberon!" she gasped.

"Splendor of God, I've thought of you so long I've conjured you!" John Campbell couldn't credit the ethereal creature of his daydreams had come to him in the form of a mermaid. He kicked out with a long stroke and grabbed her wrists before she could submerge. "You're real!" he declared.

"I'm real, and the predicament I'm in is very real too, sir. You *must* let me go!" As he held her fast he gave the impression of sheer brute strength, and her knees turned weak. A strange frisson from his strong fingers went up her arms, making her shiver. While he held her fast, all she could think of was the feel of his lips on hers. She wondered if he would do it again. *What a wicked thought! I must not let him do it again!*

"I've waited all day for you—I'm not about to let you go yet."

"Why were you waiting for me? Because I stole your salmon?"

Because you stole my senses. "If you pay me for the salmon, I can hardly say you stole it, can I?"

"But I have no money, sir." She tried to pull her wrists from his powerful hands in vain.

A delighted grin spread over his face. "I know." His grip tightened. "There's other currency between a man and a maid."

She looked at him solemnly. "Yes, there is forgiveness and there is generosity."

"Precisely! If I forgive you, you must be generous."

"What do you want?"

He rolled his eyes just thinking of what he wanted. The

water revealed much of her high-thrusting breasts, and he was enjoying the view immensely. "I only want to talk."

"We cannot talk, sir. We have no clothes on."

He laughed at such an ingenuous notion. "If we cannot talk, then I suppose I'll have to settle for a kiss."

"I'll not give it," she whispered.

"You need not give it—I'll take it."

She knew she was trapped. She knew he would never let her go until he got what he wanted, perhaps not even then. The innate actress inside her took over. Her eyes widened solemnly and shone with unshed tears. "I mistook you for a gentleman. I imagined you to be a man of decency and honor."

Damn, she was completely indifferent to his teasing charm. "I *am* a man of honor. I won't hurt you, Beth."

"Then will you give me your word of honor you will let me go?"

He hesitated for long moments as he towered above her. The tension between them stretched taut. He imagined her complete state of undress, picturing her rising from the water like Botticelli's Venus. He envisioned her lying naked beside him in the grass. The thought of her delicate, slim form was irresistible to him. He had a hungry craving to touch her, smell her, taste her. What was this fascination he felt for her? "After the kiss," he bargained.

"All right," she conceded with wary reluctance.

He released her wrists and cupped her bare shoulders. As he drew her toward him he felt her tremble and saw her eyes liquid with apprehension. A sudden wave of doubt swept over him as it began to dawn on him that perhaps his water sprite was as sweet and virginal as she looked. Though the desire to possess her raged hot in his veins, the urge to protect her waged a battle with his lust and won. As he gazed down at her beautiful face he could not bear the thought of spoiling her innocence in any way. He touched his lips to hers in a chaste, gentle kiss that took his breath away. It was as brief and delicate as the brush of a butterfly wing, yet its impact was like a blow to his solar plexus. Dazed, he lifted his hands from her shoulders. "Go. Go quickly," he ordered.

*   *   *

By the time Elizabeth arrived home it was twilight. She had missed supper, but she had also missed the explosive row that had erupted between her parents over the wagonload of turnips, for which she was profoundly thankful. She would rather endure anything than be subjected to her mother's blazing anger.

Before she went to bed, she helped her father pack the theatrical trunk with the old costumes, wigs, masks, and makeup they'd accumulated over the years. She wrapped up the small Irish harp in a shabby velvet cloak, carefully placed the pair of rapiers in their gilt leather sheaths on top, and bound the trunk securely with a rope.

In the bedroom she shared with Maria, she helped her sister pack her carpetbag before she packed her own. Each of them had a cotton dress, a shift made from bleached flour sacks, a pair of black stockings, an extra pair of drawers, and a woolen shawl. They shared a hairbrush, a flannel towel, and a lump of soap.

Maria climbed into their bed and pulled up the quilt. "You missed a battle royal tonight. Father was holding his own until she demolished him by calling him 'Jack and the Bloody Beanstalk'!"

"Please don't talk of it—it makes me feel ill. I hope Mother's not still angry in the morning."

"She won't be. Dad has a way of taking her to bed and mollifying her. Oh, Beth, I can't wait to be in Dublin again, 'tis years since I've seen the city."

Beth blew out the tallow candle and removed her smock, which was still wringing wet from the scrubbing she'd given it to remove the mud. She spread it across the back of a wooden chair then, covered with gooseflesh, slipped into bed and tried not to shiver.

"You're making the bed shake," Maria complained.

"Sorry. I'll try to think warm thoughts." The moment she uttered the words a vision of the dark male she'd encountered the last two days came to her full blown. As she pictured his muscle-ridged chest and black waving hair that brushed his wide shoulders, she began to feel quite hot. Then she remembered his mouth touching hers, and her lips felt scalded. Yet in spite of the burning heat of her body she still shivered. As she dropped into exhausted sleep, however, the shivering ceased and she drifted off in a warm pool of dreams.

She was an otter, swimming in the water with her mate. He was a sleek, brown creature with gleaming eyes, extremely bold and playful, yet always protective of her. Every evening, just at twilight, he dove into the water with reckless daring, luring her after him. She followed, unable to resist his potent attraction or the compelling hold he had over her. The game they played tonight was joyful, ever touching, teasing, taunting, until he led her from the water into the tall grasses. Suddenly, Elizabeth realized that they were not really otters, but a young man and woman having fun pretending. They were completely naked and enjoying every wicked moment of the delicious game they played. When he lifted her high she laughed down at him and allowed her golden curls to cascade and brush across his powerful chest. He slid her down his hard muscled body until her toes touched the ground, and his mouth covered hers in a long, lingering kiss that filled her heart with yearning.

The dream vanished when Beth awoke to the raucous crowing of the cock from a nearby farm, as she did most mornings. Today, however, it was still dark. She reached for her smock, which was yet slightly damp, then pulled on her black stockings and button-up leather boots. When she went down to the kitchen she met her father coming in from outside, carrying eggs.

He winked at his daughter. "I found these before they were lost. Quick, get the pan."

By the time the travelers set off they had filled their bellies with eggs, melted cheese, and goat's milk; they would remember the meal fondly over the next four days when their food consisted of boiled turnips, raw turnips, turnip greens, and more turnips.

Their spirits were high the first day as they traveled along the country roads, bathed in late-summer sunshine. They'd no money for inns and spent the first night under the shelter of a church lychgate. Jack unhitched the mule and allowed him to crop the grass of the cemetery. The girls used their carpetbags for pillows, and Maria was thankful that Elizabeth had had the foresight to pack their bedquilt.

At Ballyclare, great activity was underway. The young lords' servants and valets were busy packing their masters' trunks with everything from formal evening attire to hunting clothes, caped greatcoats and beaver hats, from riding boots to dancing slippers, and fine linen undergarments. The young aristocrats not only traveled with their own mounts, saddles, and hunting dogs but with their own snowy bedlinen and eiderdown-filled bolsters and comforters. The stack of trunks, boxes, and gun cases in the entrance hall already resembled a mountain, yet the packing was only half finished. A fortnight ago, the visitors had arrived at Ballyclare in three heavy berline coaches, two of which were used for baggage alone. Each traveling coach was pulled by a matched team of four carriage horses and driven by a seasoned coachman.

In the dining room on their last evening, the gentlemen lingered over their port and Irish whiskey, recounting tales of the great hunting and lamenting over the fish and game that had gotten away.

"You're silent tonight, brother. Don't tell me this illbegotten land has enchanted you."

John Campbell smiled. "Just thinking of a rare bird I saw by the river—far too lovely to bag."

"Speaking of rare birds," Michael Boyle interjected, "my cousin Lady Charlotte is to be presented to Will's father, the Viceroy, at Dublin Castle's drawing room next week. She's of high enough rank that she'll be able to sit on the dais with His Excellency. It will give you a damn good chance to look her over, Will."

"Go over her fine points again," William Cavendish urged.

"Let's see, a brother and sister died in infancy, leaving her the sole heiress of my extremely wealthy uncle, Third Earl of Burlington. She'll not only inherit the Piccadilly mansion and the Palladian villa by the Thames at Chiswick but will get the Boyle estates at Londesborough and Bolton Abbey in Yorkshire. Need I mention the vast tract of land in County Waterford, crowned by the magnificent Castle of Lismore?"

"No, you needn't mention Lismore, 'tis the jewel of Ireland." Will's mouth curved with desire. "I think I'm already in love."

"Love!" John Campbell mocked. "We all know there is no such thing. Love is a foolish fantasy indulged in by females only."

"Well, let's hope my valet packed my ballroom shoes so that I may dance attendance upon Lady Charlotte and lure her into indulging her foolish fantasy."

"Surely, in Dublin, it won't be all rigid formality?" Henry Campbell asked with dread.

"I'm afraid it is patterned after the Court at St. James." Will's eyelid drooped in a wink. "However, since Father's viceregal appointment as Governor of Ireland is up, he'll turn a blind eye on the final night of his term. The champagne will flow and a saturnalia will prevail to ensure a successful reign."

"Thank God for that! I wouldn't want a cold bed on my last night in Ireland," Henry jested.

"You'll have your choice of attractive matrons, or the pretty daughters of solicitors or physicians who have little social rank, but the *débutantes* who are to be presented are absolutely 'off limits' for dalliance. Marriage proposals are the only offers they may consider," John Campbell warned his younger brother.

"Mother would run mad and Father disinherit me if I even thought of bringing home an Irish bride. Being the heir, your case is even worse, John. Sometimes I believe that none less than royal blood will be deemed good enough to mate with Argyll."

"Ha! You don't imagine Hanover blood would measure up to His Grace's expectations, do you? Scots and Germans may share a battlefield but not a marriage bed, I can assure you."

"My sister Rachel has a secret *tendre* for you, John. You could do worse, you know—as the eldest daughter she'll come into a good deal of wealth and property," Will Cavendish pointed out.

"Lady Rachel was being courted by Lord Orford last time I was in London," John Campbell demurred.

"Well, she can't wait forever for you to declare yourself," m teased.

ur mother has a bevy of aristocratic ladies she is grooming as contenders to become John's wife. There's Mary Montagu, the Duke of Buccleuch's daughter, Dorothy Howard, the Earl of Carlisle's daughter, and Henrietta Neville, the Earl of Westmorland's chit."

When his friends raised their eyebrows, questioning if there was a front runner, John laughed and shook his head. "There's safety in numbers, thank God!" Though he jested, he knew it was his duty to marry well, and his family was pressuring him to stop putting it off. Even Will was coming to terms with the fact that he must marry soon and beget heirs. Duty to family was paramount.

Will stood up and stretched. "If we get an early enough start tomorrow we should make it to the Black Bull Inn. They have a large coachyard and hostlers aplenty to take care of our cattle."

"The Black Bull gets my vote," Michael agreed, "they have a very good cellar and will even roast our own venison, if bribed."

Thanks to the diligence of their servants, the travelers got an early start and the four companions were in the saddle before seven the next morning, galloping well ahead of their carriages.

The high spirits of the Gunnings had drained away by the time they'd been on the road for six hours on the second day and weariness set in. The steady diet of turnips did nothing to lift their mood, and their slow progress, which made the journey seem endless, did nothing to soothe Bridget Gunning's irascible temper.

Elizabeth felt so sorry for the mule with its heavy burden that she refused to ride in the cart. Instead she held its reins and walked beside it, encouraging it with soft words or sometimes a song. She'd known from the beginning that she'd be walking for most of the journey; it was the reason she'd put on her leather boots that first morning. In the afternoon, to make matters worse, the rain started. Once Irish rain began, it fell in a steady drizzle for days. With unwavering stoicism, Beth pulled her woolen shawl up over her head and patiently urged the mule to plod on to Dublin.

*   *   *

Long hours in the saddle had little effect on John Campbell or his brother, who were both military men. In the late afternoon, however, as the light faded from the leaden sky, they gladly joined their companions in seeking the comfort of their berline traveling coach as shelter from the bone-chilling Irish rain.

Presently, however, the entourage found itself slowed by a plodding mule cart. The coach driver made several attempts to pass, by whipping up the horses, but the road simply wasn't wide enough. Finally, William Cavendish opened the window and gave instructions to the driver. "Get the damned fellow off the road while we pass. We haven't got all night, Bagshot."

"Aye, my lord." Bagshot stopped the carriage and set the brake.

Then he strode through the rain to the wagon. "My good fellow, your turnip cart is blocking the road. Their lordships are due at the Black Bull Inn and shan't arrive until midnight at this rate," he told the farmhand in the shabby coat and soaking cap.

"My heart goes out to them," Jack Gunning replied cheerfully.

"No, you don't understand. You must get off the road and let our carriages pass."

Jack looked over at his daughter, who was patiently holding the mule by its harness and stroking its muzzle. "No, *you* don't understand. *We* have the right-of-way."

Beth pulled her shawl closer and bit her lip to keep from laughing. Her father was enjoying himself at the driver's expense.

"These traveling coaches belong to His Excellency, the Viceroy of Ireland. Surely, you will oblige him?"

"The Viceroy is a generous man, I've heard tell, and wouldn't be averse to a little compensation for such a great favor."

The coachman reluctantly reached into his greatcoat pocket for a coin. "What do you say to a shilling?"

Jack took the coin and bit down on it. "A shilling sounds about right for me. Now, what are you willing to offer the mule here?"

Purple in the face, the coachman handed over a sovereign and strode back to the carriage. He was subjected to laughter from the mule cart and laughter from the young lordlings in the coach. He cursed under his breath. "That cost me a bleedin' sovereign."

"That's why we're laughing, Bagshot. You didn't even have the presence of mind to get us a turnip!"

Within the hour the four gentlemen were seated around a roaring fire drinking mulled ale, while a haunch of their own venison turned on a spit in the inn's vast kitchen. The dozen carriage horses had been unharnessed and taken to a barn with dry straw. Their thoroughbreds were stabled, curried, fed, and covered with horse blankets. Their hunting dogs had been kenneled, and their servants were seated in the common room enjoying steaming bowls of mutton stew.

It was more than two hours later that the weary mule plodded into the yard of the Black Bull. At the kitchen door Jack Gunning bartered two dozen turnips for a night's shelter in the barn, while his wife petulantly parted with tuppence for some hot roasted potatoes. Jack unhitched the mule and brought it inside, then they all four sank down on the straw to eat their supper.

Unlike the others, Elizabeth did not devour her potato. She held it in her hands, its heat seeping into her fingers. Then she lifted it to her nose and breathed in its delicious aroma. When her belly started to rumble and her mouth began to water, she allowed herself a small bite. She relished the earthy taste of the potato's soft white inside and saved the skin until last. She chewed slowly, savoring the thick roasted outside and sighed with deep appreciation as she swallowed the last mouthful.

"There you are, my beauties, snug as bugs in a rug," Jack declared expansively.

"More like drowned rats!" Bridget countered. While their mother angrily spread their soaked shawls to dry, Maria pulled the quilt from her carpetbag and crawled beneath it. Beth, dreading her mother's mood, went over to look at the carriage horses. Though their size dwarfed her, she felt no apprehension as she stroked their necks and whispered to them. She had an affinity for all animals, wild or domesticated, and they in turn welcomed her affection.

When she returned, she was dragging a leather feed bag behind her, excited at the treasure she'd discovered. "Real oats! Would you believe they feed the carriage horses real oats?" She struggled to lift the bag over their mule's head.

"Oats? Don't let the mule eat them, you thoughtless girl!" Bridget protested angrily. "We can have porridge tomorrow."

"Oh, please don't take them away from her," Elizabeth begged. "There's plenty more over there. I'll fetch some."

Jack stood up and brushed the straw from his behind. "Well, if you're all right and tight my beauties, I'll go and try my luck in the common room."

"I'll have that sovereign before you go gaming, Jack Gunning!"

Bridget took the gold coin and gave him a shilling in its stead.

He winked at his wife. "It'll be like taking jam from a baby."

"If that coachman's in there, it might be more like getting blood from a turnip," she taunted with exquisite sarcasm.

Elizabeth shuddered. *Mother always gets the last word.* She took off her boots and slipped under the quilt beside Maria. She was asleep in minutes, far too weary to dream tonight.

Chapter Three

*T*he four noble friends were given accommodation adjacent to the Viceroy's state apartments in Dublin Castle. Though it was neither picturesque nor had much architectural merit, at least they had good views of the Liffey and the Irish Sea. Though the castle was crowded to the rafters, they secured a dressing room where their valets could sleep, but their other servants had to make do in the Quadrangle situated in the lower castle yard.

They were welcomed by the Viceroy himself, Will's father, the Duke of Devonshire. Before they even had a chance to unpack they were drinking his private stock of smoky Irish whiskey.

"Your Grace, allow me to be among the first to congratulate you on your new appointment as Lord Steward of the Royal Household." John Campbell saluted William's father with his glass.

"Why, thank you, John. Your grandfather, Argyll, was Lord Steward to King George I, if I remember correctly?"

"That's right, Your Grace, and my father is Master of His Majesty's Household for the Kingdom of Scotland."

"That's a heritable post that will come to you someday, isn't it, John? Appointments handed down from father to son are more advantageous by far." He drained his whiskey and continued, "We are in for some fun Friday evening—a command performance of David Garrick and Peg Woffington at Smock

Alley Theater. The carriages leave at seven promptly. That Peg
is a fine figure of a woman. She's staying here at the castle and,
by God, if Garrick didn't watch her like a dog with a bone, I'd
have a go, stap me if I wouldn't!" He reached for the decanter.
"Then Saturday night, to finish with a bang, we're having presentations and the grand ball. Anything at all you need, just ask
the Court staff."

As they left the Viceroy, Henry Campbell jested, "I wonder
what the staff would say if I asked for a strumpet on a crum-
pet?"

"Wouldn't raise an eyebrow—they'd simply supply you
with the address of the nearest brothel," William murmured
with a wink.

"Which happens to be the Brazen Bitch in Trollop Street,"
Michael provided. "The Irish are so literal."

"If we're not attending the theater until Friday, why waste
tonight?" Henry asked. "I'm ready for a command performance
now!"

When the Gunnings finally arrived in Dublin, they made
their way across O'Connell Bridge to the heart of the city that
was dominated by Dublin Castle. They entered Temple Bar
area, a maze of crooked, cobblestone nooks and crannies, and
rented a room off Dame Street by the River Liffey. It had two
beds, a wooden table and chairs, a wash stand with a tin tub,
and most important, a small hearth.

As the girls set their carpetbags on a bed, Jack carried in a
stack of what looked like dried sod. "Now you see why I helped
myself to the Black Bull's supply of peat. These streets by the
river are damp even in August, but with a cookshop at one end
and a pub at the other, we have everything we need. There's no
shortage of water, and we'll even be able to heat it on the fire."

"Well, what are you waiting for?" Bridget asked, thrusting a
jug at Maria and a bucket at Elizabeth. "I noticed a pump up the
street. You can use the tin tub to scrub yourselves, then we'll
use the water for our clothes. Every stitch we own needs washing."

"My love, the girls are exhausted," Jack protested. "Let
them have a good sleep before you put them to work."

"I want them to be spotless, with clean clothes and shining

hair, when I take them to the theater. They'll never get work on the stage unless they are looking their very best!"

"You are right as always, Bridget my love, but they won't look their best with pinched faces and dark smudges of fatigue beneath their lovely eyes. Why don't the three of you get your beauty rest, while I take the turnips to the market and get us our money? I've paid a week's rent and, when I come back, I'll pay for another week. You don't need to scrub clothes or wash their hair until tomorrow to prepare for their visit with your friend Peg."

Two days later, Bridget Gunning ushered her daughters into the famous Smock Alley Theater and asked to be directed to the dressing room of the leading actress, Miss Woffington. The girls' dresses were freshly laundered, their beautiful tresses washed and curled to perfection, and their spirits high with expectation at meeting the greatest actress of their time. Their faces radiated pure joy.

When Woffington's dresser opened the door to the visitors, Peg jumped up from her dressing table with a cry of delight. "Bridget Gunning, I'd know you anywhere—you haven't changed one iota!"

Bridget preened at the welcome reception by her old friend and, taking her eldest daughter's hand, propelled her to the center of the room. "*This* is Maria," she announced with overweening pride.

"You are as tall as a man!" Maria exclaimed.

Peg laughed with genuine amusement. "Well, I haven't grown since the last time I saw you, but you certainly have, child."

Elizabeth blushed at her sister's inappropriate remark. Peg was strikingly tall and slim, and though she was not conventionally beautiful, she had vivid Titian hair, expressive green eyes, and a vivacious personality that captivated in such a compelling way it was hard to pull your gaze away from her laughing face.

Peg held out both hands. "And you must be Elizabeth. What an enchanting poppet you were last time we met." She twirled her about to get a good look, then drew up a wing chair for Bridget and sent Dora, her dresser, for tea and cakes before she turned her attention back to the Gunning girls. "I simply cannot believe it! Cannot *believe* it!" She threw back her head and laughed with delight. "It is rare when one is blessed with a daughter of exceptional beauty, but you have *two* such exquisite creatures!"

"I knew it was more than motherly pride, Peg, for people stare and gape at them in the street."

"There are many beauties lauded in Society—and usually the larger the dower, the prettier the young lady in question—but your daughters are true beauties, natural beauties, without the artifice of dress, makeup, or fortune. 'Tis no wonder people stare at them. They stand out like two Thoroughbred racehorses among a stable of cart horses. Nay, a better analogy would be fine crystal vessels amidst a table filled with thick glass jars."

"I am very proud of Maria's hair. I've never seen more beautiful tresses in Ireland, or in London itself, for that matter."

"Yes, she has the classic beauty of silver-gilt hair and oval face, giving her the angelic quality to which our society aspires, but Elizabeth I think has the more unusual and arresting beauty. Her hair is the color of molten gold, and her violet eyes in her heart-shaped face hint at a burning flame hidden deep within."

"I want them to have the chance on the stage that I never had," Bridget said passionately. "They can both sing and dance and act. They practice a play every night before bed and each has prepared something from Shakespeare for you."

"How ambitious. You fair take my breath away!" The dresser came back carrying a huge tray of refreshments. "Let's have our tea first, then you can both perform for me," Peg invited.

Maria took a cake, ate it quickly, then reached for another. Elizabeth's eyes shone with delight as she gazed at the tray of confections. Simply looking at them brought her pleasure; choosing one added to her enjoyment. Finally, she picked one that was smaller than the others, but its pink icing and silver balls marked it as the daintiest. As she bit into it she raised her eyes and saw that Peg was watching her, and her cheeks turned the same delicate hue as the cake's icing and she lowered her lashes shyly. Her actions showed such vulnerability that Peg was enchanted.

When she poured the tea and handed round the cups and

saucers she saw that the Gunning daughters could have been taking tea in the finest parlor in England. Their manners would have done them credit at St. James's Palace, and Peg flashed her friend a look of admiration for teaching them how to acquit themselves well in company. When they were finished, Peg folded her napkin. "Now we are fortified, you may recite your Shakespeare, but pray don't think of this as an audition. Try to enjoy yourselves!"

At her mother's signal, Maria stood up and curtsied. "I would like to do Juliet for you." When she saw that she had Peg Woffington's full attention she clasped her hands together and recited:

> "O Romeo, Romeo, wherefore art thou Romeo?
> Deny thy Father and refuse thy name;
> Or, if thou wilt not, be but sworn my love,
> And I'll no longer be a Capulet.
> 'Tis but thy name that is my enemy;
> Thou art thyself, though not a Montague.
> What's Montague? It is nor hand nor foot,
> Nor arm nor face, nor any other part
> Belonging to a man. O, be some other name!
> What's in a name? That which we call a rose
> By any other word would smell as sweet;
> So Romeo would, were he not Romeo call'd,
> Retain that dear perfection which he owes
> without that title. Romeo, doff thy name,
> And for thy name, which is no part of thee,
> Take all myself."

Though the delivery was rather unremarkable, Peg had to admit that Maria Gunning was surely the most exquisite-looking Juliet she had ever seen. If Maria were upon a stage, she would attract every eye in the house. "Even Will Shakespeare would have to agree that you are the very image of his Juliet," she offered generously.

Elizabeth glanced at her mother and saw she was like a dog with two tails at the praise Maria had received. She was in such good temper that Elizabeth dared to abandon her pretty recitation of Ariel, the Elemental, offering the chalice in *The Tem-*

pest. She took the floor and bowed gravely. "I wish to do *Henry V* rallying his men at Agincourt." She looked quickly away from her mother before she could glimpse her displeasure and spoke directly to Peg:

"This day is call'd the feast of Crispian:
He that outlives this day, and comes safe home,
Will stand a' tiptoe when this day is named,
And rouse him at the name of Crispian.
He that shall see this day, and live old age,
Will yearly on the vigil feast his neighbors,
And say, 'To-morrow is Saint Crispian.'
Then will he strip his sleeve and show his scars,
And say, 'These wounds I had on Crispin's day.'
Old men forget; yet all shall be forgot,
But he'll remember with advantages
What feats he did that day. Then shall our names,
Familiar in his mouth as household words,
Harry the King, Bedford and Exeter,
Warwick and Talbot, Salisbury and Gloucester,
Be in their flowing cups freshly rememb'red.
This story shall the good man teach his son;
And Crispin Crispian shall ne'er go by,
From this day to the ending of the world,
But we in it shall be remembered—
We few, we happy few, we band of brothers;
For he to-day that sheds his blood with me
Shall be my brother; be he ne'er so vile,
This day shall gentle his condition;
And gentlemen in England now a-bed,
Shall think themselves accurs'd they were not here;
And hold their manhoods cheap whiles any speaks
That fought with us upon Saint Crispin's day."

For a moment, Peg could not speak for the lump in her throat. The lovely golden girl had transformed herself into proud, young King Harry as he urged his men to fight for England. She was noble, passionate, and heartbreakingly vulnerable at the same time. Peg applauded. "I am absolutely thrilled that you don't mind taking a male role. Often the best parts are written for men. I, myself, am playing the part of Sir Harry Wildair tonight in *The Constant Couple*. It's such a fun part. You must stay and see it!"

"Thank you! It's been ten years since we last saw you on stage, but I have never forgotten your performance. May we look around the theater?" Elizabeth asked with suppressed excitement.

"Of course. It's a good idea to get yourselves familiar with the place if you intend to perform here." Peg scribbled on a card and handed it to Bridget. "This tells management you are my guests and are to be given front-row seats. After the performance we'll go for a late supper and celebrate!"

Buoyed by all things theatrical, Bridget squired her daughters backstage to view the props and the scenery that moved up and down by myriad ropes and pulleys. With great authority she pointed out the exits and entrances at stage left, right, and center, and explained the lighting and how to gain and keep the spotlight. They lingered in the makeup room, lined with mirrors, and inspected all sorts of fascinating pots containing rouge, white lead face paint, powder, patches, beards, and wigs. The girls, who had never been allowed to wear face makeup, found the smell of grease paint, mixed with spirit gum, quite exotic. Eventually, they were shooed out as the actors arrived to get ready for the upcoming performance. They skirted the wardrobe room where dressers were assembling the costumes for tonight and went down to the pit to see the musicians arrive to tune their instruments and set up their music stands.

They wandered up the aisles between the rows of seats and marveled at the theater's acoustics that magnified their voices in the empty playhouse. Then they climbed to the balcony and, feeling extremely daring, entered a private box. Maria preened, pretending all eyes were upon her, while Elizabeth sat in a velvet upholstered seat and imagined how decadent it must feel to be able to view a play from such a luxurious setting. Finally, they climbed to a third level, known as "the Gods," where the cheap seats were located and learned firsthand why it was necessary to cultivate a full-bodied stage voice that would carry up to the roof.

Shortly, the Smock Alley Theater began to fill up, and Elizabeth watched, wide-eyed, as the well-dressed Dublin patrons filed in and took their seats. She felt acutely self-conscious in her cotton dress and woolen shawl and was greatly relieved that the lamps were being lowered by the time they were shown to their seats in the front row. But from the moment the curtain went up and the actors stepped onto the stage, Elizabeth forgot about herself and was transported to the make-believe world of *The Constant Couple.*

The antics of Sir Harry Wildair soon had the audience rolling with laughter. Of course everyone in the theater knew that the principal role was being played by Peg Woffington, who was equally adept at comedy or drama. The play was farce, pure and simple, and Peg, full of vitality and wit, held the audience in the palm of her hand. Beth knew immediately what her secret was: Though she was an attractive, elegant woman in reality, she did not mind appearing unattractive or inelegant, and her audience adored her for it.

Elizabeth sat enthralled as she took in every nuance, every wink, every gesture and dramatic pause. Like a sponge she absorbed the tone, the timing, the timbre of the voices, the humor, both broad and sly, and the flawless delivery. She heard the words, the music, and the laughter. She smelled the perfume, the grease paint, and the sweat of the unwashed. She felt the magic and the wonder and the joy of the performance unfolding before her eyes, and she knew that this was one of the most deliriously happy nights of her life.

After the performance, Peg took them for a late supper to the Oyster House in Fishamble Street, where she told her guests to order anything they fancied. Elizabeth was hesitant at first, worrying about the cost, but when her mother ordered chowder followed by smoked trout and Maria boiled shrimp and crab, she decided to indulge with fried oysters and prawns. Peg and her mother were drinking porter, served in big pewter mugs, and Bridget gave her permission for the girls to have a small beer for the very first time. Elizabeth was amazed at how easy it was to laugh between delicious mouthfuls of food and drink. What a lovely place the world seemed with a full belly and replete appetite!

"I'm staying at Dublin Castle—a guest of the Viceroy, no less." Peg drained her tankard and ordered another. "His Excellency has ordered a command performance for tomorrow evening. The whole Court will come in state. A retinue of eight or ten carriages will start from the castle and proceed according to the rank of the parties, and a file of cavalry with jingling accoutrements will form an escort to the colonnade of Smock Alley Theater."

"The house will be crowded to the roof," Bridget predicted.

"The Viceroy's party will sit in the box we were in!" Elizabeth's eyes were wide with wonder that she had actually sat in the state box where the Governor of Ireland would sit tomorrow.

"Exactly right," Peg nodded, trying to contain her laughter. "The Court puts on a better bloody performance than we do. The theater manager, wearing a satin suit, leads the way, holding aloft a pair of wax candles, then, at the head of his glittering staff, the Viceroy enters, blazing in gold and Garter. The Court staff in regulation uniform—coats with gilt buttons and blue satin facings, with white waistcoats—stand stiffly in a miserable state of agitation while the orchestra plays 'God Save the King' and everyone tries to ignore the vulgar and piquant observations from the great unwashed sitting up in the Gods." Peg wiped her eyes.

Bridget rubbed a stitch in her side from laughing. "You paint such an amusing picture. I can see it all in vivid detail."

"Oh, I wish we could come to Dublin Castle and really see the Viceroy and the Court," Maria said wistfully.

Peg put her head on one side thoughtfully. "Why not?" she said slowly as an idea began to form. "On Saturday, His Excellency is having a drawing room followed by a ball. It will be a grand affair to end the Season, where the *débutantes* are presented." Her gaze was drawn to Maria and Elizabeth. "Why shouldn't these beautiful young ladies be presented?"

Maria turned a radiant face to her mother. "Oh, could we?"

"It's not possible," Elizabeth said apologetically, trying to hide her humiliation. "We don't have anything to wear."

"Ah, I hadn't thought of that." Peg bit her lip, then smiled. "The theater has a whole wardrobe room packed with gowns and wigs. Come tomorrow and we'll find something that fits you—you too Bridget. In the meantime, I'll see that your names are put on the invitation list."

Suddenly, Elizabeth dared to hope for what had seemed unattainable. *There is magic in the air tonight, and Peg Woffing-ton must surely be our Fairy Godmother!*

When they arrived back at Dame Street, their father, who had been out to a gaming club, was there before them. Excit-edly, they told him about Smock Alley Theater, the play they'd seen, the supper at the grand Oyster House, and saving the best till last, finally told him that Peg Woffington was going to arrange for them to be presented to the Viceroy of Ireland at Dublin Castle. "She's even going to let us choose gowns from the wardrobe department!"

"Is all this true?" Jack asked his wife.

Bridget nodded. "I told you our luck was about to change! Peg was extremely impressed by our daughters' beauty and tal-ent. She sees no reason why they shouldn't be offered small parts and begin their apprenticeship at Smock Alley Theater."

"But what about attending this drawing room the Viceroy is giving at Dublin Castle? Don't you have to be somebody to be put on the invitation list?"

"We are somebody! Are you not the son of Lord Gunning, and do we not live at Castlecoote? It certainly sounds like a cas-tle and none need know otherwise! You girls get to bed; you've never been up this late in your lives."

Maria and Elizabeth did go to bed, but they couldn't sleep for hours. Instead they lay whispering about what it would be like to attend a ball. "We must practice our dancing tomorrow, in case someone asks us to dance," Maria decided.

"No one will ask. We don't know anyone," Elizabeth whis-pered.

Try as she might, she simply could not visualize herself in a ball gown, yet, when sleep finally did overtake her, she found herself wearing a beautiful dress and, to her utter amazement, a gentleman asked if he could partner her in the dance. His face was blank and in the dream he had no discernible features, yet, strangely, there was something dangerously familiar about him.

The following morning, much to their delight, the Gunning females spent hours in the wardrobe room of the Smock Alley Theater. Neither Maria nor Elizabeth had had the least notion that dressing for a formal affair was so involved and complicated. The things that went beneath a gown were every bit as important as the dress itself, perhaps even more so.

First and foremost came stockings, and Elizabeth was astounded when the dresser in charge brought out all her boxes of hose. They were dyed every color of the rainbow and made from many different materials. She chose a pair of ecru lace, crocheted in a flower pattern, then, to her great delight, the dresser opened her boxes of garters. Elizabeth realized that choosing garters was much like selecting cakes from a tray of confections. Some were beribboned, others were embroidered with beads or sequins, while yet others were adorned with huge flowers or bright birds. Maria immediately picked garters decorated with brilliant red poppies, but Beth lingered long over her choice and finally decided on a pair made from a delicate shade of green ribbon and embellished with snowdrops.

When she drew the stockings up her long, slender legs and fastened on the pale green garters, a sudden feeling of longing came over her. They transformed her girl's legs into the lovely limbs of a lady, and she wished she could keep them on forever.

Next, they had to be fitted for corsets, something they'd never owned. Their mother had a corset, of course, but it was nothing like these delicate garments with fine whalebone and fancy laces. Bridget fitted one around Maria's midsection and began to pull on the laces. Peg chose one of white silk for Elizabeth that reached from her hips up to beneath her breasts, and as Beth cupped her hands over her exposed bosom, Peg began to draw on the laces.

When she was done, she called to her dresser, "Dora, bring a measuring loop! I've never seen such a tiny waist in my life. It cannot be more than eighteen inches!"

Dora measured Elizabeth's waist. "Seventeen inches, ma'am!"

"My darling girl, your figure is perfection. Every female in the world will envy, hate, and detest you. How bloody marvelous!"

"Oh, Peg, I don't want other females to hate me," Beth replied.

"Well, I'm afraid they will. Your face alone will guarantee that, my darling girl. Let's see if we can find a gown small enough. It must be white, so that will cut down on our selection."

When both sisters were dressed, their gowns were quite similar in style. Each had a low neck, short sleeves, a tight waist, and a full skirt that opened down the front to show the stiff petticoat. Maria had chosen white satin brocade while Elizabeth's was made of delicate white tulle.

They undressed with care, and Dora provided the girls with cloth bags to protect their garments, hung them on a rack, then wheeled it all into Miss Woffington's dressing room for safekeeping until the appointed time. "Don't forget to come early on Saturday—you will need makeup and wigs. Here's your mother. Let's see what she's picked." Bridget had chosen royal blue lace. "Good choice. It has a look of class, which will be most apt since I put you down on the Viceroy's invitation list as the daughter of Viscount Mayo, whoever that may be!"

"Viscount Mayo?" Bridget looked alarmed.

"His family name is Theobald Burke, and Burke is your maiden name, so it seemed convenient. Not to worry, County Mayo is clear across Ireland." Peg looked at their worried faces and raised her arm in a regal gesture. "You'll carry it off—you are *actresses*!"

Chapter Four

*T*he Gunning girls spent hours practicing their dancing steps, curtsies, and Court manners beneath their mother's critical eye. She provided them with paper fans and put them through their paces regarding etiquette and the *language* of the fan. "Remember to address the Viceroy as Your Excellency. A duke or duchess is Your Grace and it will be safest to address everyone else as My Lord or My Lady. Now, do either of you have any questions?"

"How will we be announced when we are presented?" Beth asked.

Bridget had no answer for once and turned to Jack for his help.

"I will simply be announced as John Gunning, Esquire, of Castle Coote. Your mother, since her elevation to the peerage, will be the Honorable Bridget Gunning, daughter of Viscount Mayo. It will depend on what's printed on the invitation. You could be Elizabeth Gunning, granddaughter of Viscount Mayo and Lord Gunning of Cambridgeshire. The last, at least, is no lie," he said, laughing.

Bridget gave him a scathing look. "Maria, being the elder, will be presented first, Elizabeth. Don't shove yourself forward!"

Beth put her hand over her heart. Being presented at the Viceroy's ball would be too daunting. "My insides are fluttering."

"Cease such nonsense immediately, Elizabeth! You will simply think of it as a role in a play. You are both young ladies of the *ton* who are being presented to the Viceroy of Ireland. You make your curtsies, you display pretty manners, you smile, you lower your lashes demurely if spoken to, and you keep your mouths *shut*."

"Except when we eat," Maria chimed in.

"Ladies of breeding eat like birds! Have you forgotten all I've taught you? If and when you are offered refreshments, you open your fan, lower your eyes, and murmur, 'No thank you, ma'am'."

"Are we ready for off, my beauties? There's a warm breeze blowing, I don't think you'll need your woolen shawls."

As they stepped into the street, a gust of wind blew Elizabeth's skirt up to reveal her ankles clad in the black cotton stockings. She pushed it down and cast an apprehensive glance at her mother.

"Acting the role of a young lady of breeding doesn't come naturally to you, Elizabeth. How do you expect to be a success on the stage? You must imitate Maria; she has it down to perfection."

"Yes, ma'am," Elizabeth murmured, wishing with all her heart that she could make her mother proud of her.

They walked from Dame Street to the theater but hoped that once they were garbed in their finery they'd be able to ride to Dublin Castle. Beth's excitement began to rise and a bubble of laughter rose to her lips. She felt her father squeeze her hand and anticipated this would be the most thrilling night of her life.

At the theater Bridget Gunning concentrated on getting Maria ready, then attended to her own transformation. Peg Woffington's dresser, Dora, tightened the laces on Elizabeth's corset then lifted the stiff petticoat and gown over her head.

"Your skin is translucent—it would be a crime to cover it with makeup. I'll darken your brows and lashes and put a bit of color on your lips. There! Now you're ready for a wig." Dora selected one with small curls. "Your real hair is far prettier than any of this false stuff, but 'tis the fashion to wear a powdered wig, especially when you are to be formally presented to the Viceroy." Dora swept up Elizabeth's golden tresses and pinned them to the top of her head then fit the powdered hairpiece over them. She stepped away from the mirror so that Elizabeth could see herself.

"Oh, I can't believe it's me!" Beth ran her hands over the white tulle skirt then lifted it slightly so she could see her lacy stockings and satin slippers. "Thank you so much, Dora!"

"Here's the fan that matches the gown. Slip the ribbon over your wrist so you won't lose it."

Beth gazed reverently at the silk covered fan as she opened and closed it. "Oh, I promise I won't lose it, Dora." Suddenly, she caught sight of her sister. "Maria," she whispered, awestruck, "you look like a princess."

"Our English princesses are ugly! I look like an angel."

Beth saw the pearls threaded through the curls on her sister's powdered wig and the silver ribbon on her fan. Maria had on pale white face paint and red rouged cheeks. "Yes, just like an angel."

"Don't tell me these elegant ladies are my little girls?" Jack Gunning teased, as he paid homage with a low bow.

"Father, you look like a Lord of the Realm!" Beth's eyes shone with pride at her handsome father, garbed in a dark blue satin suit with lace at collar and cuff.

"Wait until you see your mother."

Official invitation in hand, Bridget swept into the wardrobe room, a vision in royal blue lace. She was never lacking in confidence, and the elegant gown and faux jewels added an air of supreme authority. No queen could have appeared more regal. "Peg has sent her carriage for us. Above all, remember your poise this evening."

A coach stood waiting at the theater's colonnade, but when Jack made to open its door, Bridget stopped him and raised her eyes to the driver. "The carriage door, if you please, sirrah! Be quick about it before this accursed Irish wind blows us into Dublin Harbor."

The coach drove quickly up Cork Hill, but the lower castle yard was congested with carriages, and the fashionably dressed guests who had alighted from them formed a jostling crowd that pressed forward toward the upper castle yard. As they joined the throng Bridget ordered, "If we get separated, we'll meet at the state apartments."

In less than a minute, Elizabeth was surrounded by a mob.

She searched the sea of faces but found none of them familiar. She did not panic because she saw there were other young ladies in white gowns who were obviously going to be presented to the Viceroy. At a sudden gust of wind the girl beside her cried out and clutched her head. Elizabeth saw that the girl's powdered wig had been snatched by the blustery sea breeze and was rolling across the courtyard. Without hesitation Beth chased after it, but the wig eluded her and rolled beneath the wheels of a carriage.

Elizabeth bent to retrieve it and to her dismay found that it was no longer white but the color of sludge. She carried it in the direction of its owner and only found her in the throng because she was crying. "I'm so sorry . . . please don't cry."

"Charlie, I should box your ears! Why were you so careless?"

Elizabeth knew this was the girl's mother. Her heart went out to the small, dark female, because she knew what it felt like to incur a parent's wrath. "It wasn't her fault, my lady. The wind snatched it, then a carriage ran over it before I could catch it."

"Well, it's totally ruined, and you cannot possibly be presented to the Viceroy without it, Charlie. You would be a laughingstock!"

The girl began to sob. She only came up to Elizabeth's shoulder, and she looked so young and vulnerable that it wrung Beth's heart. "Please don't cry . . . it will be all right. You can have my wig," she said impulsively. She immediately removed it and handed it to the young lady's startled mother.

"But, my dear, what about you?"

"I can manage without it. I've never worn one before."

The older woman, filled with gratitude, stared at Elizabeth's golden tresses. "You have beautiful hair indeed, and a generous heart to go with it." She fit the powdered wig over her daughter's dark curls then pulled out a lace-edged handkerchief and tenderly dried her tears. "My *pauvre petit.* Don't be upset, darling—you look quite lovely once again."

Charlie smiled at her mother then took Beth's hand. "You are an angel! I thank you with all my heart. What's your name?"

"Elizabeth Gunning. I got separated from my family."

"You stay close by us, Elizabeth, until we find your own mother."

Beth inwardly cringed at the thought of her mother's fury when she saw her without her powdered wig. She glanced at the older woman and knew instinctively that there was love and affection between mother and daughter. The knowledge warmed her heart.

By this time the crowd had thinned, and Beth and Charlie, hand in hand, finally made their way to the magnificent state apartments, whose ceilings were painted with scenes from Ireland's history. The outer gallery was crowded with guests, peeresses, and *débutantes*, all awaiting entrance into the Long Gallery. It took only ten minutes for Beth to come face to face with her mother.

"Elizabeth! Why on earth have you removed your wig? Put it back on immediately!" Bridget ordered.

Beth's eyes widened with apprehension. She opened her mouth to speak, but nothing came out.

"Allow me to introduce myself." Charlie's mother held out her hand to Bridget. "I'm Dorothy Boyle, Countess of Burlington, and I want to congratulate you on Elizabeth's exquisite manners and generosity of heart. My daughter, Charlotte, had an unfortunate accident with her hairpiece, and Elizabeth came to her rescue. Your daughter has the most beautiful hair I've ever seen, and she looks far lovelier without the wig."

Bridget took a deep breath. Then she actually clasped the hand of the woman without fainting. "I am delighted to make your acquaintance, Lady Burlington. I'm Bridget Gunning, daughter of Viscount Mayo."

"Not Theobald Mayo? Well, bless my soul, before I married I met Theobald on many occasions. He was a friend of my late mother. What a small world this is. How providential we have met—our daughters are already fast friends."

They heard the chamberlain begin to announce the names of the *débutantes* who were to be presented to the Viceroy. "Hurry, Charlotte, he'll be announcing the names starting with B at any moment. Don't forget to hold your head up high when you walk down the Long Gallery." She turned back to Bridget. "See you later."

"Elizabeth! Do you have any notion of who she is? She's the

wealthy Countess of Burlington, who owns a palatial mansion in London's Pall Mall. Her daughter, Charlotte Boyle, is one of the greatest heiresses in the kingdom!"

"You're not angry because I lent her my wig?"

"On the contrary. For once you used your head!" Bridget laughed at her own pun. "You must introduce Maria to Charlotte. Nothing is more advantageous than influential friends. Come, girls, let's push closer to the doors so we can see into the Long Gallery."

"Where is Father?" Maria demanded. "I shall go without him if they announce my name and he isn't here."

Bridget craned her neck to observe what was going on in the Long Gallery. "By the look of things, you won't need him. Apparently, they announce the parents' names and their rank but the young lady being presented walks down the Long Gallery alone."

Elizabeth caught a glimpse of the gallery lined with people who, in effect, were an audience for the young ladies making their debut. She realized it would be the same as being on stage. She could hear low murmurs, coughs, and the rustle of garments coming from the members of the audience as they watched the presentations with varying degrees of attentiveness.

Presently, the chamberlain announced, "Lady Fiona Gower, daughter of the Earl and Countess of Granville—"

"Maria, you will be next. Gunning comes after Gower. Get ready, and remember your poise," Bridget hissed. She handed the chamberlain the invitation card on which was printed the names and pertinent information he was to announce.

The chamberlain waited until the Viceroy, enthroned at the far end of the gallery, finished speaking with Lady Fiona Gower. Then he cleared his throat and announced, "Mistress Maria Gunning, daughter of John Gunning, Esquire, of Castle Coote, and the Honorable Bridget Gunning, daughter of Viscount Mayo."

Maria stepped into the gallery and walked slowly forward. Suddenly, the audience ceased murmuring; no one coughed and even the rustle of garments stopped. Complete silence fell over the spectators as the beautiful young lady made her way down the Long Gallery. She had the presence of a princess and the poise of a goddess. When she made her curtsy to the Viceroy, the audience let out a collective sigh then began to buzz like a beehive.

The Chamberlain intoned, "Mistress Elizabeth Gunning, daughter of John Gunning, Esquire, of Castle Coote, and the Honorable Bridget Gunning, daughter of Viscount Mayo."

Elizabeth lifted her chin and stepped forward. The buzzing had already stopped, and before she walked five feet, another hush fell over the curious spectators. As she gained confidence, the trembling left her knees, the thunder of her own heartbeat in her ears lessened, and she was able to summon a serene smile that held her audience in thrall. As she neared the end of the Long Gallery she distinctly heard a male voice murmur, "Two beauties!" When she sank down in a graceful curtsy before Ireland's Viceroy, the crowd broke into spontaneous applause.

"It is my distinct pleasure to welcome such a lovely lady to Dublin Castle and to my Court." His Excellency's eyes kindled.

She gave him a radiant smile. "The pleasure is mine, Your Excellency. You do me great honor." She moved on to the next chamber, which was St. Patrick's Hall where the ball was being held.

She expected to see Maria but it was Charlotte Boyle who stood waiting for her.

"I was supposed to sit on the dais behind the Viceroy, but I was so nervous that I forgot and came straight into the ballroom," Charlotte said with a bubble of laughter.

"Will your mother be angry with you?" Beth asked anxiously.

"Oh, no. She won't be angry, but she will tease me endlessly about being nervous, and Father will say, 'Spit in their eye, Charlie, you've the best blood in Ireland!' "

Beth laughed as Charlotte mimicked her father's voice. "Do you live in Ireland?"

"No, we were just visiting our castle at Lismore. We might be known as the 'Mad Boyles,' " Charlotte confided, "but we have more sense than to come to Ireland in any month but August!"

"The rain can be endless," Beth sympathized. "I wanted to introduce you to my sister, Maria, but she seems to have disappeared." Elizabeth searched the crowded ballroom filled with sets of dancing couples, ladies in elaborate gowns, gentlemen in formal attire, and military men in resplendent uniforms.

"Maria and I introduced ourselves, then she went off on the arm of a handsome cavalry officer."

Before Elizabeth could respond, her new friend was seized about the waist by a laughing red-haired young man.

"Here you are, little cousin! I've been looking everywhere for you. My friend William has been begging for an introduction, and I assured him you would be sitting up on the dais with his father. Thanks for making a liar out of me, Charlie."

"You don't need my help for that, Michael. You lie every day of your life. I'd like you to meet my friend Elizabeth Gunning. Elizabeth, this is my cousin Michael Boyle—definitely one of the reasons we're known as the 'Mad Boyles'!"

Michael took Elizabeth's hand and drew it to his lips. "One of the Beauties! Mistress Gunning—your servant. You caused quite a stir in the Long Gallery."

Elizabeth blushed profusely. "How do you do, my lord?"

Michael turned as a tall, blond man approached and towered at his shoulder. "I found her at last, Will. Charlie, permit me to present William Cavendish, Lord Hartington. This is my favorite cousin, Lady Charlotte Boyle."

"Lady Charlotte, I am enchanted."

Beth watched Charlie's face as the young lord lifted her fingers to his lips. Her eyes gazed upward as if she had become mesmerized, and Beth knew the handsome devil had rendered her momentarily speechless. Finally, she murmured, "My lord."

"My friends call me Will, and it is my sincere wish that you and I become friends, Lady Charlotte."

Beth was amazed at his easy manner. He was Lord Hartington, heir to the great Dukedom of Devonshire, yet he was warm, friendly, and totally unpretentious.

Michael touched his friend's elbow and said affably, "Will, may I present Mistress Elizabeth Gunning?"

When the Viceroy's son kissed Beth's hand and told her he was delighted to meet her, she realized he was completely sincere.

"They are choosing partners for the quadrille. Would you do me the honor, Lady Charlotte?"

As William led Charlie onto the dance floor, Michael Boyle

executed a bow. "Would you do me the honor, Mistress Gunning?"

Beth experienced inward panic but did not permit it to show. Instead, she smiled and placed her hand in his. As soon as the music began, her feet executed the steps she had practiced so often, and her panic receded. However, it came flooding back over her when it came time to change partners and she found herself in the arms of a man she had never expected to see again. "You!" she gasped.

"Me!" John Campbell smiled down at her. "Mistress Gunning, can you ever forgive me for the cavalier way I treated you when we met by the river? I fully deserved to be slapped in the face. I had no idea you would be coming to Dublin to be presented to the Viceroy. Will you give me the chance to make amends?"

Her knees felt like wet linen, and her heart was beating much faster than the music. In his formal black evening attire with the snowy lace at his throat, he looked devastatingly handsome. "How will you do that, sir?" she demanded in a cool voice.

"By taking back my kisses?" His dark eyes glittered dangerously as he tightened his hold on her.

His words were so outrageous they sparked the desire to tease him in return. "I'll not give them back. I'd rather keep them."

Once more, it was time to change partners. A dark young man held out his hand to her, but Campbell did not release her. "Go to the devil, Henry." He bent his head and confided, "My brother. No young lady is safe with him."

The corners of Beth's lips lifted. "It must run in the family."

"I'm taking you off the dance floor. It's the only way I'll be able to keep possession of you. Every man here wants to partner the most beautiful *débutante* at the ball." He kept firm hold of her hand as he led her off the floor and into another gallery. "You are quite possibly the loveliest *débutante* ever."

Her eyes sparkled with mischief as she confided, "I'm not a *débutante* at all, John. I told you I was going to be an actress. I'm just playing a part! Peg Woffington is my mother's dearest friend. She arranged our invitation, and this gown is a costume from Smock Alley Theater's wardrobe department."

John Campbell was stunned. For a moment he suspected that the lady was being an unmerciful tease. Then he realized that she was far too ingenuous for that, and he was overcome with a desire to preserve her sweetness and protect her innocence. He covered her hand with his. "Are you enjoying yourself, Beth?"

"Oh, 'tis the most wondrous night of my life, John. I've never seen anything like these state apartments with their liveried staff, scarlet carpets, and painted ceilings."

He followed her upward gaze. "That's King George, being supported by Liberty and Justice—two strapping wenches!"

Remembering her appetite, he led her past lavender scented fountains to long tables filled with wines, platters of cold food, and sweetmeats. "Would you like something to eat?" His mouth curved. "Not that you're the least bit hungry, of course."

She laughed up into his face, thrilled that he had remembered her words, and answered as before: "Since it would be impolite to refuse, it would be my pleasure to taste everything, sir."

"But not the wine?" he asked, amused.

"Of course the wine! It cannot steal my senses tonight. You have already done that," she admitted shyly.

He wanted to keep her to himself to enjoy the sensual pleasure of watching her eat, but they were joined by William and Charlotte, followed by his brother, Henry, who was now escorting Maria Gunning. Then along came Michael Boyle with Charlie's mother, Lady Burlington, on his arm. Before John could introduce Beth, he discovered that everyone had already met and spoke like friends.

Elizabeth glanced at him quickly, and he easily read the plea in her eyes: *Please don't reveal my secret.* He handed her a glass of wine and touched his own glass to hers in a pledge. "To confidences shared," he whispered intimately.

Elizabeth took a sip and almost choked as she saw her mother and father moving toward her with plates in their hands. She drained her wine and set the glass aside before they saw her, then heard Lady Burlington's distinctive voice. "Mrs. Gunning . . . Bridget, I declare you are monopolizing the most attractive man here tonight. I insist you introduce me."

"Lady Burlington, may I present my husband, John Gunning?"

With amazement, Beth saw her handsome father take the hand of the countess to his lips and heard the peeress say, "Dorothy! You must call me Dorothy, and I shall call you John." Elizabeth could clearly see that her mother was in her element, socializing with the nobility as if she rubbed elbows with the *ton* every day. Beth, wanting to escape from the gathering, sent a desperate signal to her companion, but before they could move away they were joined by none other than the Viceroy himself.

"Hello, Father. The presentations must be over at last. I believe you know Lady Charlotte's mother, Lady Burlington?"

"'Course I do. Good to see you, Dorothy. Thirsty work, receiving *débutantes*. Get me a drink, Will!"

Dorothy took the Viceroy's arm. "William, allow me to introduce John and Bridget Gunning. Would you believe Bridget is Theobald Mayo's daughter?"

Elizabeth held her breath as the Duke of Devonshire peered through his quizzing glass at her mother. "Ahh, mother of the Beauties! Easy to see your daughters get their looks from you. How is old Theo?" He took the wineglass from his son and drained it.

"You young devils are monopolizing these beauties. Take them back to the ballroom immediately. There's a score of viscounts and uniformed officers lined up to dance with these pretty gels!"

As bidden, the young devils dutifully escorted their partners back to the ballroom and reluctantly relinquished them to the eager nobles who had been waiting to dance with the *débutantes*.

John Campbell waited exactly five minutes then tapped Lord Sackville on the shoulder and looked into Elizabeth's eyes. "I believe the lady is promised to me."

She smiled up at him. "I believe I am," she said breathlessly.

Chapter Five

Since it was dawn before they arrived home, the Gunning sisters did not awaken until noon. Elizabeth stretched and smiled as the indelible memories of last night's presentation and ball came flooding back to her. Peg Woffington had arrived after her performance at Smock Alley and had told them they needn't return their borrowed clothes until today. She was the most generous friend anyone could ever have. Without her, Elizabeth knew that last night would never have happened.

Before Maria started chattering, Beth closed her eyes and thought about John. He had finally told her his last name was Campbell—a good Scottish name. A picture of the darkly handsome male with broad shoulders flashed into her mind, but she knew it was far more than his looks that made her pulse quicken. It was the fact that he made her feel special and that the attraction between them was mutual. She sighed, remembering that he was returning to England, but her toes curled as she relived the good-bye kiss he had given her when they parted at dawn. Before she opened her eyes she made a wish that someday they would meet again.

"Maria! Elizabeth! It is time to get up. Breakfast is on the table, and we have a great many things to discuss." Bridget's voice was brisk and brooked no argument.

Elizabeth's eyes flew open. Last night she had done many things of which her mother would not approve, and now she would have to pay for them. As she threw back the quilt she ad-

mitted that she didn't care. It had all been worthwhile. Glori-
ously worthwhile!

When she sat down at the table Beth glanced at her father
and saw that he had a look of disbelief on his face, as if he had
heard some shocking news. Her heart sank as she realized they
must have been discussing a most serious matter.

"At least thirty gentlemen asked me to dance last night,"
Maria boasted, taking her seat at the table.

"And you, Elizabeth?" her mother demanded.

"Per—perhaps a dozen," she said, apprehensive about the
consequences of her answer.

Bridget turned to Jack. "There you are, then! Do you need
more proof that my decision is the right one?" she demanded.

"What decision?" Maria asked, taking a bite of soda bread.

"I have decided that we are returning to England to take our
rightful place in Society."

Maria squealed with delight. Elizabeth remained silent,
wondering what their rightful place in Society was but certain
that their mother was about to enlighten them.

"Last night I had a *revelation*! My eyes were opened! I kept
a close watch on both of you, and what I saw astounded me.
The Gunning sisters, Maria and Elizabeth, were the center of
attention. Your beauty attracted men like a lodestone! And they
were no ordinary men. They were wealthy, titled gentlemen!"

"We've always known their beauty was exceptional," Jack
said.

"Yes, but now they are of marriageable age, it would be a
disservice to our daughters not to take advantage of that beauty.
I have decided that we shall go and live in London."

"Oh, how wonderful! Do you think David Garrick would let
us act at Drury Lane Theater?" Maria asked excitedly.

"You can both forget about becoming actresses!" Bridget
decreed. "We are going to London so that you can make good
marriages. Titled, wealthy men do not marry *actresses,* let me
assure you. The highest an actress could aspire to is becoming
a mistress. Look at my friend Peg, if you want living proof of
that!"

Elizabeth blushed. Maria had told her that Peg was Garrick's
mistress, but she hadn't really believed it.

"Titled men marry young ladies with dowries. Moreover,

living in London will cost a great deal of money. Where do you expect to get it? From your father, Viscount Mayo?" Jack asked dryly.

Bridget turned on him with blazing eyes. "It doesn't matter a damn that my father isn't Viscount Mayo! What matters is the perception! You saw what happened last night. The Countess of Burlington *perceived* that I was Mayo's daughter, then even His Excellency, the Duke of Devonshire, *perceived* that I was *Old Theo's* offspring. As an actress I know that what is paramount in this world is the *perception,* not the *reality,* Jack Gunning!"

"We'll need real money to set up in London. Not just the perception of money, Bridget."

"That's your job, Jack. You must return to Castlecoote and sell it immediately. We'll stay here. With any luck you can be back in a week, two at the most. I'll give you a list of things to keep, such as our books, and you can sell everything else."

"You're serious, then?"

"I've never been more serious in my life. Maria and Elizabeth already possess beauty, breeding, brains, and youth. As you saw last night, all they need are the right clothes and a few invitations to Court functions and our future will be set. Remember the words of the Bard: *There is a tide in the affairs of men, which taken at the flood, leads on to fortune.*"

Within the hour, Jack set off for Roscommon. Elizabeth went with him as far as the nearby stable so she could say good-bye to the mule. Inside, she was terrified that her world was going to be turned upside down and that her chance to become an actress, to lose herself in acting out roles, was being snatched away from her. As her father harnessed the animal between the shafts of the wagon, she ventured hopefully, "You do disagree with Mother's decision?"

"My only concern is for you and Maria. If by some miracle you could make good marriages, it would be far better than a life on the stage. We'll try it her way." He touched her cheek tenderly then laughed. "What bloody choice do we have? When Bridget issues her orders none dare to disobey. Good-bye, Beth. Be a good girl."

"Good-bye, Dad. Be careful!" She closed her eyes for a quick prayer: *Please make him come back to us . . . don't let him run away!*

*   *   *

When the Gunnings returned the fancy clothes to the theater, Peg greeted them warmly. "What an outstanding performance you gave last night. Your daughters made quite an impression, Bridget, and you didn't do so badly yourself, old girl!"

"It turned out so successfully that we've decided to return to England. Our goal for Maria and Elizabeth is marriage!"

"By God, Bridget, I admire your ambition. Their faces very well could be their fortune! But if you want husbands for them, they must abandon their aspirations to become actresses."

"Do you think so?" Bridget asked, as if such a thought had never occurred to her.

"I *know* so," Peg said with conviction. " 'Tis a ramshackle life, and actresses soon acquire notorious reputations, deserved or not. The only proposals Maria and Elizabeth would receive would be dishonorable ones. Not a hint of scandal must touch them if they are to make good marriages. But if you can successfully pull the wool over Society's eyes, it will be a gamble worth taking."

"We need to earn some money to get us to London. If they cannot work as actresses, perhaps you could give them jobs behind the scenes?" Bridget suggested, counting on Peg's generous nature.

"Well, let's see. You could be my understudy for the part of Sir Harry Wildair . . . you learn lines quickly, Bridget. I intend to perform every night for the next fortnight, until we return to England, so it's just a precaution against an unforseen accident."

"Thanks, Peg. Give me a script and I'll know it by tomorrow."

"The girls can work in the wardrobe department. There are always costumes to be sewn, garments to be cleaned, wigs to be repowdered. You'll soon have enough for passage across to England."

Elizabeth curtsied. "Thank you, Miss Woffington. Last night was like a magical dream. We are so lucky to have a friend like you. May we begin work today?"

"If you are good with a needle, the wardrobe mistress will soon put you to work, Elizabeth."

As Beth and her sister made their way to the wardrobe room

Maria protested, "I don't want to clean costumes. I want to be an actress up on stage!"

To banish her own fear and reassure herself as much as her sister, Beth said, "Don't you see, Maria? In England, we *will* be actresses, but instead of performing on a wooden platform with a curtain, our stage will be the whole of London, and our audience will be the entire upper class of Society. We are to pretend to be *débutantes*, having a first Season, and try to make good matches."

"Well, I certainly shan't have trouble catching a husband. I know what men like. You might have difficulties, though. You are far too unworldly and innocent for your own good," Maria declared. "Oh, I can't believe we're going to London! I've wished for it so often. Perhaps wishes really do come true."

Elizabeth fleetingly thought of the wish she'd made about John Campbell, and her knees turned to water. "I told John I was going to be an actress. What if I meet him again in London?"

"Dismiss it as a flight of fancy. Men are easily handled, Beth, if you go about it the right way."

During the next two weeks the wardrobe department of Smock Alley Theater became Elizabeth's entire world. She loved working with the costumes, especially the ladies' garments, and she absorbed like a sponge all the tricks the wardrobe mistress taught her about changing the look of a gown. With a froth of lace, some bright satin ribbons, or the addition of delicate artificial flowers, the appearance of a dress could be transformed from plain to fancy. Changing a matching petticoat to one whose color contrasted with its overdress produced a gown that would not be recognized. Sleeves could be added or removed, necklines raised or lowered, and a gown with a fitted waist could be turned into a sacque or half-sacque with a full, flowing back.

When the fortnight was up the Gunnings bade good-bye to Peg Woffington and David Garrick, who were returning to London's Drury Lane Theater a week before the opening of Parliament in September. This date marked the beginning of the busy social Winter Season, when politicians and the *ton* returned to London after spending the summer at their country estates.

Elizabeth and Maria each received five shillings in wages, and Bridget immediately relieved them of their money and added it to the ten shillings that Peg had paid her to understudy. She put it in the bag she had sewn into her petticoat along with the money Jack had made by selling the turnips. Back at their room off Dame Street, she took out all their money and counted it. Including the sovereign she had taken for safekeeping from Jack and the crown she got when she pawned Elizabeth's harp, they now had seven pounds. "Your father could have been back by now if he wasn't so feckless!"

Elizabeth fought a feeling of panic, wondering if he would return at all, but knew better than to voice such a doubt. The next day was spent packing their carpetbags, while their mother went to inquire about the cheapest passage to England. That night, when her father returned, Beth burst into tears.

"Stop that sniveling immediately, Elizabeth. We'll have no melodrama. Anyone would think you were off to be executed, rather than embarking on the most advantageous journey of your life."

Jack winked at his daughter, knowing she shed tears of relief. "No need to cry, beauty. I brought more than turnips this time."

"How much did you get?" Bridget sounded ready to murder him if he had let them down.

"When Thomas Longford offered me a hundred pounds for Castlecoote, I informed him Lord Lanesborough had offered me double for the land alone. It was a bit of an untruth, but I reasoned Tom Longford couldn't very well rush up to his lordship and question him. Next day Longford offered two hundred, cash on the barrel!"

"Two hundred!" Bridget was pleased, but she couldn't bring herself to praise him. "We should've sold Castlecoote long ago!"

Early the next morning, the Gunnings boarded a boat that was transporting cattle to the Liverpool stockyards. There were no passenger cabins on the livestock barge, but the captain agreed to give them passage for a few shillings, if they were willing to sit up on deck. While Elizabeth went to befriend a calf, Maria complained that the smell was making her sick. For once she got short shrift from her mother. "*Mal de mer* is a fashionable complaint. Stick your head over the rail. I wasn't about to waste money on a fancy sailing ship, when we still have to buy stagecoach tickets from Liverpool to London."

That night, when they arrived at the Liverpool docks, Elizabeth and Maria sat on their carpetbags while their parents argued. "We should take a room, Bridget. The girls need sleep."

"They can sleep in the coach. If we travel on the overnight coach, we'll be in Stoke-on-Trent by morning and Coventry by tomorrow night. We can take a room there."

"I wish you weren't so hard on the girls, Bridget."

"If wishes were horses, beggars would ride! One of us has to have a plan of action. You seem to forget I'm doing this for them, Jack Gunning. Pick up that trunk and let's go."

Four days later the Gunnings arrived at the White Horse Inn, in London's Piccadilly. Jack bought them all bread and cheese, then Bridget led the way into nearby Green Park. "Your father and I are going to search for a house we can lease. It might take all day to find one with a good address that we can afford. The park is the safest place for you until we return. Stay together, speak to no one, and keep your heads covered. We don't want anyone to remember your beautiful hair."

The prospect of having to stroll around a park for hours when she was exhausted didn't sit well with Maria. "I hope the house they get has beds. I never closed my eyes in that wretched coach. When we get to the house, I'm going to sleep for a week."

Elizabeth, aching all over, tried not to think about sleep. She fed her crumbs to the pigeons and gazed about. "This is a lovely park. It would be wonderful if the house was close by. The trees and grass remind me of Ireland."

"Ugh, I hate Ireland—it's always damp and raining. This is the most exciting city in the world, and all you want to do is walk in the wretched park and feed dirty pigeons and squirrels. I want to explore London. We're here to catch husbands, but you'll never do it unless you grow up!"

"You make it sound like catching salmon." Elizabeth thought of John Campbell, and her lips curved in a smile. "Men aren't fish."

"Aren't they? You set out your bait and let them have a little nibble. You hook them and play them on your line until they are gasping before you reel them in. Then you devour them at leisure."

The afternoon light was fading from the city's sky by the time Jack and Bridget Gunning returned to collect their daughters. Their mother's mood was one of outrage at the prices that London commanded for its accommodation. "It's barefaced robbery! There isn't a house in Mayfair going for less than two hundred pounds a year. Imagine them wanting us to spend every last penny we have to our name on the first day that we arrive!"

"So you didn't get us a house?" Maria asked with dismay.

"Of course I got us a house, and with a prestigious address, but we could only afford to lease it for six months. The Gunnings now reside in Great Marlborough Street. The house comes furnished and with a small staff—a cook-cum-housekeeper and an aging footman. Come girls, the walk will do you good, and it's the last fresh air you'll be getting for awhile. You will remain indoors and out of sight until we can transform you into young ladies of fashion. Thank God it's going dark and no one will see you arrive looking like beggar girls. With only six months to accomplish our goal, we've got our work cut out for us. Jack, first thing in the morning you can make the rounds of the moneylenders!"

In Pall Mall, the huge black traveling coach swung through the gates of Burlington House and pulled up at the marble steps of the mansion. The coachman jumped from the box and opened the carriage door for the earl and countess as the butler, housekeeper, maid, and footman descended the steps to welcome the family home.

"Take Lady Charlotte—she's fallen asleep. Traveling is so utterly exhausting." Flanked by her London ladies' maid and her housekeeper, the Countess of Burlington followed the footman carrying her daughter into the house and up the grand staircase.

"Use the bedwarmer on Lady Charlotte's sheets. I don't want her coming down with a cold just as the Winter Season starts."

As the footman placed her in a gilt chair while her bed was

prepared, Charlie awoke in time to see her own ladies' maid come through her chamber door carrying a Dandie Dinmont terrier. "Hello, Dandy. I've missed you so much!" Charlie held out her arms and laughed as the little dog jumped up to lick her chin.

"Don't unpack Lady Charlotte's trunks tonight. It will take hours, and she needs her rest. But you can get her some nice warm chocolate." Dorothy Boyle dropped a kiss on her daughter's dark curls. "Good night, darling. You must stay abed until noon tomorrow to regain your strength from the rigors of travel."

The journey from Ireland had been far less rigorous for the Boyles than it would have been for lesser mortals. They had crossed the Irish Sea aboard their own yacht then ridden in their well-sprung traveling coach, with outriders for protection. They had not slept at inns but at their own residences of Bolton Abbey, Londesborough Lodge, and Uppingham Manor in Rutland, all of which had their own full staffs of servants to feed and pamper them.

As the Countess of Burlington entered her own bedchamber, her maid asked, "Would you like hot water for a bath, your ladyship?"

"Yes, thank you." She scribbled a note and handed it to her.

The maid passed the note to the earl's valet, who in turn took it to his master's bedchamber and delivered it. Presently, Richard Boyle made his way to his wife's private bedroom. "You wanted a word, my dear?"

"Yes, Richard. Charlie has confided in me that she has taken a fancy to William Cavendish, Lord Hartington. Now, I know she is only sixteen, but I don't think we should let this opportunity to make a dynastic marriage slip away. William might become Duke of Devonshire sooner than we think, by the looks of the old duke. The Devonshire property is even more vast than our own."

Boyle frowned. "Hartington's at least twenty-eight. Don't you consider that a little mature for a sixteen-year-old, Dorothy?"

"Maturity is a welcome quality in a husband. He's likely sown all those disgusting wild oats and is ready to settle down. I suspect he's in the market for a wife and if we don't *snare* him, another prominent family will. If he shows the slightest interest in Charlie, we should encourage it in every possible way."

"You make it sound like setting a trap for the poor devil."

"Exactly so! No male voluntarily asks to be leg-shackled. I believe a six-month relentless campaign will result in victory!"

Bridget Gunning lost no time visiting her friend at Drury Lane Theater. "I managed to lease us a house in Great Marlborough Street, on the fringes of Mayfair," she told Peg.

"Oh, that's a most acceptable address. I believe Lord Charles Cavendish has a house in that street, and Horace Walpole, the gossip, lives within spitting distance in Hanover Square."

"Lord Charles Cavendish is one of the Duke of Devonshire's sons, but not the heir, correct?"

"Correct. William Cavendish, Lord Hartington, is the heir and, naturally, he lives at Devonshire House in Piccadilly. I have a copy of *Burke's Peerage* to keep the players straight. Garrick and I have a house in Soho Square, not quite as fashionable but handy to the theater district." Peg threw back her head and laughed. "My hat is off to you, Bridget. You've set yourself a goal to which few would dare aspire. I hope you pull it off, old girl. If I can help in any way, don't hesitate to ask."

"Thank you, Peg. From time to time I intend to hire the services of some of your bit players, but I'm getting before myself. The first item of business is our wardrobe. Do you suppose one of Drury Lane's seamstresses would be interested in coming to Great Marlborough Street?"

"Any of them would be glad to earn extra money, I'm sure. Come, we'll go and see Mary. She works magic with a needle."

"Do you ever sell any of the garments from the wardrobe department?" Bridget hinted.

"Very seldom. The costumes are reworked again and again. But there is a marvelous secondhand shop in Covent Garden where the actresses from all the theaters buy and sell their clothes. Most of the styles would be inappropriate for young girls, but I have no doubt you could acquire some fashionable outfits for yourself."

Mary moved into Great Marlborough Street for a week, and

with the help of Maria and Elizabeth, sewed all night long, creating undergarments, day dresses, cloaks, and bonnets so that the Gunning daughters could make their debut into Society.

At the secondhand shop Bridget found some smart outfits for herself that looked as if they had hardly been worn. Admiring her slim figure in the shop's mirror, she concluded that the woman must have sold them because she had gained weight and couldn't fit into them. She bought stockings and gloves that all of them could wear, then selected three fans. They were rather shabby but she knew the sticks could be recovered with new material.

By the end of the week, the only garments lacking were ball gowns. The cost of such dresses was exorbitant, but Bridget was adamant that her daughters must have gowns from one of the best *modiste* shops in London, rather than something stitched by Mary.

Wearing their lovely new day dresses and accompanied by their liveried footman, Maria and Elizabeth emerged into the sunshine for the first time in a week. They drew every eye as Bridget ushered them past Hanover Square to Bond Street where the ladies of the *beau monde* did their shopping.

They entered Madame Madeleine's, a fashionable establishment renowned for its copies of Worth gowns. Maria and Elizabeth were in seventh heaven trying on the exquisite silk and satin creations, and each girl had no difficulty selecting her favorite. The difficulty arose when Bridget learned what they cost. It was twice as much as she had anticipated—but the solution was obvious.

"We'll take this one." Bridget indicated the gown that Maria had chosen. "The two of you will simply have to share it!"

When they arrived home Bridget confronted Jack. "Our money is melting like snow in summer. I want you to visit your family in St. Ives. Inform them of our daughters' extraordinary prospects in the marriage market and tell them bluntly that you expect them to contribute to the expense of their Season."

At last, Bridget Gunning was ready to launch her campaign, and she intended to open it with a salvo. She went to the newspaper offices of the *London Chronicle* and paid five shillings to have a notice placed in a prominent position on the social page:

The beauteous granddaughters of Lord John Gunning, of St. Ives, and Theobald, 6th Viscount Mayo, recently arrived from Castle Coote, Ireland, to take up residence at their London home in Great Marlborough Street. Maria and Elizabeth were recently presented to His Excellency the Viceroy, Lieutenant Governor, where their incomparable beauty took Dublin Castle by storm. They are expected to have a similar impact on London Society. The Gunning sisters, swamped with social invitations, are in great demand for the fashionable entertainments being planned for the Winter Season.

Chapter Six

*B*efore Parliament opened, George II, King of England, held a levee at St. James's Palace. Now that everyone was back in London, these would be weekly events attended by courtiers, politicians, the nobility, and wealthy landowners seeking favors from the Crown.

The Duke of Devonshire, newly appointed Lord Steward of the Royal Household, stood talking with the king, graciously acknowledging the monarch's thanks for his "prudent administration" in Ireland. Devonshire's heir, William, Lord Hartington, ambitious for the post of Master of the Horse, was also present at the levee. He greeted his friend John Campbell and enquired why his brother, Henry, was absent.

"Henry was called back to active duty with his regiment."

"He's a captain with the infantry of the Argyll and Sutherland Highlanders isn't he? There's no trouble in Scotland, I hope?"

"Posted to the Continent as a warning to the French, I warrant."

John and Will were joined by James Douglas, Duke of Hamilton, who held a seat in Parliament. Hamilton hated the king with a passion, though he attended his levees without fail. Hamilton had courted renowned beauty Elizabeth Chudleigh until widowed King George fell in love with her and stole her affections. The blow to his pride had been monumental.

"Hello, James. You missed a damned good hunting trip to

Ireland. The game and the salmon were abundant, and even the weather cooperated until the last couple of days," Will said.

"I prefer a gaming hell to the hell of Ireland, any night of the week." Hamilton had come into his dukedom at the tender age of eighteen and, as a result, led a dissolute life of drinking, whoring, and gambling. "If I want bleak weather and uncivilized company, I can always visit my ancestral seat in Scotland."

Will, who had an easygoing temperament, laughed, but John Campbell did not find Hamilton amusing. Argyll was the most powerful Highland clan; Hamilton was the leading Lowland clan, and there had always been an unspoken rivalry between the two.

John, hand on his smallsword, said, "Borderers do tend to be uncivilized." *None more so than the Douglases!*

Will laughed again, enjoying the cut and thrust of their byplay.

"At least uncivilized Borderers are superior to barbarian Highlanders," Hamilton drawled.

"I concede they are superior at cattle raiding and whiskey imbibing," Campbell countered.

"Did I hear the word *whiskey*?" asked George Norwich, Earl of Coventry, who also held a seat in Parliament and had declined the hunting trip to Ireland. "I hope you brought a good supply of the smoky stuff back from Bogland."

"Well, Father certainly did," Will Cavendish informed him. "You can sample it at the reception we're having Friday evening at Devonshire House to celebrate Father's new appointment."

"Will your sisters be there?" Coventry inquired, constantly on the prowl for a noble wife.

"Yes, they'll hostess the affair. We can't get Mother to leave Derbyshire. She hates London only slightly less than Ireland."

"You can't fault her for loving Chatsworth. It's by far the loveliest stately home in England," John Campbell declared.

"Why, thank you, John."

"Don't thank me, Will. Thank Bess Hardwick who had the foresight to build Chatsworth two hundred years ago."

"Now *there* was a *woman!*" Coventry declared.

"A dominant, red-haired virago, according to history."

Hamilton sneered. "A wife should be beautiful, docile, and obedient."

"That's why none of us are wed . . . they're devilish hard to find! Beautiful women are often fickle and usually have a mind of their own." Coventry's words were a deliberate dig at Hamilton's loss of the beauteous mistress Elizabeth Chudleigh.

"At least you and I are free to chose our own wives since we acceded to our titles long ago, George. Pity poor Will and John who must have their brides approved by Devonshire and Argyll."

"Amen to that," Will Cavendish acknowledged, while John Campbell cursed silently because Hamilton spoke the unpalatable truth.

"Now that we've all managed to insult each other, I think we can declare the levee a success and move on to more important business. Anyone care to accompany me to White's tonight?" Hamilton invited.

"Well, since I'm already in full Court dress, why not put it to more productive use than a royal levee? White's sounds far more entertaining to me," George Coventry agreed.

"Thanks, but I have a previous engagement," Campbell declined.

"You don't have to dine with me if you'd rather go to the club," Will said as Hamilton and Coventry departed.

"My idea of an enjoyable evening isn't watching Hamilton gamble. He can't bear to lose. When he does, he proceeds to drink himself into a savage temper then visits a brothel to work off his fury."

"Well, I'm glad you're coming to Devonshire House. You can aid and abet me into persuading my sisters to invite Lady Charlotte Boyle to the entertainment Friday night. I don't want to come right out and ask them, or they will take perverse delight in teasing me to distraction about her."

"Why don't I ask them to invite her on my behalf? That way they won't suspect a thing."

"Thanks, John. I was hoping you would suggest that. Perhaps I can return the favor sometime. Are you in Town until Friday?"

"No, I have pressing business tomorrow at Sundridge. I'll be back Friday—it's only a twelve-mile ride from Kent, after all."

* * *

Hamilton and Coventry entered White's club room for a drink before dinner. Though both nobles wore formal attire and powdered wigs, the similarity ended there. Hamilton, of medium height, had the stocky build and hazel eyes of his Border ancestors, while Coventry was tall and slim with narrow shoulders. The paneled room with its comfortable leather chairs provided its members with all the London newspapers published each day. Hamilton ordered a double brandy then idly picked up the *London Chronicle* to scan its headlines. "The front page is full of Devonshire's appointment," he said with disgust.

"Will you attend the entertainment Friday night?"

Hamilton glanced over the top of the newspaper. "I think not. All the kowtowing to Devonshire would make my gorge rise."

Coventry leaned forward to read the social notices on the back page. It was filled with names of the *beau monde* who had returned to Town for the fashionable Winter Season. He tapped the paper with his quizzing glass. "Did you see this, James?"

Hamilton turned over the paper, and his eyes scanned the names.

"The 'beauteous granddaughters'?" he questioned.

"Yes . . . 'their incomparable beauty took Dublin Castle by storm.' "

"The Gunning sisters. Have you seen them, George?"

"As a matter of fact, I have," Coventry lied, taking perverse pleasure in stealing an advantage over Hamilton where a beautiful woman was concerned. "At the theater last night," he improvised.

"Did you meet them?" Hamilton demanded.

"No, James. I simply paid homage to their beauty from afar."

Hamilton downed his brandy and ordered another. "Ten guineas says I manage to procure an introduction before you do, George!"

"Do you always associate females with *procuring,* James?"

"To procure for promiscuous sexual intercourse . . . why not?"

"Let's get this straight, James. Are you betting me ten

guineas that you gain an introduction before I do, or that you bed one of them before me?"

"I'll wager you ten guineas on the introduction . . . ten *thousand* guineas that I fuck one of them before you do, Coventry!"

"By God, you're on! You never could resist a beautiful woman."

Rachel and Cat Cavendish poured over the guest list for the entertainment they were giving at Devonshire House to celebrate their father's appointment as Lord Steward of the Royal Household. They had made sure that invitations had gone out to the guests of their own choice who would further their marital ambitions. Rachel was being unofficially courted by the Earl of Orford, nephew of Sir Robert Walpole, the late Prime Minister. Cat, however, fancied herself in love with John Ponsonby, who had no title, much to her chagrin.

"The Earl and Countess of Burlington are on the list, but not Lady Charlotte. I had no idea she was old enough to be included in social functions." Cat picked up a pen and blank invitation.

"Will and John Campbell said she was among the *débutantes* presented to Father in Dublin, so she must have turned sixteen."

Rachel bit her lip and tried not to feel jealous. For the last two years she had attempted to engage John Campbell's attention, but he still treated her as a sister. She knew she must stop holding off the Earl of Orford and make a sensible marriage. Becoming a countess was nothing to sneeze at. "Why don't we pay a call at Burlington House and drop off the invitation?"

An hour later, the Cavendish sisters stepped from their carriage to the portico of Burlington House. The majordomo admitted them to the reception hall and took their calling card to the countess.

"Lady Rachel, Lady Catherine, how kind of you to call!" Dorothy Boyle kissed their cheeks. "Come, you're just in time for tea."

"Thank you, Lady Burlington. Actually, we came to address an oversight. We forgot Lady Charlotte's invitation for Friday."

"Oh, Charlie will be thrilled to receive a formal invitation to

Devonshire House." She turned to the liveried majordomo. "Ask Lady Charlotte to join us for tea."

When Charlie entered the drawing room Rachel Cavendish was shocked. The dark-haired Charlotte was pretty enough, but she was a short five feet and looked no more than fourteen years old. *Surely John Campbell cannot be interested in this child!* Rachel hid her surprise and handed over the invitation. "Lady Charlotte, I understand you were presented to our father at Dublin Castle?"

"Oh, yes! I had the most marvelous time! His Grace was so kind to me, and I danced with your brother, Will . . . I mean, Lord Hartington." Charlie's cheeks colored when she said his name.

The Cavendish sisters exchanged a glance. "Yes, at dinner last night he and his friend John Campbell spoke of meeting you there."

"John Campbell partnered my friend Elizabeth Gunning. We all had such a wonderful evening."

"Gunning? Where have I seen that name recently?" Cat puzzled.

"It was in the social news of the *London Chronicle* yesterday," Rachel supplied. "It announced that the Gunnings have arrived from Ireland and taken up residence in Great Marlborough Street."

"Truly? Elizabeth Gunning is here in London?" Charlie asked, unable to hide her excitement at the prospect.

Rachel turned to Charlotte's mother. "Are you acquainted with the Gunnings, Lady Burlington?"

"Yes . . . a charming couple. Your father met them. Bridget Gunning is Viscount Mayo's daughter. We hit it off instantly! I am delighted they are in London for the Winter Season."

Rachel felt an insatiable curiosity to see this Elizabeth Gunning whom John Campbell had partnered in Dublin. "Why don't I send the Gunnings an invitation to Devonshire House for Friday?"

"Why, that would be delightful, Lady Rachel. You are too kind."

*   *   *

An hour after dawn, as John Campbell rode over his own acres at Combe Bank Manor, Sundridge, he realized how much he loved Kent and how much he'd missed it. The county had a rural tranquillity that belied its close proximity to the City of London. He stood in his stirrups to admire his lovely valley and took in a deep, appreciative breath, detecting the scent of hops on the breeze.

After his ride he bathed, donned fresh clothes, then went down to his library to go over the accounts of the estate, read letters from Argyll, and sign business correspondence prepared by his secretary, Robert Hay. Shortly, his house steward announced the visitor he had been expecting. He stood and cordially shook hands with William Pitt, whom he'd invited to Combe Bank when they met at the king's levee. Pitt had been in Parliament for twenty years; though he was a magnificent orator and popular with the people, King George and the Whig party leaders heartily disliked him. "Thank you for coming all this way, Mr. Pitt."

"Far better that we meet here, my lord, where I may speak bluntly, away from prying eyes and ears." He accepted a glass of claret. "Hostilities have again broken out in Europe and, at the risk of speaking treason, the king agitates for war with France."

"The king formed the coalition army of England, Hanover, Austria, and Holland for the invasion of France, Mr. Pitt."

"Under the present Secretary of State, neither England's army, navy, nor diplomatic service are well organized. In a war with France, England will suffer calamity!"

"I agree with you, Mr. Pitt. And doubtless Newcastle will advance from Secretary of State to being our next Prime Minister. England is not best served by Dutch and German troops. We need a strong *British* army and navy. Argyll and I think we need regiments recruited in the Highlands, not in foreign countries!"

"The king and his ministers fear all Scots are Jacobites."

"That's utter rot! It was Scottish regiments under command of my father, Argyll, who defeated, nay *crushed,* the Jacobites at the Battle of Culloden Moor. Recruits from the Highlands, given regular pay, would faithfully support the government."

"I myself am ambitious for more power in the administration. Lisping, effeminate, indecisive incompetents such as Newcastle only get elected by bribery. I am working to change the system. Can I personally count on the support of you and Argyll?"

John Campbell saw the minister's energy, his patriotism, and his devotion. "You can, Mr. Pitt."

"Where the devil have you been?" Bridget Gunning was furious that her husband, who had gone to visit his family in St. Ives, Cambridgeshire, had been absent for three days.

"My father is seriously ill, Bridget. It's providential that I visited St. Ives—his days are numbered, I fear," Jack said sadly.

Her eyes narrowed. "Did you get the money?"

"I could hardly bring up money at such a time."

"What better time? I can assure you that your brothers' thoughts will be on money if your father is dying! Will you be named in the will?"

"Bridget, you know I am not his heir. I am the youngest. I can only hope for a couple of hundred, at best."

"Your brother Peter will be the new Lord Gunning. At least we'll be able to drop his name socially, especially if he takes his seat in the House."

"Peter was happy to see me. He insisted on providing me with a mount when he realized that I had no horse."

"A horse requires stabling . . . one more expense. You must make another round of the moneylenders now that you have prospects of being named in Lord Gunning's will. If you make them think your inheritance will be substantial, you should have no problem borrowing more funds. The first thing we need is a ladies' maid. It is imperative that young ladies of fashion be accompanied by a maid when they are not in the company of their mother."

"Invited to the Court of St. James, are they?" Jack asked dryly.

"As good as!" Bridget picked up the two invitations that had arrived in the morning's post and wafted them beneath his nose with an air of triumph. "The girls are readying themselves this very moment for afternoon tea with the countess and Lady Charlotte Boyle at Burlington House." She paused for dramatic effect then announced with a fanfare, "Ta-da! Tomorrow night we are invited to a gala reception at Devonshire House, no less!"

"You've done well, Bridget," Jack acknowledged. "Don't let this go to your head. Proceed with caution, as will I. No doubt there will be gaming at Devonshire House tomorrow night."

"I'll just get my bonnet. When the girls come down, don't you dare tell them that their grandfather is dying!"

"I won't be here. I must secure a place for my horse in the Great Marlborough Street livery stable."

As Bridget Gunning ushered her daughters down Regent Street toward Piccadilly, she gave them strict instructions. "Do not forget to address the countess as Lady Burlington at all times. Do not put yourselves forward. Do not speak until spoken to. Address her daughter as Lady Charlotte unless she gives you permission to be less formal. Above all, do not gape at the splendor of Burlington House. I can guarantee we have seen nothing before like it. The mansion's interiors have been designed by William Kent, the most renowned architect in all of England and a close personal friend of the earl. Lord Burlington is reputed to be a man of extraordinary taste and an inspired collector of art."

When a gentleman on Regent Street tipped his beaver hat to the ladies, Maria rewarded the gallant with a smile. "A lady never, *ever* bestows her smile upon a man on the street. It is simply not done! It is downright common—something an *actress* would do." Bridget said the word *actress* as if it were anathema.

Maria, who didn't like being chastised, complained, "My new shoes are making a blister on my heel. How much farther is it?"

"We shall take a cab at the corner. We must arrive by carriage, but I wasn't going to pay a driver to bring us all the way from Great Marlborough Street." Bridget looked over the handsome cabs critically and chose the one that was the least shabby. It gave her a great deal of satisfaction to give the driver directions.

"Burlington House!" She swept into the cab with regal *hauteur.*

The public conveyance was scrutinized by the porter and only allowed to pass into the courtyard after he had assessed the occupants and found them worthy. When the cab drew up at the portico, Bridget paid the driver then ascended the marble steps and lifted the door knocker. Maria followed in her mother's confident wake, while Elizabeth tried not to feel overwhelmed.

As the liveried majordomo led the way toward an elegant sitting room furnished with blue silk gilt chairs and satinwood tables, Charlie, with her dog at her heels, came running down the spiral staircase, overjoyed to see her friend. "Elizabeth! I'm so happy to see you!" Remembering her manners, Charlie bobbed a curtsy to Bridget Gunning. "Thank you for coming to London, ma'am!"

"You have a dog!" Elizabeth exclaimed with delight then heard her mother clear her throat. "Thank you for inviting us to tea, Lady Charlotte. What's his name?"

"His name is Dandy and please call me Charlie." She looked at Maria, who was quickly backing away from the dog before he could jump up and paw her new pink afternoon dress. Charlie bent and scooped up the dog. "I'm sorry, Maria. He won't hurt you."

"Welcome to Burlington House." The countess bent toward Bridget's cheek and kissed the air. "Such punctual guests put me to shame. Everyone will tell you I have no notion of time."

"We've been so inundated with invitations since we arrived in London I'm losing track of time myself." Bridget settled in the chair facing Dorothy Boyle. She removed her gloves but not her stylish bonnet. Following her mother's lead, Maria also took a gilt chair and removed her gloves. Elizabeth and Charlie sat on a gilt settee with Dandy between them and grinned at each other.

"You must learn which invitations to decline and which to accept, or you will be run ragged," the countess advised as a uniformed maid rolled in a tea cart holding a magnificent Georgian silver tea service and a three-tiered server filled with dainty lobster *pâte* and cucumber sandwiches. "Of course, certain invitations are obligatory." She poured the tea and told them to help themselves to the refreshments.

"I could use some advice in these matters. I haven't lived in England for ages." Bridget knew most females loved to offer advice.

"Well, naturally, one doesn't refuse to attend any Court

function or invitations from the ruling Whig families. Then, of course, Wednesdays are taken up with Almack's. The place is a must when you have daughters of marriageable age, as we do."

"I haven't had a moment to see about subscriptions to Almack's." Bridget spread her hands helplessly.

"I'll have a word with Sarah Jersey. I'll be happy to sponsor Elizabeth and Maria. They'll be good company for Charlie. She has more confidence when she's with friends."

"How can I thank you for your trouble?"

Dorothy waved a languid hand. "No trouble at all. What are friends for? How is that handsome husband of yours?"

"Been visiting his father, Lord Gunning, for the past three days. I'm relieved he got back in time to escort us to the reception at Devonshire House tomorrow night."

Dorothy, dying to gossip, needed to get rid of their daughters first. "Charlie, I believe Dandy needs to go to the garden. Daddy doesn't appreciate his little turds on the new Turkish carpets."

Charlie and Elizabeth jumped up immediately, eager to escape to the garden so they could talk freely. Maria was more reluctant. "May I look at your paintings, Lady Burlington?"

"Of course, my dear." Dorothy turned to Bridget. "Imagine one so young taking an interest in art."

"I've been thinking of having Maria's portrait painted . . . haven't decided on an artist yet, though Reynolds is highly recommended."

"Devonshire House is filled with portraits of the Cavendish daughters, though none of them are what you would call raving beauties." Dorothy leaned forward and spoke to Bridget confidentially. "When Rachel and Catherine were here to tea I couldn't help thinking it was a pity they got their looks from their mother. The duchess was plain Catherine Hoskyns when the duke wed her, and I do mean *plain!*"

"Perhaps she had other attractions!" Bridget said, laughing.

"Money, of course, but no breeding. Her father was a middle-class businessman, and Devonshire had enormous gambling debts."

Bridget listened avidly as Lady Burlington indulged in her second favorite pastime: gossip.

Once in the garden, Beth and Charlie hugged each other and

didn't stop talking for quarter of an hour. Out from beneath her mother's disapproving eyes Elizabeth became animated. She laughed with delight as she watched Dandy sniff every flower then cock his leg up to pee on every tree. "Charlie, you are so lucky to have a dog. May I hold him?"

"Of course. Dandy loves attention!"

Beth scooped him up, held him close, and let him lick her chin.

"I'm so excited about tomorrow night. At first, the Cavendish sisters forgot to invite me and I think it was Will who prompted them to bring me an invitation. I hope it was Will! I can't stop thinking about him, Beth," Charlie confessed.

"Did they mention Will, I mean, Lord Hartington?"

"Yes, they said that John Campbell and Will had dinner with them at Devonshire House. I told them about you and what a marvelous time we had, and Mother suggested they invite you to the reception."

"Do you think John Campbell will be there?" Elizabeth could hardly breathe at the thought of seeing him again.

"Of course he'll be there. He and Will are best friends."

"Will there be dancing?" Elizabeth asked breathlessly.

"I'm not sure. It isn't a ball—it's a reception for His Grace—but there should be lots of opportunities to talk and stroll in the gardens beneath colored lanterns . . . and flirt!" Charlie lowered her voice to a whisper. "I dreamed about Will last night . . . I dreamed that he kissed me!"

Beth closed her eyes, remembering, as her hands caressed the little dog. "Everything seems like a dream to me. I cannot believe I'm going to Devonshire House tomorrow night!"

That night when she went to bed, Elizabeth Gunning barely slept for the excitement bubbling inside her. They had ridden home in the shiny Burlington coach with the crest on its door, because their mother had cleverly said that though the Gunnings had ordered a carriage, it had not yet been delivered.

Elizabeth thought about her mother for a moment. She was certainly a force to be dealt with. Bridget had seemed so at ease, talking with the Countess of Burlington as if they were bosom friends, and she had even managed to get them subscriptions to Almacks. It was nothing short of a miracle!

At breakfast the next morning, Elizabeth knew her excitement had not diminished; if anything, it had grown. She felt as if her heart was singing. "I asked Charlie if there would be dancing tonight. She said that she didn't think so, because it's a reception for the duke, but she said the guests could stroll in the gardens beneath colored lanterns! Oh, I can't wait to see Devonshire House!"

"Well, I'm afraid you're going to have to wait," Bridget said.

Elizabeth looked at her mother, and her heart jumped into her throat. "What do you mean?" she whispered as apprehension dug in its sharp claws.

"Have you forgotten, Elizabeth? We have only one ball gown. Maria shall be the one to wear it to Devonshire House!"

Chapter Seven

*E*lizabeth pinned Maria's silvery-blond curls securely to the top of her head then teased tiny spirals to frame her lovely face, made even paler by paste and powder. "I'm glad Mother is letting you wear your own hair tonight; it's far more lovely than a wig."

"And will garner me far more male attention," Maria added.

"Please make my excuses to Charlie . . . tell her I have a sick headache and beg her forgiveness."

"I shan't *beg* Charlotte Boyle for anything! She's a pampered little chit who won't have to lift a finger to get a husband. Because of her father's wealth and property, titled men will fawn on her. I don't know how you can be such friends with her!"

Beth was startled at her sister's vehemence. "It's not Charlie's fault that her father is an earl. And it is because of my friendship with her that our family has received invitations."

"Well, I agree the Burlingtons are a great social connection."

"That isn't the reason Charlie is my friend. I truly like her."

"Help me with my gown, I don't want to disturb my curls."

Elizabeth lifted the exquisite white gown over Maria's head, adjusted the full skirt over the petticoat, and stepped back. "You look absolutely beautiful. Don't forget a fan." Beth had recovered the old fans with silk and added ribbons.

Maria pulled on her evening gloves and selected the prettiest fan. "I must go and show Mother how beautiful I look."

Jack Gunning entered Elizabeth's bedchamber with a look of regret on his face. "I'm sorry you're not able to go, my beauty. It's very generous of you to let Maria wear the gown tonight. There is sure to be gaming at Devonshire House—I promise to win enough to buy you a ball gown of your own."

"You look very grand, Father. Have a wonderful time and don't worry about me." She picked up a bodkin threaded with pale green ribbon. "I'm going to make the Gunning ladies some garters."

There was such a crush of carriages in the Devonshire House courtyard that none would notice they had come by hired cab, Maria realized with relief. The massive mansion looked like a barracks from the outside but, when the Gunnings went inside, Maria saw that it was even more opulent than Burlington House. A connoisseur would have known the elegant rooms of Burlington House were furnished in better taste, but the *beau monde* in general knew little about taste. Greeted by their hostesses, Maria followed her mother's instructions and sank into a graceful curtsy. "Lady Rachel, Lady Catherine, I am delighted to make your acquaintance."

"Mistress Elizabeth," Rachel murmured with narrowed eyes.

"Ah, no, this is my elder daughter, Maria," Bridget Gunning explained. "Elizabeth could not be with us tonight."

Rachel's glance swept Maria from head to toe. She did not look reassured, and as the Gunnings passed into the marble-pillared salon Rachel whispered to her sister, "Her beauty is angelic—what must the other be like?"

A liveried footman presented a silver tray of champagne. Bridget swept up a glass and looked at Maria with approval as she opened her fan and demurely lowered her lashes. "No, thank you."

As half a dozen males lifted quizzing glasses to observe the exquisite creature who had just arrived, Charlotte Boyle found them. "You're here at last! Where's Elizabeth?"

"She sends her apologies, Lady Charlotte," Bridget said.

"She's not coming?" Charlie was aghast. Her face fell with the acute disappointment she felt.

The Countess of Burlington materialized. "Bridget! John!"

She turned to the man beside her. "I want you to meet the Gunnings. This is Charles Fitzroy, the Duke of Grafton."

Bridget struck up a conversation immediately. Dukes were few and far between. Though he wasn't in the first flush of youth, it was possible that the duke could be a widower.

The countess tucked her arm beneath Jack Gunning's and gave him an arch look. "Shall I show you where the gaming room is?"

"Dorothy, you read my mind." Jack winked at his wife. "I'm sure you will excuse us Bridget, Grafton."

Bridget waved them off, and Grafton managed to escape. "Your father can be a smooth devil when the mood takes him," she told Maria then lifted her fan to cover her mouth. "All the gentlemen in the room are gaping at you."

Maria opened her fan. "They are all dying for introductions!"

Bridget glanced aside and saw that Charlie Boyle looked forlorn. "Lady Charlotte, I know you must be eager to introduce Maria to your friends, so off you go, you two. Try to behave yourselves!"

Maria eagerly moved away from her mother.

"Mistress Gunning! I had no idea you were in London." Michael Boyle made a leg, then waggled his eyebrows at Charlie.

"Maria, you remember my cousin Michael Boyle?"

She looked into his eyes and gave him a sly smile. "I remember that I slapped you, my lord."

He took her fingers to his lips. "Your servant, mistress."

"In that case, you may get me some champagne."

Michael took two glasses from a passing footman, bestowed one upon Maria, then sipped the other himself.

"Thanks for nothing, Michael!" Charlotte declared.

"I'm looking out for you, Charlie. Champagne steals the senses."

"Along with the manners, obviously." She took her courage in her hands. "Is your friend Will . . . Lord Hartington here?"

"Since this is Devonshire House, you know damn well he's here. Deep in conversation with John and Cumberland when I left them."

Maria blinked. "Do you mean the *Duke* of Cumberland? His Royal Highness?" she asked with disbelief.

"Yes, he and John fought in Scotland, at Culloden."

"But now they're friends again?" Maria asked inanely.

It was Michael's turn to blink. *Much beauty . . . few brains!*

"Boyle, trust you to monopolize the most captivating beauty in the room . . . I mean beauties." The man bowed to Lady Charlotte.

"Hello, George. I believe you know my cousin, but allow me to introduce Mistress Maria Gunning. This is my friend George Norwich, Earl of Coventry."

Coventry's jaw almost dropped. "Mistress Gunning, I'm delighted."

"Coventry? Do you know Lady Godiva?" Maria asked eagerly.

The earl laughed. "Your wit is only exceeded by your beauty, Mistress Gunning! May I have the honor of escorting you to the supper room?" Her mention of Lady Godiva filled his head with dazzling visions of her riding naked upon a white horse. He took her hand and placed it upon his blue satin sleeve.

As they walked, Maria twirled her empty glass. "Will there be more champagne in the supper room, Lord Coventry?"

"I sincerely hope so, my dear. Could you not call me George?"

She arched an eyebrow at him. "Not on such short acquaintance. My mother would never approve, my lord."

"Ah, you are here with your mother?" The earl sounded regretful.

"After supper, perhaps we could become better acquainted as we stroll in the gardens beneath the colored lanterns?"

Coventry caught his breath. "Your mother would never approve."

She gave him a sidelong glance. "No, she would not . . . George."

Her glance, coupled with the way she said his name, made him harden instantly. He covered her hand possessively. "Your lovely hair is the color of moonlight." His eyes roamed over her with appreciation. She was the most beautiful female he'd ever touched.

John Campbell thanked the king's son, the Duke of Cumberland, for placing some of the army recruits his father had sent down from Scotland. "Argyll has been funding the education of some young men from the west Highlands with a view to getting them into the army or the navy. Most are already experienced sailors. Would you be willing to use your influence with the king on their behalf?"

"I often have trouble persuading my father in military matters, though he says he trusts my judgment implicitly. Unfortunately, he also trusts the judgment of his ministers who advise building up the military with German rather than British fighting men. Between us, we will have to prove them wrong."

John was pleased with Cumberland's response. During his reign George II had allowed his wife, Queen Caroline, and Prime Minister Robert Walpole to rule by a corrupt system of bribery that kept the wealthy Whigs in power. Now that both the queen and Walpole were deceased, the king would do well to rely on Cumberland, the undisputed military leader. "If you can arrange a private meeting with His Highness, I'll do my best to persuade him to our cause."

John's eye was caught by a lady wearing a diamond tiara, who had her handsome son in tow. "Here comes the Princess of Wales and the heir to the throne. George seems to have left his boyhood behind."

"By God, yes. The lad is fourteen and already has an eye for the ladies. The king dotes on him! Young George can do no wrong."

John made a gallant bow. "Princess Augusta, Prince George."

She bestowed a gracious smile upon him and spoke to Cumberland.

"George craves masculine company. Insists he's too old to be seen with his mother hovering about. Keep an eye on him, Cumberland."

As she walked away, Prince George said, "On the contrary, I crave *female* company. The most heavenly creature just went into the supper room. Her name is on everyone's lips—a Mistress Maria Gunning, I believe. I'd like an introduction."

John Campbell felt his heart give one great thud. Surely it wasn't possible that the Gunning sisters were in London? *If by*

*some miracle Maria is at Devonshire House tonight, Elizabeth
must be here too!* He excused himself from Cumberland and
went in search of the young woman who had set his pulse racing. As he glanced about the salons, he could not believe the
eagerness he felt. The anticipation of seeing her again filled
him with yearning. No female had affected him this way before.
John grew impatient when he couldn't find her and told himself
that young George must have been mistaken. Then suddenly he
caught sight of Bridget Gunning in animated conversation with
Princess Augusta and the Duke of Devonshire. She wore a sophisticated gray gown and black feathers in her Titian hair. A
frown creased his brow. Beth had told him she wasn't a *débutante*, that her clothes were borrowed and that she was about to
become an actress. It didn't add up, when her mother was on intimate terms with royalty.

He stalked upstairs to the supper room, his keen glance ex-
amining every lady he passed as he searched for the elusive female who now consumed his thoughts. He saw Maria Gunning
immediately—she would stand out in any crowd—but Elizabeth was nowhere to be seen. As he approached Maria, he was
surprised to see that she was with his friend the Earl of Coventry.

"Sundridge, allow me to introduce Mistress Maria Gunning,
here for the Winter Season from Castle Coote, Ireland."

John bowed. "I have already had the pleasure, George." His
glance took in the costly gown and the delicate matching fan,
and he measured them against the smock Beth had been wearing the first time he had encountered her by the river.

"Sundridge? I thought your name was John Campbell,"
Maria said.

Coventry shook with laughter. "Mistress Gunning has the
most delicious sense of humor, John."

"I've been looking for Elizabeth."

"Ah, my sister chose not to come to Devonshire House
tonight. She had a previous engagement."

"On the stage of Drury Lane, no doubt." John was stung that
Beth Gunning had made a fool of him.

Maria laughed prettily. "Ah, that is a little game Elizabeth
loves to play with gentlemen. She pretends she wants to be an
actress. She has these wicked little flights of fancy. At our cas-

tle in Ireland she loved to run wild, like a child of nature. Mother despaired of controlling her. Since we arrived at our London house in Great Marlborough Street, she has been swamped with invitations. In spite of her teasing ways, she is very popular."

"No doubt her popularity is *because* of her teasing ways, not in spite of them," Coventry pointed out.

"Do you have a message for Elizabeth?"

"No, no message," John murmured politely. "Excuse me." He felt the need for fresh air, so stepped out into the gardens. Couples strolling beneath the colored lanterns made the atmosphere far too romantic for John's mood. He cursed beneath his breath as he fought the urge to go directly to Great Marlborough Street and confront Elizabeth Gunning with the preposterous stories she had offered him. Then he remembered that she wasn't at home. Mistress Gunning, it seemed, had a previous engagement. The knowledge did nothing to improve his savage mood. As he made his way out to Piccadilly, he decided to sleep at his town house in Half-Moon Street tonight rather than return to Sundridge.

In Great Marlborough Street, Elizabeth stood pensively looking from her bedchamber window. She knew she should go to bed, since it would be hours before her family returned from the entertainment at Devonshire House, but she doubted she would be able to sleep. She had sewn half a dozen pairs of pretty garters to pass the time, but though this occupied her hands, it did nothing to keep her mind busy. Her imagination took wing, seeing the luxurious rooms, the ladies in fashionable gowns, and the gentlemen in formal attire. She pictured Charlie's disappointment over her absence and hoped that when John Campbell learned she was in London, he would find a way to contact her. *Perhaps he will write me a note!*

It was midnight before the Gunnings arrived home. Elizabeth was eager to hear about Devonshire House and learn about all the people they had encountered there. Her mother took center stage, listing all the important members of the *ton* with whom she'd conversed. She saved the best till last. "I spoke at length with Princess Augusta. I have no doubt she will invite us to Leicester House."

"The Princess of Wales was only widowed at the beginning

of the year. I doubt she'll be entertaining until she's out of mourning," Jack pointed out to his wife.

"Rubbish! Her son George will be the next King of England. She likely mourned her husband for no more than five minutes!"

"I met Prince George tonight . . . he couldn't take his eyes off my bodice. He is a very mature fourteen-year-old. He will most likely insist that the king invite me to Court," Maria said smugly.

"It wasn't only Prince George who had his eyes on you, Maria. I swear every male present was agape at your beauty. The Duke of Grafton, who is widowed, did more than glance at you, and I believe you made a particular conquest of the Earl of Coventry."

"I'm certain I did. I told him I would be walking in the park tomorrow. I'm willing to bet that he will be there too!"

"Speaking of bets, I had a successful evening in the card room. Won every hand I played against the Duke of Grafton. I think I have enough to buy you a ball gown, Elizabeth."

"Jack Gunning, we need a carriage! Then Maria won't have to walk in the park—she can ride as befits a lady of fashion."

"Bridget, it's Elizabeth's seventeenth birthday next week. She needs a gown of her own if she is to catch a wealthy husband." He winked at his favorite daughter. "The carriage will have to wait."

Beth smiled a secret smile. For once her father was putting his foot down. She couldn't wait to get Maria alone to ask her about Charlie—and about John Campbell too, she secretly admitted. "Come, Maria, I'll help you remove your gown and your makeup."

Upstairs in the lovely bedchamber they shared, Elizabeth unfastened the costly white gown and petticoat, carefully lifted them off, and hung them in the wardrobe. She poured water from the jug into the china washbowl and handed Maria a face flannel.

"I'm too tired to wash my face tonight. I'll do it tomorrow."

"You shouldn't leave that white paste on overnight, Maria. It might spoil your delicate skin." Elizabeth unfastened her sister's corset strings. "Did you see Charlie?"

"Of course I saw her, and her cousin Michael Boyle. Actually, it was Michael who introduced me to the Earl of Coventry. The earl asked me to call him George and begged to take me to the supper room. I had him panting by the time we walked in the gardens."

"Did Charlie seem disappointed that I didn't go?"

"She seemed far more disappointed that her cousin Michael wouldn't allow her to drink champagne. But her thoughts were on Will Cavendish, Lord Hartington, until she finally hunted him down. Perhaps I should engage Will's affections. He'll be the next Duke of Devonshire, and I would love being addressed as 'Your Grace.'"

Beth felt alarm. She knew Maria was perfectly capable of doing such a thing, and she was far more beautiful than Lady Charlotte. Beth, however, kept a wise silence, knowing that if she attempted to dissuade Maria, it would have the opposite effect. She took her courage in her hands. "Did you see John Campbell?"

"I most certainly did. He lied to you, Elizabeth! His name isn't Campbell at all. His name is John Sundridge. He happens to be a friend of the Earl of Coventry's, who introduced us."

Beth went pale. "Sundridge?" She wished Maria didn't sound quite so triumphant. "What did he say when you were introduced?"

"When I told him you had a previous engagement, he asked sarcastically if it was on the stage of Drury Lane!"

Beth's cheeks turned warm. "I should never have told him I was going to be an actress," she murmured miserably.

"I soon disabused him of such a silly idea. I told him your pretended interest in acting was a little game you played. Then I assured him you were swamped with invitations. That appeared to make him angry, but it served him right for lying to you."

Beth lay awake after Maria's breathing told her she was asleep. She was glad they didn't share a bed, for her restlessness would keep Maria awake. Then, with a heavy heart, she drifted into sleep.

They were alone in a ballroom. "I'm not a débutante *at all, John. This gown is from the theater's wardrobe department."*

"Let me help you remove it, then we can talk." His fingers began to unfasten the gown, and suddenly it pooled at her feet. His possessive hands moved up to caress her bare shoulders, and she realized that he too was naked.

"We cannot talk, sir. We have no clothes on."

"If we cannot talk, then I'll have to settle for a kiss."

"I'll not give it!"

"Stop pretending to be a lady. You're a common little actress."

"No, my interest in acting is just a game I play."

"If you like playing games, I know one we can both enjoy." He lifted her high above him, so that her golden curls brushed across his powerful chest. Then he slid her down his hard muscled body, until her toes touched the floor and his mouth covered hers in a long, lingering kiss that filled her heart with yearning.

Early the next morning a footman from Burlington House delivered a note for Elizabeth. Before she could read it, her mother snatched it from her fingers. "I shall first read any correspondence you receive, then pass it along if I deem it fitting." Bridget scanned the letter. "It is from the countess. Seems that Lady Charlotte missed your company so much last night she invites you to stay at Burlington House for the weekend so that the two of you can spend some time together."

Elizabeth held her breath, hoping against hope. Yet she very much doubted her mother would give her consent for the visit.

"There is no mention of Maria," Bridget fumed. "If she had invited both of you, I would be happy to let you go."

Elizabeth's heart sank.

"I don't want to visit Charlie Boyle!" Maria protested. "I told the Earl of Coventry I'd walk in the park today, and I know he will go out of his way to be there too."

"Don't fret, Maria. We shall certainly walk in the park today."

Bridget glanced at Elizabeth and decided it would be preferable if she was not with her sister at the rendezvous with Coventry. "I think you'd better accept Lady Charlotte's invitation. The countess may take offense if we decline."

Elizabeth's heart soared.

Bridget scribbled her acceptance on the bottom of the letter and took it to the front door where the footman stood awaiting a reply. "Ask Lady Burlington to send the carriage for Mistress Elizabeth."

Within the hour Beth was hanging the afternoon dress she had brought for Sunday in Charlie's spacious wardrobe. She spied a white ball gown and asked, "Is this what you wore last night?"

"Yes, but I'd like a new one that has some color. White is so childish, don't you think? I want to look more grown-up."

"I'm to get a ball gown for my birthday next week. I'm sure Mother will insist it be white because it's traditional."

"And *virginal*," Charlie whispered, wrinkling her nose. "I wish I were going to be seventeen, but I've only just turned sixteen." She sighed. "Will must think I'm such a baby."

"You saw him last night! Did you walk in the gardens?"

"Yes, he asked me to walk in the gardens! He also asked me if I would be driving in the park this afternoon."

"Then he doesn't think you're a baby but a lady of fashion!"

The Countess of Burlington popped her head around the door. "Hello, Elizabeth. Charlie, if you want to drive in the park this afternoon, you need a new parasol. Would you ladies like to go shopping this morning?"

"Yes, please!" Charlie was eager. "Perhaps Elizabeth can help me chose a gown that will make me look more grown-up. She's getting a new ball gown for her birthday next week. Perhaps she'll see something she likes at Madame Chloe's."

As she donned her bonnet, Elizabeth found herself as eager as Charlie for the shopping excursion. She had no money, but it didn't cost anything to look, and looking at clothes brought untold pleasure to any female worth her salt.

Madame Chloe displayed every style and shade of parasol in her *élite* establishment for her wealthiest customer. The countess chose one of black-and-white-striped silk, while Lady Charlotte decided on a forget-me-not blue to match her new afternoon dress.

"Which one will you have, Elizabeth?" the countess asked.

"Oh, I couldn't, my lady," she declined quickly.

"Nonsense, it's just a frippery. How about the pink? Every lady should have a rose-colored parasol to make her face glow."

"Thank you," Elizabeth said shyly.

"Lady Charlotte would like a gown that makes her look a little more fashionable," Lady Burlington told Madame Chloe.

Charlie picked out two gowns and took Elizabeth into the dressing room with her. Hung in the spacious room was a gown of gold tissue. "Oh, Elizabeth, this gown was made for you!"

Elizabeth touched the gilt threads with her fingertips and fell instantly in love with it. She couldn't resist trying it on.

"It brings out all the golden lights in your hair. You look like a goddess, Elizabeth." Charlie held up a dress. "I think I like this peach-colored one for myself. Help fasten me up."

"The color is wonderful with your dark hair, Charlie, and the drape of the silk makes you look much taller."

Charlie rushed out to show her mother. "Elizabeth thinks this gown makes me look taller, and pale peach is my favorite color!"

"All right, the pair of you have convinced me. Anything that makes you look taller is a godsend." She glanced at Elizabeth. "That gold tissue is spectacular on you. Would you like it?"

Beth went pale. "Oh, no, my lady, I have enough gowns, thank you."

Back at Burlington House they enjoyed a delicious lunch of cracked crab with drawn butter, asparagus tips, and cheese *soufflé,* followed by Charlie's favorite dessert, blackberries and cream. When they were finished lunch, Dorothy Boyle stood up. "How very providential that the sun has come out. I shall have the open carriage readied for your drive in the park. I shan't play gooseberry in case young Hartington turns up— your maid will be sufficient *chaperon.*" The countess smiled slyly. "If you ladies will excuse me, I have a previous engagement of my own. Don't forget your parasols!"

"Elizabeth, it's so good of you to come and keep me company. It's like having a sister. Maria will miss you today."

"Maria won't even notice I'm gone. She has her own rendezvous planned in the park—with the Earl of Coventry, no less!"

Upstairs they washed their hands and faces, then Charlie sat down at her dressing table to powder her face and put on lip rouge. "You're beautiful without paint but would you like some?"

Elizabeth caught her breath at the array of pots and powder puffs laid out before her. She darkened her lashes with a tiny brush, then put on rose-colored lip rouge and powdered her nose.

The maid came to the door. "The carriage is ready, my lady."

"Shall we take Dandy?" When Elizabeth nodded eagerly, Charlie asked her maid to get the dog's leash.

Elizabeth and Charlotte climbed into the carriage and opened their frilled parasols. They sat facing the horses with Dandy between them, while the maid, Jane, took the seat opposite. The driver tooled the open carriage along Piccadilly in the direction of Hyde Park, turned at Park Lane, then slowly circled onto the Serpentine Road. It was a warm, sunny afternoon, and the park was crowded with ladies walking and riding in their carriages.

Lady Charlotte was greeted by everyone they passed, while Beth received a great number of curious stares. It was the first time she had been in the fashionable park, and as they crossed the bridge over the Serpentine, she searched the crowd to see if she could spot Maria and her mother. Suddenly, Elizabeth froze. Riding toward them were Will Cavendish and John *Whateverhisnamewas!*

Chapter Eight

*E*arly that morning when Will had entered the Devonshire House stables, he was surprised to see that John's horse was still there. It told him that his friend had not returned to Sundridge, Kent, last night, but must have stayed at his townhouse in Half-Moon Street. At lunchtime, when John came for his black Thoroughbred, Demon, Will told him he was hoping to encounter Charlie in Hyde Park and begged his company.

As the two riders left Rotten Row and cantered toward the Serpentine Bridge, Will turned to John with a triumphant grin. "Here comes Charlotte, and if I'm not mistaken she is accompanied by a lady of *your* acquaintance."

John turned accusing eyes on Will. "You knew they'd be together when you asked me to ride with you."

"I didn't *know* . . . I simply surmised from something Charlie said."

The men immediately reined in and waited for the carriage to clear the bridge. Charlotte instructed the driver to stop. When he did so, Will Cavendish urged his mount to Charlie's side of the coach. John guided Demon to the opposite side, removed his tall beaver hat, and gave a curt nod. "Mistress Gunning."

Elizabeth's violet eyes blazed with fury. "My sister informs me that your name is *Sundridge* not Campbell!"

"It is both. I am John Campbell, Baron Sundridge."

Her eyes widened. "You are a *lord*? I had no idea!"

"There are likely many things you don't know about me."

"Such as?" Her challenge was direct.

"I am a soldier," he said simply, omitting that he held the military rank of major.

I should have guessed! He has the dangerous, savage look of a warrior. "You might have told me these things, Lord Sundridge."

"And you might have told me that becoming an actress was only a flight of your imagination . . . a game you like to play." Her face beneath the rose parasol glowed with a tantalizing translucent beauty that played havoc with his senses.

Elizabeth's lashes fluttered to her cheeks, then she raised them and smiled into his dark eyes. "I'm sorry."

By God, if you enjoy playing games, Elizabeth, there's a few I'd love to play with you! "A truce. Shall we begin over, proud Titania?"

She laughed. "We shall, my Lord Oberon." Dandy barked his approval and they laughed together.

Will leaned down from his saddle to speak confidentially with Lady Charlotte. "If you rode tomorrow, at an early hour, it would make me extremely happy."

"Elizabeth is staying with me. Perhaps a ride would amuse her, especially if we encounter other riders of our acquaintance."

Will grinned down at her, taking her meaning. "I shall do my best to keep him in Town until tomorrow."

As the carriage bowled down Piccadilly, Charlie asked, "You do ride, Elizabeth?"

Lost in a dreamy reverie, Beth twirled her parasol. "Yes, I ride," she answered absently, imagining the compelling John Campbell in military uniform, astride his black Thoroughbred.

"Wonderful! I've accepted an invitation for us to ride in Rotten Row tomorrow morning," Charlie said breathlessly.

"What?" Beth cried. "I mean, I beg your pardon, Charlie?"

She had ridden farm horses and lots of ponies in Ireland but always bareback, never with a saddle. "I . . . I didn't bring my horse with me nor did I pack my riding habit." *Both of which are nonexistent!*

Charlie laughed merrily as the carriage slowly turned through the gates into the Burlington courtyard. "Our stables are filled with riding horses. Come, we'll go now and choose a mount for you."

Elizabeth felt dismay. Even the sight of Dandy cocking his leg up against the carriage wheel didn't divert her apprehension. Once inside the stables, however, her anxiety was swept away when she saw the horses close-up. She had an affinity for all animals, and soon she was stroking their necks and murmuring soft words.

"Amber seems to like you," Charlie prompted.

"She's a beauty. Her coat is like satin. May I really ride her?" She glanced over at the saddles. "I suppose you ride sidesaddle here in London. In Ireland I always rode astride."

"Oh, how exciting! I'm afraid it will have to be sidesaddle on our morning ride in Rotten Row. Come on, let's find you a habit and some riding boots."

Elizabeth stood on a chair while a Burlington House sewing woman took down the hem on one of Lady Charlotte's habits. The jade green riding dress fit her slender figure to perfection except for its short length. Charlie's boots also were not a bad fit, as both girls had rather small feet.

They took dinner trays in Charlotte's chamber, since the earl and his chief architect, William Kent, were eating in the formal dining room, going over plans for a new house they were building on the vast Burlington acreage that her father had decided to call Burlington Gardens. After dinner, Charlie took her on a tour of the picture gallery and into the library. Elizabeth was overawed at the number of books on the shelves. "I could spend a year in here without ever leaving." She didn't envy Charlie's clothes, servants, or mansion, but she certainly coveted the books.

The two friends talked late into the night, discussing everything from Royal Court presentations to Almack's, but finally Elizabeth retired to the adjoining bedchamber. No sooner did she put her head on the pillow than it seemed a maid was knocking with her breakfast tray. Then it was time to dress for their ride.

Her reflection in the oval mirror told her that jade green was a most flattering color. She quickly gathered her hair into a Grecian knot, firmly pinned on the matching small hat with its jaunty feather, and felt extremely elegant.

At the stables a groom led Amber to the mounting block and, feigning confidence, Elizabeth climbed into the saddle as if she had done so every morning of her life. She positioned her legs exactly the same as Charlie did and took the reins into her gloved hands. The groom mounted his own horse and led the way across Piccadilly into Green Park. They cantered to the end of the park, crossed back over Piccadilly, and entered Hyde Park. At this early hour on Sunday morning there were no pedestrians or carriages, only a few mounted riders. By the time they slowed to a trot, Elizabeth had gained full confidence. By the time they spotted the two gentlemen riding toward them and their well-trained groom fell back to give them privacy, she felt ready for anything.

Almost anything.

She was not prepared for John Campbell to dismount, stride to her stirrup, and raise his powerful arms to her. She was not prepared to be lifted from the saddle and held aloft by sheer brute strength. She was not prepared for the excited rush of her blood as he slowly lowered her to brush against his muscled thighs until her feet touched the ground. Nor was she prepared for his murmured, "Good morning, my beauty," or the brush of his hot mouth against her cheek as his dark, intense gaze devoured her.

It is exactly like in my dreams, except we are not naked! Elizabeth suddenly blushed as if that's exactly what they were. She swayed against him, dizzied by the intimate closeness and her own wanton thoughts. She felt his strong hands gripping her waist, steadying her, and imagined she felt his heat through the cloth.

They walked slowly, side by side, leading their horses along the bridle path. "Beth, I want to spend time with you, and Will wants to spend time with Lady Charlotte, but such an arrangement takes a deal of planning and plotting, or the gossips will have a heyday."

"As we plotted and planned for this ride today?"

"Exactly. But in the middle of Hyde Park, all I can do is lift you in and out of the saddle. I'd like us to spend time alone."

"My mother would never permit that, my lord."

His mouth curved in a smile at her innocence. "There's safety in numbers. Will has a plan for next weekend. The

Boyles have a Palladian villa at Chiswick on the Thames. Charlie will get her mother to invite everyone—the Cavendish sisters, the Gunning sisters, perhaps the Ponsonby girl, and naturally an equal number of the opposite sex. Then the following weekend, the Cavendishes will reciprocate by inviting everyone to their country place at Oxted in Surrey, which happens to be just a short four-mile ride from my home at Sundridge, Kent."

"Where we can be alone? Such an ingenious plan. What happens if I don't accept these invitations?" Elizabeth teased.

"Then you leave me in the clutches of Lady Rachel Cavendish who has pursued me shamefully for the past two years."

"If you've managed to elude her for two years, I don't believe you are in any danger of succumbing to her charms, my lord."

"I feel in imminent danger of succumbing to *your* charms, Beth."

I am the one in danger, and we both know it, you wicked devil. I've been in danger since your first predatory glance.

Rotten Row was no longer deserted, and other riders cantered by.

"I believe it is time for me to lift you into the saddle."

She glanced up and impulsively confided, "This is the first time I've ever used a sidesaddle. I usually ride astride."

He pictured her mounted on a Thoroughbred. It was only a short step for his imagination to picture her astride him, and he hardened instantly. He captured her tiny waist between his hands and deftly managed to brush her against his hard length as he lifted her into the saddle. He watched her lashes sweep to her cheeks; when she lifted them, the impact of her violet eyes took his breath away. He kissed her fingers then touched his heart. "I shall see you in Chiswick, if not before."

She smiled a secret smile. "Perhaps, Lord Sundridge."

On the way back to Burlington House, Charlotte told Elizabeth about the plan Will Cavendish had concocted.

"Will your mother agree to invite everyone to Chiswick?"

"Of course she will. Mother is an angel, and I think she is secretly hoping for a match between Lord Hartington and me."

"Unless my sister, Maria, is invited, I doubt my mother will allow me to come to Chiswick."

"Of course we will invite Maria. Do stop worrying, Elizabeth."

They were back in time to attend a short service in the Burlington House chapel, then it was time for Beth to bid Charlie good-bye. She felt reluctant to leave but knew deep down inside it was actually reluctance to go home. Out from beneath her mother's critical eye, she had been filled with carefree exuberance and vitality. Lady Boyle was indeed an angel, when compared with her own mother.

Charlie urged her to keep the green riding habit, insisting that she'd never wear it herself since jade made her skin look sallow. But when Maria saw the rose pink parasol and the riding dress, she became petulant.

"If Elizabeth can have a parasol, I want one too! I don't want a riding habit, because I hate horses, but I think I should get a new afternoon dress."

"We will go shopping soon," Bridget assured her, "but in the meantime I'm sure Elizabeth will lend you the parasol. Now, tell us all the details of your stay at Burlington House."

It was a command. Beth knew full well that her mother would criticize her carriage drive in the park, when she and Maria had had to walk. She also realized that the early-morning horseback ride would earn her mother's disapproval. Over the years she had learned to protect herself by being selective. She recounted every dish she had eaten and every word she had exchanged with the countess. "We spent last evening in the Burlington House library. They have so many books it would take a year to read them all." She watched Maria shudder at such a notion, then added, "Today we attended a church service in their very own chapel."

"It's a wonder you didn't die of boredom!" Maria looked smug. "I walked in Hyde Park, and it was no coincidence that I encountered the Earl of Coventry. He invited Mother and I to ride in his carriage. She cleverly let it drop that we would be attending the theater tomorrow night and Almack's on Wednesday."

"There is no guarantee that he'll be at the theater, Maria.

Don't forget that Parliament opens tomorrow," her mother warned.

"What does that have to do with the earl?" Maria asked blankly.

"As Earl of Coventry, he has a seat in the House, but George Norwich is also a professional politician. You should know these things, Maria. If you encourage him to talk about himself, you will hold him in the palm of your hand."

"I've been thinking," Maria said. "I cannot wear the same gown to the theater and then to Almack's."

"It is paramount for my plans that all three of us attend the theater tomorrow night. Mary left a bolt of lovely brocade. It shouldn't take you long to sew evening capes. None will know what is beneath the capes if you keep them on throughout the play. Then on Wednesday Maria can wear the white ball gown to Almack's."

In spite of the wretched tight feeling in her chest, Elizabeth summoned her courage. "My birthday is Wednesday . . . will I have my new gown in time?"

"Ah, Elizabeth, I've been meaning to talk to you about that. I'm afraid it won't be possible to lay out the money for your ball gown just yet. Your father had a run of bad luck and there are certain expenses, such as employing a ladies' maid, that I deem necessary for your future success. Oh, and speaking of birthdays, I've decided that you may turn seventeen, but Maria shall remain eighteen for another year. Seventeen and eighteen are ideal ages for marriage, whereas nineteen gives the definite impression that a young lady is desperate."

How can you possibly control how old we are? But Elizabeth knew it was not only folly to protest but utterly impossible to challenge her mother's decisions.

That night, when the Gunning sisters retired to their bedchamber, Maria stood in front of the mirror wearing the new evening cape Beth had sewn for her and twirling the new parasol, admiring the effect. "Mother thinks to teach me how to hold a man in the palm of my hand." Maria laughed slyly. "I already know how to hold a man in my hand *and* curl my fingers around him." She demonstrated on the handle of the parasol. "It works far better, and faster, than talking politics."

Elizabeth blushed profusely. She knew what Maria meant

because of her intimate encounter with John Campbell this morning. "Take care. Mother wants us to get *marriage* proposals, not indecent ones."

"Oh, little Miss Chastity teaching *me* about marriage proposals. I've already got an earl on my line . . . and I shall allow him lots of *play* before I ever attempt to reel him in."

"I can't wait to meet your earl. Does he make your pulses race and steal your breath away, and does his touch make you weak at the knees, Maria?"

"Of course not! I'm considering him as a husband, not a lover. It is the idea of becoming a countess that makes my heart beat faster. A duchess would be even better. Just the thought of being addressed as Your Grace takes my breath away."

Later, after they retired and Elizabeth's dream began, she found herself alone with John Campbell.

He lifted her from the saddle, and she went down to him in a flurry of petticoats. As she stood captive in the circle of his arms, she brushed her hand against his hardness, curled her fingers, and squeezed.

"You are acting like a little whore! Is this one of the tantalizing games you like to play, Elizabeth?" he demanded.

"I am not a whore! I am a lady!"

"You are an actress, pretending to be a lady. You may be able to fool others, but you cannot deceive me. I know all your shameful secrets, Elizabeth Gunning!"

The next morning Bridget left the house early. She had a busy day ahead of her. The first stop she made was at an employment agency that specialized in providing ladies' maids to the well-to-do matrons of the *ton*. When she voiced her needs, she was shown into a room where half a dozen women, with hopeful looks on their faces, sat waiting to be employed.

Bridget's sharp eyes were critical as she assessed each female. She found all of them to be cut from the same cloth. Each looked genteel, amenable, and shabby. She had definite ideas of what a ladies' maid should look like and none of them fit the bill. She took her leave and made her way to Drury Lane. She went directly to the casting hall used by all the theaters, where actors and actresses flocked in hope of being chosen for a small supporting role in one of the stage productions. Early in her career she and Peg Woffington had sat in this hall hours on end. "I'm looking for someone who can play the role of ladies' maid."

When a dozen eager females stood up, Bridget explained, "You won't be acting your part on the stage but out in *real* Society. I need someone with the confidence to mix with lords and ladies, earls and countesses, perhaps even royalty." When all twelve of the actresses remained standing, Bridget looked them over carefully. She wanted a woman around thirty, on the plain side, though not ugly. She also must have an air of command mixed with a little disdain. "You will have to act as ladies' maid and companion to two beautiful young ladies for the Winter Season. If your authority is questioned by anyone, you must be able to stand your ground, and you will, of course, report to me."

Bridget selected three women and asked them questions so that she could not only hear their voices but assess the manner in which they spoke. She finally chose a tall woman with a ramrod-straight back and a flat chest, who held her nose in the air as if she smelled something offensive. "The pay is five shillings per week, and you will live at Great Marlborough Street. Agreed?"

The woman bobbed a stiff curtsy. "Yes, madam."

"You may start today. Your name will be Emma. Wait here."

Bridget walked to the opposite end of the hall where the male actors congregated. "I need some actors tonight for a crowd scene outside Drury Lane Theater. The job pays sixpence apiece. I shall arrive at theater-time accompanied by two beautiful young ladies. When we step from the carriage, I want you to mob us. You must jostle and push each other to get a glimpse of the Beauties. I'm sure that's all the direction you need—you've all played in mob scenes on the stage, I warrant." Bridget opened her reticule and handed out coins to a score of men. "Show up, do a good job, and I shall use your services again soon."

Bridget walked back down the hall. "Come, Emma. We'll visit my friend Peg Woffington. Consider this your audition."

Emma walked one step behind Bridget as she made her way

into Drury Lane Theater. Tonight was opening night and by afternoon backstage would be like Bedlam. Bridget knocked on Peg's dressing room door, which was opened by Dora. "I've come to wish you well!"

"Bridget, come in and sit for a few moments," Peg invited.

Emma followed Bridget and tried not to gape at the famous star. "May I take your cloak, ma'am?"

"No, thank you, Emma. This is opening night, so I shan't stay."

"We're doing *She Stoops to Conquer.*" Peg glanced at Bridget's ladies' maid and arched an approving eyebrow. "We try to coordinate with the opening of Parliament. The critics will call my performance *coarse extravagance,* but I prefer to think of it as *exuberant high spirits.*"

"My daughters and I plan to attend, Peg. I just wanted to warn you that wherever they go these days, they create a sensation." Bridget lowered her eyelid in a wink.

"You clever minx, the critics report on everyone and everything that happens opening night." Peg grinned. "Have a care or the name Gunning will be as famous as Woffington."

"Newspaper people can be as tenacious as bloodhounds."

"It is a burden we must endure," Peg said dramatically.

"I'll be off. Emma's wardrobe is appalling. I must get her fitted with some decent uniforms."

Bridget took Emma to the secondhand shop and between them decided on a plain black silk dress and a gray one. They were more elegant than uniforms and must have been expensive when new. She also bought her a smart black cloak trimmed with braid. "You can come to Great Marlborough Street now. This evening you will help my daughters to dress and perhaps fashion their hair. After we leave for the theater, you can go and fetch your belongings."

On the opening day of Parliament, none of its members expected to accomplish much in the way of the country's business. They showed up, greeted one another, either warmly or distantly, sized up their opponents, and huddled with their cronies. The members noted who had died since the last session and speculated on who looked most likely to do so during this session.

The Earl of Coventry could not wait to greet his friend the Duke of Hamilton. "James, you're looking a bit worse for wear today. Have a taxing weekend, did you?"

"Don't remember, actually," Hamilton drawled. "Woke up this morning at the Cloister in Pall Mall. Must have enjoyed more than one nun by the size of the bill the good abbess presented to me."

George, accustomed to Hamilton's boasting about his virility, had a little boasting of his own to impart, to say nothing of the bet he would collect. It was sure to wipe the smug sneer from Hamilton's face. "James, shall we meet as usual in Bucks' Coffee House, Parliament Square, after the session?"

"Why not? I'll need a bloody eye-opener by then."

Two hours later, James Hamilton entered the smoke-filled coffeehouse and slid into the booth where Coventry sat awaiting him. "Who showed up at Devonshire House Friday evening? All the usual toadies, including yourself, George?"

"You'll want to kick yourself for not being there, James."

"And why is that, pray?" Hamilton stifled a yawn.

"I was formally introduced to *Mistress Maria Gunning*!" He grinned. "You owe me ten guineas, James. Perhaps you should see your doctor—you've turned a peculiar shade of green."

Hamilton's look of boredom vanished. "You sly bastard, Coventry! Did you know she was going to be there?"

"I swear I didn't have an inkling. But I tell you what, James, the rumors weren't exaggerated. Maria Gunning is the most beautiful creature I've ever laid eyes on."

"So you haven't laid hands on her yet?"

"I don't think either of us will be collecting on that particular bet anytime soon. Her mother watches her like a hawk!"

"Perhaps I should try tupping the mother," Hamilton half jested.

"Attractive woman, but dominant and controlling in the extreme. Took them up in my carriage when I encountered them walking in Hyde Park Saturday. She keeps her daughter on a very short leash."

"There's another one, isn't there?" Hamilton's tone was rife with speculation.

"Elizabeth . . . even younger than Maria. I haven't yet had the pleasure, but the Gunnings are attending Drury Lane tonight."

"Then so are we, James, so are we."

Chapter Nine

*D*ressed in identical dark sapphire-blue evening capes that contrasted so vividly with their bright tresses, Elizabeth and Maria stood before their mother and Emma for critical inspection.

"Masks, I think." Bridget opened the old trunk that held theatrical paraphernalia and produced a pair of masks on sticks. "Do not cover your faces with them," she warned. "We want everyone attending the play tonight to get a good look at you both. Just carry them for dramatic effect. Emma, what do you think?"

"Absolutely stunning, ma'am."

"Good, that's the effect we are aiming for. Maria, Elizabeth, keep yourselves aloof from the riffraff tonight," she ordered.

A half hour later, when they arrived in Drury Lane by hansom cab, the entire theater district was crowded. Opening night was *the* fashionable place to be for London's *élite*. Bridget emerged cautiously from the carriage, followed by her daughters. The moment Maria set her foot to the pavement, cries went up.

"It's the Gunnings!"

"Let me see!"

"Look, it's them! It's the Gunnings!"

The cries were accompanied by a great deal of jostling, pushing, and shoving, mingled with shouting and cursing. The throng outside the theater was rapidly becoming involved in a *mêleé*.

Coventry and Hamilton had just purchased box tickets for the performance, when the crowd around them erupted. "What the devil is going on?" Hamilton demanded. "Bloody rabble should be shot!"

Coventry, taller than most in the crowd, caught a glimpse of silver-gilt hair. "James, it's them . . . it's the Gunning ladies! By God, they will be trampled."

Hamilton carried a silver-headed malacca cane, which he wielded effectively as he ordered, "Make way, make way there!" The crowd fell back enough for the two men to clear a path to the ladies.

"Lord Coventry, how can I thank you for your gallant rescue? We should not have come! It is getting to the stage where my daughters cannot appear in public without being mobbed!"

Elizabeth looked at the Earl of Coventry whom Maria claimed was already hooked on her line, but then her eyes were drawn to the man who accompanied him. He was staring openly at her and made no attempt to hide his blatant interest. She lowered her lashes to break their eye contact, but when she raised them again, she found his unblinking gaze transfixed upon her. His hazel eyes devoured her. She covered her face with her mask in a protective gesture.

"Let us get inside the theater lobby, away from this unruly crowd," Coventry urged, genuinely concerned for Maria.

Once inside, they were no longer being pushed, but they were certainly being stared at and whispered about.

"We have a box. I suggest you ladies join us for your own protection," Hamilton invited.

Bridget arched her brows. "I rather think not, my lord. Sitting in a box would be tantamount to putting my daughters on display for the audience to gape at!"

"Permit me to introduce my friend, James Douglas, Duke of Hamilton. This is the honorable Bridget Gunning, her daughter Mistress Maria, and I assume Mistress Elizabeth."

"Your Grace, I am delighted."

Hamilton saw the look of speculation on Bridget Gunning's face and pressed his advantage. "I must insist! I believe you ladies will be far safer in our box than sitting in the audience."

Bridget inclined her head. "Your Grace is too kind."

It was her first concession; he vowed it would not be her last.

They were led to the box by an usher, who was all deference to the noble gentlemen. He held aside the plush curtain, and Maria Gunning stepped in and took a front-row seat as if she owned it. Elizabeth held back, awaiting directions from her mother. When Bridget indicated where she should sit, Beth quietly took her seat and shook her head when the duke offered to remove her cape.

Maria's fingers fluffed out her hair as she looked over the audience. She felt quite complacent at the number of people who were gazing up at her with frank curiosity. Her beauty had caused quite a stir tonight, and she liked the way it made her feel. Elizabeth, on the other hand, felt vaguely suspicious. It was almost as if her mother had arranged for them to be mobbed the moment they arrived. She also wondered if this meeting with a Duke of the Realm was contrived. She recognized immediately that Lord Hamilton and her mother were two of a kind. Both were strong-willed and used to taking control. A small curl of fear constricted her breathing.

When the curtain went up, Elizabeth focused on Peg Woffington.

She Stoops to Conquer was a comedy that poked fun and often ridiculed the manners of Society. Somewhere in the middle of the first act, Beth became immersed in the play and began to laugh.

James Hamilton never took his eyes from the golden-haired female. Her beauty easily eclipsed that of his former *fiancée*, Elizabeth Chudleigh, but this lovely young girl had an indefinable air of chaste innocence about her as well. The sister also was undeniably beautiful, but she was fully aware of it, and it lessened her charm. Of the two, Maria would be far easier to bed and therefore less of a challenge. James Hamilton's appetite was whetted. He had a sudden desire to own Elizabeth, body and soul.

The first act ended, but before the lights went up, Beth became aware of the duke's eyes upon her. The spiral of fear curled tighter inside her chest. When she recognized the occupants of two boxes across the theater, some of her anxiety left her. The Countess of Burlington and Lady Charlotte sat in a box next to the Cavendish sisters, who were accompanied by their brother, Will, Lord Hartington. She watched as he visited Charlie's box, feeling acute disappointment that his friend John was not with him.

Before the lights went down, Charlie waved to her. She was about to wave back when Beth found her mother glaring at her as if she had committed an unforgivable social blunder. "A lady never draws attention to herself, Elizabeth."

Beth quickly lowered her lashes before her mother could see the resentment flash in her eyes. *You are a hypocrite! You want us to draw the attention of all London. Why else are we sitting here on display in this theater box with a duke and an earl?*

When the theater darkened, Elizabeth felt a hand cover hers. Her lashes flew up, and she looked directly into the duke's eyes. Ostensibly, the hand was to comfort her, but Beth knew otherwise. It was to gain her trust. She poked it with the stick of her mask and was disconcerted when it did not have the desired effect. Hamilton gripped her hand more firmly and squeezed. When she stared coolly into his eyes, he smiled. She knew he was showing his power when he did not remove his hand until he was good and ready.

The play was spoiled for Beth since she could no longer focus on anything save Hamilton's overpowering presence. She was greatly relieved when her mother declined a ride home in his carriage. "Thank you, but we shall join my friend Lady Burlington. We are to discuss plans to attend Almack's on Wednesday night."

Bridget Gunning bade the gentlemen good night, her daughters dropped curtsies, and the three ladies took their leave.

Dorothy Boyle gave Bridget a faux embrace. "I swear the name of Gunning is on everyone's lips tonight. People were jostling just to get a glimpse of you."

"If we hadn't been rescued by His Grace, the Duke of Hamilton, I don't know what we should have done."

Dorothy changed the subject. She would save the gossip about Hamilton for when they were more private. "We are having a house party this weekend at Chiswick. Maria and Elizabeth's invitations are in the post but I wanted to assure you that I shall *chaperon* them every moment. No need for you to worry at all." She winked. "You may be sure that any young men included will have coronets."

Bridget pressed her lips together. Dorothy Boyle was making it clear that only her daughters were invited; she was not. But if this was the way things were done by the families of the *ton*, she would acquiesce. Emma, of course, would accompany them to Chiswick.

When they had returned to Great Marlborough Street, Elizabeth waited until she and Maria were in their bedchamber. "I quite liked the Earl of Coventry. It is easy to see that he is ready to lay his heart at your feet."

"I much prefer *your duke* to *my earl*. Perhaps I'll steal him!"

"He isn't *my* duke!" Elizabeth protested. "Coventry is a far more amiable gentleman and would be more amenable, I believe."

"But I would much rather be a duchess than a countess, and it would be far more fun bringing a duke to heel than an earl."

"It isn't a game, Maria."

"Between a man and a woman, it is always a game. And it is a game I shall win, because I set my own rules!"

Mother sets the rules. "You shouldn't pit two friends against each other."

"Whyever not? I love men to fight over me. Tonight, my beauty almost caused a riot!" Maria was inordinately pleased.

Her vanity blinds her to Mother's manipulation.

"White's or the Kit-Cat Club?" Hamilton asked Coventry before they climbed into the carriage.

"Drop me off at home, if you don't mind, James. I'm preparing a speech for the House tomorrow."

"Bolton Street." Hamilton gave his coachman the address of Coventry's townhouse then climbed in after his friend.

"Well, what do you think?" George asked eagerly.

"The Gorgeous Gunnings! Indeed, you did not exaggerate their beauty. There wasn't a man at the theater who wouldn't have given his left ball to be in our shoes tonight! Pity the mother is such a fucking dragon. Knows the value of her merchandise, I'm afraid."

They soon arrived in Bolton Street. As Coventry climbed

from the carriage he asked, "Will I see you at Almack's, James?"

"*Almack's?* I'd as soon be buried alive, George!"

At Sundridge, John Campbell, who had been debating with himself for the past two days, finally summoned his secretary to Combe Bank's library. "Robert, how would you feel about a quick trip to Ireland? I need some inquiries made and know I can count on your discretion."

"I am completely at your service, Lord Sundridge." Hay grinned. "The Irish Sea should be free from gales until late October."

"I would like you to visit County Mayo and make inquiries about Theobald Burke, Viscount Mayo, or, more precisely, about his daughter, Bridget."

Hay wrote down the information his lordship required.

"Then I need you to travel to County Roscommon and make inquiries about the family of John Gunning, who own Castle Coote."

"Is there anything in particular you wish to know, my lord?"

"Just general information. Their social connections—where the Gunnings stand in the pecking order, that sort of thing. Take a good look at the castle and its landholdings to see how well it prospers." John picked up the invitation to Chiswick and banished the twinge of guilt he felt. "I'll have your money and maps ready by the time you are packed." He scribbled his acceptance across the invitation and set it with his other letters to be posted.

On Wednesday when Elizabeth opened her eyes, her very first thought was that she was finally seventeen. Her second thought was that she would see John Campbell this weekend at Chiswick. Both thoughts filled her with happiness.

Maria forgot that it was her sister's birthday and at breakfast chattered on about her upcoming visit to Almack's this evening. "Did you know that it is absolutely *de rigueur* to arrive at Almack's after eleven o'clock? May I stay until dawn, Mother?"

"We shall take our cue from the Countess of Burlington. When she decrees it time for Lady Charlotte to leave, we shall leave. That way, we are guaranteed a ride home, since we *still* don't have a carriage of our own. Ah, Jack, there you are. Almack's has a gaming room. Are you planning on joining us tonight?"

"No, I plan to take Elizabeth out for a birthday supper." He dropped a kiss on his younger daughter's golden curls and gave her a scroll wrapped with ribbon. "Happy birthday, my beauty. I'm sorry I couldn't buy you the ball gown I promised."

Elizabeth unwrapped the scroll and smiled with delight. "It's a Virgo horoscope! How lovely! Thank you, Father."

"Everyone knows a Virgo is a paragon of virtue!" Maria said sweetly. "To say nothing of being demure and always proper."

"Maria, you would do well not to sneer at such qualities. Gentlemen find them enchanting," her father said pointedly. "Go on, read it aloud. Give us a list of your virtues, my beauty."

Elizabeth wrinkled her nose at Maria and began to read. "A Virgo is conscientious, tactful, thoughtful, and endearingly sincere. A Virgo also is punctual, prudent, unfailingly discreet, and knows how to keep secrets. She loves animals, nature, and writing poetry. She is modest, self-effacing, yet ultrafeminine."

"Enough virtues! Read us your vices, Elizabeth," her mother said.

"A Virgo arrogantly applies her lofty standards to others. A Virgo has skittish emotions and fragile nerves. High-strung Virgo requires harmony and tranquillity to thrive. She often daydreams and indulges in fantasies that try the patience."

Bridget concurred. "Well, that hits the nail on the head. You certainly do your best to try my patience at times, Elizabeth."

The footman appeared at the dining room door, holding a large box. "This was just delivered, madam. For Mistress Elizabeth."

Bridget took the box and he withdrew. Jack motioned for his wife to give it to Elizabeth and with reluctance she did so.

Beth read the card. "It's from Charlie! It's a birthday present." She unwrapped it slowly and lifted the lid. For a moment, she couldn't believe her eyes. It was the gold tissue ball gown she had tried on at Madame Chloe's. "Ohhh," she sighed softly, blinking back tears.

"My God, it must have cost the earth," Jack marveled.

"Money means nothing to these people! Now do you see

why I am willing to dedicate my life to ensuring that you marry into wealth? No matter the sacrifice to myself?"

"I want to wear it to Almack's!" Maria could not hide her envy.

"And so you shall, but not tonight, Maria. After all, it is Elizabeth's birthday."

"Now we can all go to Almack's, and I'll win us a fortune!" Jack grinned.

"Mmm, my desire for a carriage will soon be fulfilled, I warrant," Bridget said with exquisite sarcasm.

The Gunning sisters spent the afternoon washing their hair. Bridget had soon realized that their glorious tresses gained her daughters the lion's share of attention at any gathering. She wisely refused to hide their crowning splendor beneath powdered wigs. Emma, amazingly gifted as a *coiffeuse,* fashioned Maria's silver-gilt hair in a high pompadour to show off her long, slim neck. When she was done with Elizabeth, her golden hair cascaded down her back in a hundred glossy ringlets.

It was after the hour of eleven when the Gunning family stepped down from the hired cabriolet in Pall Mall and swept into the hallowed halls of Almack's. The Gunning sisters were the *on dit* of the moment, and their entrance brought a gasp or two from those assembled. Other *débutantes* felt dismay; their mothers felt resentment. The men felt their bodies stir at such exquisite youth and tantalizing beauty.

Dorothy Boyle introduced Bridget to Almack's patronesses, Sarah Jersey and Emily Cowper, who were avid to meet her, then took Jack Gunning's arm. "John, the gaming room awaits you." She laughed up into his handsome face. "This is becoming a habit with us. Too bad our meetings are always public, never private."

Jack squeezed her hand. "Lead on, and I shall follow."

"Is that a promise?" she asked archly.

She was not the first titled woman who had made overtures to him, and he quite enjoyed charming the ladies. He knew that if he rebuffed the countess, he would not only make a deadly enemy but sound the death knell to his daughters' social aspirations. Jack lifted her fingers to his lips. "Perhaps it is."

When she came back downstairs, she saw William

Cavendish arrive with his sisters. "Lord Hartington, it does my heart good to see such a dutiful brother."

"Please call me Will, Lady Burlington." He bowed over her hand and murmured, "My sisters gave me a perfect excuse to come and dance attendance on Lady Charlotte, but I don't see her."

"That is because Charlie and the Gunning sisters are surrounded by an adoring throng of admirers. If you don't make haste, their dance cards will be completely filled."

Will hurried off, leaving Rachel and Cat Cavendish to their own devices. "Lady Burlington, I hope this warm, sunny weather lasts through the weekend. We are so looking forward to Chiswick."

"September is always a lovely month. I invited Orford, but is there someone special you'd like me to invite, Lady Catherine?"

When Cat flushed, her sister Rachel suggested, "If you invite Harriet Ponsonby, perhaps her brother, Johnny, will accompany her?"

So, Cat Cavendish, you are hot for John Ponsonby, who is without a title. Your mother will be livid, but here is my chance to gain your undying gratitude! "Since the Ponsonbys are our closest Chiswick neighbors, their invitations have already been posted." *Or will be the moment I get home.*

When the Cavendish sisters arrived in the crowded ballroom, Rachel was dismayed to see the Earl of Orford worshipping at the shrine of Maria Gunning, along with many other infatuated males. "I have decided that I have pined for the attentions of John Campbell long enough," she murmured to Cat. "From now on I shall devote myself to Orford until he makes a commitment!"

Maria Gunning, deciding an Earl of the Realm wasn't quite good enough, was doing her utmost to ignore the attentions of George Norwich. Since word had spread like wildfire about her being mobbed at the theater, tonight she had attracted a throng of gentlemen, and she flirted with everyone save the Earl of Coventry. Finally, like a kicked hound, he slunk off to join her sister, Elizabeth, who stood amidst a gathering of her own, receiving birthday wishes. He greeted his friend Will and envied him the adoring looks young Charlotte Boyle was bestowing upon him.

"Hello, George. Seems everyone is here tonight."

Coventry brightened. "Everyone is right. Even Hamilton deigned to attend, though the other night he swore he'd rather be buried alive. He's up in the gaming room." George elbowed aside the young man who was talking to Elizabeth. "Would you do me the honor of the next dance, Mistress Gunning?"

"Oh, I'm sorry, Lord Coventry, the next dance is taken, but I will save you the one after that," she promised with a smile.

"I warrant m'sister Cat's dance card isn't full yet, George."

"Really, Will?" Coventry brightened still further. A Cavendish lady, though no raving beauty, was a prize indeed.

Elizabeth stayed on the ballroom floor for twelve dances in a row. The gold tissue gown made her feel beautiful, and each time she spoke to Charlie, she thanked her again for the generous gift. She was thoroughly enjoying herself; her only regret was that John Campbell was not there to see her and dance with her. Before the night was over, she suspected that she would dance with every young man present. She had no idea which men were titled and which were not and, in fact, never thought about such things, unlike most young ladies, who could quote verbatim from *Burke's Peerage*.

Elizabeth and Charlotte were accompanied to the supper room by George Coventry and Will Cavendish. The ladies were happy with the almond-flavored ratafia, while their partners settled for sherry. When the men looked askance at the dainty sandwiches and seed cake, Charlie laughed and promised more substantial fare at Chiswick.

It was around two o'clock in the morning when Jack Gunning left the gaming room in the company of the Duke of Hamilton. Jack had lost most of his money to the nobleman, who was an habitual gambler. Then, an hour ago, when the duke learned his name was Gunning, his luck turned and Jack recouped all his losses.

Maria Gunning saw the Duke of Hamilton the moment he stepped into the ballroom. She had been watching for him ever since Coventry had told her the duke was upstairs in the gaming room.

Maria glided to his side and touched his hand. "Your

Grace," she whispered seductively, giving him a provocative sideways glance, "you have kept me waiting for three hours."

His hazel eyes swept her from head to toe. "Mistress Gunning, let me be blunt so that I do not waste any more of your time. I am not in the market for a duchess. A *liaison,* however, is another matter entirely, and I am at your disposal."

Maria gasped as if she'd been slapped in the face. "You must be drunk, sir!"

He bowed. "After midnight, dearest lady, I am always drunk."

She turned on her heel and walked off with disdain. She searched out Coventry and found him about to partner Elizabeth. She placed a proprietary hand on his arm. "I have neglected you shamefully tonight, Lord Coventry, but I am free for this dance."

Elizabeth saw that the earl was torn between desire for Maria and duty toward her. She said graciously, "Do partner Maria so that I may ask Father to dance."

Jack Gunning took Elizabeth's hand and led her onto the floor. "Happy birthday, Beth. You're the prettiest lady here tonight."

She laughed up at him, happily. "It's the gown, Father."

"No, it is not the gown, my beauty."

As they danced, she had the eerie feeling that someone was watching her. She glanced uneasily into the shadowed recesses that dotted the perimeter of the ballroom, but saw no one. She concentrated on the music to keep time, but the feeling became so strong that she felt the back of her neck prickle. Her glance once more searched around the room. And then she saw him, half hidden by a pillar. It was the Duke of Hamilton. His attention was riveted upon her, his unblinking stare relentlessly followed her about the ballroom. A shudder rippled down her spine.

"Surely you're not cold, my beauty? It's warm in here."

"No, just a little tired, Father."

"Let's find your mother. I think it's time we went home."

"Thanks, Father." She smiled gratefully and squeezed his hand.

Chapter Ten

*N*ext day, Elizabeth and her father were in the livery stable behind Great Marlborough Street where the residents kept their horses. It was one of the few places Jack and his favorite daughter could spend time alone, knowing Bridget and Maria had no love of stables.

"I rode in the park on Sunday with Charlie. She let me ride one of their horses. It was the first time I'd ever used a side saddle, but it wasn't difficult at all."

"How would you like to have your own mount at Chiswick?"

"Do you mean Cavalier?" Elizabeth had loved the bay gelding on sight, the day her father had brought him from Cambridgeshire. "That would be splendid, but we are going in the Burlington carriage with Charlie tomorrow at ten."

"I could ride him down there for you and come back by river. The countess told me that she was going a day early to prepare for her guests. She can show me around Chiswick House."

"It would be wonderful! But do you think Mother will approve of your visiting Chiswick without her?"

"Since the countess is our *entrée* to the *beau monde,* your mother has suggested that Dorothy Boyle and I become intimate friends." He shook his head ruefully. "Bridget is determined that we climb the social ladder along with her, whether it suits us or not."

Elizabeth stroked Cavalier's reddish-brown coat and sighed. "Maria seems far better suited to social climbing than I am."

Jack set down the currycomb. "She is very like her mother."

"And I am like you . . . thank heaven above!"

Bright and early Friday morning, Jack Gunning rode Cavalier along the Great West Road to the County of Hounslow, then rode south along Burlington Lane to Chiswick House, which sat on the bank of the River Thames. The Earl of Burlington had designed it in the simple symmetrical style of Palladio's Villa Capra, and his friend, William Kent, had done the interiors.

Dorothy Boyle lay supine in her big bed, staring up at the classical painting on her bedchamber ceiling as her partner labored above her. The act had become tiresomely routine, and she had to stifle a yawn. He had been pumping for half an hour but by the feel of things wasn't going to bring either of them satisfaction any time soon. Deciding she'd been both patient and accommodating long enough, she slid her forefinger along the cleft between his buttocks and deftly inserted it. With a gasp, he spent immediately and rolled off her, exhausted.

Feeling restless and dissatisfied, she arose from the bed and slipped on a loose morning gown. Through the long French windows she caught sight of a rider headed in the general direction of the stables. She frowned, knowing it was far too early for any of her guests to arrive. She glanced at her bed partner of many years. "No, no, don't exert yourself further—you need the rest, darling."

Her servants were well trained to be unobtrusive and to attend her only when summoned. She strolled out across the side lawns toward the stables and was pleasantly surprised to find John Gunning dismounting from a glossy bay.

He glanced at her *dishabillé*. "I hope I haven't disturbed you at such an early hour. I thought I'd bring Elizabeth's mount to Chiswick for her."

She gave him a sly smile and purred, "You disturb me at any hour, John, especially in those tight riding breeches. Come, let's put him in a stall." She followed as he hitched Cavalier's bridle and slid off the saddle. She ran her hand down the animal's satiny flank. "What a pity he's gelded . . . has it lessened his spirit?"

Jack grinned and reached for her, knowing it was *his* spirit she was questioning. When his mouth came down on hers, she opened her lips, inviting him inside. She slid her arms about his neck and pressed her body into his, enjoying the feel of his erection as it grew against her. His hands came up to cup her heavy breasts, and in a heartbeat he unfastened the loose gown so that her flesh was bared to his hands and his mouth. He teased her nipple with his teeth until it became turgid and swollen to the size of a marble.

His hand moved between her thighs, and when he found her wet and ready, he slid two fingers deep inside her and at the same time thrust into her mouth with his tongue. When she moaned and opened farther for him, he pressed her up against the side of the stall and thrust in a third finger. He felt her sheath, hot and throbbing, grip his fingers as he buried them deep. He pushed her to the edge, then, with one last driving thrust, brought her to shuddering climax. He watched as she leaned back against the wooden stall, panting.

"There's something about the smell of a stable that is definitely arousing, but perhaps we should go inside, where you can show me the many chambers of the villa."

She caught her breath, wishing with every fiber of her body that they could indeed repair to a bedchamber. Then she began to laugh. It was low and sultry, and filled with irony. "Your timing is rather awkward, John."

"Good God, Dorothy. Don't tell me your husband is here?"

"Rather more complicated than that."

They heard someone enter the stable and call her name. Jack watched her face suffuse with amusement she couldn't hide.

"Here I am. John Gunning has brought his daughter's horse so she may ride this weekend. This is Charles Fitzroy, the Duke of Grafton. I believe you've met before."

The young guests who had been invited to Chiswick for the weekend began to arrive at eleven o'clock, and by the hour of noon they were all seated around the huge dining room table for lunch. The talking and laughing reached a crescendo before the first course was served, and the countess had to hold up her hands for silence. "Welcome to Chiswick, everyone. We want you to enjoy yourselves this weekend, so after I've made my little speech, I shall disappear as any *chaperon* worth her salt should do."

A chorus of *"Hear! Hear!"* came from the young men.

With tongue in cheek she continued, "There's lots to do to keep you out of trouble. There are rowboats and punts for on the river, there's tennis and shuttlecock, as well as archery butts. Anyone who doesn't have a mount may borrow one from our stables. The woods hereabouts are alive with rabbits and game birds, and if you want to organize a shoot, there are plenty of guns in the gun room. The staff will be happy to pack you lunch baskets for picnics, and dinner won't be served until eight o'clock to give you plenty of time to wear off all that disgusting energy you young people seem to have in abundance. If you fall in the river, don't call me."

"You have the most understanding mother in the world, Lady Charlotte. If she were not married to your father, I would offer for her on the spot," William Cavendish said with a wink.

"Oh, please, let's not use silly titles this weekend. Just our first names? Everyone must call me Charlie!"

"I rather like titles," Maria Gunning whispered to the Earl of Coventry, "especially yours, George."

"I'll call you mistress if you wish, but I much prefer Maria."

"Since I'm not your *mistress,* I see no reason to call me such," she teased wickedly. "What would you like to do, George?"

Coventry, obsessed with the thought of making love to her, tried desperately to think of something more acceptable to suggest. He was not the athletic type, but he did enjoy hunting, and a walk in the woods with such a beautiful female, who was in a playful mood, seemed heaven-sent. "Would you care to watch me shoot, Maria?"

"I'd love to watch you! Perhaps you could give me some lessons and teach me how to handle a gun."

Her suggestion sounded somehow provocative and aroused him instantly. He swallowed hard. "It would be my pleasure, Maria."

The couples paired off quite naturally by unspoken, mutual consent, just as the countess had planned. Charlie was partnered by Will, Elizabeth by Sundridge, Maria by Coventry, Rachel Cavendish by Orford, and her sister, Cat, by Johnny Ponsonby. That left Harriet Ponsonby, and the countess knew she could count on her nephew Michael Boyle to be accommodating. The shrewd young devil knew on which side his bread was buttered, and she never forgot to reward him handsomely for his trouble.

Elizabeth sat quietly beside John Campbell, luxuriating in his commanding presence and deliriously happy to be out from under her mother's critical eye.

He smiled down at her. "I've missed you, Beth. I always forget how beautiful you are, then I see you and it takes my breath away."

She blushed at his compliment. "I celebrated my seventeenth birthday on Wednesday."

"I knew it was soon, but I didn't realize it was this week. Happy birthday, sweeting."

"Do I look any older?"

His dark eyes searched her lovely heart-shaped face. She looked beautiful, sweet, vulnerable, and impossibly young. He covered her hand with his. "You don't believe me now but there will come a day when you will want to look younger, Elizabeth."

She laughed happily at the absurdity of his words.

"I know you love the water—will you come out on the river?"

She nodded eagerly. "I should run up and get my parasol."

"I'll go and get us a boat before they're all gone. Meet me down at the river landing."

When she went upstairs to the chamber she was sharing with Charlie, her friend also was searching for her sunshade. They found them in the wardrobe where their maids had put them when they unpacked. "John is taking me on the river."

"Will wants me to go on the river too. It's the first time we will actually be alone. I think it's sooo romantic!"

They walked down to the river together and were glad to see they were the only two females adventurous enough to go out on the water. The small watercraft had been fitted with padded leather seats, with cushions piled against the backboards so ladies could recline in comfort.

Will waited on the wooden landing holding his boat's mooring rope, but John stood in the boat he had chosen, with his legs braced apart to keep it from rocking.

Charlie climbed in, and the boat rocked from side to side in spite of Will's efforts to hold it steady. John, with supreme confidence, held up his arms to lift Elizabeth from the landing. She went down to him without hesitation, showing that she put complete trust in his ability to keep her safe. When he took full advantage of the opportunity to snatch a quick kiss, she wondered if her trust was misplaced and smiled a secret smile. She sat down amidst the cushions and opened her rose-colored parasol, while John removed his jacket and took up the oars.

She noticed a picnic basket tucked beneath his seat. "We've only just finished lunch. What's in the basket?"

"Something to drink in case we get thirsty." He rowed out into the current but not all the way to the middle where the Thames' tide flowed too rapidly. They drifted downriver as swans glided away from them toward the safety of the bank.

"Look, a pair of black swans! Perhaps it is Jupiter and Leda."

"Your knowledge of mythology tells me you've had a classical education. I'm hungry to learn more about you, Elizabeth."

Since her "classical education" consisted of stories her father had told, she gave him a teasing reply. "I shall remain a mystery." She watched him through half-closed eyes. "It is you I wish to explore."

Does she realize that's a double entendre? She looked so innocent it was impossible for him to decide. "I much prefer exploring you but perhaps it would be fun to explore each other." He could tell she blushed, in spite of the glow from her parasol.

"Do you enjoy saying wicked things to me?"

He laughed. "I must confess that I do. It gives me pleasure to see the roses bloom in your cheeks. Now it's your turn—say something wicked to me."

She tilted her head, watching his muscles flex beneath the fine lawn shirt. "I have an affinity with animals and find that you have an animal magnetism that attracts me."

He was stunned at the honesty and intimacy of her words. *Lord God, I may have to protect her from herself!* "Eliza-

beth . . . Beth, you really shouldn't go around saying things like
that to the opposite sex. You will be meeting a lot of men at social functions this Season, many of whom will try to take advantage of you."

"Will *you* take advantage of me, John?"

Is she extending me an invitation? He had the decency to
flush, for indeed he had every intention of taking advantage of
her sooner or later. Since she was being honest with him, he
warned, "Given half a chance, you know I will."

His words, coupled with his predatory glance, sent a shiver
of anticipation racing through her blood. A delicious heightened tension shimmered between them. It was like a game that
only two could play, and though she was unsure of the rules,
she had every intention of participating. Her lashes fluttered to
her cheeks as suddenly she recognized that what she felt for this
dark, powerful man was desire. The knowledge did not frighten
her; it emboldened her. "I attended Almack's on my birthday
and received more male attention than I've ever had before. I
don't think any of them wanted to take advantage of me."

"Believe me when I tell you that they did, Elizabeth. It is
simply that at Almack's the proprieties must be observed and
the mothers are the predators. Males prefer other hunting
grounds."

The corners of her mouth lifted. "Such as Chiswick?"

John threw back his head and laughed, displaying the corded
muscles in his neck. "Such as Chiswick," he admitted.

"When does the hunt begin?" she challenged.

"It has begun. The predator has already separated his prey
from the pack and the water prevents her escape."

She began to sing the popular hunting ballad "John Peel":

"For the sound of his horn brought me from my bed
And the cry of his hounds which he oft times led,
Peel's 'view halloo' would awaken the dead
Or the fox from HER lair in the morning."

"If you play the role of vixen, Elizabeth, which shall I play,
the hound or the gallant John Peel?"

"I hope you will play the gallant John Campbell."

"*Touché* . . . you disarm me at every turn."

"I doubt that, Lord Sundridge. A relentless hunter like you most likely keeps a concealed weapon about his person."

His concealed weapon immediately hardened and lengthened. "You know all my secrets." He steered the boat toward the bank where weeping willows dipped their branches into the water. As they drifted beneath the leafy green boughs, he joined her among the cushions and reached for the basket. He produced a bottle of champagne and two glasses. He popped the cork and poured the wine then unwrapped a linen napkin that held chocolate truffles. He lifted a tempting bonbon to her lips and murmured intimately, "You know I cannot resist watching you eat, Elizabeth."

She bit down with sharp teeth then licked the luscious soft center and thrilled as his dark eyes devoured her.

He lifted the glasses of champagne, one to her lips, one to his own. "Happy birthday, sweetheart."

She drank deeply and sighed with pleasure. Then she closed her parasol and took her champagne from him. As her hand touched his she felt a little shock. "A spark flew between us."

"It happens every time we touch." He waited till she drained her glass then took it from her. "Let me show you." He slid his arms about her, bringing her closer so that the tips of her breasts momentarily brushed against the fine lawn of his shirt. The sensitivity of her nipples amazed her and indeed it did feel as if sparks flew between them. Then he crushed her breasts against his hard muscled chest. His gaze was intense as slowly, deliberately, he softly brushed his lips against hers and murmured, "Feel the fire." Then his mouth took possession of hers in a fiery, hot kiss that burned her lips and scalded her heart.

As she felt his body's heat seep into her, the flame of her desire flared up in a brilliant flash that blinded her to caution or discretion. Her fingers threaded into his black hair, holding him captive for her mouth's ravishing.

Finally he lifted his mouth and gazed down at her half-closed eyes. "I wanted to give you your first taste of passion." He stroked the back of his fingers across her delicate cheek. "Once tasted, never forgotten."

The hunt had ended, the seduction begun. Unbidden words from "John Peel" ran through his head: *From a find to a check, from a check to a view, from a view to a death in the morning.*

John felt a pang—nothing so puritanical as guilt—but it caused him to pause in his headlong rush toward sensual satisfaction. She was a gift to be savored, cherished. In an encounter with a female as lovely and innocent as this one, there should be a prelude . . . a long, lingering, pleasurable prelude to the mating dance.

He released her and refilled her glass. "Sip your champagne and eat your chocolates, while I take us up the river to Kew. Since you are a wood nymph, I know the gardens will delight you."

John moored the boat at the wooden landing and, without asking permission, picked up his lady and carried her onto a broad expanse of sweeping lawns. "Here are three hundred acres to wander at your heart's content with thousands of varieties of plants." He swung her around playfully before setting her feet to the ground.

"Why are you deliberately trying to make me dizzy?"

"So that you will stagger and cling to me."

She laughed up into his face, and he slipped his arm about her and drew her close to his side. They walked past flower beds ablaze with autumn color. Yellow and bronze chrysanthemums towered beside white and purple asters and black-eyed daisies. Pink lupins nodded beside mauve larkspur and blue delphiniums. Late-summer roses bloomed next to beds of heliotrope, filling the warm afternoon air with their heady fragrance.

She urged him toward an area of intricate pathways edged with herbaceous borders whose intoxicating scent drew a myriad of tiny butterflies. She could name all of the herbs, while he could name none, but he took delight in her enchantment and was bemused at how young and carefree she made him feel. "Would you like to go through the greenhouses where the more exotic plants are grown?"

She glanced across the gardens toward the glass hothouses and shook her head shyly. "There are too many people there. I don't like crowds . . . and I'd much rather be alone with you."

He looked down at her quizzically. "From what I hear, the Gunning ladies attract crowds wherever they go. Surely that is most flattering?"

"It's Maria's beauty that attracts crowds. She loves the attention when people stare and whisper, but there are many times when I would much rather be private."

He weighed her words for sincerity. How could she possibly believe that Maria was more beautiful? "To avoid people, we'll keep a safe distance from Kew Palace. Let's walk through the orchards and see if I'm better at naming fruit than herbs." With a perfectly straight face he said, "These I believe are apples and those over there are pears."

He bent to pick up a small, hard fruit that had fallen to the ground and held it on his open palm so they could inspect it. When Beth reached for it and lifted it to her nose, he cautioned, "Don't taste it. Unripe persimmons are nasty, bitter fruit. Here, have one of these instead." He reached up and picked a Persian plum for the sheer pleasure of watching her eat it.

"Surely it is against the rules to pick the fruit!"

"Some rules cry out to be broken, and forbidden fruit is always sweeter." He grinned wickedly. "Sin now; beg forgiveness later." He dipped his head to steal a kiss and tasted plum on her lips.

When they returned to the boat, he pointed across the river. "That's Syon House. It's rather plain on the outside but the Adam interiors are magnificent."

"Plain? I would call it square and ugly. Didn't it belong to the Dudleys in Elizabethan times? I expected Syon to look more romantic, because of its stirring history. Instead, it's like a fortress . . . I feel sorry for whoever lives there."

Again he weighed her words, wondering if they were sincere. Surely every *débutante* in Society was seeking a husband with a large, magnificent house, crammed with objets d'art and a staff of a hundred servants to wait upon her hand and foot? Perhaps Beth was the exception to the rule—a female not ruled by ambition. John began to realize that, ambitious or not, Elizabeth had beguiled him. He knew he wanted her and intended to have her. Marriage, however, never entered his mind.

By twilight, most of the couples had returned from their various pursuits, and by the time dinner was served at eight, the only male and female conspicuously absent were Rachel Cavendish and the young Earl of Orford. Everyone was seated around the dining room table when the couple finally made their appearance.

Rachel, breathless and more than a little disheveled, drew every eye. Orford held her chair and when she sat down, he cupped her shoulders in such a proprietary manner that she burst out, "Orford asked me to marry him—and I said *yes!*"

The earl looked quickly toward her brother, Will, as the men began to congratulate him. "Of course I still have to approach your father and ask His Grace for his daughter's hand."

Everyone laughed and began to talk at once. Elizabeth murmured to John, "Will the Duke of Devonshire give his consent?"

"Absolutely. The duke was the best of friends with Orford's uncle, Robert Walpole. It was the late Prime Minister who gave Devonshire the governorship of Ireland."

As Elizabeth glanced around the table she knew a moment's panic. What on earth was she doing with all these wealthy, titled, famous people? One was the nephew of a Prime Minister, the Devonshires were the next thing to royalty, and even her dearest friend, Charlie, was the wealthiest heiress in the country. How long could she keep up this preposterous *charade* of pretending to be one of them? She glanced down the table at Maria and caught her sister's look of raw envy as she stared at Rachel Cavendish.

Maria Gunning, seething with jealousy, was completely free of the misgivings that assailed her sister. She swirled a pretty curl about her fingers as she turned speculative eyes upon the Earl of Coventry and brushed her leg against his. "George, do you have ambitions to become Prime Minister of England?"

George knew that it took influence and money beyond his means, but he was extremely flattered by Maria's suggestion, and aroused by her touch. "I'm not without ambition, my dear." His first and foremost ambition, of course, was to get her to lie with him.

As John Campbell looked down the table at Rachel Cavendish he felt a great deal of relief. Her relentless pursuit of him was over. At long last Rachel had given up on the chase, and brought Orford to earth. Words from "John Peel" again ran through his head: *From a check to a view, from a view to a death in the morning.* He lifted his wineglass. "A toast to the happy couple." Everyone saluted them, then John touched his glass to Elizabeth's and murmured low, "To us, sweetheart. To this moment and the moments we have yet to share."

Elizabeth's panic dissolved. John made her feel so special.

Chapter Eleven

*A*fter dinner, a suggestion of cards was voted down by the
ladies. The gentlemen were not too disappointed, since a
game of hide-and-seek was proposed instead. Michael Boyle,
accommodating as always, volunteered that he and Harriet
Ponsonby would be first to hide their eyes and do the seeking.
There were so many rooms in the villa, with numerous places
of concealment, that the tantalizing game could be drawn out
for hours.

Each male had an identical goal: to find a place of privacy
where he and his female companion could be alone and undis-
turbed for the best part of an hour. Will Cavendish and Charlie,
hand in hand, made their way into the far recesses of the conservatory. In the dimly lit room, fragrant with fuchsia, they
found a garden seat set amidst concealing palm fronds and sat
down to cuddle.

Maria Gunning led the way to the second story, with George
eagerly in tow. With finger to her lips, she entered the bedchamber she was sharing with Harriet, divining that her own
room would be the last place she would look. When Maria
scorned a chair and sat down on one of the beds, George
thought he was in paradise.

John Campbell took Elizabeth down a central hallway to the
east wing then led her up the back stairs and along to a walk-in
linen closet. At one end, lavender-scented sheets, bolsters, and
towels lay on shelves, while stacked at the other end were piles

of soft blankets and feather pillows. Once he drew her inside and closed the door, they were in pitch blackness.

Elizabeth stretched out her hands before her. "John, I cannot see anything. Where are you?"

With his mouth close to her ear, he murmured, "Sshh! We must whisper or they will hear us. I know we cannot see, but we have our other senses that will be heightened in the darkness. We can still hear and smell and . . . touch."

His voice, soft as black velvet, insinuated itself inside her, luring her to imagine wicked fantasies. She drew in a swift breath as she felt his fingertips touch her face, tracing her eyebrows, her cheekbones, the outline of her lips. Then she felt him thread his fingers into her hair.

"Whenever I see you, I want to touch your beautiful hair. You have the most alluring golden curls I've ever seen, and my fingers always itch to play with them."

"You cannot see it now," she whispered.

"All I have to do is close my eyes and I can always see it." He dipped his head and brushed his lips against hers. "I picture you naked, cloaked in your golden hair."

She went faint at the thought. "You really do enjoy saying wicked things, and it isn't to see the roses bloom in my cheeks."

"Sshh! Feel the fire, sweetheart." His arms enfolded her and pressed her softness against the hard length of his body. His mouth took hers in a possessive kiss that sent her blood running hot through her veins like wildfire. The tip of his tongue insinuated itself between her lips then thrust deep inside, filling her mouth and her senses with the taste of him.

The sensual darkness and the knowledge that she would be unable to voice her objections inflamed his imagination. When he felt her stiffen and try to pull away, he would not allow it. Instead, he caressed her back with long, slow strokes, and gradually he felt her rigid muscles relax. The rough, soft slide of his tongue worked its magic, until she lifted her arms about his neck and melted against him.

Though Elizabeth had tried to withdraw, her own longing to be held in his arms made it impossible. She learned exactly what it felt like to wage a losing battle against him and against herself. When he lifted his mouth from hers, he took hold of her hands and stroked them with the ball of his thumb. This reminded her of just how attractive his powerful hands were. Slowly, he raised one to his mouth and kissed each finger with reverence, then repeated the delicious process with her other hand. When he lifted it to his face and touched her fingertips to his brow, she began to trace his features, outlining the straight nose and muscled jaw. She touched his hair, remembering its night-black color, and knew that even in the darkness his brown-black eyes were devouring her.

Slowly, tenderly, he lifted her against his heart and carried her to the pile of soft blankets and feather pillows. He set her down gently and followed her. Again, he threaded his fingers through hers and lifted her arms above her head, so that she reclined beneath him in a captive position that thrust her breasts snugly against the broad expanse of his muscled chest.

Gradually, she became aware of his scent. It was a mixture of leather, sandalwood, and something male and dangerous. Yet as she lifted her mouth for his kiss, she had never felt safer in her life. The total blackness hid their provocative behavior, and she wished that the night could go on forever. Lying in his arms felt so right. Surely this was the way it was supposed to be between a man and a woman. She had longed for this closeness all her life.

The silent darkness became thick with unrequited need.

Suddenly, the door was flung open and lamplight streamed in.

"Uh . . . nobody in the linen room!" Michael Boyle declared emphatically and quickly shut the door.

"Beth, I'm so sorry." John's intense words, coupled with their discovery, acted like cold water and she struggled to sit up. "Boyle's a good friend . . . I promise you he won't betray us." He squeezed her hand and lifted it to his mouth in a pledge.

In the boat, when she had asked him if he would take advantage of her, he had replied, *Given half a chance, you know I will.* Well, she had given him more than *half a chance,* so she could not blame him—she could only blame herself for her wanton behavior. "We'd better go," she said softly.

"I'll go first, sweetheart. Try not to blush when you go downstairs. What we did was lovely and unbelievably innocent. Please don't regret the moments we shared tonight."

A short time later, the ladies retired and left the men to their cards. Beth and Charlie went up together, both of them flushed because of the game they had played. Charlie closed the bed-chamber door and turned to Elizabeth. "I let Will kiss me tonight and take all kinds of other liberties. Oh, Beth, I'm so head over heels in love with him that I got carried away. I know it sounds wicked, but I *wanted* him to make love to me!"

"Where did you hide?"

"We went into the conservatory. It was dimly lit and our garden seat was hidden from view by tall palm fronds. The atmosphere was so romantic and secluded—it was as if the whole world receded and there was just the two of us. When he kissed me and . . . caressed me, it felt so right, but now I know my behavior was wanton!" Charlie was covered with guilt. "Where did you hide?"

"In the linen room," Beth confessed, remembering the feel of the soft pillows and blankets.

Charlie gasped as she pictured the intimate hiding place. Then the two friends looked at each other and burst out laughing. "Would you mind terribly if we stayed together tomorrow? If I'm left alone with Will, I know I shall behave recklessly again—I simply cannot resist him."

Elizabeth agreed. She knew exactly how Charlie felt.

Next morning, the two girls went down to breakfast wearing riding habits and were happy to find that John and Will were clad in buckskin breeches and boots. The two couples agreed to ride together and have a picnic lunch in the woods. John and Will exchanged a rueful look but made no protest. They had next weekend to look forward to at the Devonshire's country house in Surrey, where they fully intended to continue their mating dance.

Elizabeth and Charlotte had a delightful day in the woods, with their escorts behaving most gallantly toward them. When it was time to eat, each couple found a private spot, by tacit agreement, where they could feed each other and exchange kisses in sublime solitude. Then, in the afternoon, the four riders tracked a small herd of deer that led them through the heavily wooded valley of the Thames to Richmond.

When they returned to Chiswick, Elizabeth thanked John for giving her such a lovely day. "I love being in the country so much more than London. The woods today reminded me of Ireland."

He lifted her from the saddle and held her captive far longer than he needed to. "If you enjoyed this, you will love Kent. Promise you will ride with me to Sundridge next weekend?"

She smiled her secret smile. "How can I resist when you have played the gallant all day?"

He whispered in her ear, "On my own turf I might play master."

"Just so long as you don't expect me to play mistress."

Her words, so direct, disarmed him and threw him off balance.

On Sunday, the Chiswick guests awoke to rain. Low clouds had moved in from the sea and the weather threatened to worsen before it improved. As a result, the weekend house party broke up early. The Countess of Burlington assured Elizabeth that a groom would return her horse to London along with her own and Lady Charlotte's. On the carriage ride home the presence of Emma and Charlie's maid, Jane, discouraged conversation. Elizabeth was overcome with anxiety about what Emma would report to her mother. John's words danced in her brain—*Sin now; beg forgiveness later*—but suddenly the phrase was no longer amusing. If Emma divulged any of what had gone on at Chiswick, there was no way that Bridget would allow them to go to Surrey.

When they arrived at Great Marlborough Street, the footman came out to help Emma with the luggage, and Elizabeth bade Charlie a wistful good-bye. Maria dashed into the house before she got wet, and by the time Elizabeth entered the drawing room, her sister was already telling her parents about Rachel Cavendish and the Earl of Orford. "He asked her to marry him the first day, but he still must face old Devonshire to formally ask for her hand."

"Maria, you must not refer to His Grace as 'old Devonshire' outside this house."

"The Duke of Devonshire will certainly give his permission, since Orford is the nephew of the late Prime Minister," Jack said.

"So," Bridget glanced knowingly at her husband, "these

country house parties foster proposals of marriage among the nobility." She spoke to Emma. "I'd like a full report. I trust you watched over my daughters at all times?"

Elizabeth went pale and held her breath.

Emma sketched Bridget a curtsy. "I took a page from Lady Charlotte's personal maid, ma'am. Jane is extremely strict where the proprieties are concerned. I used her as my guide and copied her words and actions in every way." *We had a bloody good time with the Chiswick footmen, drinking expensive wine and gorging ourselves on fancy food!* "Mistress Maria and Mistress Elizabeth were models of decorum, ma'am. You taught them very pretty manners indeed. You can be proud of them."

Elizabeth felt her jaw almost drop, then relief washed over her. "Father, the countess arranged for a groom to bring Cavalier from Chiswick with the other horses. Now, speaking of manners, I must immediately write the Countess of Burlington a thank-you note."

"Very good, Elizabeth. You may convey your sister's thanks also." Bridget turned to her elder daughter. "Now, Maria, tell me all about your progress with the Earl of Coventry."

An hour later when Maria came into their bedchamber, Elizabeth said, "I was so afraid of what Emma would report, but she said exactly the right thing to appease Mother. Actually, I never saw her the entire weekend."

"That's because the gentlemen gave all the maids money to keep out of sight and keep their mouths shut. That's the way it's done. Honestly, Beth, you are so naive!"

On Monday, at Sundridge, John Campbell received a summons from King George to present himself to His Royal Highness the following day. He was pleased that the letter had come directly from the king to him, rather than through the Duke of Cumberland. In a one-on-one meeting, Campbell was confident he could persuade the king to his way of thinking in certain military matters concerning the Crown. He was aware, however, of the delicate subject matter. Convincing a German that German troops were inferior to British troops would take a great deal of diplomacy. John knew he would have to handle George with kid gloves, for he had seen his royal rages where he had torn off his wig and kicked it across the room when someone dared to differ with him.

John contemplated wearing his military uniform for his interview with the king, since his father was the commander of all troops in Western Scotland but then decided against it. He was loath to conform to the delicate artifice of formal Court dress of satins and powdered wig, so instead chose to wear Argyll plaid, kilt and all. The dark green tartan would remind His Royal Highness of Argyll's power.

With his steward, John rode out to the tenant farms of Combe Bank and together they decided that the hop fields were ready for harvesting. He inspected the farmhouses and authorized the necessary repairs be made as soon as the crops were picked, before the bitter winds of winter played havoc with the thatched roofs.

Next morning at sunrise, he rode to his town house in London's Half-Moon Street. Once there, he bathed, donned his kilt and Argyll badge, and made his way to St. James's Palace.

After a thirty-minute wait, His Royal Highness sent for him. King George held his private audiences in a spacious room known as the King's Bedchamber, though it boasted no bed. John waited for the king to speak first, as protocol demanded.

"Lord Sundridge, we are pleased to see you answer our summons today." George scrutinized the boar's head on his Argyll badge, with its latin inscription NE OBLIVISCARIS, then his eyes looked askance at the kilt.

John Campbell bowed. "Your Majesty is most gracious to allow me a private audience."

George began to pace the room. "My son, Cumberland, tells us that Highlanders are amongst the best fighting men on earth, what?"

"That is true, Sire. The Argyllshire Highlanders' motto is *Without Fear,* and I assure you that no fiercer soldiers exist."

"They put fear in the hearts of the enemy with their naked, hairy legs and screaming bagpipes, what?" He looked again at Campbell's bare knees.

"Sire, they do put fear in the hearts of the enemy but with raw courage, fearsome weapons, and unmatched physical strength."

"Just so, just so!" George accompanied his words with a half dozen rapid nods of his head. "They were part of the coalition army we formed to fight for the Austrian Succession."

John bit down on his tongue. The war of the Austrian Succession was one of the most useless and destructive wars in history. King George had only taken part because of his possession of Hanover in Germany and, before a truce was signed, the French had soundly thrashed the coalition army of English, Austrians, Dutch, and Germans.

"At the risk of being blunt, Sire, we are still fighting our ancient enemies Spain and France, in India and America. Though war has not yet been declared, I believe that you and I know that it is inevitable, not just in those distant lands but in Europe too."

"Keep this between ourselves. Walls have ears! Walls have ears, what?" The king was becoming agitated.

Campbell began to soothe him. "While time is still on our side, I propose you allow me to go to the Highlands and recruit Scottish fighting men. Argyll, and I myself, are prepared to train these soldiers into a great military fighting force." John hesitated, for here was the part where the Hanoverian could take offense. "Britain should be able to fight her own wars without depending upon foreign mercenaries." Though the thought ran through his head he did not come out and say: *Send the bloody Germans packing!*

King George's bulbous eyes stared at him, long and hard. "How do we know we won't be harboring Jacobite sympathizers, what?"

"At Culloden, Argyll and Cumberland crushed the Jacobites once and for all time, Sire. If the Scots are given the opportunity for warlike glory and regular pay, I pledge that they will faithfully support Your Majesty's government."

"Your father, Argyll, has great wealth as well as power. Will you bear the cost of training these Highland recruits, what, what?"

Campbell's jaw clenched like a lump of iron. *The parsimonious swine wants it both ways!* "Argyll will bear the cost of training, if when they are ready for war, they will be inducted into the British army and receive regular pay."

The king pointed to the door. "Summon our man and we will

draw up a document authorizing you to go immediately and recruit in the Highlands, what?"

Campbell swallowed his surprise. "Would next week be soon enough, Sire?"

The king's head nodded rapidly. "Next week. No later. War could be imminent."

When John left St. James's Palace, he had the document with the king's signature upon it tucked away safely in his breast pocket. As he cut through St. James's Park and walked toward Parliament, he heard the Westminster chimes announce that it was one o'clock. Reasoning that the members would still be at lunch, he made his way to Bucks' Coffeehouse in Parliament Square. The man he wanted to see had finished his lunch and was on his way out.

John placed his hand on his breast over the document and nodded politely. "Good day, Mr. Pitt." He lowered his voice. "I have the king's authorization to recruit in the Highlands."

Pitt returned the polite smile. "A *good* day indeed, Sundridge."

John's glance traveled down the room and, as he had half expected, saw Will Cavendish having lunch with Coventry and Hamilton. It was fortunate that Mr. Pitt had shrewdly kept on walking.

"Ah, the Argyll Boar has arrived," Hamilton drawled, glancing at John's kilt and badge. "The definition of boar, I believe, is uncastrated male swine."

The other men laughed good-naturedly.

John smiled. "The Hamilton coat of arms bears three acorns. I've often wondered, d'you have three nuts, James?"

The other two guffawed, enjoying the pricks of their friends' verbal swordplay. "Must fascinate the whores," Coventry remarked.

"It's the size that fascinates 'em, not the quantity."

"Sounds like the boast of a schoolboy. You'll be challenging us to a pissing contest next," Campbell declared.

Hamilton conceded and rose to his feet. "Since you're in Town, John, why don't the four of us go to White's tonight?"

"Sorry, can't be done. I have to return to Kent. The hops are ready to be harvested."

"Well, that lets out Farmer John but it doesn't excuse the rest of you. Shall we say ten o'clock?"

Coventry and Hamilton departed together, leaving Will behind. "Do you really have to return to Combe Bank?"

"I do if you want me in Surrey this weekend."

"Oh, absolutely! Rachel sent off a letter posthaste to Mother about Orford's proposal, so I'm expecting her in London by the weekend. Devonshire House will be taken over by females issuing their infernal orders and arranging engagement parties and whatnot. I much prefer to be in Surrey when she arrives."

"You don't seem in any hurry to get back to Parliament. Nothing of interest going on?" John inquired.

"I'm not going back at all. Lord Halifax wants money for military protection of the new colony in Nova Scotia, and whenever the government wants money, the first name they think of is Devonshire!"

On the ride back to Kent, John wished he hadn't sent his secretary running off on a wild goose chase to Ireland. Elizabeth Gunning's background didn't need investigating. She was well-bred and highly educated, and her family were minor nobles. Elizabeth had truly captivated him, and he knew he would miss her far, far too deeply. When he got to Scotland, his mother would again pressure him to make a match with the daughter of one of the great Scottish nobles such as the Duke of Buccleuch. Mary Montagu was a great heiress and attractive enough, but she wasn't Elizabeth. With resolution he dragged his thoughts from her. He had many business matters that needed attention and much paperwork before he was free to leave for Scotland. He hoped Robert Hay would return from Ireland shortly. John's thoughts drifted once again to Elizabeth. Would she be unhappy to learn that he was leaving for Scotland? He hoped so. A sensual smile curved his mouth. They would have this weekend together, and John Campbell vowed to make the most of it.

Chapter Twelve

*O*n Wednesday afternoon the Gunning sisters, accompanied by Emma, visited Dunne's Perfumery and Ornamental Hair Shop in Charing Cross Road. Bridget had learned there was to be a royal drawing room planned for next week and anticipated an invitation. Since powdered wigs were *de rigueur* at Court entertainments, Maria had insisted she needed a new one as well as a fresh supply of pale *maquillage* with which to paint her face.

Inside the shop they encountered Peg Woffington, who was buying an outrageous shade of lavender hair powder. She advised them about various products and warned against lead paste. "It invariably causes face eruptions if used too long. Far better to use face powder than paste, my darlings."

Elizabeth heeded her advice and bought face powder, along with some irresistible black beauty patches. Maria, however, blithely ignored the warning and purchased the white paste.

"It was lovely to see you both. I see your names on the Society pages, more and more. Say hello to Bridget for me and do drop in to Soho Square, so we can have a natter and a laugh over tea."

Emma was awestruck by the encounter and on the way back to Great Marlborough Street asked Elizabeth, "If you do decide to visit Miss Woffington, would you allow me to accompany you?"

"Of course, Emma. Theatrical people are truly fascinating."

When they arrived home, Maria rushed upstairs ahead of her sister so that she could try on her new wig and monopolize the mirror. As she set the wig box on her bed, she heard a carriage outside. From the window, she saw a footman in royal livery and realized the much coveted Court invitation was being delivered.

Maria rushed from the room and ran headlong down the stairs, pushing aside her sister who was on her way up. Elizabeth fell back down three steps and Maria ended up on top of her.

"What an unseemly display! Did you trip your sister deliberately, Elizabeth? Get up immediately, both of you." Bridget waved off the elderly footman and opened the door herself. When she saw the messenger in royal livery, she accepted the invitation with a regal nod, as if it were her due. "I shall send the reply with my own man."

She closed the door and turned to see Elizabeth sitting on the bottom step. "I thought I told you to get up!" she raged.

"I turned my ankle," Elizabeth said faintly. She paled, not from the pain but from her mother's anger.

"That serves you right for pushing Maria aside so that you could grab the invitation. Such behavior ill becomes a lady!"

"Please don't be angry at her, Mother. She's hurt herself. Let me help you upstairs, Elizabeth."

With Maria's help, she limped upstairs and sat down on her bed.

Emma took a look. "I think it's swelling a little. Put your foot up, and I'll get a cold cloth."

"You certainly shouldn't go dancing tonight."

"No, but don't worry too much, Maria. It isn't that bad. It will be fine by tomorrow."

"Since you won't be going, may I wear the gold ball gown to Almack's tonight?"

Beth bit her lip. "Of course you may."

Late that evening at White's the trio of young nobles encountered the Earl of Orford playing faro and sat down at the table to join him. Hamilton won consistently until about eleven o'clock; when his luck changed he suggested that they move on to the Divan Club in the Strand, where they turned a blind eye to illegal games such as evens and odds, and écarté.

His companions—Cavendish, Coventry, and Orford—decided that they preferred to go to Almack's, which was close by, where they would find the young ladies to whom they were paying court. "I visited Almack's last week. Once per Season is all I am prepared to endure," Hamilton drawled. The four men departed White's together; Hamilton signaled his carriage, while the other three walked down St. James's Street toward Pall Mall.

When Hamilton climbed from his carriage in the Strand, he immediately recognized John Gunning entering the Divan Club. He had played cards with Gunning on two separate occasions before and knew him to be an inveterate gambler, as he himself was. Hamilton checked his watch then had a quiet word with his driver, who acted as henchman as well as coachman. As he entered the club, Hamilton smiled. It would be a simple matter to allow Gunning to win against him for the next two hours.

Before midnight, Elizabeth told Emma that she could go to bed. She assured the maid that when Maria came home, she would help her remove her ball gown and makeup. Then Elizabeth sat down to sew some silk roses on the *décolletage* of Maria's white evening dress. Around two o'clock, when she heard the front door open downstairs, she assumed it was her mother and Maria returning from Almack's.

Elizabeth set her sewing aside and went to the top of the stairs. "Father!" Her hand flew to her throat as she saw the bright red blood on his white evening shirt. Jack Gunning was being helped through the door by another man. She was halfway down the stairs when the man looked up at her and she saw that it was the Duke of Hamilton. "Your Grace! Whatever happened?" she cried, alarmed that her beloved father had been injured.

"I'll be all right, Elizabeth. Go to bed, my dear."

"I shan't go to bed! You have been hurt!"

"Let's get you upstairs, Jack." Hamilton explained, "When he left a gaming club, he was set upon for his winnings, Mistress Gunning. Fortunately I saw it happen. When I drew my sword, the thief fled into the night." He drew Jack's arm over his shoulder and half carried him up the staircase.

Elizabeth, white-faced with anxiety, indicated her parents' chamber. "Let me look at the wound," she insisted when Jack sat down on the end of the bed.

"I shall tend him, Mistress Gunning. It will be far too distressing for a young lady of tender years and sensibilities."

"Elizabeth's a brave girl, James. She won't faint."

The fact that these two men were on a first-name basis did make her feel faint. She gently parted the fair hair on the back of her father's head and saw a nasty gash. She didn't think it was too deep, however, for it had already crusted over and stopped bleeding. "Thank heaven, it isn't a sword wound." She felt weak with relief. "I'll get some water to clean it."

She came back in less than a minute with water and towels.

"The thug used a billy-cosh." Jack touched his head gingerly. "Knocked me senseless for a moment and felled me to my knees."

The duke produced a silver flask. "Take a few swallows of brandy." Hamilton's tone was fatherly, "Allow me, my dear. You hold the water." She watched in amazement as the duke dipped the end of the towel into the water, gently cleansed the wound, then wiped the dried blood from the blond hair. "You were lucky, Jack. By tomorrow only a headache will remind you of your close call."

"Lucky that you were there to aid, Your Grace." Elizabeth was overwhelmed with relief and gratitude. This was the second time that the Duke of Hamilton had come to the Gunnings' rescue. Her cheeks flushed, remembering how ungracious she had felt toward him at the theater. "I thank you from the bottom of my heart for helping my father, Your Grace."

"Think nothing of it, I pray, Mistress Gunning."

She led the way down the stairs, again smiled her gratitude, and bade him good night. Then she ran back upstairs to her father. "Let me help you to bed, then I'll soak the bloodstains from your shirt before Mother sees them." She spotted a small leather pouch on the tallboy. "What's this?"

Jack frowned, then winced. "Hamilton must have left it."

Elizabeth picked it up. "It's filled with gold sovereigns!"

"Well, I'll be damned. In his great generosity, Hamilton has replaced my winnings that were stolen!"

Elizabeth was filled with remorse. She had completely misjudged His Grace, the Duke of Hamilton.

Early Saturday morning, when the Burlington carriage arrived to pick up the Gunning sisters, Charlie's mount was tethered at the rear, with a groom to tend it. Jack brought Cavalier from the stable and made sure he was safely secured beside the other horse. By this time, the luggage had been stowed, and Emma ushered her charges inside the coach and sat down beside Lady Charlotte's maid.

"How is your ankle? I missed you so much at Almack's!"

"It was nothing, Charlie. The swelling was gone in hours."

"Did you receive an invitation to the royal drawing room at St. James's Palace?" Maria only asked to show that she had one.

"Yes." Charlie wrinkled her nose. "Unfortunately, royal invitations cannot be refused without giving offense."

"Why would anyone, with any sense, want to refuse?" Maria asked. "I imagine I was invited at the insistence of Prince George. He couldn't take his eyes from me at Devonshire House."

"Prince George is extremely precocious for his age; he's only thirteen," Charlie said from the lofty heights of sixteen.

"He turned fourteen," Maria informed her, "and he is quite physically mature. Whoever marries him will become a royal princess," Maria added dreamily.

"Whoever marries him will already be a royal princess," Charlie pointed out. "A Prince of the Realm can only marry royalty."

"Rules can always be broken," Maria said haughtily.

Charlie laughed. "I *know* . . . let's break some this weekend!"

When the carriage arrived at Oxted Hall, Will Cavendish helped Charlotte from the carriage, kept hold of both her hands, and drew her close. His lips brushed her temple. "I couldn't wait."

Charlie gazed up at him with stars in her eyes.

Rachel Cavendish, acting as official hostess for the weekend, welcomed the sisters. "Elizabeth, I've put you with Charlotte again, and Maria, you may—"

"Have a chamber to myself, since you have so many bedrooms?"

"Why, of course, if that's what you would prefer."

Elizabeth glanced at Charlie and Will, who only had eyes for each other. He was untethering the horses. "I'll see that our things get to our bedchamber. You take the horses to the stable."

She gazed up at the house that was more mansion than country manor, then caught up with Maria and Rachel.

"Why are Devonshire houses bigger and better than others?" Maria asked artlessly.

Rachel laughed. "Actually, this isn't a Devonshire house at all. Mother was Catherine Hoskyns and this Tudor house belonged to her parents. My late grandfather was known as Miser Hoskyns."

She turned to address Jane and Emma, who followed with the luggage. "I've put you two together in our servants' wing. You will do your utmost to be invisible this weekend, I trust?"

Elizabeth stopped Emma from unpacking. "I can hang my own clothes in the wardrobe. You go along and help Maria. I'm sorry Lady Rachel spoke to you like that."

"Most ladies speak to servants like that, and your mother and sister are no exception. But I don't mind making myself invisible. Jane and I will enjoy a quiet weekend with no duties."

When Elizabeth was alone she unpacked then washed her hands and face. As she looked in the mirror to brush her hair, she saw that her own eyes sparkled like stars and knew that with every moment her excitement grew. The anticipation of seeing John sent her blood singing in her veins. *Is this what it feels like to be in love?* Suddenly, she was filled with apprehension. *What if he doesn't come?* She banished the thought and smiled her secret smile. *John will come. He wants to take me to Sundridge.*

Meanwhile, Maria gave Emma her orders. "Don't tell Mother I had a chamber all to myself. In fact, don't tell her anything. She thinks that Lords of the Realm are attracted to virtuous ladies, but nothing could be further from the truth in my experience. If you keep your mouth shut, I'll get Coventry to make it worth your while again."

She slipped the door key into her reticule, departed her room, and deliberately took a wrong turn to explore the east wing. Norwich, Earl of Coventry, walking down the hall, saw her immediately.

"Maria, you came!" His relief was transparent.

"George!" She touched her hair to draw his attention to it. "Emma was able to secure me a chamber to myself." She showed him the key and saw his eyes dilate. "If you give her an extra reward, perhaps I'll do the same for you." Smugly, she watched his body react to her suggestive words.

Elizabeth gave Charlie and Will time to be alone then went down to the stables to make sure Cavalier had been fed and watered. She looked at the horses carefully to see if John's Demon occupied any of the stalls. When she didn't spot him, she wondered anxiously what was taking John so long.

Will welcomed her to Oxted. "I'm not a very good host, but I know that you of all ladies understand my inattention." His possessive arm anchored Charlie to his side. "Good, John's here!"

Elizabeth spun around, her face lit with a radiant smile. When his eyes sought her before his friend, her heart filled with joy.

He dismounted, led Demon into a clean stall, then strode to her side and handed her a small branch that sported three large leaves and small greenish-yellow fruit that looked like tiny artichokes. "Ripe hops. I had to get the crop in before it rained."

"They have a strong aroma, but it's quite pleasant."

"I think so, but I am biased because I grow them."

"You have a proclivity for them," she said breathlessly.

"I have a proclivity for you, Elizabeth." He dipped his head and stole a quick kiss before Will and Charlie strolled over.

"We could go for a walk in the woods before lunch to escape the tennis and shuttlecock games my sisters have planned," Will said.

"Oh, Will, I adore shuttlecock!" Charlie exclaimed.

John gave Elizabeth a rueful glance, much preferring a secluded walk in woods ablaze with autumn colors.

She smiled shyly. "I'd like to watch you play tennis."

138 *Virginia Henley*

Will waggled his eyebrows suggestively. "Not as much as we'll enjoy watching you ladies play shuttlecock."

Charlie gave him an affectionate shove, and it dawned on Elizabeth that he was hinting that their breasts would bounce.

When the two couples arrived at the house, Rachel and Cat, their arms filled with racquets, balls, and feathered shuttlecocks, were greeting another couple who had just arrived.

"Ladies, this is my brother, Charles, and his lovely wife, Margaret. May I present Mistress Elizabeth Gunning and Lady Charlotte Boyle?"

Lord Charles Cavendish bowed. "Mistress Gunning, I believe we are neighbors in Great Marlborough Street. Lady Charlotte, I haven't seen you since you were a child."

"She's little more than a child now," Lady Margaret said archly.

Elizabeth saw Will clench his fists at the uncalled for remark but his sisters quickly deflected further remarks by handing each lady a racquet. "C'mon, we're off to the court!"

Maria Gunning refused to play, pretending she was the one who had hurt her ankle a few days ago. So Rachel, Cat, and Margaret Cavendish were pitted against Charlie, Elizabeth, and Harriet Ponsonby. As a child, Elizabeth had played with a shuttlecock, but she had never been in a match with partners and rules. Nevertheless, she was willing to give it a try. When the game began, she was rather inept, but it didn't really matter. Charlie played like a fiend, returning the bird every single time it came on their side of the net. Soon the men were rooting for her, and when she soundly trounced Lady Margaret and her partners, a great cheer went up. Will and John hoisted Charlie onto their shoulders and gave the laughing, blushing girl a victory parade.

When the men played tennis, Will and John easily beat Charles and Orford. Elizabeth never took her eyes from John Campbell. He had the lithe speed of an athlete, combined with the strength and power of a military warrior. In every way she found him to be head and shoulders above every other male of her acquaintance and she knew without a shadow of a doubt that he was her heart's desire.

Lunch wasn't served until one o'clock and lasted more than an hour and a half. John, impatient to be alone with Elizabeth, held her hand beneath the table. Finally, he could wait no longer for her answer. "You will ride with me to Sundridge?"

She lifted her lashes and looked into his eyes. "You know I will. I'll go up now and change."

John rose to his feet, and Will followed suit. "My duties as host may be remiss, but Charlie and I are going for a ride before the rain comes."

Upstairs, Elizabeth changed into the jade riding habit. "I'm going to Sundridge to see John's home. I know it's not proper, Charlie, but I don't care!" *Sin now; beg forgiveness later.* The thought stole her breath and made her dizzy with excitement. She looked in the mirror and decided to wear one of her beauty patches. She carefully placed a tiny black heart beside her eye on the tip of her cheekbone. "What do you think?"

"Very seductive!" Charlie grinned mischievously. "He won't stand a chance. May I have one?"

They walked down to the stables together, where the men had already saddled the horses and stood awaiting them. John set his hands to Elizabeth's waist and lifted her into the sidesaddle. The moment he touched her, threads of fire spiraled from her belly into her breasts, and the mingled scent of leather, hops, horse, and male animal filled her senses.

"The moment we are out of sight, I intend to take you up before me on Demon." His murmured promise set her nerves ashiver.

Side by side, they rode directly east toward threatening clouds. Before they had galloped a quarter mile, John drew rein and dismounted. "It's only four miles—far too short a distance to have you in my arms." He lifted her from Cavalier and fastened him to his own saddle with a long leading rein. Then he remounted, leaned down, and with sheer brute strength, picked her up and set her between his thighs. "Have I told you today that you are the loveliest woman on earth?"

"No," she said breathlessly.

"You are the loveliest woman on earth, Elizabeth Gunning."

It isn't true, but you make me feel like the loveliest.

John touched his heels to Demon and settled him into a rhythmic, slow gallop. He was acutely aware of Elizabeth and the delicate scent from her warm body aroused him instantly. He shifted slightly in the saddle to ease the pressure of his swollen cock as it bulged the whipcord of his fawn riding breeches. As she reclined against his body he became aware of how small she was. Desire pulsed at his groin with a sweet, almost unendurable ache. The heat from her body mingled with the heat between his thighs, turning him marble hard in a delicious agony of need. A long tendril of her beautiful golden hair brushed against his face, making him quiver.

Suddenly, big raindrops splashed down onto their faces. He quickly gauged that they were closer to Oxted Hall than they were to Combe Bank. "Do you want to go back?" he offered gallantly.

She looked up at him with raindrops glistening on her eyelashes. "Of course not. 'Tis unlucky to turn back."

"I don't want to shelter beneath the trees in case it lightens." No sooner did he speak than a zigzag of lightning lit the darkening sky. He set his spurs to Demon and they thundered into Kent where the air was redolent with the strong fragrance of hops.

By the time they arrived at Combe Bank Manor, they were drenched to the skin. He dismounted and led the horses into the stables where he told a groom, "They need a good rubdown."

He lifted Elizabeth from Demon, set his lips to her ear, and murmured wickedly, "Us too!" Then handclasped and laughing like children, they made a mad dash from the stables to the manor house.

Inside, the great hall had thick beams, a massive stone fireplace and polished, black oak floors. The air was fragrant with lavender beeswax and masses of yellow lilies that overflowed from Chinese porcelain jars. "Oh, John, it is so lovely!" She moved toward the welcoming fire, but his words stayed her.

"I'll light you a fire upstairs. Come." He held out his hand and trustingly, without hesitation, she curled her fingers into his.

They laughed at the puddles they left on each stair, reveling in irresponsibility, as they cast off all care. All that mattered to them at this moment was that they were together. Together alone.

He led her into a spacious bedchamber with a red Turkish carpet and a white marble fireplace. He knelt down and lit the fire that was already laid. "Wait right here," he ordered then disappeared through a connecting door that led into another chamber.

Elizabeth's glance traveled around the room, noticing the padded window seats beneath the mullioned panes and the wide bed hung with wine-red velvet curtains. John returned carrying a thick white towel and a black bedrobe. "Get that wet riding habit off and put this on. The fire will give off heat in a minute or two." He went back into the adjoining chamber and pulled the door so that it was almost closed, but not quite.

As quickly as she could, Elizabeth removed the jade green habit and hung it to dry over the brass fender. Slightly dismayed, she realized that her petticoat and underclothes were soaked also. She stripped them off and slipped on the huge black velvet robe, then wrapped the towel, turban-fashion, about her wet hair. She removed her riding boots but hesitated to set them on the costly white marble hearth without asking permission. On stockinged feet she padded toward the adjoining door and pushed it open. "John—"

She saw him kneeling before the fireplace, lighting his own fire. He was stark naked. "Oh . . . I'm so sorry!"

He stood up, turned, and looked at her. "I'm not."

She stood rooted to the spot as slowly, deliberately, he walked a direct path to her.

Chapter Thirteen

*O*vercome with shyness, Elizabeth raised her hands, which were hidden inside the long velvet sleeves, and said the first thing that came into her head. "The robe is much too big."

His mouth curved as he gazed down at her. "Big enough for both of us." With deliberate hands he opened the black robe and stepped inside, drawing her naked flesh against his. As his possessive hands slid about her back, he realized that her skin was softer and smoother than the velvet of his robe. Slowly, his palms moved lower to the swelling curve of her bottom, and he felt his phallus pulse against the warm softness of her belly. "Beth!"

Elizabeth gasped and raised her hands to his shoulders to steady herself. It lifted her breasts against his hard muscles and the crisp black curls on his chest abraded her nipples. She cried out from the strange sensation and from sheer excitement. He dipped his head and took possession of her lips, taking her cry into his mouth hungrily. Her hands slid up to the nape of his neck, and she threaded her fingers into his black hair. His kiss deepened, and she yielded her mouth willingly, eagerly, generously, and felt his tongue master her. Heat leaped between them, almost scalding her as he pressed her against his granite hard thighs, flat belly, and his rigid, unyielding erection. When he lifted his mouth, she raised her lashes and saw his face, hard with passion. "John, we must not . . ."

"Beth, we must . . ." His lips moved hungrily down her

throat, leaving a trail of kisses over the swell of her breast, until his mouth took possession of its delicate pink tip, almost devouring it whole. He felt her shudder—the towel about her hair loosened and fell to the carpet, and it shocked him into realizing he must go much more slowly in his foreplay. He stooped to pick up the towel, then led her before the fire. "Let me dry your hair." He sank to his knees on the hearth rug and tugged on her hand, drawing her down before him, so that she faced the fire with her back toward him. Gently he began to towel her long golden hair as he knelt at her back, where she could not see his nakedness.

No longer intimidated by the sight of his rampant maleness, Elizabeth calmed. She sat before him, gazing into the leaping orange and blue flames, as his powerful hands rubbed the wetness from her hair and worked their magic. She became almost mesmerized by the fire and by his touch as they knelt together in the intimate warm glow. He tossed away the towel and she felt his fingers comb through her tresses, lifting and separating the strands and tendrils until they formed a myriad of curls that tumbled over her shoulders.

"The reflection of the fire turns your hair to pure-spun gold."

Lightning at the mullioned windows momentarily lit up the darkened chamber, making Elizabeth jump. As thunder crashed above them, she felt him drop a kiss on the top of her head then place his hands on her shoulders. Slowly, he drew off the black velvet robe, so that only her cascading hair covered her nakedness. She felt his hand sweep it aside, and his lips begin a fiery trail down the curve of her back, causing a delicious shiver to run down her spine. When he kissed her bottom, she gasped with shock.

He stopped immediately and diverted her attention by slipping his arms about her waist to draw her back against him. It was his turn to shudder as the soft curve of her bum brushed against his muscled thighs. His palms cupped her lush, full breasts, loving their weight, and his thumbs brushed across her nipples, turning them into tiny thrusting spears. He heard her soft cry at the new sensations he was arousing in her body, and the sound made his own passion flare. His lips brushed her ear as he murmured, "Your breasts are exquisite. I've pictured them ever since we were naked together in the loch, but I had no idea they would feel so lush and lovely and fit so perfectly in my hands." Still cupping her left breast, he stroked his other hand down across her soft belly and his fingers drew slow, tantalizing circles around her navel.

Elizabeth began to realize that all her most vulnerable and private parts were open to his seeking hands. Surely the wicked devil would not dare to touch her secret place? Her answer came immediately as she felt him cover her mons with his warm palm. She instinctively eased back but met the inexorable barrier of his iron-hard thighs pressing against her from behind. She stiffened as his fingers began to separate the curls between her legs.

"I know you are virgin, Beth . . . I promise I won't tear your hymen, sweetheart. Yield to me."

His fingertips circled the tiny bud inside the folds of her cleft, and she was swept with a burning desire to let him do whatever he wanted. She stopped resisting and opened slightly, knowing that he would not hurt her.

Cupping her mons, he slowly, gently slid his middle finger into her sheath. She was so tight and hot he had to close his eyes to control the raw desire that urged him to carry her to his bed. He held still so that she could get used to the sensation of fullness, then began to move his finger in and out, a movement that matched what he wanted to do with his cock. Each time his finger stroked over the tiny bud of her womanhood, she arched back against him and brushed the sensitive, swollen head of his shaft, arousing him to savage need. He felt her sheath tighten on his finger, then he felt a small implosion inside her and heard her gasp out her pleasure. He withdrew his finger but still cupped her tightly until her last tiny spasm was spent. Gradually, he felt her breast soften in his hand and her body relax as she reclined against him.

"I feel boneless," she murmured shyly.

Deftly, he pulled the robe from beneath her bottom, spread it before the fire and gently pushed her down to lie upon it. She was naked, save for her lace stockings and green ribbon garters adorned with snowdrops. He spread her hair in a golden halo about her shoulders. Her pale skin, also touched by gold in the flickering firelight, was a startling contrast against the black velvet. "You are so beautiful—you steal my breath."

Her lashes fluttered to her cheeks, veiling her eyes from his nakedness. After a full minute, she raised her lashes and looked at him. He was propped on one elbow, his eyes ravishing her. "You have stolen my breath and my senses, John Campbell." Almost against her own volition she reached out to touch him, drawn inexorably by his dark, compelling male beauty. She traced along his collarbone with one finger, then outlined the contour of a chest muscle. She stroked the crisp black pelt of hair, feeling its texture, so different from the soft curls at the nape of his neck. The corners of her mouth lifted. "Your animal magnetism attracts me. I am unable to resist touching you." Her fingers trailed across his rib cage then boldly descended to his belly, where they circled his navel, as he had done to her.

"Touch all of me."

She raised her eyes to his. "I dare not."

"Do I frighten you?"

"A little," she confessed breathlessly. *A lot!*

She was so delicate, so vulnerable, it brought a lump to his throat. He lifted her hand to his mouth and dropped a kiss into her palm, then he guided her fingers toward the nest of curls that covered his groin and from which sprang his rampant manhood.

With great daring she touched the head of his shaft. "It feels like velvet." Her voice was filled with wonder. At his hand's urging she closed her fingers about his shaft. "It is so thick. Is it always so?" she asked shyly.

"No, sweetheart. When you are not about, it actually behaves itself and lies soft and quiet. But the moment I see you it becomes aroused and longs to bury itself deep inside you."

She loosened her fingers immediately and withdrew her hand. "I couldn't resist touching you."

"And I cannot resist *tasting* you." He began at her temple, feathering kisses where the tendrils of hair fell over her brow. The tip of his tongue traced her cheekbone, where she had placed the black beauty spot. His fingers removed the little patch and stuck it beside her lips, then he dropped a quick kiss at the corner of her mouth. He covered her lips possessively and explored her mouth sensually, tasting its sweetness. When he finally lifted his mouth from hers, he moved the tiny black heart to the curve of her breast. His tongue licked a path down the arch of her throat, her shoulder, and finally across the swell of her breast. He licked and tongued her nipple until it peaked, then sucked it whole into his mouth as if it were a ripe berry.

Elizabeth was breathless at the game he played, moving her beauty patch to the place where he intended to kiss and taste her. It was tantalizing, filling her with anticipation mixed with apprehension, especially when he placed the beauty mark beside her navel. As his tongue licked across her belly and dipped into the indentation, she was torn, wanting him to stop, yet wanting him to never stop. She watched, fascinated, as he moved down her body.

He lifted his head, and his eyes met hers as he moved the small black heart to sit atop her pubic bone. Aware that she watched exactly what he was doing, he blew softly upon the golden curls covering her mons and dipped his tongue to taste her. With a shocked gasp, she raised her knees in a reflexive move. Gently, he pushed down the knee closest to him but left the other one raised, allowing him to delve more deeply into her honeyed sheath.

Elizabeth, stunned at the wickedly erotic thing he was doing to her, reached down to stay the dark head, but the moment her fingers touched his hair, the pleasure his plunging tongue gave her was so intense she arched up into his mouth with an uninhibited little cry. Perhaps because it felt so forbidden, she gave herself up to him with blissful abandon, allowing the rough primal thrust of his tongue to breach her last defense until she lay beneath him in a wanton sprawl as she dissolved in exquisite liquid tremors.

He came back up over her and enfolded her in his arms as she cried out her release, burying her face against his shoulder. He stroked her hair and murmured endearments that he meant with all his heart. As she clung to him so sweetly, she was unbelievably precious to him in this intimate moment, and he knew in all conscience that he could not take her virginity then leave for Scotland. He raised her chin and kissed her quickly, then removed himself from temptation. "Your petticoat should be dry by now." He went into the adjoining room and lifted it from the brass fireguard. The heavy ache in his groin made him momentarily fear a case of blue balls. He took a deep breath to control his raging lust and returned to his bedchamber. She stood up, and he slipped the petticoat over her head. Then he shrugged into his black velvet bedrobe. "There's something I must tell you, Beth."

She looked at him with trusting eyes and waited.

"I have to go to Scotland. The king has asked me to recruit soldiers for his Highland regiments. I shall probably be gone for a couple of months."

His words made her feel forlorn. "When are you leaving?"

"My orders were to leave immediately, but I couldn't go until you had seen Sundridge. Elizabeth, I swear I didn't plan the rain but I'm not sorry we got drenched. What about you, sweetheart?"

She shook her head and said shyly, "I'm not sorry, John." Then she smiled at him. Her face was radiant and her eyes sparkling. "I want to see you in your uniform."

He threw back his head, laughing. "Careful what you wish for." When she sat down on his bed to watch, his jaw clenched like a lump of iron as he tried to control his rampant cock. He took underdrawers and stockings from his tallboy then removed his uniform from the wardrobe. As he took off the bedrobe their eyes met, making his arousal buck and throb, and he knew for her own safety it was good that she was across the room. He pulled on his smallclothes and the white riding breeches of his major's uniform. Then he donned a linen shirt, buttoned it, and tucked it in. He left off the vest that went over the shirt and slipped his arms into the sleeves of his scarlet jacket with dark green facings and brass buttons. He indicated the yards of dark blue and green plaid as he fastened on his sword and dirk. "The kilt is alternate dress to my uniform, but when I must spend hours in the saddle, I prefer the riding breeches."

She jumped down from the bed and drew close to examine his crest, with its Campbell shield and boar. Her fingers traced the Latin motto, NE OBLIVISCARIS. "What does it say?"

"Do not forget."

She wrapped her arms about him. "I cannot bear you to leave. Do not forget me, John."

He enfolded her against his heart. "Don't cry, sweetheart." After a moment, he removed one of the brass military buttons from his uniform and pressed it into her hand. "Do not forget, Beth."

"I have no keepsake for you."

Quickly, he withdrew his dirk, sliced off a small golden curl and tucked it into his jacket pocket. Then he kissed the teardrops from her eyelashes. "My own sweetheart, I'm not going to war! Come, you need some food inside you to banish the darklings."

"I cannot leave this chamber in my petticoat!"

"Nonsense, the only servant in the entire manor at the moment is my cook, and Mrs. Craufurd will keep to her kitchens. Did you know that Combe Bank has a ghost? A lady in gray!" He removed his weapon belt and jacket. "Come, and I'll show you the place where she has been seen."

The temptation was too great for Elizabeth to resist. As he took her hand, drawing her along the beamed corridor and down the polished oak staircase, she said, "I love this house! Its welcoming warmth wraps itself about me, almost as if it knows me."

He took her to the old hall. "My lady ghost moves from the window to warm herself at the fireplace."

"I sense only happiness here . . . no great sorrow or tragedy. Do you have any idea who the lady in gray is—was?"

"She was the mistress of the lord who owned the manor in the last century. The lovers could not marry, perhaps because he had a wife. Supposedly, she always watched for him at the window. Legend says this manor was where they spent their happiest hours."

Elizabeth sighed and touched the bright yellow lilies in the blue jar. She imagined that she too could be happy here.

He sat her down at the polished refectory table before the stone fireplace. "Wait here . . . I'll go and see about some food."

While she waited, she glanced at the window. Though the thunder and lightning had abated, rain still pelted against the panes. He seemed to be gone a long time; when he returned from the kitchens he was carrying a huge serving tray laden with food, which he set before her. He got plates, silverware, and glasses from the tall Welsh dresser then slid in close beside her on the bench.

He lifted a silver cover and pretended surprise. "What a co-incidence . . . partridge!"

She laughed happily. "You asked Mrs. Craufurd to prepare them special." She watched as he carved them and put the choicest pieces on her plate. "They're stuffed with chestnuts! The aroma is making my mouth water." Under another cover were small roast potatoes, a dish of leeks, and pieces of buttered marrow.

"I want to see you eat the partridge with your fingers."

She obliged by picking up a wing and slowly tearing the tender meat from the bones with sharp white teeth. Before she could lick her fingers, he took possession of her hand and did it for her.

"I love to watch you eat. You enjoy every morsel as if it were a sensual experience." He took up the bottle of red wine, filled a glass, then lifted it to her lips. "And you already know that wine steals the senses," he teased.

She took half a dozen slow, deliberate sips then watched him drink from the same glass, making sure his lips touched the spot where hers had been. Then he kissed her, deeply, and she tasted the wine on his tongue. The sensation was intoxicating.

He deliberately finished his food before her, then slid beneath her so that she was sitting in his lap, and he proceeded to feed her with his fingers. When she playfully bit his fingertip, she felt his arousal swell beneath her bottom. "Now, see what you've done." He kissed her ear. "I don't dare let the wild beast out of his cage . . . he would devour you."

She slid from his lap and stood up. "Thank you for feeding me, and warming me, and telling me about your ghost, John. Perhaps I had better go and see if my clothes are dry."

He picked up another bottle of red wine and a glass. "Lead the way, and I shall follow."

When they arrived in the bedchamber where she had undressed, she walked a direct path to the brass fireguard to feel her garments.

The skirt of her jade riding habit was still quite damp. "I feel so exposed," she said self-consciously.

She was in danger of withdrawing from him, and he refused to let that happen. "Then you shall wear my shirt." He removed it quickly and slipped her arms into it, so that her bare shoulders were demurely covered, then he poked up the fire. "Another half hour will thoroughly dry your clothes. In the meantime, let's have another glass of wine." He took her hand and led her into the adjoining chamber. Then he took pillows and cushions from his bed, tossed them before the fire, and sank to his knees to fill the glass with wine. "Do you remember the words to our own special toast?"

She sat down beside him and nodded shyly. "To this moment and the moments we have yet to share." They sipped the wine and shared kisses. "When you removed your shirt, I believe I saw that you have a beauty mark of your own."

He touched the black mole in his armpit, and grinned. "It's a birthmark, passed down for generations from a father to his sons. It was known as the mark of Argyll."

"Let me see!"

He lifted his arm, but the moment she touched him he revealed that he was ticklish, and they both dissolved into laughter. His playful kisses soon turned passionate, and his need to again have her naked in his arms overcame her reluctance. His hot, hungry mouth trailed down across the scented, soft flesh of her belly and then his tongue delved deep to taste her lovely essence.

The rough, soft slide of his tongue aroused a myriad of pleasure points and exquisite sensations deep within her woman's center, making her moan and writhe with passion until at last she peaked with a sensual shudder that left her languorous with love.

John quickly moved up over her body until he straddled her with his muscled thighs. He had faithfully promised not to tear her hymen, but at the moment his body's needs were rampant. He had thought he could control himself, but her pale enticing loveliness had aroused him beyond his endurance. He pressed her lush breasts together and slid his marble-hard cock into the valley between. He thrust between her satin-smooth flesh until a great cry was ripped from his throat as he spent.

When he could move and think again, he brought warm water to bathe her breasts, then enfolded her in his arms and cradled her against his heart. "Forgive me, Elizabeth."

"There is nothing to forgive, John. I love you."

As they finished the wine, she leaned against him, gazing

into the fire. Its warmth mingled with her wine-heated blood and the heat of John's body made her languid and drowsy. Her eyelids closed, and she drifted into sleep—happy, content, and safer than she had felt in years.

John held her secure, feeling extremely protective toward her, then as they lay curled together, he too drifted into sleep.

Many hours later, when a log in the fireplace fell into ash, Elizabeth awoke with a start. She became instantly aware that it was full dark. "John, John, what time is it?"

He roused beside her and stretched. "Late . . . long past midnight, I warrant. Let me light a lamp."

"Oh, my God, you shouldn't have let me fall asleep! I should have been back at Oxted Hall hours ago!"

The lamp illuminated the chamber, and the clock on the wall indicated that it was almost four o'clock in the morning.

Elizabeth clutched his arm. "John, it *cannot* be that time. Whatever am I going to do?"

"Sweetheart, you're trembling. It will be all right. I'll take you back now. We couldn't ride back earlier; it was pouring rain."

"You don't understand. My mother will fly into a rage . . . her punishment will be terrible!"

"Are you afraid of your mother?" he asked, incredulous.

"Afraid?" she whispered. "I am terrified." Though she tried valiantly, she could not stop trembling.

"Beth, sweet, your mother won't find out." He squeezed her hands to reassure her.

"Of course she will!"

"Your maid, Emma, won't say a word. I'll make sure of it."

"My sister, Maria, will make sure Mother learns of what I've done." Her face was filled with panic, her eyes desperate.

"Elizabeth, I'll get you back into Oxted Hall without anyone knowing," he pledged. "Only Charlie will know what time you returned, and you know you can trust her. Hurry and get dressed."

John was as good as his word. After they stabled Demon and Cavalier, he smuggled Elizabeth up to her room without encountering any of Oxted Hall's staff or guests. Then he returned to the stable to tend the horses. He had dressed in riding clothes and, since it was around five in the morning, a claim that he had arisen early for a morning canter would be perfectly believable.

As Elizabeth closed the door of the chamber she shared with Charlie, she was panting with apprehension. When her friend sat up in bed, Beth murmured, "I'm so sorry to disturb you."

"You're not disturbing me," Charlie whispered. "Will only just left. I'll keep your secret, if you'll keep mine!"

Five hours later, as the weekend guests enjoyed a leisurely, late breakfast, William Cavendish was unpleasantly surprised by the arrival of his mother, the Duchess of Devonshire. He had known she would rush to London the moment she heard of Orford's proposal to his sister Rachel, but why the devil had she come running to Oxted? He immediately suspected someone had tipped her off to the cozy arrangement the young couples had planned for themselves, and his suspicion settled on his brother Charles's wife, Margaret.

"A dozen young people at a weekend house party without a *chaperon* is highly irregular." The duchess looked pointedly at the females as if detecting an unsavory smell. "An explanation is in order."

A muscle ticked in William's jaw. "Mother, you are mistaken. We have a married couple to *chaperon* us."

Her eyes hardened as they flicked to Will and the small female sitting beside him. "Charles is younger than you are. I hold you responsible for this, William."

John Campbell saw his friend flush with embarrassment. He was a man grown, being castigated by his mother before his guests. John rose to his feet immediately. "Your Grace, how lovely to see you again. Please join us for breakfast . . . take my seat." He bowed gallantly and brought another chair to the table for himself.

Slightly mollified, she accepted his offer. "Lord Sundridge, John, I trust your family is well?"

"Very well, thank you. I shall convey your felicitations when I arrive in Scotland next week."

Rachel Cavendish spoke up quickly. "I'm so glad you are here, Mother. I can safely place the arrangements for our engagement party in your hands."

The duchess looked at the man now standing beside her daughter. "Orford, congratulations seem to be in order." Her glance traveled to her other daughter, Cat, and the man sitting beside her. "And this gentleman is . . ."

"May I present John Ponsonby, and his sister Harriet?" Cat said quickly, almost defiantly.

She lifted her lorgnette to examine him. "*Lord* Ponsonby?"

Cat's defiance fled. "No . . . just . . . John Ponsonby."

Will jumped to his feet, determined to deflect his mother's censure from his sister Cat. "Mother, may I present Lady Charlotte Boyle? I don't believe you've had the pleasure."

"Boyle?" She peered through her lorgnette at the creature and her face went stiff. "Not the Earl and Countess of Burlington's offspring?" The duchess looked in danger of apoplexy.

"I am delighted to make your acquaintance, Your Grace," Charlie said faintly.

Sensing impending disaster, Coventry got to his feet and reintroduced himself. "I hope you remember me, Your Grace. May I present Mistress Maria Gunning and her sister, Elizabeth?"

Up went the lorgnette. She hated them on sight because of their flawless beauty. "I shall speak to your mother. A word to the wise would seem to be in order." Her eyes flicked to Coventry. "Politicians have rather tawdry reputations."

"With the exception of my friend George Coventry." John Campbell smiled pleasantly, and the Duchess of Devonshire smiled back. He had seen Elizabeth's hands begin to tremble the moment the duchess said she'd have a word with her mother. He silently cursed the ugly old bitch and wondered how in God's name Will's father put up with her.

After breakfast, the duchess made a point of speaking with all the ladies' maids, so that she could give them a tongue-lashing for being derelict in their duties to their young mistresses.

Most of the male guests took the opportunity to retire to their rooms and instruct their valets to pack their bags. John touched Elizabeth's hand and murmured, "Meet me in the stables."

After a few discreet minutes had passed, Elizabeth made her way to the stables where John was saddling his horse. When he took her hand, she opened her palm to show him that it held the button from his uniform. He kissed her brow tenderly, then she went on her toes and offered up her mouth in a lingering good-bye kiss.

"*Ne obliviscaris,* Beth."

She shook her head. "I won't." *My heart already whispers your name. Do not forget me, John.*

Chapter Fourteen

*T*he following day, John Campbell began packing for his
journey to Scotland. He'd spent the morning with his
steward making sure the hops were on their way to the brew-
eries with which he had contracts, and all loose business ends
were dealt with until his return. After lunch, he returned to the
library to write a letter to his parents, advising them when he
would arrive at Inveraray and was much relieved to see his secretary walk through the door.

"Robert, thank heaven you are back today! King George has
finally given me consent to recruit in the Highlands. After
months of indecision and procrastination he has ordered me to
leave immediately. I hate to spring this on you the moment you
return, but do you think we could be ready to travel tomorrow?"

"Of course, Lord Sundridge. As soon as I deliver my report
on Ireland, I'll gather the files and papers pertaining to Scotland."

"Ah, yes, Ireland." John leaned back in his chair, not wanting Hay to learn that he now believed the trip had been unnecessary. He reached for a decanter of port on the side table and
filled two glasses. "Sit—wash the dust of the road from your
throat."

Hay drained the glass and shuffled his papers. "First, as you
suggested, my lord, I traveled to County Mayo to inquire about
Theobald, Viscount Mayo, and his daughter, Bridget. I have to

report that the viscount has no such daughter, unless of course she is illegitimate. 'Tis rumored he has a number of by-blows."

"I see." John steepled his fingers.

"In Roscommon I had a little difficulty finding Castle Coote, mainly because it isn't a castle at all. *Castlecoote* is a small manor house in need of repair. John Gunning, more suited to gambling than farming, recently sold the house and land to a nearby farm. The family had no social connections whatsoever, but the unusual beauty of their two daughters was spoken of by everyone in the district. The family reportedly moved to Dublin so that the Gunning sisters could earn their living as stage actresses."

"Thank you, Robert," John said calmly. "We'll leave at first light if you can be ready."

When Robert Hay left the library, John Campbell sat quietly for a full minute. Then he picked up the decanter and hurled it across the room with a foul oath. He strode to the stables, saddled Demon, and rode from the valley as if the devil were on his tail.

After a bruising gallop, he finally drew rein. *What the hell is the matter with you? Did you have some ridiculous plan in the back of your mind to make Elizabeth Gunning your wife? Christ Almighty, man, even if she were from minor nobility, your family would never accept her!* Suddenly, Elizabeth's scent filled his nostrils and he knew that the things Robert Hay had told him made no difference to his feelings for her. Familial duty made marriage out of the question, but she enchanted him and he intended to have her. John laughed mockingly at his own foolishness. *Surely, even secretly, you never dreamed of making her your wife?*

Bridget Gunning paid another visit to the Drury Lane casting hall and distributed sixpences to the out-of-work actors, then she penned anonymous notes to the fashionable newspapers, tipping them off about where the Gorgeous Gunnings could be seen. The day before they were to attend the royal drawing room at St. James's Palace, Bridget insisted that she and her daughters take an afternoon walk in Hyde Park, before the weather turned cold.

Accompanied by their maid, the Gunning ladies took a carriage to Park Lane. When they arrived, Bridget instructed the cabman to wait for them. Elizabeth and Maria no sooner opened their parasols and began their stroll when a crowd began to gather, shouting and pointing at them. The crowd quickly became unruly, and it turned into a mob scene. Emma valiantly struck out with her umbrella at the men who were trying to touch the girls, and a throng of genteel ladies gathered to defend the Gunnings. By the time the police were summoned, Bridget had ushered her daughters back into the carriage, and the culprits vanished.

On the drive back to Great Marlborough Street, Bridget pressed her lips together in outrage. "The king shall hear about this!" she declared, much to Maria's delight and Elizabeth's horror.

The crush at the royal drawing room at St. James's Palace was a testament to the unwritten law that such invitations could not be declined. Though it was fashionable for Society's matriarchs to complain in public, in private they were prideful as peacocks to parade themselves and their pubescent daughters at Court.

Maria Gunning, in her new powdered wig, preened by fingering the white roses that Beth had sewn onto her gown. Elizabeth followed with tentative steps, wearing the gold tissue ball gown. She wore her own hair, which garnered stares and prompted one matron to gush, "Do tell where you bought the glittering gold hair powder!"

Receiving the lion's share of attention from King George and Augusta, Princess of Wales, was the Duchess of Devonshire and her two daughters, Rachel and Cat. In point of fact, it looked as if the duchess were the one holding court, even though her gown was as nondescript as her face, and her wig was an old-fashioned gray.

Elizabeth dreaded the moment when the duchess and her mother were introduced, for God alone knew what accusations the Devonshire Dragon would make about the Gunning sisters. She was greatly relieved when Charlie arrived. "You look so pretty in your pale peach gown." They had chosen it to complement Charlotte's dark hair, but this evening she wore the requisite wig.

Dorothy Boyle greeted Bridget and immediately whispered behind her fan, "The fellow coming this way in the puce satin is Orford's cousin, Horace Walpole. He's the greatest gossip in Society, with a rapier wit and a tongue that can cut glass. Show the cynical swine deference, unless you wish to be eviscerated." Dorothy lowered her fan. "Horace, darling, do allow me to introduce the honorable Bridget Gunning and her daughters, Maria and Elizabeth."

"Lady Burlington, you have anticipated my desire, but then you've had so much practice." He raised his quizzing glass and examined the sisters. "The Beauties!" He swept Bridget with a glance. "Undoubtedly take after their father."

When Bridget laughed at his audacious remark, he was flattered. "Allow me to present your beautiful daughter to the king, madam. My cousin Orford has strutted before him long enough. Once he is wed to a Devonshire, he'll think himself a Prince of the Realm."

Maria simpered, placed her hand on Walpole's puce sleeve, and glided forward to meet her monarch.

Elizabeth stepped back, hoping to make herself inconspicuous yet feeling slightly rebuffed. She jumped nervously at a voice from behind her and turned to face the Duke of Hamilton.

He bowed formally before Elizabeth. "May I have the honor of presenting you to the king, Mistress Gunning?" Garbed in pewter-gray silk, he made Walpole look garish.

"Your Grace . . . there is no need." She lowered her lashes demurely, wondering why he had come to her rescue yet again.

"There is every need for the most beautiful lady at Court to be presented to His Royal Highness," he said gravely. "Come, my dear." His words sounded avuncular, and because of dissipation he looked much older than his twenty-nine years.

Elizabeth suffered the pinch her mother delivered without flinching, then she placed her hand on the duke's silk sleeve.

As he led her forward, he was aware that every eye was upon them. "Never hide your beauty," he murmured. "Lift your chin."

Used to obeying authority, Elizabeth immediately complied. They arrived at the king's side just as Walpole introduced Maria. Beth almost gasped at the words that came from her sister's mouth.

As she arose from her curtsy, Maria said, "Your Royal Highness, I've always longed to see a coronation!"

A blanket of silence fell as everyone realized she could not see a coronation unless the king died. Suddenly, Walpole tittered at the *gauche* remark, then King George's bulbous eyes popped back into his head, and he laughed at the beautiful girl's social blunder.

Hamilton stepped forward. "Your Majesty, it gives me great pleasure to present to you Mistress Elizabeth Gunning."

As Elizabeth sank into a graceful curtsy, King George's appreciation for female beauty was visible to everyone. He gazed at the golden goddess then stared hard at Hamilton, misliking the duke's proprietary attitude. "We are indeed pleased. Mistress Gunning shall remain at our side."

Hamilton bowed and stepped aside to join his friend Will Cavendish. "I don't dismiss so easily," he drawled. "The lady is far too innocent for the king's lechery."

Will's eyebrows rose in astonishment. "Since when did you consider innocence a virtue, James?"

"Since I met Mistress Gunning." He turned and saw the look of jealousy on Maria Gunning's face because her sister was receiving attention from the king. He tucked the information away in hope that he could make use of the rivalry. The Earl of Coventry joined Hamilton, and he too was consumed with jealousy.

"Why the devil has Horace Walpole attached himself to Maria? Not even a title, yet he insinuates himself into royal circles!"

"Your precious Maria is safe with Walpole, George. The inveterate gossip's wrist is too limp to even masturbate."

The fourteen-year-old heir to the throne approached Maria Gunning and lifted her hand to his lips. When she bobbed him a curtsy, he stared down her rose-strewn bodice.

Maria spied her opportunity and told the impressionable youth about how she had been accosted yesterday while walking in the park. As she hoped, the outraged Prince of Wales immediately reported the incident to the king. Within minutes, Maria and her mother were summoned to the king's side.

Elizabeth wished the floor would open up and swallow her as her mother answered the monarch's questions, displaying histrionic outrage as if she were acting the lead role in a drama, which of course she was. Elizabeth stood mute, unable to control the blush that suffused her cheeks. Inwardly, she shrank even farther at the solution King George proposed.

"By order of the king, you shall have an armed guard of a dozen soldiers with halberds each and every Sunday afternoon, so that you may walk in our Hyde Park unmolested, what!"

Since Bridget Gunning had received royal attention, the Duchess of Devonshire condescended to acknowledge her. Dorothy Boyle, however, was not so fortunate. The duchess cut the countess dead.

"I don't believe it," Lady Burlington declared to the assembly at large. "When I spoke to Catherine Hoskyns," Dorothy used her maiden name, "she looked through me as if I were invisible!"

"I've always found the Duchess of Devonshire delightfully vulgar," Horace Walpole drawled. "Far be it from me to repeat gossip, but I believe I overheard her call your delightful daughter, Lady Charlotte, a *baby face*."

"Baby face?" Usually shrewd, Dorothy Boyle was at a loss.

"Well, she is little more than a child, after all. Perhaps she fears Will is in danger of robbing the cradle," Walpole supplied.

The Countess of Burlington flew into a rage. "Since when did robbing the cradle ever stand in the way of the Devonshires when it came to marrying wealth? She's apparently oblivious to the number of *baby faces* the Devonshires have married in their time!" She saw that Walpole was drinking in every word and gave him something he could repeat. "Middle-class! That's what the Hoskyns were. She'll never be an aristocrat if she lives to be a hundred, which is precisely the age both she and her clothes look these days!"

The royal drawing room was talked about for months. Not only had it introduced the Gorgeous Gunnings to the Court of St. James, it also had been the setting where the deadly, virulent feud began between the Duchess of Devonshire and the Countess of Burlington.

Dorothy Boyle had not suffered such a personal affront since she had discovered her husband's peculiar predilection for his own sex.

Conversely, Bridget Gunning was the happiest of mothers.

The king's decree guaranteed the fame of her daughters, as Londoners began to gather outside their house in Great Marlborough Street hoping for a glimpse of the beauteous Gunning sisters. Bridget reasoned that where there was *fame*, surely *fortune* would follow.

Rachel and Orford's engagement party was held in early October, and the wedding date was set for November 15. When Bridget Gunning opened their wedding invitation, she was disappointed to learn that the daughter of the Duke and Duchess of Devonshire was to be married at Chatsworth, their ancestral home in Derbyshire.

"We are not going to the wedding," she informed Maria and Elizabeth. "We cannot possibly afford to travel to Derbyshire. We'll have to think up some plausible excuse."

To Bridget's delight and her husband's sorrow, fate provided one in the death of Jack Gunning's father. Her delight turned to fury, however, when the will was read and everything was left to her husband's oldest brother. The moment they returned from St. Ives, she gave her husband his orders. "You must make the rounds of the moneylenders and borrow on the strength of your inheritance."

"I've already borrowed on my nonexistent inheritance once," he said dryly, "and repayment is overdue."

"They don't know it's nonexistent. You must borrow from Peter to pay back Paul. Why are you so feckless?"

The couple sniped at each other for hours, and when Lady Charlotte stopped by to invite Elizabeth to go for an afternoon carriage ride in the park, she jumped at the chance to escape from the distressing atmosphere.

"I'm so sorry your grandfather passed away," Charlie murmured.

"I hardly remember him. We went to live in Ireland when I was a little girl, but I know my father mourns him." She changed the subject. "When are you leaving for Derbyshire?"

"We're not." Charlie hesitated, then confided, "We didn't get an invitation, and my mother is absolutely livid at the insult."

"But your mother and the Duke of Devonshire seemed like

old friends in Ireland, and Will and his sisters accepted your mother's invitation to Chiswick. What has happened?"

"Mother tries to keep it all from me, but I believe I am to blame for the sudden enmity. The Duchess of Devonshire is not pleased that Will wants to court me."

Elizabeth was shocked. Charlie was the epitome of what every *débutante* should be. Not only was she exceedingly pretty, sweet, and innocent, she was one of the wealthiest heiresses in England.

"She called me a *baby face*. She obviously thinks I'm far too young to become her son's wife. Will sent me a note, asking me to meet him in the park. I hope you don't mind, Elizabeth?"

"Of course I don't mind, but won't you want to be private?"

Charlie blushed. "We've been private too often, I believe."

Will Cavendish spotted the carriage as soon as it turned in to the park. He had practiced what he would say to Charlie several times. The last thing in the world he wanted was to hurt her. When the driver stopped, he rode alongside. He was relieved to see she had Elizabeth with her rather than her maid. He was urbane enough to know that servants could not always be trusted.

"Hello, Elizabeth." His eyes immediately sought Charlie. "I must apologize for my mother's unforgivable breach of manners in not issuing a wedding invitation to your family. She's lived in the country so long she doesn't realize her rustic, provincial ways are unacceptable in London Society."

"It's all right, Will, I understand. It's Mother who is angry."

"And so am I . . . I only just learned of it, and I let her know exactly how I felt about such a slight. Please forgive me, love?" *God, it's a damn good thing you have no idea of the vitriol that gushed forth from her when I announced that I was serious about you, Charlie. Her words are still ringing in my ears: "The Burlingtons are a family who attract scandal! Both the earl and the countess are morally bankrupt! For years, the woman has conducted a blatant liaison with the Duke of Grafton, while it is common knowledge that Richard Boyle enjoys a physical relationship with his architect, Kent. We'll not be tainted by them!"*

When Charlie flushed with pleasure at the endearment, a wave of protectiveness swept over Will. She was so innocent it brought a lump to his throat. "Once this wedding is out of the way, and Father and I return to London, I mean to ask your parents for your hand in marriage. My intentions are completely honorable, Charlie, and my father supports me in this, despite what my mother thinks."

"What does she think, Will?" Charlotte asked softly.

It was his turn to flush. "She thinks you are too young for me, Charlie, but we know better, don't we, love?"

She nodded trustingly.

"Elizabeth, may I give John Campbell a message for you?"

"John will be at the wedding?"

"I expect he and his family will be there."

Tell him I miss him. Tell him I want him to come home. Tell him I love him! "Tell him . . . just tell him . . . I remember."

In Scotland, John Campbell could not forget Elizabeth Gunning. Asleep or awake, her image haunted him. All during October and early November he and his captains rode over Argyll, through the craggy Grampian Mountains, recruiting troops for Argyll's Highland regiments. It was a race against time before the snows came to block the mountain passes. There was no lack of eager volunteers who weighed the advantages of regular army pay against eking out a living that often verged on starvation, especially during the long, cruel winter months, fast approaching. So Campbell had the task of selecting the fiercest, fittest, and finest men and sending them to Inveraray for a month's training under his father's exacting eye. After that they would winter in Glasgow with other Highland regiments, where they would complete their training.

Long hours in the saddle riding through the majestic mountains gave John much time for thought and introspection. The magnificent vistas of purple mountains made him realize that all this land would one day belong to him. Invariably, whenever he crossed a wild stream where stags watered, he wished he could share its breathtaking beauty with Elizabeth. He never saw a loch without remembering them naked together in the water. The thought triggered his body's response to her and left him with a hungering ache in his groin that sometimes reached his heart.

Cold rain brought back memories of riding to Sundridge

with Beth held captive between his thighs, and at night, if they made a campfire to cook or stay warm, the flames conjured visions of him making love to her with his mouth as they lay before the fire. Before he slept, he always fingered the golden curl that lay in his breast pocket. Once sleep claimed him, his dreams were so sensually erotic he awoke with a savage need that felt like torture.

John knew no other female had ever affected him in this way. He told himself it was likely because he had never previously hesitated to slake his passion and rid himself of his sexual energy before it built into an obsession.

John arrived back home at Inveraray Castle the second week in November, in time to settle a mild dispute between his parents. His mother whisked him into her private sitting room, before his dominant father had a chance to influence his opinion.

Mary Bellenden Campbell handed her son the invitation to the Devonshire wedding being held at Chatsworth. "I have to send my response no later than today, and your father is being stubborn."

John grinned. "When was he ever anything else?"

"Well, that's the pot calling the kettle black! You're every bit as stubborn as your wretched father."

"I'm putty in your hands when you flatter me like that." His arm went about her shoulders. "What is it you want me to do?"

"Persuade him to take me to Chatsworth. You go and tell him you'd like to see your friend William, while I accept this invitation and give it to a courier."

He watched her sit down at her desk and pick up a pen. "You are a devious, manipulative woman, pitting a son against his father."

She gave him back his words. "I'm putty in your hands when you flatter me like that. Besides, you pit yourself against him on a regular basis . . . and against my wishes too," she added.

"First I'm stubborn, then I pit myself against your wishes."

She tapped the invitation with a long, elegant finger. "You know, John, you could have married Rachel Cavendish if you'd played your cards right. I believe she had a *tendre* for you."

He schooled his face in serious lines. "Do you really think

so? The thought of marrying Rachel Cavendish never entered my mind."

His mother's mouth curved in an indulgent smile. "Don't mock me. Has the thought of marrying *anyone* ever entered your mind?"

"How could it not, when you are forever thrusting potential wives upon me?"

"I wish you would be serious, John. You are not getting any younger . . . you'll be twenty-nine, or is it thirty, next birthday? By the time your father was your age, he had given me two sons and planted a daughter beneath my heart. As the heir to Argyll, it is your duty to marry and have children."

"I am aware of all my duties, Mother." His tone told her the discussion was over. He changed the subject. "Pen your acceptance. I'll go and persuade Father."

"Christ Almighty, I'm up to my arse in raw recruits. I've no got time fer muckle nonsense like weddings"—Argyll raised a bristling white brow—"unless it's *yours!*"

"Your saving grace is your sense of humor, Father."

"I'm no jesting. I'm serious."

"That's what makes it so bloody funny. Anyway, you know you'll take her to Chatsworth. Why are you pretending otherwise?"

"Ye think Mary Bellenden has me wrapped round her finger?"

I know she has. "An old warhorse like you? Of course not! But it does give you pleasure to indulge her upon occasion."

"Why is she so set on visiting the Duchess of Devonshire?"

"Perhaps because as Duchess of Argyll she will put her in the shade? But more likely it's Chatsworth she enjoys visiting, and weddings hold such an irresistible fascination for women."

"They enjoy watching the condemned mon go to his execution!"

"And you wonder why I'm in no rush to put my neck in the noose?"

Chapter Fifteen

*O*n November 15 in the ancient church at Eyam near Chatsworth, most of England's and a few of Scotland's aristocratic families witnessed the nuptials, as Rachel Cavendish became the Countess of Orford. Will acted as best man, then joined his friend John Campbell when the wedding party entered Chatsworth for the lavish reception.

"John, I'm so glad to see you. I desperately need your advice."

"First things first, old man." He reached into his pocket and took out a letter for Elizabeth. "Do you have any message for me?"

"Yes. She said, *Tell him I remember.* Does that make sense?"

"Perfect sense." John gave him the letter. "Give it to Charlie, and she'll pass it along to Elizabeth."

"I will, but therein lies the trouble. Mother threatens to disown me if I continue to see Charlie. She is adamant that I not even think of marrying Charlotte Boyle. She is being a downright bitch about the whole thing," Will said unhappily.

"How could she possibly object to Lady Charlotte?" John was at a complete loss. Charlie was the best marriage prize in England.

"Well, for one thing, she raves on about Dorothy Boyle being an *adulteress,* for God's sake!"

"Well, ruling out adultery would eliminate almost every matron of the *ton* with eligible daughters. Perhaps if you give her time, you can overcome her objections."

"If I give her time, she'll come up with more ammunition. She's being a bitch, but she forgets that makes me a son of a bitch! I refuse to let her ride roughshod over me."

"It seems like you don't need my advice at all, Will. It is quite obvious you have already made up your mind."

Will grinned sheepishly. "I have. My brothers and sisters are all on my side in this. They have taken to calling me Guts Cavendish, because I dare stand up to Mother. Thanks for listening. I'd better go and play the dutiful son and propose a toast to the happy couple."

As dusk fell on Chatsworth, John walked outside through the vast gardens, now covered with fallen leaves from the trees, and gazed up at the moon. Subdued and reflective, he unsuccessfully tried to ignore the empty ache inside. The Devonshires' objection to someone as noble and wealthy as Lady Charlotte made him realize the futility of expecting the Argylls to accept someone as utterly unsuitable as Elizabeth Gunning.

Elizabeth jumped at the chance to visit Charlie at Burlington House, hoping with all her heart that John Campbell had sent her a message by way of Will Cavendish. She was relieved that Maria showed no interest in joining her, preferring instead to go for a carriage ride with her latest conquest, Henry St. John, Viscount Bolingbroke. He was a Tory politician, and Elizabeth knew that her sister had chosen him to make George Coventry, who was a Whig, madly jealous—or, more to the point, so he would ask her to become his countess.

Charlie had sent the carriage for her, but when Elizabeth arrived she was surprised when her friend, wrapped in her new fur cape, ran out, spoke to the driver, then climbed in beside her.

"I've asked him to drive us over to Burlington Gardens. They've started doing the interiors, and we can be private over there."

Elizabeth saw the pinched look on Charlie's face and felt apprehensive. *John didn't send me a message, and she needs privacy so she can deliver the bad news.*

They entered the magnificent new house, which smelled of

damp plaster, and walked past some workmen doing decorative work on the mouldings. When they reached an empty chamber, Charlie handed her the letter.

"Oh, thank you!" Elizabeth whispered John's name in her heart and went weak at the knees. "Did William bring it?"

Charlie nodded and Beth sat down on a window seat to read it.

> Elizabeth:
> I dare not put my thoughts down on paper. Suffice it to say that I miss you with all my heart. I wish you were here with me in Scotland, for I know how much you love the countryside. The Highlands are far wilder than Ireland but I feel sure you would appreciate their beauty.
> I will try to be back in London by Christmas.
> Ne obliviscaris!
> John

She sighed. "He misses me, and he'll be home by Christmas."

Charlie gave her a tight little smile then said, "Elizabeth—"

"Yes?"

"Um . . . how do you like the house?"

"It's absolutely splendid. I love the sweeping staircase we passed. What color will this room be?"

"Daddy says I may choose the colors . . . he hinted that Burlington Gardens would be mine when I marry."

"Oh, how wonderful, Charlie!"

"Yes." She bit her lip. "Elizabeth—"

"You want to tell me something. What is it?"

"I . . . I think I'm with child!" Charlie blurted, her face chalk white. "What am I going to do?" she whispered.

Elizabeth, stunned, stared at her in disbelief for a moment then took her hand as realization dawned that she spoke the truth. "You're going to marry William, of course."

Charlie nodded eagerly. "You were with me, remember, when he said that once his sister's wedding was out of the way, he intended to ask my parents for my hand in marriage?"

"Of course I remember. Have you told Will?"

Charlie's hand went to her throat. "Oh, I couldn't."

"Of course you can! Will is a man, not a boy. He will take care of everything, Charlie. You love each other, and you already have a house. I don't see any insurmountable problem."

"You're forgetting his mother. She hates me!"

"She doesn't know you. Once she does, she will love you."

Charlie shook her head. "I overheard Mother raging over the Duchess of Devonshire's remarks. She called it 'an accursed match' and a '*mésalliance*.' Mother says she's like a relentless steam-roller, determined to destroy everything in her path."

"You are shivering." Elizabeth took her hands and chafed them. "You are icy cold. The house isn't heated. You can't stay here."

They got back into the waiting carriage for the short ride back to Burlington House. "Can you tell your mother, Charlie?"

"No, no, she would run mad."

Beth understood her reluctance; she would never dare confide anything to her own mother. "Then promise me you will tell Will?"

Charlie nodded miserably.

At Devonshire House, William and his father were having yet another serious discussion about the duchess's opposition to her son's union with Lady Charlotte Boyle.

"I've pointed out to her that you are about to achieve the dynastic marriage of the century, but she won't budge!" He threw down the letter he had just received from Chatsworth. "Read it."

William scanned the pages with a growing disgust. "It's filled with self-pity and self-righteousness. Mother is obsessed over some imagined 'wrong' I will do to her with this 'monstrous marriage'!"

The duke downed another whiskey. "Since I can make no headway with her, I don't suppose I can dissuade you, William?"

"Absolutely not! I am as inflexible as she. I am twenty-eight. I am Marquis of Hartington. I insist on my right to marry as I please. Any other mother would be over the moon at such a brilliant match."

Devonshire raised his glass. "I bow to the inevitable—you have my blessing. Just give your mother time to come round."

William immediately dashed off a note to Charlotte's parents.

The following day the Earl and Countess of Burlington greeted Lord Hartington warmly. Seated in their exquisitely furnished formal drawing room, Dorothy Boyle swallowed her rancor over the Duchess of Devonshire's objections, and when William asked for their daughter's hand in marriage, they both assured him that they welcomed him as a son-in-law.

Richard Boyle quite naturally began to discuss money and property. "Charlotte's dowry is thirty thousand pounds, and I've promised her yearly 'pin money' of a thousand. I shall have a bank draft drawn up."

"There is no hurry for that, I assure you, Lord Burlington. If you will agree to an immediate engagement, I thought perhaps a wedding in the spring, once Charlotte turns seventeen, would please the ladies."

Richard beamed at his future son-in-law's consideration.

Dorothy smiled at her husband. "Darling, why don't you go and get the plans for Burlington Gardens to show William? While you're off to the library, Will and I can have a cozy chat."

Since Richard's great passion was building houses, he rushed off to get the plans.

"The real reason for wanting to wait until the spring is your mother, is it not?" Dorothy spoke with sympathetic understanding.

"Yes," William admitted. "I'm hoping she will give us her blessing, but if she doesn't, it will make no difference."

"Good. Charlotte's maid, Jane, has confided to me that my daughter's menses have stopped. Waiting until spring isn't an option, I'm afraid."

William, momentarily shocked, colored. "Forgive me, Lady Burlington."

"Nonsense, my lord, there's nothing to forgive. December is a lovely month for a wedding. I beg you not let Charlie know I have the faintest notion."

Richard Boyle returned, his arms filled with plans. He cleared off an eight-foot refectory table and eagerly spread them out.

"Lord Burlington, I fear I am too impatient to wait until spring. Would you be amenable to a December wedding?"

"Certainly, my boy. Come and look at Burlington Gardens. I intend to assign the house to my daughter's husband for life."

William gazed down at the plans in disbelief. "You are most generous, Lord Burlington."

"But not very romantic, I'm afraid. Houses are all very well, Richard, but William wants to propose." Her eyes met Will's with understanding. "You'll find Charlie upstairs."

The second week of December, Burlington House was filled with a profusion of white hothouse carnations, chrysanthemums, and lilies for the wedding of Lady Charlotte Boyle to William Cavendish, Marquis of Hartington.

Elizabeth Gunning handed the bride her bouquet of white rosebuds and lifted the long train so her friend wouldn't trip as she descended the staircase in the Pall Mall mansion. Elizabeth, along with William's sisters, Rachel and Cat, wore identical bridesmaids' gowns of ice-blue satin over Irish lace. Her heart was overflowing with happiness for Charlie, a stark contrast from the anguish she had felt for her friend a fortnight ago.

Elizabeth had lain sleepless for two nights before she had received Charlie's note. She shuddered as she remembered her mother snatching it from her fingers before she could read it.

"Have I not made it clear that I will be the first to read any correspondence you receive, Elizabeth?"

Beth's hands began to shake uncontrollably as her mother read the note from Charlie. She would never breathe a word of her friend's secret, but that would not matter if Charlie's words revealed her plight.

"It seems your friend is getting married." Her mother's eyes gleamed with envy as she thrust the note at her daughter. "Ask her to teach you how to catch a husband!"

Elizabeth sagged with relief as she read the note.

Elizabeth:
William proposed to me last night. I am the luckiest and the happiest girl in the world!
Love,
Charlie

That night Elizabeth burned the note, along with the one she had received from John. Regretfully, there was nowhere she could keep private letters safe from prying eyes.

Now, as the bride took her place beside the groom, Elizabeth's thoughts turned to William. Though his father, his brother, and sisters were present, his mother was conspicuously absent. Rumor was rife that the Duchess of Devonshire was so incensed her husband had taken his heir's side against her wishes that she had decamped from Chatsworth and moved into the rectory at Eyam. Her Grace hoped to become a martyr in the eyes of Society but, instead, the *ton* whispered that the old duchess had gone mad.

As Elizabeth looked at the handsome groom she fervently hoped his mother hadn't taken the joy from his union with Charlotte. Her glance traveled to his brother, Charles, standing beside him, and she wished with all her heart that his best friend, John Campbell, could have returned in time for the wedding. John had sent her another letter explaining that since his brother's regiment was overseas, his mother had begged him to stay in Scotland for Christmas and that he would return to London in January. Sadly, it was another letter she had had to burn.

The Boyles spared no expense on the lavish reception for more than two hundred invited guests. Wedding gifts were displayed in the long picture gallery, a full orchestra played in the ballroom for dancing prior to the formal wedding dinner, and liveried footmen proffered trays filled with flutes of champagne for toasting the newlyweds.

When Maria Gunning danced twice with the young Prince of Wales, George Coventry, madly jealous, asked Elizabeth if he could partner her. Hamilton, guarding his own interests, cut in on his friend George. Then red-haired Michael Boyle, deciding to sow a little mischief among his friends, deliberately cut in on Hamilton. When the music stopped, William's male friends encircled him, and reached for champagne to offer toasts.

"Too bad John couldn't be here," William declared. "Let's drink to our absent friend."

Michael Boyle laughed and waggled mischievous eyebrows at Charlie. "Probably couldn't bear to see Will leg-shackled!"

"He could come back from Scotland leg-shackled himself, for all we know," Coventry jested.

Boyle saw the fleeting look of distress on Elizabeth's face. "The ladies of Scotland are reputedly cold with ice in their veins. You're a Scot, Hamilton, isn't that true?"

"Yes, but there isn't one of them who wouldn't melt at the thought of an estate, or a fine set of bagpipes playing 'The Campbells Are Coming, Hurrah, Hurrah!' "

William laughed. "John does have a fine set of bagpipes!"

Hamilton saw Elizabeth's cheeks turn a delicate pink. "The party is getting bawdy. Please forgive us, Mistress Gunning— such coarseness is unforgivable." He led her off to her parents.

When he left, Bridget looked with speculative eyes at Elizabeth. "Dare I hope that you have made a conquest of His Grace?"

"No, Mother," Elizabeth said faintly. "He was just being kind."

"Dukes *are* rather elusive. They've had lots of practice eluding the marriage trap. You might have more luck with the Duke of Grafton. He's been a widower for years."

John Gunning took his daughter's hand. *He's also been Dorothy Boyle's lover for years.* "No, Bridget, the Duke of Grafton is completely unsuitable for Elizabeth," he said firmly.

Hamilton joined Coventry to rub salt into his wounds. "Maria giving you the cold shoulder these days, is she, George? Doesn't seem like you'll be winning our wager any time soon."

"I've had her on the brink a couple of times, James, which is far closer than you've gotten with her sister, I warrant."

"You and I go about things differently, George. But I warn you, I play to win."

"Everyone knows you can't bear to lose. If you do start to lose, you change the rules. If that doesn't work, you take your cricket bat and go home."

His mouth curved in a saturnine smile. "Precisely."

It was almost midnight when Charlotte, the new Marchioness of Hartington, went upstairs with her bridesmaids to change out of her wedding gown. The newlyweds were spending their wedding night in their new home, Burlington Gardens, and a sleigh with a team of white horses stood ready to transport them across the snow-covered acres that separated the two mansions.

Before Charlie went downstairs, Elizabeth wrapped her in her fur cape and whispered in her ear, "I hope you will always be as happy as you are tonight."

"Oh, Beth, I don't think that will be possible. My heart is overflowing with love. I hope John comes back soon. When he does, you will be able to meet here at Burlington Gardens."

Elizabeth slipped on her winter cloak so that she could follow the newlyweds outside and see them off. Though she stood amidst the crowd of guests who were laughing and waving until the sleigh disappeared through the snowflakes, Elizabeth felt utterly alone.

Shivering, she closed her eyes and fingered the brass button that she had sewn into the lining of her cloak. Suddenly, she was no longer alone, or cold, as John's warm presence enveloped her.

Inveraray Castle's great hall was filled to the rafters for the Christmas celebration. Guests staying for the holidays and visiting neighbors from miles around had gathered for the feasting and revelry. The din of raucous laughter mingled with the skirl of pipes grew more deafening with each hour as the Campbells of Argyll lifted horns of October ale and drams of whiskey to mark December 25, 1751.

A forty-foot Douglas fir, trimmed and decorated, stood at one end of the hall, and the air was redolent with the aroma of roasting meat and game. Highland cattle, stags, geese, grouse, and partridge had been on the spits since before dawn, making stomachs growl in anticipation of the Christmas feast.

John's sister, Anne, and her husband, the Earl of Sutherland, had brought their two children, Fiona and Grace, who dogged John's footsteps wherever he went. He had just hoisted Gracie so she could reach a piece of marzipan from a silver dish on a high table.

"You seem to like children, and 'tis obvious they adore you."

John turned to see Mary Montagu, daughter of the Duke of

Buccleuch, at his elbow. They were visiting from Buccleuch Castle, their pink sandstone fortress that housed innumerable treasures, including an art collection that boasted dozens of Van Dycks, a Rembrandt, and a Leonardo da Vinci painting. Campbell and Buccleuch ancestors had intermarried, and John was well aware that his mother had invited young Lady Mary in hope of making a match.

John laughed. "Gracie takes shameless advantage because she knows I will indulge her passion for sweets."

She touched Grace's chin with her finger. "Lucky girl! What lady would not wish to have you indulge her passion?"

John was saved from the sally by young Fiona trying to steal the dirk from his boot. He cuffed her gently. "Stop that!"

Lady Mary laughed. "Your niece's passion is weapons. At Boughton House in Northamptonshire we have an armory with a collection of weapons that rivals that of the Tower of London. I would love to show it to you, John."

His mother, whom he realized must have been watching, joined them and lifted little Gracie from his arms. "John, after New Year, Lady Mary is planning to visit her aunt in London, an arduous and risky journey in wintertime. I told her she must allow you and your captains to act as her escort."

John bowed. "Mistress Montagu, it would be an honor to escort you safely to London."

Her glance lingered on his mouth. "How gallant you are! Surely we have known each other long enough for you to call me Mary? We can break our journey at Bowhill in the Borders and Boughton House in Northamptonshire, if you and your captains will accept our hospitality. I shall be able to show you the armory after all."

I have already been exposed to your weapons, and they are formidable. John knew that he had been outflanked by his mother and the attractive daughter of Buccleuch, which was hard to swallow for a military man. He cursed himself for an unsuspecting fool. He knew he should have kept up his guard; for days his mother had been cataloging the Buccleuchs' wealth, priceless collections, and property. Her words came back to him now: *They say Boughton House resembles a great gray Versailles set down in the heart of England. What a pity it*

*is only occupied for a month each year when they are not in
Scotland.*

"Ah, you must excuse me. They are about to drag in the Yule
log and I'd like to help. It's supposed to be lucky, you know."

His mother's eyes sparkled with mischief. "You are already
lucky, John. I have seated you and Lady Mary together at dinner."

Long after midnight, when Inveraray Castle finally lay
shrouded in silence, John Campbell climbed to the turrets of the
north tower. The icy-cold wind whipped the snow about so that
the visibility was nonexistent, but it was a good place to think
without distraction. He shook his head at his own folly of offering his dinner partner grouse instead of partridge, as if the
game bird must only be eaten by Elizabeth.

Mary Montagu was a great marriage prize, suitable in every
way. In a couple of years, when he could no longer put off taking a wife, he had no objection to considering her, if she was
still in the market for a husband. But that was for the future. At
the moment, he was only interested in the present, in returning
to London and taking up where he left off with Elizabeth Gunning. She was his heart's desire.

Chapter Sixteen

*I*n London, the social whirl over Christmas and New Year
built in a crescendo of invitations to Court entertainments
and private parties by the reigning families, and climaxed in
January with the New Year's Honors List from the king. This
was to be celebrated at the first drawing room of the year at St.
James's Palace.

Bridget Gunning, who had been watching for the royal invitation, easily intercepted a note addressed to Elizabeth from the
newly married Lady Hartington. She opened it quickly and
scanned its contents:

> Elizabeth:
> I am so excited about William's appointment as
> Master of the Horse, which will be announced at the
> king's drawing room for the New Year's honors.
> J sends regards, and we all look forward to seeing
> you at St. James's Palace.
> Love,
> Charlie

Bridget handed over the note. "Who is J?" she demanded.

"Jane . . . Charlie's maid," Elizabeth improvised quickly,
swallowing her guilt over the lie.

"He would never have gotten the appointment if his father
wasn't the Duke of Devonshire!" Bridget said with malice.

Elizabeth skipped over the first part of the message and concentrated on the second. Charlie was telling her that John was back in London and looked forward to seeing her at St. James's. Her heart did a somersault as she rushed upstairs to dress.

John Campbell graciously agreed to escort Lady Mary Montagu to the drawing room at St. James's Palace. He felt it his social duty to introduce the young *débutante* to the Court, then his obligation would be finished. Upon his arrival in London, he had immediately visited his best friend, Will Cavendish, and his bride at Burlington Gardens. He was delighted that Will would be Master of the Horse, an appointment he had long anticipated, and attending the drawing room would give John a chance to report to the king. He asked Charlie to let Beth know he was back in London and most eager to see her.

When John arrived, he lost no time in escorting Lady Mary to the king. He glimpsed Maria Gunning close by, and his pulse quickened as he realized Elizabeth must be somewhere in the chamber. "Your Majesty, it is my honor and my pleasure to present the Duke of Buccleuch's daughter, Lady Mary Montagu."

King George looked her over. "The pleasure is ours, Sundridge. Welcome to our Court, Lady Mary."

She sank into a deep curtsy. "You honor me, Gracious Majesty."

"We trust your journey from Scotland was uneventful, what?"

"Lord Sundridge gave me safe escort, Your Majesty."

"Quite! Couldn't be in better hands!" King George's speculative glance moved over the couple, then he made eye contact with Campbell and indicated that he would see him in his privy chamber after the reception.

The king wasn't the only one speculating. George Coventry and James Hamilton watched John return the lady to her aunt then walk across the chamber to greet them. As Hamilton began to hum "The Campbells Are Coming," Coventry jested, "By God, I told you he might return from Scotland leg-shackled!"

"She has such lovely manners . . . Buccleuch, Bowhill, Boughton."

"I'm glad I amuse you," John said dryly. "If her manors interest you, please feel free to pursue the lady." His dark glance swept relentlessly around the room until it found the object of his desire. "Excuse me, gentlemen."

As he walked a direct path to her, he saw her mother join Dorothy Boyle, leaving Elizabeth in the company of Charlie and Will. John took her fingers to his lips, and his eyes drank in the smile of radiant joy she bestowed upon him.

"Lord Sundridge," she said breathlessly.

She wore a new gown of ice-blue satin over a lace under-dress; her golden curls remained unpowdered. She was a thousand times more lovely than he remembered. "My beauty," he murmured for her ears alone. Then he proceeded to press his newlywed friends to arrange a rendezvous at Burlington Gardens.

Across the room, Dorothy bent close to Bridget. "You'd think the duchess would be here to see her son honored with the appointment of Master of the Horse. Her actions prove she is neither aristocrat nor even plutocrat." Dorothy shuddered. "Middle-class!"

"She should be ashamed to embarrass the duke and her son in such a manner. Gossip about her is rife!"

"The *ugly duchess* is without shame. In all the years her husband was Viceroy of Ireland, she spent only a month there. Stuck her nose up at the Irish and decamped back to Chatsworth. Is it any wonder he turned to his two other loves?"

Bridget's eyebrows lifted in inquiry.

"Gaming and drink!" Dorothy laughed at her own joke. "I see Johnny Ponsonby's name on the Honors List. Old Devonshire has managed to get him appointed Baron Duncannon. That's strictly to appease the old bitch. When Cat Cavendish weds him, she'll have the title of Lady Duncannon."

Bridget Gunning was incensed that so many weddings were taking place among her daughters' acquaintances. Her girls were far more beautiful than any of the chits who were becoming brides, especially Maria. Bridget's resolve hardened. She would have to take matters into her own hands. Time was of the essence.

Unwittingly, King George became her ally when he beckoned Maria and lightly scolded her about her newfound friendship with her Tory admirer. Even Maria understood that the king preferred Whig supremacy in Parliament and on the spot decided it was time to stop giving George Coventry the cold shoulder. She assumed that all she'd have to do was crook her little finger and he'd come running. She felt a small frisson of panic when she found the earl laughing with the female John Campbell had presented to the king as Lady Mary Montagu, daughter of Duke Somebody-or-other. Her mother had warned her: *If you chase two rabbits, you end up losing both!*

Maria placed a proprietary hand on Coventry's sleeve. "George, are you going to introduce me to your friend, Lady Mary?"

"It would be my pleasure. May I present Lady Mary Montagu, daughter of the Duke of Buccleuch? Mistress Maria Gunning."

Determined to separate George from Lady Mary, she asked sweetly, "Isn't John Campbell escorting you this evening?"

Lady Mary laughed. "Actually he's escorted me all the way from Scotland. John and I've known each other since we were children."

Maria plied her fan. "George, I'm thirsty, could I impose upon you to help me find a glass of ratafia?"

"Certainly." He covered Maria's hand with his and bowed to Lady Mary. "May I get you some refreshment, my lady?"

"No, thank you, Lord Coventry. It was lovely to see you again."

"I suppose she's a wealthy heiress," Maria asked acidly when they were barely out of earshot. "An ideal wife?"

George's pulse began to race. Was it possible that Maria was jealous of his attention to another lady? "An ideal wife for John Campbell, no doubt. Hamilton and I were baiting him about the property of Buccleuch, Bowhill, and Boughton."

His words did not ease her panic. What man in his right mind would choose her over a bride who would bring castles and wealth? She sipped the ratafia he handed her and fished for an invitation.

"I would love to see *The Rival Queens* at Drury Lane. I haven't been to the theater since before Christmas."

"Would you do me the honor, Maria, of allowing me to escort you on Friday evening? Your Mother and sister too, of course."

"I would love to. But why Elizabeth? The play is *The Rival Queens* not *The Rival Sisters!*"

"You have a delicious sense of humor, Maria," he said fondly.

On the hackney ride home Bridget forbore lamenting their lack of a carriage and instead focused on her latest resolve. "I have it on good authority that Cat Cavendish will be the next bride. Old Devonshire has bribed Ponsonby with the title of Duncannon to become her husband. Gentlemen, it seems, need to be bludgeoned! We have been in London five months—our time is running out!"

"It's difficult to bring a man up to snuff when we have nothing to bribe him with. We are in direct competition with the daughters of dukes such as Devonshire and Buccleuch!" complained Maria.

"You have your beauty! A clever woman wields it as a weapon!"

"Yes, that's exactly what I did tonight. As a result, the Earl of Coventry is taking me to the theater on Friday evening."

"Your sister and I are included, I take it?"

Elizabeth came out of her happy reverie. "Charlie invited me to Burlington Gardens on Friday evening to . . . to help her plan her first entertainment as a married lady," she improvised.

"What the devil would you know about entertaining on the lavish scale of the Burlingtons and Devonshires, pray tell?"

Her mother's acerbic tongue usually rendered Beth speechless, but it was her only chance to see John. "Charlie values my opinion. She assumes we lived on a grand scale in Ireland, and when I'm acting a role I'm not tongue-tied or shy."

"Far better that you attend the theater. Perhaps Coventry could invite the Duke of Hamilton to partner you," Bridget suggested.

Elizabeth withdrew into silence in the corner of the carriage.

"I believe it would be more intimate if George and I did not have another couple along. I mean to bring him up to the mark!"

"You are probably right, Maria. We should concentrate on making you a countess. A far easier task, I warrant, than snaring a marriage proposal for your sister."

They arrived home around eleven o'clock, just as Jack was about to leave to go gaming. Bridget, already in a peevish mood, pounced. "It is downright humiliating to take a hackney to and from St. James's Palace! I have waited five months for that carriage you promised, Jack Gunning! Five long months!"

It'll be five long years before I can afford a carriage and horses, my girl! Jack had so many gambling debts he didn't know which way to turn. He made the rounds of the gaming hells every night, hoping for that one big win that would deliver him from *dun* territory. As did all gamblers, he won many small wagers that paid his way into high-stakes games, where he hoped to make a killing from wealthy addicts like the Duke of Hamilton. However, the nobleman had had the Devil's own luck of late, and Jack prayed that tonight was the night it would change.

"Lady Luck is with me tonight." He winked at Bridget. "I feel it in my bones!"

Relief washed over Elizabeth as she closed their bedchamber door. "Thank goodness Father was on his way out. Mother was spoiling for a row."

"Father and I have learned to say just the right thing when she unsheathes her claws. You always end up getting scratched."

Elizabeth picked up the wig Maria had flung onto the dressing table and fit it over its stand. "Thank you for saying you preferred going to the theater without me, so I can visit Charlie."

"If you're hoping to see John Campbell, be prepared for disappointment. Not only did he present Lady Mary Montagu to the king this evening, he escorted her all the way from Scotland. Did you know she is the wealthy Duke of Buccleuch's chit? They own Buccleuch Castle, Bowhill, and Boughton House in Northamptonshire. George told me that John's friends expect him to marry her."

Elizabeth felt as if she had received a blow to her solar plexus. Her hand went up to cover her heart in a protective gesture. Her inner voice warned: *Maria is trying to hurt you. Don't believe her!* Her vulnerability made her feel devastated for a moment or two, then she remembered the look on John's face when he had seen her tonight. It had been both fierce and tender, and completely possessive. The pain in her heart melted away. "Good night, Maria. I hope you enjoy the play."

The liveried servant opened the door, took Elizabeth's cloak to reveal her gray chiffon dinner dress, then disappeared quickly as the new Marchioness of Hartington came to greet her guest. Dandy welcomed Elizabeth with a wildly wagging tail and three short barks. She bent down, picked him up, and dropped a kiss on his head, then she followed Charlie into the elegant sitting room. "Does he like Burlington Gardens?"

"He likes it very much—what he's seen of it." John was standing by the fireplace mantel with a drink in his hand.

Elizabeth caught her breath. He looked taller, darker, and more devilishly handsome than any man had a right to, and his glittering brown eyes devoured her as she stood cradling the dog.

Charlie ignored John's remark. "Dandy took to the house immediately, and Will has already taught him to go outside to do his necessary."

Will slipped his arm around his diminutive wife. "Now if I could just teach you not to leave little turds on the new carpets."

Charlie slapped him playfully then raised her eyebrows to her husband when neither John nor Elizabeth laughed at his outrageous remark. Apparently they could hear or see nothing but each other.

Charlie took Dandy. "Elizabeth, why don't you give John a grand tour of the house, while I see about dinner?"

"My bride is so domesticated she has already learned from cook there are three meals each day—breakfast, lunch, and dinner."

Charlie gazed up at her husband with adoration. "Never mind, darling—I'll laugh at your jokes."

John set his glass on the mantelpiece and walked toward Elizabeth, and together they left the room as if they were in a trance. When the door closed behind them and they found themselves alone, John let out a whoop, swept her up in his arms, and swung her about then lifted her high.

As she looked down at him, her laughter bubbled up and spilled over, flooding them with happiness and joy.

"Lord God, how I missed you."

"I missed you too, John."

"How much?" he demanded. "Show me how much you missed me!"

Laughing, she held up her fingers about half an inch apart.

"Heartless little wench!" His fingers dug in to tickle her, then suddenly his laughter fled and his face hardened with need. He slid her slowly down his body until her feet touched the carpet, then he cupped her face with reverent hands and his mouth covered hers in a kiss that was fierce with pent-up demand.

His lips were warm and tasted of brandy; his male scent, a mixture of leather, tobacco, and heather, was intoxicating. He kissed her hungrily, murmuring love words, for half an hour, before they drew apart and it came back to them where they were. He slipped his arm about her, and they began to wander through all the elegant chambers of the newly built mansion. At least once in every room, John pulled her into his arms to let his fingers run wild through her golden curls or glide his hot lips along her neck. If they encountered a mirror, he pulled her before him so she could watch him cup her breasts possessively, while she rubbed her bottom against his arousal, teasing and tempting each other to the limits of their endurance.

When they came to the magnificent spiral staircase, John swept Elizabeth into his arms and carried her up to the bedchambers. His lips playfully nuzzled her ear. "If I had my way, I'd do this every night of your life." He stepped into the newlyweds' chamber, with its marble fireplace and big curtained bed, and stopped dead in his tracks, wishing with all his heart it could be their bedchamber tonight. He set Elizabeth on her feet, and together they retreated, knowing the room's intimacy was too overwhelming for them in the vulnerable state they were in tonight.

John looked down ruefully. "I wish we were in Kent tonight."

She rubbed her cheek against his shoulder wistfully. "The lady in gray will be standing at the window, waiting for her lover."

"You are my lady in gray." His brushed his fingertips across her cheek. "I wish you were waiting at the window for me tonight."

They looked down and laughed. Dandy was sitting watching them with his head cocked on one side, and it brought them out of their wishful fantasy.

"Will and Charlie look extremely happy together."

"They are," she agreed. "In spite of the duchess's disapproval of the marriage, they are a well-matched couple in every way."

Charlie watched them descend the staircase with their arms entwined about each other. "Did Beth show you the nursery?"

"Nursery? Do you plan on a family soon?"

"Sooner than you think." Charlie laughed as her husband joined her. "I'm already breeding."

"Well, congratulations, you old Devonshire Dog! Your appointment should have been Master of the Bedchamber, not Master of the Horse."

"Oh, he's both . . . quite a stallion," Charlie said with a wink.

Elizabeth blushed, and it was brought home to John just how innocent she was. He lifted her fingers to his lips, knowing he was a lucky man. He was the one who would continue to initiate her in the rites of love, and he was in an agony of anticipation.

The four enjoyed an intimate dinner filled with toasts to the newlyweds and a good deal of companionable laughter.

"I'm so glad you could come tonight. You are our very best friends," Charlie declared.

"I almost didn't. Maria went to the theater with George Coventry, and Mother wanted me to join them. I said you needed me to help you plan your first entertainment as a married lady."

"Why, that's a splendid idea! I don't know why I didn't think of it myself. What do you think, Will?"

"You'd like to throw a party a week from this Saturday night?"

"Yes! Oh, I know, a masquerade party! What do you say, Beth?"

"Well, I don't have a costume," Elizabeth said hesitantly.

"Think of the fun you'll have creating one," Charlie declared. "Will, I want enough plants brought from Chiswick to fill our conservatory, and we'll borrow footmen from Devon-shire House."

Will lifted his hands in helpless appeal to John and Eliza-beth. "What can I say? She rules the roost like a termagant!"

Charlie confided to Beth, "I've always wanted to disguise myself as a male. I imagine myself in a tie-wig, wearing a black formal suit so that I could circulate among the men and hear what they say when they think no ladies can hear them."

Beth thought of the many times she had dressed as a boy while rehearsing the male role in a play. "Why don't you?"

"I couldn't possibly! People would gossip, and I would em-barrass my husband. It would give my mother-in-law just cause to hate me."

Elizabeth and Charlie spent the next hour making plans for the party, while Will and John talked quietly, enjoying each other's company. At a sign from Will, John stood and stretched. "These children should be abed. I'm taking you home."

"Oh, I couldn't . . . Mother—"

"—will still be at the theater. Come, I'm not taking no for an answer."

John told his driver, who had spent the evening in the warm kitchen eating the same food as his master had been served abovestairs, "Great Marlborough Street."

Inside the carriage, Elizabeth almost asked him about Lady Mary Montagu, but fear held her tongue. She didn't want to spoil the perfect evening. Eventually she would find out the truth of their relationship, but tonight it was better not to know. Elizabeth, enfolded in John's arms, allowed his warm, com-pelling presence to engulf her. When his possessive hands slipped inside her cloak, she led his fingers to the place where she had sewn his military button in the lining. "I touched it a thousand times while you were gone."

His hand moved up to cup her breast. "In my dreams, I've touched this a thousand times. Do you dream of me, Beth?"

"Yes. I sometimes dream about us swimming in the loch."

"I can never look at water without becoming aroused." His arms tightened, and his lips pressed kisses into her lovely golden hair. "I wish I could take you home with me tonight."

"I love Combe Bank," she said softly. "Is that where you are going tonight?"

"Yes, but I shall be back next Saturday for the party," he promised. The carriage ride was far too short. He wanted more, he needed more, and he intended to have more. His mind was busy conjuring plans for Saturday night's masquerade. In costume it should be a simple matter to slip away without detection. He knew he couldn't spirit her all the way to Sundridge, but he did have a town house just minutes away in Half-Moon Street.

Chapter Seventeen

A few days later when Bridget and Maria received the hand-delivered invitations for Lady Hartington's ball at Burlington Gardens, Elizabeth apologized. "I'm sorry, but I couldn't dissuade Charlie from deciding on a masquerade ball."

"Sorry?" Maria exclaimed, "I think it's exciting!"

"But it will mean the expense of costumes," Elizabeth said.

"Not at all! What the devil is the point of having the star of Drury Lane as your friend if she can't cough up some costumes?" Bridget asked with her usual expediency. "I shan't be going cap-in-hand this time but as a *lioness* of Society."

Later that day the Gunning ladies were given *carte blanche* of the theater's wardrobe department in exchange for Bridget's promise that Elizabeth would wangle an invitation to the party for Peg Woffington and David Merrick.

"Merrick and I are acquainted with the Devonshires. It's not as if we were strangers. And of course we won't be able to attend until late, after our performance," Peg explained.

Elizabeth knew it would be easier for her to ask Charlie than to say no to her mother.

Because of her red hair, coupled with her delusions of grandeur, Bridget decided that she would make a magnificent Queen Elizabeth. She picked out a starched neck ruff and a purple brocade gown whose sleeves were sewn with a profusion of glittering glass beads.

Maria spied a silvery tulle whose low-cut bodice and di-

aphanous cape were trimmed with white fur. It had been used
in a performance of *The Snow Maiden,* and she kept the
wardrobe mistress busy for an hour searching out the icicle-
hung headdress that went with it.

The moment Elizabeth saw the black gown with its bodice
of black feathers, it reminded her of Leda, who had been turned
into a swan. The headpiece had its own mask, all fashioned
from black feathers, and she hoped her mother wouldn't voice
disapproval, as she usually did over the choices Elizabeth
made. Bridget, however, was too absorbed in Maria's costume
to give hers more than a glance.

"Thank you, Peg, and we shall see you on Saturday night."
Bridget kissed the air and herded her daughters from the theater.

When they arrived home, Elizabeth sent off a note to Charlie, and Bridget insisted that Maria write a *billet-doux* to
Coventry to make certain he would be attending the masquerade ball. During the following days it seemed to Elizabeth that
her mother and Maria constantly had their heads together, whispering and plotting something or other, from which she was
happy to be excluded.

A couple of days before the party, Elizabeth was surprised
when her mother asked her to describe in detail Burlington Gardens, then gave her pencil and paper and told her to draw a
floor plan of the mansion showing all the chambers adjacent to
the ballroom. She was also surprised that Bridget was not badg-
ering her husband to escort her. It almost seemed as if she
didn't want him to join them. Elizabeth concluded that her
mother would rather he try to win money to buy them their own
carriage.

At Sundridge, John Campbell inspected the repairs on his
tenant farms. January and February were quiet months in rural
Kent. This would change once spring arrived, when the vast
acreage of hop vines would be pruned then fertilized.

He read his correspondence from Argyll and penned a report
to the king and another to the king's son, the Duke of Cumberland, advising that the Highland recruits wintering in Glasgow
would be fully trained and ready for duty in March. Then he answered a letter from his brother, Henry, whose infantry regi-

ment was patrolling the border connecting the Netherlands to England's enemy, France. John regaled him with an amusing account of the Christmas festivities at Inveraray and emphasized how much they had all missed his wicked practical jokes and depraved humor. He omitted any reference to the Highlanders he had recruited for the king, in case the correspondence fell into the hands of the enemy.

On Friday, he went up to London to make preparations for Saturday night. For the masquerade ball, he planned to wear neither his military uniform nor his Argyll kilt, since both would make him too conspicuous. Instead, John decided to wear black doublet and breeches beneath a black cloak. A black panther mask from a long-ago Venetian *carnival* would complete his disguise.

When Saturday arrived he ordered flowers for Half-Moon Street, asked his cook to prepare a simple supper of lobster and champagne, and gave the servants the night off. He made sure he was one of the first to arrive at Burlington Gardens and was pleased when Will didn't recognize him.

John stationed himself where he could observe those arriving, since he had no idea what costume Elizabeth would be wearing. The house began to fill rapidly with guests, and it was only because Bridget Gunning had chosen to masquerade as someone so like herself—and there was no disguising Maria's silver-gilt beauty—that he realized the female in black was Elizabeth. Her golden tresses hidden beneath the feathered headdress, coupled with the mask concealing her exquisite beauty, made her impossible to identify away from the other members of her family.

The ladies were soon swallowed by the crowd, though Elizabeth seemed to hang back, hesitantly looking for someone. John came up silently behind her. "Leda will not be joined by Jupiter tonight."

She turned slowly, looked up at him, and whispered sensually, "Your animal magnetism attracts me. I am unable to resist touching you." She slid her hand beneath his black cloak and ran her fingers over the musculature of his chest.

Through the slits in the mask, her eyes glittered with a recklessness he had never before seen in her. He took firm hold of her roaming hand and reversed their direction, walking away from the ballroom rather than toward it. Her eyes became wary.

"Where are you taking me?"

"A swan is fitting prey for a panther. I have stalked you and captured you. Now I intend to drag you to my den and devour you."

"I don't dare leave . . . Mother is here."

"No one will even notice. I'll bring you back in a few hours." His predatory glance swept over her feathered breast. "After I've plucked you!"

Elizabeth gasped at the wicked devil's promise, then her eyes glittered like amethysts. "Pledge we won't leave London?"

"I promise. I also promise you pleasure."

She took a deep breath and nodded, unable to speak. Suddenly, she was so filled with excitement she wanted to scream and allowed him to lead her where he chose. Handclasped, they slipped from Burlington Gardens unnoticed and ran toward his waiting carriage.

The host and hostesses wore magnificent medieval costumes; Charlie's veiled steeple headdress lent her needed height and Will's long, muscled legs were showcased in knightly hose. Michael Boyle, with wide shoulder padding and red beard, came as King Henry VIII, and George Coventry was dressed as a cavalier. Whoever had told him he looked dashing had lied.

Maria Gunning found George drinking a toast to Cat Cavendish and the newly titled Lord Duncannon, who were telling all and sundry of their engagement. She made coy, thinly disguised allusions about how she too longed to be a June bride, like Cat, to which George seemed oblivious. She clung to him like a cocklebur when they repaired to the ballroom, and after she had one dance with the young Prince of Wales, rushed back to Coventry's side as if she could not bear to be separated from him.

George, more flattered than he had felt in weeks, hoped that perhaps tonight would be his lucky night. Feeling positively *cavalier* when Maria brushed against him for the second time in as many minutes, he murmured, "I have my carriage outside, Maria. Would you like to go for a ride?"

"I much prefer to stay and dance, my lord, but later perhaps I could be persuaded to let you drive me home . . . alone."

His arousal lengthened and hardened at the promise, and beads of sweat rose on his forehead along the edge of his Charles II wig. "It's devilish warm in here."

"Yes, why don't we go and get a drink, before my icicles start to melt?" *Mother said to make sure he drank a lot tonight.*

George took her fingers to his lips. "It is your heart I am longing to melt, Maria."

"You have already melted my heart, George. Would you like to feel?" She took his hand and pressed it to her breast, where the white fur ended and an expanse of creamy skin began.

Maria accepted a glass of wine but goaded George to stronger spirits. "Cavaliers were *real* men, who drank *real* liquor." She took a glass of whiskey from the footman's tray and lifted it to his lips. "I warrant you have a strong head for drink, my lord."

"It is you who goes to my head, Maria. You intoxicate me."

"You say the most romantic things, George." She saw her mother with the Princess of Wales and raised her eyebrows in a question. Bridget shook her head, and Maria remembered that her mother had told her not to make her move until Peg Woffington arrived. "Let's go back and dance, George. I long to feel your arms about me."

At the cozy town house in Half-Moon Street, John and Elizabeth sat across from each other at a small table before the fire. He picked up a lobster tail and extracted it from its shell. Then he dipped a succulent piece in drawn butter and lifted it to her lips.

She closed her eyes in appreciation. "Mmm, ambrosia."

"Most fitting for a goddess."

"I forgot Leda was a goddess."

"Not Leda . . . the goddess I refer to is Elizabeth."

Her eyes shone with love. "Why do you always feed me?"

"To whet your appetite for other things . . . for me."

"I'm always hungry for you." She licked the butter from her lips and lifted her napkin. "I mustn't drip on my feathers."

"No." He moved around the table and began to unfasten the

buttons on the back of her gown. His lips brushed her ear. "I told you I would pluck you. Stand up."

She obeyed, but her knees felt weak as water. When they had first arrived, he had removed her mask and feathered head-dress, freeing her hair, so that he could play with it as it cas-caded about her shoulders. Now he removed the feathered gown and carefully laid it aside for safekeeping. Then he pulled her down into his lap and commenced feeding her lobster, kiss-ing the butter from her lips between bites.

She wore only a tiny busk that cupped her breasts and a half petticoat from the waist down. His hand slid up inside the shift to stroke the silken skin on the inside of her thighs where her stockings ended. To distract her he lifted the glass of cham-pagne to her lips. The moment she took a sip, he slid a finger into her tight sheath and thrust in and out until she moaned with pleasure.

Once he had brought her to her first peak of arousal, he re-moved his hand. Then he lifted his fingers to his mouth and tasted. "Mmm, ambrosia."

She buried her face against his shoulder, aghast yet de-lighted that he thought her body delicious. "John, you are so wicked!"

He lifted her chin and looked into her eyes. "Not wicked, love, just enchanted by everything about you." Their food was forgotten as he removed her busk and petticoat then shed his own garments. He carried her to his bedchamber, laid her on the bed, then spread her glorious hair across the pillows. "You are so unearthly fair. To have you alone for a few hours is like par-adise."

"We cannot stay away too long. We mustn't fall asleep like we did last time."

John's mouth curved. "I promise we won't sleep."

The scent of narcissus and white hyacinths stole to her as he made love to her with his eyes. He lifted her foot and dropped a kiss upon her instep, then the slow, hot glide of his lips moved upward, kissing every inch of her skin until her body hungered for him. When he stretched out beside her, she was reeling from his foreplay and the overwhelming intensity of his dark beauty. He took possession of her lips and showed her how to make achingly perfect love with her mouth.

His arms held her tightly as he rolled with her until she was above him in the dominant position. "Straddle me." He felt his pulse beat in his throat and the soles of his feet. When his rigid cock lay in her hot cleft, he knew that one driving thrust would take him deep inside her. His jaw turned to iron as he controlled the savage urge to impale her. "Love me, Beth."

She bent forward until her hair tumbled over the muscles of his shoulders and chest. She felt him buck as the rough slide of her tongue thrust deeply into his mouth. Then she heard herself moan as his hands cupped her bottom and his fingers dipped into the cleft of her bum cheeks. She rubbed her hot center back and forth along his shaft in a tantalizing rhythm that drove them both to the edge of delirium.

"Take me inside you."

His words brought her back from the brink. *We mustn't make a baby. That's what Will did to Charlie!*

Without going inside, he thrust once along her cleft. He continued the movement, and her thighs tightened about his hips. She threw back her head as a wave of pleasure swept her body from her breasts to her toes. Her climax was strong and drawn out as ripple after ripple pulsated deep inside her sheath and up into her belly. Then she collapsed onto his hard body.

His possessive hands caressed her back with long sensual strokes, circling her bottom cheeks with the tips of his fingers, while his marble-hard cock throbbed against her sensitive mons and his lips feathered kisses into the tousled curls at her brow. He whispered love words designed to inflame her desire to the point where she would yield to his body's demands. When he felt her tongue lick his flat nipples and she began to nip his flesh with tiny love bites, he quickly rolled her body beneath his and he straddled her in the dominant position.

He gazed down at her lovely face, saw her eyes smoky with passion, her lips half parted and swollen from his kisses, and knew she lay in silken torment, aching for fulfillment. Every instinct told him that this was the perfect moment to make her his. He reached down and spread her hot cleft apart with his thumbs, then thrust the blood-proud head of his shaft slowly but firmly into her scalding sheath. "Open for me, love . . . wrap your legs about me."

With a small whimper she obeyed, arching against him with

a need for she knew not what. For a frightening moment the pressure inside her seemed too much . . . he was too big, too hard, too thick for her slim body. She gasped for breath, then miraculously he slid all the way inside her and held still. Amazingly she loved the fullness and the weight of him, and when he covered her mouth with his and thrust his tongue in deep, matching what he had done with his cock, she moaned with pure sensual pleasure.

He moved slowly at first, then unable to help himself, began to plunge savagely with hot, drugging strokes until the night exploded. Fire snaked through his groin, and he spilled with a primal growl deep in his throat. They lay still, pulsating together in a mating that had been cataclysmic in its perfection.

With a groan he rolled his weight from her and gathered her close.

His lips reverently brushed her temple. "Did I hurt you, love?"

"Yes . . . no . . . I wanted to scream with pleasure," she panted.

"You did, sweetheart." His arms tightened protectively. "I don't think I can live without you. I want you to come and live with me at Sundridge. Do you think you could be happy there?" He placed his fingers over her lips. "No, don't answer now. I want you to think about this very carefully."

Elizabeth's heart was singing with love and happiness as John bathed and dressed her. Then, her eyes slumberous with newly awakened sensuality, she watched him put on his black clothes. He tucked her hair beneath the black feathered headdress, and when he slipped a white flower into her *décolletage*, she lifted her lips for one last lingering kiss before they returned to the masquerade.

Peg Woffington and David Garrick came to the party as soon as they came off stage at Drury Lane. They did not change from the costumes they wore in *The Rival Queens*. Garrick made a beeline for Will Cavendish, whom he already knew, and Peg had no difficulty recognizing Bridget. "We look like rival queens," she jested.

"We shall never be rivals. We are best friends. Do me a favor, Peg, and stick close to me, then follow my lead."

The actress spotted Maria with a proprietary hand on the Earl of Coventry's sleeve and waved to her, then laughed as Bridget also waved. "I don't see Elizabeth."

"The silly girl is no doubt helping her friend Charlotte look after the guests instead of helping herself by husband hunting."

Across the room, Maria took her mother's wave as a signal and went up on tiptoe to whisper into her cavalier's ear. "George, the crush in here is making me feel faint. Why don't we find a secluded spot that is more private?" She took his hand and led him from the ballroom. They passed through a small chamber being used tonight as a cloakroom, then Maria opened the door to the dimly lit conservatory and led her eager partner inside. She hadn't taken him too far into its green depths before she reached out to stroke the bulge in his breeches. "I love your costume, George. Cavaliers were so . . . rampant."

"Maria," he gasped, "you make me feel rampant." He pulled her close and rubbed his arousal against her soft belly.

She lifted her face, inviting his kiss, then sucked his tongue into her mouth. After a moment she pulled her mouth away and caressed her breasts suggestively. "In those days, ladies' gowns were cut deliberately low so that a gentleman could lift out her puppies and play with them."

In a trice, George eased the silvery gown from her shoulders, and before it fell to her waist, he had her puppies in his hands, stroking and fondling them. Then he dipped his head and captured a little pink nose in his mouth.

The conservatory door opened and Maria gasped, "Mother!"

Stunned, George stared into the accusing eyes of a regal Elizabeth Tudor and feared the Tower of London.

Bridget yanked Peg into the conservatory. "Shut the door quickly before the world sees my innocent daughter being *ravished*!"

She staggered back in a momentary faint into Peg's arms.

Peg thought that both Bridget and Maria had missed their calling by not following through on a stage career.

George stepped away from Maria and moved as a supplicant toward an outraged Bridget. "My dear Mrs. Gunning, I would never ravish your daughter. I *love* Maria. My intentions have never been dishonorable, I assure you, madam."

Bridget recovered instantly and snatched the offensive. Staring him down, she demanded, "You intend to do the honorable thing?"

"Indeed . . . indeed, I was about to ask Maria to become my wife."

"Oh, George, I would love to be the Countess of Coventry!"

Maria's pets were back in their basket, tucked beneath their fur cover, and she looked the epitome of a virginal *débutante*.

"And the wedding date?" Bridget had not yet blinked.

"Er . . . perhaps Easter . . . yes, Easter . . . it's early this year."

"Early?" Maria puzzled. "Isn't Easter the same every year?"

George, startled at such a notion, found he could not bring himself to disagree with a Gunning lady on any subject just then.

"Yes, indeed, the same every year . . . right after Lent."

As if she were delivering a dramatic line onstage, Peg stepped forward and held out her hand. "Allow me to be the first to congratulate you, Lord Coventry. Your bride will surely be the most beautiful countess London has ever seen."

In a daze, George realized this was probably true. Gathering his wits to belatedly observe the proprieties, he looked at Maria. "I should speak with your father."

"No need for that, Lord Coventry," Bridget assured him, "I speak for my husband. We are delighted to bestow Maria's hand in marriage. Shall we return to the party? News travels so swiftly, I warrant the secret of your proposal will soon be out!"

The first person Maria saw when she returned to the ballroom was her sister, Elizabeth, in deep conversation with Charlie. She left George hovering at the entrance and rushed to her sister's side. "You may congratulate me," she said smugly. "George just proposed. I am to be the Countess of Coventry!"

Both girls kissed her and wished her every happiness. Charlie went to tell Will, and Elizabeth took Maria's hand and led her back toward George.

"Will my title of countess outrank Charlie's title of marchioness?" she asked eagerly.

"No, Maria, the pecking order is duchess, marchioness, countess."

"Damnation! Some people have all the luck."

Elizabeth took Coventry's hand. "Congratulations, my lord.

There's none I would rather have for my brother than you, George."

He took her fingers to his lips. "You honor me, Elizabeth."

Charlie found Will playing host in the supper room. "Your friend George just proposed to Maria Gunning!"

"Well, I'll be damned. Your party will be deemed a roaring success by the *ton*. Too bad you didn't get here a minute sooner. John just left. Oh, well, he'll find out soon enough. I must go and congratulate the bridegroom. Misery loves company!"

Charlie slapped him. Something she did on a regular basis.

After the ball, when Coventry drove Maria home in his carriage, they were far from alone. Elizabeth sat silently in a haze of happiness for both herself and her sister. She did not wish to steal Maria's thunder by mentioning anything about herself and John. She had lots of time, because John hadn't formally proposed yet, though he had asked her to think about living at Sundridge. She couldn't wait to tell him yes.

Chapter Eighteen

*W*hen the Parliamentary session broke for lunch, George Coventry, as usual, gravitated toward his friend and rival Hamilton. Since his engagement Saturday night, George had come to embrace the idea of marrying Maria Gunning, the most beautiful young lady in Society. The ten thousand guineas he would collect from his bet with Hamilton would be icing on the wedding cake.

"You didn't attend Will and Charlie's party on Saturday."

Hamilton gave him a look of disdain. "I accept invitations to balls but I am a fucking *Duke of the Realm,* George. I do not attend masquerades and play silly buggers by dressing in costume."

"I asked Maria Gunning to marry me . . . an Easter wedding."

"The devil you say!"

"Looks like I shall be collecting that bet after all, since you've made little headway with her sister. I'm surprised you've not snatched her away from Sundridge by now."

"Sundridge! Was John Campbell at the masquerade?"

"No, I don't recall seeing John."

"I have *never* seen him with Elizabeth Gunning. He wasn't dancing attendance on her at Almack's and at the king's New Year reception he escorted Buccleuch's daughter, Lady Mary."

"Before he went up to Scotland, John was completely enamored of Elizabeth. Trust me, James, I know when a man desires a woman."

Hamilton smiled inwardly. It whet his appetite to think of stealing the prize from his arch rival, Campbell, but he said repressively, "Half of London's male population, including the king, are enamored of Mistress Gunning, but my dealings have found her to be both shy and innocent. A far cry from other females I could name."

George colored, remembering Maria's eagerness in the conservatory. Then he sobered. She hadn't yet been eager enough to yield all, even after a proposal of marriage.

Hamilton eyed his friend shrewdly. It was obvious he hadn't yet plucked the flower or he'd be demanding his money. Saturday's all-night gaming session had proved far more productive than the masquerade ball. It had put Jack Gunning in debt to him for seven thousand pounds. But Hamilton knew he had no time to lose if Campbell desired her and if he was to win the wager with Coventry. Since losing was not in his repertoire, win he must, and win he would.

Bridget rushed Maria to the Bond Street *modiste* shops to equip her trousseau. She would open accounts for the soon-to-be Countess of Coventry so the bills would be paid by the earl once they were married. Emma went along to help carry their immediate purchases.

As soon as they departed, Elizabeth decided to return the black feathered gown and mask to Peg Woffington. The costume was an excuse to talk with Peg, since she was so much easier to converse with than her mother. Elizabeth walked the short distance from Great Marlborough Street to Peg's house in Soho Square.

"Elizabeth, my darling girl! I was just in the mood for a good gossip. Come and have some tea and we'll have a cozy natter."

"Thank you so much for the lovely costume. From the very beginning, I don't know how we would have managed without you."

"Well, obviously the costume did the trick for Maria, although I believe Bridget did a little prodding with her magic wand," Peg said with a wink. "My hat is off to your mother. She has pulled off a miracle! One down, one to go, my dear girl, what about you?"

"Well, there *is* someone I care about," Elizabeth said softly.

"Do tell! Or is it a secret?"

"It's sort of a secret. I haven't said anything to Mother yet. Actually, I want to see what you think before I say anything."

"Poor child. Bridget has you under her thumb."

You know that she bullies me because I am not her favorite. Peg poured the tea. "I am extremely flattered to have you confide in me, Elizabeth."

She took the cup and explained, "He isn't an earl like Maria's fiancé, but he *is* titled. He's a lord!"

"Really? Are you going to tell me his name?"

"It's Sundridge . . . Lord Sundridge," she said breathlessly.

"Sundridge?" Peg put her head on one side. "But Lord Sundridge is John Campbell."

"Yes, that's his name! Do you know him?"

"My dearest girl, all the world knows him." Peg's expression turned serious. "I don't want you to be hurt, Elizabeth. He cannot possibly return your affection seriously."

I have more than his affection. I have his love. "Why not?"

Peg got up, went to the bookcase, and pulled out a thick volume of *Burke's Peerage*. She leafed through it. "Here it is. John Campbell is the heir of the Duke of Argyll; the Marquis of Argyll, Kintyre, and Lorn; the Earl of Argyll, Campbell, and Cowal; the Viscount Lochow and Glenilla; and the Baron of Inveraray, Mull, Morven, and Tyrie of the Kingdom of Scotland. He will be heritable keeper of Dunstaffnage and Carrick, and heritable Master of His Majesty's Household for the Kingdom of Scotland."

"Argyll?" Her hand shook; the tea spilled into its saucer.

"His father is the Fourth Duke of Argyll. John Campbell will be the Fifth Duke of Argyll."

Elizabeth set the cup down; her face drained of all color.

"John Campbell will have to marry someone with as much wealth as Charlotte Boyle and a great deal more blue blood. You mustn't expect a proposal from him, Elizabeth. Dalliance perhaps, but marriage, never."

"It cannot be the same John Campbell," she said through bloodless lips.

Peg's finger moved down the page. "John Campbell, Baron Sundridge of Combe Bank, County of Kent, eldest son and heir of the Duke of Argyll." She glanced up. "Are you all right, my dear?"

"Yes . . . yes. I must be going. Thank you for—"

Somehow, Elizabeth found herself outside on the street. She took in great gulps of fresh air to keep from fainting. She knew she needed to sort out her tangled emotions, but as her footsteps carried her toward home, her thoughts were in disarray, her feelings were in chaos, and her assurance had completely vanished.

For the next two days she withdrew inside herself to a place where no one could hurt her. The swirling vortex of wedding plans swept up her mother and sister to such a degree that they did not notice. Then flowers arrived without a card.

Bridget handed them to Maria. "These are from your bridegroom."

But Elizabeth knew the narcissus and white hyacinths were from John. His message was clear. *I cannot live without you!* How foolish she had been to doubt him. Her heart ached with longing to see him, so when her mother and Maria went for an afternoon fitting of her bridal gown, Elizabeth gathered her courage and set off for Half-Moon Street. She was oblivious to the stares a lady walking alone in Mayfair received. It was a two-mile walk and by the time she arrived the afternoon light was fading from the sky. There was enough light, however, for her to recognize Lady Mary Montagu and her aunt as they left John's town house. Her doubts came flooding back, but she resolutely pushed them away as she lifted the door knocker. A servant opened the door and stared at her.

She blushed. "Elizabeth Gunning to see Lord Sundridge."

His eyes widened. "Forgive me, Mistress Gunning . . . your beauty—"

John came to the top of the stairs and, when he saw who it was, came down at full speed. "Elizabeth! Come up." He urged her forward with a firm hand at the small of her back then closed the door. "You should not be visiting me alone, in daylight." He sounded like a military commander issuing orders.

"But it's perfectly acceptable after dark when none can see me?"

"Not then either." He took her cloak, laid it aside, and tried to take her in his arms. "I'm only thinking of your reputation."

She stepped aside. "Yet it's perfectly acceptable for Lady Mary Montagu to visit you?"

"She had her aunt, the Countess of Carlyle, with her," he explained. "I take it for granted you know what is acceptable."

"Just as you take for granted that I know you are the son and heir of the powerful Duke of Argyll?" Her voice held an edge.

"Elizabeth, everyone knows my father is Argyll. Surely you—"

"Everyone except poor naive Elizabeth Gunning." She lifted her chin and tossed her hair back over her shoulder. "Naive enough to think you intended marriage when you asked me to come and live with you at Sundridge." Her heart stopped while she waited for his avowal that indeed he *did* intend to make her his wife.

"My own love, you have all my heart! But marriage is impossible because of my familial duty." He reached for her hands.

"Don't you dare touch me." She spoke with regal *hauteur,* as if she were delivering the lines of a play. She paced across the room then swept around and pierced him with an accusing stare.

"I'm good enough to *bed* but not good enough for an Argyll to *wed!*"

In the rustling sapphire taffeta, tossing her glorious golden hair about her shoulders, she had never looked more beautiful to John nor more desirable. He wanted to sweep her into his arms and master her. He had the urge to push her down on the rug before the fire, mount her, and ride her. He knew a need to have her yield to him and tell him she loved him. Her challenge was irresistible. He reached out and dragged her into his arms. "Damn it, Elizabeth, I know you don't have a castle in Ireland. I know you are dirt poor and that this is all a *charade!*"

She stilled in his arms. "And if I did live in a castle and was exactly who I say I am, would you marry me?"

"You know I could not."

"Then your remark was unnecessary, ungallant, and bloody unkind!" She drew back her hand and slapped him hard across the face. Violence was against her nature. She had never hit anyone in her life, save this man. And she had struck him twice. She tried to pull away, but he grasped her wrist and held it securely.

"Sweetheart, I mean you no dishonor. I adore you! I will give you anything you desire if you will come and live with me in Kent."

"And be your gray lady, waiting endlessly at the window while you lie to your aristocratic wife, Lady Mary?"

Her arrow pierced his heart. He loosened his fingers from her wrist. "Forgive me, Elizabeth." He waited for her words: *There is nothing to forgive, John. I love you.* But the words did not come.

"Do you realize what the date is?" Bridget had stayed awake into the small hours, waiting for Jack to return from gambling. At his blank stare, she answered her own question. "It is the month of February. February! Our lease is up on this house at the end of the month and no money to renew it!"

Jack thought of all the markers he had given Hamilton and felt trapped. "We'll manage somehow. Maria is marrying money."

"The wedding isn't until Easter, when Parliament has its recess. It comes early this year in March, but the lease is up in February! Where on earth will we hold the wedding? If the bailiffs put us out on the street, there will be no wedding!"

"We'll wait until the first of March, then visit the leasing office and convince them that we want to renew for another six months."

Bridget didn't look convinced. "There is no problem paying for all the wedding finery. I've opened accounts in the Countess of Coventry's name, and George will pay the piper. Maria is urging him to buy them a mansion here in London. His ancestral home is in Coventry, unfortunately. He owns a town house in Bolton Street, adequate for a bachelor but not for a countess and family. Perhaps if he buys a place soon, we can have the wedding there."

"It is not customary for the bride to be married from the groom's home," Jack pointed out dryly.

"Nor is it customary for the bride to be wed from the

debtors' ward at the Fleet, which is where we could be by Easter!"

Jack sent up a silent prayer that Bridget stayed in ignorance of just how much in debt they really were.

A few days later, Bridget was both surprised and delighted when she opened the note from James Douglas, Duke of Hamilton. It was an invitation for her and Jack to join him for dinner at his home, which overlooked the park at Grosvenor Place. She had no idea they would be the only guests, assuming his friends would be there.

Jack wasn't as delighted as Bridget and tried to get her to send their regrets. His efforts were in vain. On the appointed night he had no choice but put on his formal attire and beard the lion in his den, though he feared that, with Bridget on his arm, he would be between the lion and the lioness. The pair of carnivores would separate flesh from bone and devour his carcass.

When they arrived at the magnificent Hamilton House on Grosvenor Place and Bridget realized they were the only guests, she was overawed. Though she had been in opulent homes before, such as Devonshire House, she had been part of a crowd and found it easy to blend in.

Tonight was different. It was like starring in the lead role of a play that had only three actors, with the spotlight on her.

Bridget squared her shoulders, pasted on a confident smile, and sipped the expensive sherry Hamilton poured for her. When they sat down to dine, she replied to his small talk as best she could, dropping such names as Princess Augusta. She mentioned the princess's invitation to a Valentine's entertainment at Leicester House, to bolster her self-esteem. Bridget found Hamilton intimidating with his square, stocky build and pouched hazel eyes that made him look both shrewd and calculating. She wanted to throttle Jack, who was more interested in whiskey than conversation. He was as much use as a chocolate teapot!

Hamilton, like a spider, watched the couple who dined with him as if they had just entangled themselves in his web. He took perverse pleasure in their struggle with conversation and ornate cutlery and in their suffering through long silences of course after course. He assessed Bridget from behind hooded eyes. Her breasts were full, her mouth generous. She was no lady, but that's what would make her a good fuck, if she wasn't such a dominant bitch. He waited until dessert before he made his move. "You are no doubt on tenterhooks wondering what I want." He watched Jack squirm.

Bridget affected a laugh. "Not at all, Your Grace."

He hid a smile. "I want your daughter's hand in marriage."

Christ Almighty, if we'd only waited a few more days, she could have been a duchess instead of a countess! "Your Grace, Maria is betrothed to the Earl of Coventry. You must have missed the wedding announcement in yesterday's newspaper."

His look and his tone were sardonic. "I have no interest whatsoever in your daughter *Maria*."

Bridget sat stunned as a bird flown into a stone wall. *Elizabeth . . . he wants to marry Elizabeth!* She noticed that Jack's attention had finally been dragged from his glass. Her inborn expedience came to the fore. Hamilton was without doubt the wealthiest man with whom she would ever have personal dealings. And he wanted something that she had. Naturally, Bridget would let him have her, but at her price. She sensed his acquisitive nature and guessed he wanted to trump his friend Coventry in the bride game. "Elizabeth is very young, Your Grace. Perhaps an engagement . . . a long engagement," she suggested.

"Out of the question." His eyes were hard as agates; his tone implacable. "I wish to marry immediately."

"Your Grace, we have the expense of our elder daughter's wedding," she hinted. "The cost is high."

"Elizabeth's wedding will cost you nothing. It will be private and must be kept secret until it is a *fait accompli*. I'll deposit funds in your name—held in trust of course until the wedding."

"What is the figure you have in mind, Your Grace?"

"Three thousand pounds."

Bridget knew she would be a fool not to bargain. "Only three?"

He looked her directly in the eye. "Do not push me, Mrs. Gunning. I am prepared to cancel your husband's gambling debt to me of seven thousand, bringing the total to ten thousand pounds."

Bridget schooled her expression, but her thoughts screamed inside her head. *You whoreson, Jack Gunning! Your brains are in your cock and always have been. As usual, it's left up to me to be the man of this family! Once my assets are snatched away from me by marriage, I'll be out on the bloody street again.* She smiled at Hamilton. "The great honor you do my daughter almost persuades me, Your Grace. But as I said, she is extremely young to leave the nest. My daughter and I are very close. I do not believe she could manage without her mother just yet."

Hamilton, smelling victory, tossed back his brandy. "This house is immense. I have not even been inside the north wing in five years. What better caretakers could I ask for my young bride?"

Once the two main players had settled things to their mutual satisfaction, Hamilton sent the couple home in his carriage.

"I'll deal with you when we get home, Jack Gunning. In the meantime I don't want Maria to learn of her sister's miraculous good fortune just yet. It will obviously rankle her that Elizabeth is about to become a duchess, and I don't want Maria upset. Besides, she cannot keep a secret and the duke demands secrecy. As a matter of fact, I don't think we should tell Elizabeth just yet either. Not until he's put that money in our names."

"What if Elizabeth doesn't want to marry James Hamilton?"

"Don't be ridiculous! And don't you dare put odd notions into her head—she's odd enough. This is the golden opportunity of a lifetime, for all of us! We don't need to worry about renewing that wretched lease now. In fact, we don't need to worry about anything, ever!" Bridget, about to smile, changed her mind. "No thanks to you, Jack, you feckless bastard!" As the carriage turned into Great Marlborough Street, her face lit up. "By Jupiter, this solves the problem of Maria's wedding. She can be married from the new Duchess of Hamilton's mansion!"

Elizabeth had been silent and withdrawn since the devastating scene with John, and finally Maria noticed. "There's no need for you to sulk because I've received a proposal of marriage and you haven't. We've always known I would marry first."

"Oh, Maria, I feel only happiness for you. I believe George

is a true gentleman. I'm sorry I've been in a wretched mood, but it has nothing to do with you. It's a personal matter."

"Ah, then it must be about John Campbell. George told me about the rumor that he is expected to wed Lady Mary Montagu."

I don't give a damn! Elizabeth told herself fiercely. *Then why does it feel like a sword has been plunged into your heart?* her inner voice asked.

"Oh, and speaking of weddings," Maria enthused, "I have decided you shall wear pink as my maid of honor. When you go for your fitting, you'll die of envy when you see my bridal gown. It has a train and a veil like a cloud of mist. I have to run. George and I are going to look at mansions. I'm taking Emma along to make sure my eager bridegroom keeps his hands to himself."

With Maria out of the house for the afternoon, Bridget decided the time had come to apprise Elizabeth of her glorious future. "Come and sit down. Your father and I have some unbelievable news to tell you."

Elizabeth sat and cast a wary glance at her father. Bridget's announcements sometimes had a way of making the earth tremble.

Bridget took center stage. "You may or may not be aware that your father and I were invited to dine with the Duke of Hamilton a few days ago. The magnificence of his mansion on Grosvenor Place surpassed my expectations. You can imagine my curiosity over why we had been invited, but I never could have guessed the reason in a million years." Bridget raised her hands dramatically, like a magician producing a rabbit from his hat. "James Douglas, Duke of Hamilton, asked us for your hand in marriage!"

Elizabeth felt the floor move beneath her feet, and she gripped the arms of her chair. Her senses swam, and her mouth went completely dry. A voice inside her head screamed, *No! No! No! No!* All the fear she had instinctively felt when she first met him came rushing back to her. A picture of his stocky build and hooded, hard eyes flashed into her mind, and she knew he was capable of cruelty. She licked bloodless lips and whispered, "I cannot accept his offer."

"Don't be ridiculous." Bridget dismissed her words without a blink. "We have accepted for you since you are not of legal age. I know the thought of becoming Her Grace, Duchess of Hamilton, is overwhelming for you, Elizabeth, but you must become accustomed to it. I realize such wealth and title are beyond your wildest dreams, but the honor and the prestige, not only for you but for your whole family, is nothing short of a miracle. You are blessed, Elizabeth. This is a gift from the gods!"

Beth rose in such agitation that her chair fell over. She fled and did not stop until she reached the sanctuary of her bedchamber.

When Jack stood up to follow his daughter, Bridget said, "Leave her! You've spoiled her all her life. What Elizabeth needs is a good dose of ignoring."

That night when Maria came into their bedchamber, she began to chatter about the houses she and George had looked at. Beth, pretending to be asleep, felt deeply relieved when Maria gave up and went to bed. Elizabeth could not sleep, but lay wide awake fighting a fear that threatened to overpower her.

For hours she managed to keep thoughts of the Duke of Hamilton at bay, but eventually they penetrated through the barrier she had erected and began to overwhelm her. *I will never agree to marry him*, she vowed adamantly, yet underneath her defiant resolve a fear lurked that her mother's decisions would rule her life, as always. *I will not marry Hamilton! I don't love him, and I never could! When he asks me, I shall tell him the answer is NO!*

Gradually memories of John Campbell intruded and steadily, forcefully, implacably drove out all thoughts of Hamilton. Just before dawn sleep overcame her and Elizabeth began to dream. She was at Combe Bank, John's house in Kent. She was arranging yellow lilies in a blue-and-white Chinese jar. Joy and happiness danced in the air like dust motes bathed in rays of sunbeams slanting in through the leaded windowpanes. She turned, saw him standing with open arms, and ran, laughing, to be enfolded safely against his heart.

When Elizabeth awoke, she knew that her dreams had supplied the answer to her dreaded dilemma. It was suddenly so simple. She would go to John and tell him that she wanted to

live with him at Combe Bank in Kent. Under the powerful protection of Argyll, she would be able to escape the attentions of
Hamilton. She would also be free of her mother's domination.
The fact that John could not marry her no longer seemed the
terrible impediment it had been up until yesterday. She *loved*
him, and that was really all that mattered. It was a thousand
times preferable to live with a man without marriage than live
with a man without love. Later this morning they were going to
the dressmakers so that she could be fitted for her maid of
honor gown for Maria's wedding. Somehow, she would find a
way to slip away and go to John.

Chapter Nineteen

*F*or the past few nights John Campbell had slept only fitfully. When Morpheus did claim him, his dreams were filled with sensual visions of Elizabeth. Even while he was awake, she was never far from his thoughts, and since their angry parting, a growing emptiness had begun inside him. He had lingered in London, hoping against hope that she would change her mind and come to him. Today, he decided to return to Kent. It was February and signs that spring would be early were everywhere. He penned a note telling his steward at Sundridge to expect him and gave it to Robert Hay to post.

"My lord, this just arrived." His secretary handed him an envelope with the royal seal of the Duke of Cumberland.

John slit the wax with his fingernail and read the note. "I'm summoned to the War Office. I shouldn't be long. When I return we'll leave for Kent. Pack up my paperwork, Robert. We'll do the correspondence at Combe Bank."

When John got to Whitehall, he made his way to the Horse Guards where Cumberland occupied quarters next to the War Office. A guard in uniform saluted and ushered him inside. The moment the king's son, William, Duke of Cumberland, saw him he strode to his side. "John, I have bad news, I'm afraid. I wanted to tell you in person rather than have you receive it through official channels. Your brother and two of his men have been killed in action."

"Henry? Killed? But we're not at war!"

"Not officially. He was on a sortie along the French border. There was a skirmish. Captain Campbell and two of his lieutenants got separated from their men and were killed by enemy fire."

"Is there any chance the report is false?" he asked tersely.

"I checked immediately . . . it's been confirmed. I'm sorry."

John closed his eyes. *Dear God, not Henry. He was too young, too hungry for life!* He opened his eyes and looked bleakly at the man with whom he'd faced death so many times on the battlefield. "Could you arrange for his body to be shipped home to Inveraray?"

Cumberland nodded. "I've already done so."

How will Mother bear the loss? Then he thought of his father, who already shouldered the twin burdens of age and power. John cursed the Fates who had placed his brother too close to enemy lines. A soldier stationed in the Netherlands in peacetime was not supposed to lose his life. "Thank you for telling me in person. I'll leave for Scotland today."

Though Elizabeth enthusiastically complimented Maria on her choice of wedding dress at the *modiste* shop, her focus drifted elsewhere while she was being fitted for her pink maid of honor gown. All she could think about was seeing John. She would tell him that she would go to Combe Bank as soon as Maria was married because she was to be her sister's maid of honor. What if John wouldn't wait? What if he asked her to go before Easter? Then it would have to be today, she decided recklessly. If he wanted her now, she would go and never return to Great Marlborough Street!

Elizabeth saw that her mother was preoccupied looking at gowns suitable for the mother of the bride and was paying scant attention to her. She crossed her fingers and hoped Bridget's disinterest continued until she made her planned escape. Finally, her mother and sister were ready to leave and, outside the shop on Bond Street, Bridget hailed a hackney cab. Halfway home, Elizabeth took a deep, steadying breath and declared boldly, "I need some fresh air. I have a terrible headache and believe I shall walk home."

She heaved a sigh of relief when her mother hardly batted an eye as she rapped sharply for the driver's attention and told him to stop.

The moment the cab disappeared into traffic, Elizabeth turned and hurried in the opposite direction toward Half-Moon Street. Her heart lifted with every step, knowing that soon she would be with John. She would put herself completely in his hands, and he would keep her safe. Elizabeth ran up the town house steps and lifted the brass knocker. The door was opened by the same servant who had stared at her beauty. She smiled at him and tried not to blush.

"Lord Sundridge, please."

"Mistress Gunning, I am sorry, but his lordship left London an hour ago." He did not return her smile and looked most solemn.

"Oh, dear. Has he gone to Kent?" She tried not to let her disappointment overwhelm her; Combe Bank was only twelve miles away.

"No, mistress, he's gone home to Scotland." She felt as if the doormat had been pulled from beneath her feet. She saw the closed look on the servant's face and knew he had been trained to keep his lordship's business private. "Thank you," she murmured politely, outwardly composed but inwardly at sea. She did not remember descending the steps or walking down Half-Moon Street, but when she came to the corner, she stopped and asked herself where she was going. The answer came back: *Great Marlborough Street.* Elizabeth was devastated. She had nowhere else to go but home.

When Elizabeth left the carriage to walk off a headache, Bridget decided it would be an opportune time to tell Maria that the Duke of Hamilton had asked for her sister's hand. When they arrived home, she removed her bonnet and broached the subject carefully. "Your sister has been very quiet the last few days. It is because she is feeling overwhelmed."

"Oh, I know all about Elizabeth!" Maria removed her hat and fluffed out her hair. "She fancied herself in love with John Campbell. Then she heard the rumor that he was to wed Lady Mary Montagu, the daughter of the Duke of Buccleuch, and began to sulk."

"John Campbell? She's in love with John Campbell?" Bridget demanded, grabbing Maria by the shoulders. "What do you mean?"

"She met him at Dublin Castle, in Ireland, remember? Then she met him again at Chiswick and has been lovesick ever since. George told me that John Campbell is heir to the powerful Duke of Argyll in Scotland, and is expected to marry Lady Mary Montagu. Imagine Elizabeth thinking a duke's son would propose marriage?"

Bridget pushed Maria into the drawing room, trying to contain a feeling of panic. "Sit down. Now think carefully. Has Elizabeth been nauseated? Do you think she could be having a child?"

"No . . . no, I don't think so," Maria said in a shocked voice.

"Emma! Emma! Where is that blasted woman?" Bridget cried.

Emma came running. "Whatever is it, madam?"

"Your job is to *chaperon* my daughters! At Chiswick was Elizabeth ever alone with that John Campbell?"

"Absolutely not, Mrs. Gunning." Emma shot Maria a warning glance. "I made sure that Elizabeth was never alone with Lord Sundridge, just as I made certain Maria was never alone with the Earl of Coventry."

"Out, both of you," Bridget ordered. "I wish to speak with Elizabeth privately when she arrives."

Elizabeth's steps lagged all the way home. She felt almost as if she were sleepwalking. She didn't know what she could do other than wait until John returned from Scotland. She did know, however, what she would *not* do. She would not marry Hamilton.

When she opened the front door she saw her mother standing with her arms folded and a grim look upon her face. Elizabeth put her hand to her brow. The headache she'd pretended suddenly descended.

"Come in here, young madam. I've been waiting for you."

Elizabeth, who had thought nothing worse could happen to her, immediately realized she had been wrong. She quietly entered the drawing room and took the chair Bridget indicated. Her mother stood before her, seeming to take up all the space in the room. "Now I know the reason you coldly rejected the opportunity of a lifetime. You've been playing the whore to John Campbell! Have you given him your virginity, the only thing you have of any worth? Come, we shall go and confront him now!"

"No, I have not given him my virginity, and you cannot go and confront him. He has gone to Scotland," she said quietly.

Bridget heaved an inward sigh of relief and seized upon her words. "And do you know why he has gone to Scotland, you silly, naive girl? He has gone to marry Lady Mary Montagu, the daughter of the wealthy Duke of Buccleuch!"

Elizabeth felt as if a cruel hand reached into her breast to crush her heart. She closed her eyes against the sharp pain. *It's not true! It's not true!*

"I read it myself two days ago in the Society pages," Bridget lied. "The wedding of the two powerful families that will unite their clans is the talk of the *ton*." Bridget watched Elizabeth's reaction with satisfaction. "We will say no more on the matter. How providential that you have received your own offer of marriage to a Duke of the Realm."

Elizabeth, who was adept at repressing the anger her mother aroused, deeply resented being forced to be submissive. She longed to take the dominant role and scream, *I shall never marry Hamilton! Come, we shall go and confront him now!* But she did not dare use a defiant tone to her mother. She clasped her hands tightly to ease their trembling, then said politely and honestly, "I do not wish to marry the Duke of Hamilton."

Bridget's temper ignited. She lashed out and slapped Elizabeth hard across the face. "Seek your room!"

Jack Gunning, about to leave the house, had overheard his daughter's words and the subsequent slap she had received for uttering them. As Elizabeth ran past him, he saw the livid mark on her delicate cheek. Instead of confronting his wife, Jack Gunning decided to go and express his daughter's wishes to Hamilton.

He was admitted to Hamilton House by a liveried major-domo and made to cool his heels outside the library for quite some time before he was allowed audience with the duke.

"Just the man I wanted to see." Hamilton held up an envelope he had just sealed. "I have written out precise instructions for your wife. Make sure they are followed to the letter."

"I've come to speak to you about Elizabeth. She is not happy with the arrangements we have entered into for her marriage. My daughter is extremely young, Your Grace. I believe that she is somewhat overwhelmed. I ask that you give her time to become used to the idea."

"Are you aware that I have deposited money in your name?"

"I am, Your Grace, but—"

"Then you must be aware that Elizabeth is bought and paid for." Hamilton's eyes were as hard as pebbles. He stood up, walked to Jack's side, and handed him the envelope. "Follow these orders or be prepared to spend the next year in debtors' prison, Gunning. The choice is yours. Know that I can and will press charges."

Jack returned to Great Marlborough Street feeling defeated and cursing himself for a coward. When he handed the envelope to Bridget, he did not try to explain his visit to Hamilton House or his reason for seeing the duke. "If we don't follow his orders to the letter, he's threatened me with the Fleet. Hamilton will make a deadly enemy, I fear."

Bridget tore open the letter and scanned the instructions. "There is no need for us to be enemies, Jack! I know which side our bread is buttered on, if you don't. I realize Elizabeth is your favorite child and you want only what is best for her. But if the Duke of Hamilton desires her enough to get her at any cost, you know he will be good to her."

He clutched the straw she held out to him like a drowning man. "She'll never want for anything again. She'll be set for life."

The Gunning ladies were readying themselves for Princess Augusta's Valentine Ball at Leicester House. For once, Bridget paid more attention to Elizabeth than she did to Maria. "No, no, not the gold ball gown again. You have worn it to the last two receptions. Tonight I think you should wear the white."

"Perhaps I should stay home tonight. I have a headache, and I don't want to spoil your evening."

"I have the very thing for head pain. You are indisposed far too often lately." Bridget went to her own chamber and returned with a small bottle of laudanum. She mixed a couple of drops with water and bade Elizabeth drink it. "Hurry and finish dressing. Your father is escorting us tonight." She slipped the laudanum into her reticule. "Emma, come and help me with my hair."

When the sisters were alone Maria said, "You don't want people to pity you because John Campbell has spurned you and gone off to marry Lady Moneybags. Hold your head high, laugh, and pretend you are enjoying yourself tonight."

It was obvious to Elizabeth that her sister knew nothing about the proposal she had received from the Duke of Hamilton, and she was relieved not to have to discuss the matter. Elizabeth hoped and prayed that Hamilton would not be at Leicester House.

The Gunnings arrived fashionably late. The royal residence was decorated by gilt cupids brandishing bows and arrows in honor of St. Valentine. Elizabeth greeted the Countess of Burlington, who informed her that Charlie was suffering from breeding sickness and would not be there tonight. She entered the ballroom where every chandelier was hung with red hearts to signify the theme of love. She pasted a smile on her face but inside felt only numbness.

Leicester House had always been a bastion for the Tory members of government, and Elizabeth was soon surrounded by young men eager to partner the renowned beauty. She wondered why they were not dancing with Maria instead, then realized that her sister was being partnered by her *fiancé*, George Coventry. Her thoughts were rather muddled, so she stopped thinking and smiled and danced by rote.

An attentive gentleman escorted her to the supper room, but she could not recall his name. She refused all offers of food with a polite murmur: "Thank you, I'm not hungry." Elizabeth was mildly surprised when her mother placed a glass of wine in her hand.

"Drink up. It will put roses in your cheeks. You are pale as a corpse, Elizabeth."

She sipped the wine dutifully and seemingly did not notice any odd taste, but afterward experienced a numbness about her lips.

Her mother said it was time to leave and that her father had gone to see about the carriage. "What about Maria?" she questioned.

With a coy look Bridget replied, "I have given the Earl of Coventry consent to escort Maria home in his carriage tonight."

Her mother wrapped Elizabeth in her cloak and ushered her from Leicester House, then helped her up into a sleek black carriage. Jack climbed in, pulled the door shut, and the coach set off.

Elizabeth's eyelids felt heavy. She yawned twice, leaned back against the velvet squabs, and closed her eyes. When she opened them and climbed from the coach she was disoriented. They didn't seem to be at home, and none of the buildings looked familiar, yet her parents obviously knew where they were going. She saw a sign that said CHAPEL but clearly the building was not a church.

The door was opened by a woman who said, "Dr. Keith is expecting you. Follow me, please."

Once inside, her father stayed behind, while her mother followed the woman through two small rooms. *Is Mother taking me to a doctor because of my headache?* Then a man in a clerical collar stepped forward. "Welcome to Keith's Wedding Chapel."

Elizabeth blinked. Then she saw him. Hamilton stood at the far end of the room in front of an altar that held lit candles. Suddenly, she came out of her trance. *"No!"* She turned and fled.

Her mother caught up with her in the first anteroom. "Stop this defiance immediately, Elizabeth!" She took her by the shoulders and shook her. "We have promised your hand in marriage to the Duke of Hamilton, and the ceremony is to take place tonight."

"I won't marry him!"

"You are the most willful creature God ever made! I have sacrificed my entire life for you and done my utmost to find you a noble husband. My reward is ingratitude! Our lease is up, our money is gone, and we will be out on the street. You will ruin your sister's chance of becoming Countess of Coventry! If you refuse to marry His Grace, your father will be thrown in Fleet Prison for debt. You are an unnatural daughter to allow this to happen."

Elizabeth wrenched free and ran through the next room to

her father. "She says you'll be thrown in the Fleet if I don't marry him. Is this true, Father?" she cried wildly.

Jack took Elizabeth's hands and squeezed them, then he raised his eyes to Bridget. "Leave us alone for a few minutes." When he and his daughter were alone he said, "I won't lie to you, my beauty. I have enormous gambling debts, which Hamilton has most generously offered to settle. But we shall put that aside for a moment and consider only you. I want what is best for you, Elizabeth. Trust me, child. This is your destiny. Once you become Her Grace, Duchess of Hamilton, your future and ours too will be secure. To climb to such a height is beyond my wildest dreams for you. Do this for me, Elizabeth, and you won't ever regret it."

"Dearly beloved, we are gathered together to join this man and this woman in matrimony. James George Douglas, will you take this woman to be your wedded wife?" Dr. Keith inquired.

"I will." Hamilton's voice was emphatic.

"Elizabeth Gunning, will you take this man to be your wedded husband, to love, honor, and obey so long as you both shall live?"

Elizabeth stood apart, detached, watching Dr. Keith marry the couple who stood at the altar. She saw the girl in the white gown, her golden head bowed, and heard her whisper, *I will.* Vaguely, she realized that the girl was her, yet not her. She was merely a silent observer watching the ceremony. She heard the vows, but they did not touch her heart, nor touch her soul. She remembered Charlotte's wedding. The exchanged vows had been beautiful, promising to have and to hold, for richer for poorer, to love and to cherish. Her thoughts returned to the present as the Duke of Hamilton began to search his pockets.

Dr. Keith spoke up. "It is of no consequence. We are prepared for any eventuality, Your Grace." He produced a box and held it out to Hamilton. "Repeat after me: With this ring I thee wed . . ."

Suddenly, Elizabeth was no longer standing on the sidelines. She was at the altar beside Hamilton, who had just slipped a ring onto her finger. She heard Keith declare: "I now pronounce you man and wife." With the acrid smell of candle wax in her nostrils she gazed down at her hand in disbelief. She had been married with a brass curtain ring.

"Elizabeth!" Her mother came forward to embrace her and she recoiled. Hamilton took her hand and anchored her to his side.

"You will address my wife as Duchess or Your Grace." His tone was firm. Then he dismissed them. "We bid you good night."

To Elizabeth, everything had an element of unreality about it, as in the play *A Midsummer Night's Dream*. Hamilton helped her into the well-sprung carriage and took a seat opposite her. Though it was dark she knew he never took his eyes from her as they rode the short distance from Shepherd's Market to Grosvenor Place.

Elizabeth felt emotionally exhausted and physically numb, frozen as if her heart were encased in ice, yet fear kept her mentally alert and wary. Protectively, she refused to allow her thoughts to anticipate what might happen later tonight and instead focused on the present moment. When they arrived at Hamilton House, the duke helped her from the carriage and escorted her into the mansion. She blinked at the blaze of lights and saw that a dozen servants were gathered in the entrance hall.

"It gives me great pleasure to introduce my beautiful wife, Elizabeth Douglas, the Duchess of Hamilton. I know you will serve her well."

Each male servant bowed; each female curtsied to her and murmured, "Your Grace."

My name is no longer Gunning. I am Elizabeth Douglas— how strange. "Thank you for your lovely welcome." Elizabeth saw that the duke had a satisfied, self-congratulatory look on his face. He touched her elbow and led her up the magnificent curved staircase. A narrow-faced maid followed them at a discreet distance.

"You have pretty manners. I'm well pleased with you, Elizabeth." Implicit in his words were that she should keep him well pleased.

He led her into a lovely suite of rooms consisting of a sitting room, bedchamber, dressing room, and bathing chamber. The bedroom had a deep-piled, cream-colored carpet, and the walls were covered with pale blue silk. "These rooms will be yours, Elizabeth. My suite is in another wing where I won't disturb you. I keep late hours."

He signaled for the servant to come forward. "This is Kate Agnew, your ladies' maid. I shall leave you in her capable hands."

A tidal wave of relief washed over her. "Good night, Your Grace."

His eyes met hers. "I shall try not to be long."

Relief ebbed away, and she was engulfed by fear and dread.

Chapter Twenty

*J*ames went straight to the library to search his desk drawers. "Where in hellfire did I put those rings?" He had had the rings designed by the best jeweler, had taken delivery of them, then forgotten to take them to the chapel. "Bloody memory lapses happen too frequently of late." When he did not find them he went to his bedchamber where Morton, his valet, awaited him.

"Congratulations on your marriage, Your Grace." When he learned the duke would be bringing home a duchess, he had been cynical, expecting the new mistress to be a bitch of the first water. Downstairs, however, when he saw the beautiful, innocent girl, who could not be above seventeen, his heart went out to her.

Hamilton threw him an accusing look. "You let me go without the rings. Find them." He watched him open the top bureau drawer and take out a velvet box. He allowed Morton to remove his coat and his shoes. "Get my brown robe. That will be all . . . for now."

As he disrobed, he chuckled at the rarity. He hadn't undressed himself for the last two years. Didn't even remember arriving home in the small hours during that time. His coachman delivered him, then Morton put him to bed. He paid well for their services.

He donned the robe and opened the velvet box. The pigeon-blood ruby surrounded by white diamonds was perfect, just as his bride was a perfect jewel. He'd provide the setting that would show off her exquisite beauty, so that everyone, from the king down, would covet the prize he alone possessed. She was everything he demanded in a duchess—young, beautiful, soft-spoken, and innocent.

James refused to believe that his young wife aroused lust in him or decadent sexual desire. These things were reserved for whores. He never wanted her touched by carnality or base sensuality, because she would be the mother of his sons. He smiled with satisfaction. His chaste bride, as beautiful inside as outside, was perfection. She had just become his most precious possession. He slipped the box into his pocket and made his way to his bride's chamber.

Elizabeth, in a white silk night rail, her hair brushed into a cloud of gold, sat in the huge bed like a doll. As the duke sat down on the bed, her violet eyes widened, their black pupils still dilated from laudanum. She wanted to run from the chamber, from the mansion, from London—but her paralyzed legs would not move. She saw him open a velvet box, felt him remove the brass ring from her finger, then watched him slip on a gold wedding band followed by a jeweled ring. She gazed down at the red heart surrounded by glittering gems. *It's St. Valentine's. So many red hearts . . . the symbol of love. How ironic.* She said what he expected her to say and knew it would become a pattern. "Thank you. It's lovely."

"You have delicate hands. They were made for jewels."

She glanced at his hands. They were square with spatulate fingers, a sign of one who would have his way at any cost. She glanced away quickly; they were hands that could inflict pain.

"Elizabeth, you are extremely young and innocent. I must consummate the marriage, and I regret that I may hurt you. I understand that physical union is naturally distasteful to a well-bred lady but I'm sure you will endure it bravely."

Elizabeth was far from sure. They were strangers. James Hamilton had never even kissed her, nor did she want him to. Nay, they were more than strangers—they were adversaries. With growing panic she watched him snuff only some of the candles. She lowered her lashes so he would not see the raw fear in her eyes. She heard the rustle of his robe as he removed it then felt the mattress dip. She was shocked to find him naked as he moved over her. She tried to separate herself as she'd done in the chapel but could not escape. She lay motionless as he slid the night rail to her waist.

He gazed down at her as if mesmerized. She was unearthly fair and delicate, finer in every way than any other female he had known. Her skin was like porcelain, her flesh translucent as pearl, her breasts sheer perfection. He drank in her ethereal beauty like a man parched and reached out to stroke her softness. Suddenly, his hand stilled. If he caressed her, he'd lose control. If he allowed himself to slake his lust and lose himself in her body, all his power would be transferred to her. She would be the one in control. For long moments he let himself look without touching, then he drew her night rail back up to cover her breasts.

Elizabeth feared he would remove her night rail completely, but he merely inched it up over her thighs. Then his hands urged her legs apart, and he lay between them, breathing heavily. When he tried to penetrate her, she was fever dry and knew he was having difficulty. On the third attempt he entered her partway.

"Am I hurting you?"

"No," she murmured and bit down on her lips to prevent from crying out, determined to endure in silence.

He thrust farther, and Elizabeth doubted she would be able to endure his body inside hers. His rigid shaft would not be denied and, in spite of her resolve, she could not hold back a cry of distress as he seated himself to the hilt.

"I *did* hurt you." His voice held a note of satisfaction. "There should be pain, Elizabeth, when a virgin bride's hymen is penetrated. Don't hold back your cries."

A sudden panic engulfed her. *I'm no longer virgin. Dear God, what will he do to me when there is no blood?* She felt him begin to move. There was nothing tentative about the onslaught as he thrust forcefully. Though it hurt immensely, her pride refused to let her cry out. But by the time he spent, she had reached the end of her endurance. Her fists clenched tightly, and she became aware that the jeweled ring had slipped around her finger to the inside and was cruelly cutting into her palm. She squeezed her hand tighter, realizing it would draw blood. As she pushed the white silk night rail down to cover her thighs, she prayed desperately that the drops of blood would save her from Hamilton's wrath.

He rolled off her, but before he left the bed, he gazed down with hooded eyes, saw her tears, and smiled. "I *did* hurt you, but you were afraid to cry out." He kissed her brow. "Sorry, Elizabeth."

She heard the chamber door close and knew at last she was alone. She lay absolutely still, drained of all emotion. She did not dare allow herself to think of John Campbell or her heart would break.

Morton was astounded when Hamilton returned to his own chamber and began to dress. *The bastard is going out on his wedding night!*

It had taken the duke less than an hour to consummate the marriage with his lovely young bride. Then Morton realized that a virgin would be of little use to a debauched profligate like Hamilton. Though he knew he could not protect the young duchess from her husband, he decided to let her know that she had an ally in him.

When Elizabeth awoke the next morning, she realized with a sinking heart that it had not been a nightmare. It was very real. No matter how much she wished otherwise, she was married to the Duke of Hamilton. She was served breakfast in bed, then she took her bath. She saw Kate Agnew whisk away the night rail with the telltale drops of blood upon it and set out a new one. It too was embroidered with a coronet and the initials EH for Elizabeth Hamilton. Then Kate brought her a morning gown to wear.

"The tradespeople are waiting, Your Grace. Three dressmakers, a boot maker, a wig maker, and a jeweler. If you will go into the sitting room, I will show them in."

The *modiste* took measurements of her height, waist, and bust, then in quick succession Elizabeth had her foot, head, and even her wrist measured. The dressmakers presented books filled with dress designs for daytime and evening wear and showed her dozens of samples of material in every shade under the sun. The wig maker vied for her attention with his own designs and samples, while the jeweler knelt to one side trying to tempt her with a display cabinet filled with gem-studded necklaces and bracelets.

She cast a look at Kate Agnew that clearly asked for help.

"His Grace left instructions to choose anything you desire."

Perversely, Elizabeth did not want the things Hamilton's money could buy her. Yet instinctively she guessed that if she refused them, he would find a way to punish her. She turned from the goldsmith and began to examine the material. Silks, satins, laces, taffetas, tulles, and velvets ran the gamut from pale pastel through vibrant bold colors to deep rich jewel tones. She had never seen anything as lovely as the cloth before her, which had come from such far-off lands as France, Italy, and the Orient. Tentatively, and not without pleasure, she made some selections.

Just before noon the Duke of Hamilton strode into her sitting room. Ignoring everyone else, he walked a direct path to her.

Elizabeth stood immediately. She did not want him towering over her. She did not curtsy, but murmured politely, "Your Grace."

He lifted her fingers to his lips. "Good morning, Elizabeth." After gazing at her possessively for a full minute, he deigned to notice the others. He instantly took exception to the samples of one dressmaker. "These won't do at all. The quality is totally unacceptable. This lady is the *Duchess of Hamilton*," he said with emphasis. "Only the best is good enough for my wife." He turned to Elizabeth. "Show me what you have chosen."

Hesitantly, Elizabeth pointed to the apricot silk, the turquoise satin, and a black velvet. She realized her mistake immediately, when he rejected them in favor of his own selections.

"The blush-colored silk will show off your flawless complexion to perfection, and the dull gold satin, when trimmed with sable fur, will be a striking contrast with your glorious hair. I forbid you to wear black—it is too sophisticated, too worldly-wise."

Elizabeth knew it was the control, not the colors, that was paramount. She watched him select styles with extremely low-cut necklines, and he chose the material and shades.

"I have a luncheon appointment, so I'll leave you to it. Indulge yourself, Elizabeth. Whatever you desire."

She gathered her courage. "I desire . . . that is, I should like to visit my friend Lady Charlotte this afternoon."

His brows lowered, and he took her aside so his words would not be overheard. "I'd rather you didn't visit Lady Hartington today. The king's drawing room is in a few days. I've sent word that the Duke and Duchess of Hamilton will be attending. The Court will be agog to learn who my bride is, and I want to surprise them."

She lowered her lashes so that he would not see her resentment. "As you wish," she acquiesced.

Hamilton's luncheon appointment was with George Coventry, and he couldn't wait. He hadn't attended the morning session in the House, since he'd been out until dawn, but knew his friend wouldn't miss it. He spotted Coventry at their usual table.

"James, I'm surprised you weren't at Leicester House last night. Quite a crush. Mistress Elizabeth Gunning was in great demand."

"You enjoy taunting me, George. How long until your wedding?"

"Only three weeks. If you'll do the honors and consent to be my groomsman, we can make the final arrangements."

"Of course. It's only fitting since we will be brothers-in-law." He gave him a large envelope with the Hamilton crest on it.

"Brothers-in-law? Don't tell me you intend to follow my lead and ask Mistress Elizabeth Gunning to marry you?"

"She is Elizabeth Gunning no longer, George. She is Elizabeth Douglas, Duchess of Hamilton. We were wed in a secret ceremony last night at the wedding chapel in Shepherd's Market."

"You are jesting! Surely this is a hoax, James?"

"Look in the envelope."

George slit the wax seal with his thumbnail, expecting to see a marriage license. Instead, it was a silk night rail embroidered with a coronet and the initials EH. It had spots of blood on it.

"You bastard! You had to trump me, no matter what it took!"

"Don't be a poor loser, George. It's bad form."

"It's not the money, it's the principle of the goddamn thing!" He could not hide his disgust. "You'll have my bank draft today."

"That's civilized of you, old man."

"Yes, but don't expect John Campbell to be civilized when he learns you have snatched the prize while his back was turned."

"Anticipating his reaction gives me even more pleasure than anticipating yours did. What, you're not leaving, George?"

"I'm not hungry. You make my gorge rise."

John Campbell saddled a mount in Inveraray stables and rode out across Argyll, keeping to the well-worn tracks. He had been a soldier since he was fifteen, and commanded men for more than a decade; though battle had hardened him to death, he found it difficult to lose men under his command. But it did not compare with losing a brother. He had lost part of himself with Henry's death, yet conversely a part of Henry would be with him always. They rode together now across their land. It was not yet spring in the Highlands, but winter had loosened its cruel grip and the deep snows were beginning to melt. He spotted a red stag with a majestic rack of antlers and knew they would soon be in rut, seeking mates.

John had been amazed at how brave his mother had been at the news of her son's death. His father too had shown his mettle and his courage over the devastating loss. When Henry's body arrived and they laid him to rest, John had vowed to be strong for them. But in truth they had turned to each other, and it was their deep and abiding love that had carried them through and comforted them in their darkest hour. All his life he'd scoffed at love. Perhaps he'd been wrong. Perhaps, on rare occasions, it was possible for two people to fall and stay in love. As he drew his fur-lined doublet close about his neck, he envied his parents their marriage.

His duty to take a wife and beget an heir weighed heavily upon him now that his brother was gone. Though his parents had said nothing on the subject, his sister, Anne, had not been reticent.

"John, it is time you wed and produced an heir. You're the

last of the male line. It's selfish and immature for a man your age not to settle down with a wife and family. It is your duty, in fact."

Cynically, he wondered if she'd be pressing him if she had produced sons rather than daughters. "You always did have a penchant for the obvious, Anne." The moment he said it, John felt guilty. His sister too was mourning.

He filled his lungs with the icy air and lifted his eyes to a bank of dark clouds that was gathering ominously above. It matched his mood. Then suddenly, the sun broke through and a bright beam of light shone down, illuminating a craggy outcrop of rock that towered before him. It enlightened his thoughts. Life was fleeting and unpredictable—why should he waste it in a dreary, dutiful marriage without affection? For the first time he allowed himself to seriously consider making Elizabeth Gunning his wife.

Though her background was unimportant to him, his family would be shocked and disapproving for a pedigree was paramount to the nobility. But once it was a *fait accompli,* there would be nothing they could do about it, and eventually they might come to accept her. Tucked in his shirt pocket, the golden curl he had stolen from her lay against his heart. He missed her so much he ached from it. Was it possible that he had fallen in love? As he turned his horse back toward Inveraray Castle, he mocked himself for a lovesick fool. But he knew he'd return to London with all speed.

At Grosvenor Place, Elizabeth was being readied for Court. She had bathed, and her body had been powdered all over. Next she had sat in her shift in the dressing room for two hours while her nails were buffed and polished, her *maquillage* applied, and a specially trained *coiffeuse* styled her hair. From time to time the Duke of Hamilton came to approve the effect they were creating.

"Let me see her in the blush-pink silk," he instructed Kate Agnew, who in turn signaled two maids to begin the dressing. First came a boned corset that emphasized her tiny waist and thrust her breasts upward and outward most provocatively. Next came a full-skirted petticoat, then they lifted the gown over her head and stood aside so the duke could apprise their efforts. "No, that isn't the effect I desire. Try the ivory damask." He returned to his own dressing room where Morton, his valet, waited to shave him.

When he came back he seemed happier. "Exquisite." Yet still he wasn't satisfied. "Isn't there a wig just that shade of ivory?"

"May I wear my own hair, Your Grace?" Elizabeth asked softly.

He looked ready to grant her wish, then smiled. "No, the wig."

The *coiffeuse,* who had spent more than an hour on her hair, fitted on the elaborate ivory powdered wig without demur.

Hamilton handed Agnew a small key. "Try the ruby necklace."

When the duke returned he was dressed in satin breeches and an ivory brocade coat. He too wore a wig, and his outfit was completed by an ornate small sword. "Not the rubies. Get the pearls . . . not the short ones. I want the expanse of her breasts left uncovered." The creamy pearls fell in a waterfall from her indecently low-cut neckline to down below her waist. When Hamilton selected a beauty spot and placed it on the curve of her breast, Elizabeth blushed, vividly remembering the last time she had worn one.

He handed her an ivory fan and led her before the cheval glass. "You are perfect."

As she gazed at the creature in the mirror, she thought that Elizabeth had disappeared and someone else had taken her place. But she admitted that the effect of ivory and cream was arresting.

"I'll get her cape," Kate Agnew said.

"There's a new one on her bed," Hamilton directed.

The servant held the fur with awe. "It's ermine!"

"A Duchess of the Realm is entitled to wear ermine."

James made sure the royal reception was well underway before they arrived. The Spring Season had begun in earnest— everyone who was anyone had returned to London and, by the carriages crowded in the courtyard, obviously had flocked to St. James's Palace. At the doors of the presence chamber he gave their names to the liveried flunky.

"The Duke and Duchess of Hamilton."

The amazing announcement caused the crowd of courtiers to turn from the door where the king was to enter toward the new arrivals. Until this moment most had not known there *was* a Duchess of Hamilton and all were eager to see the paragon he had chosen. A buzz went up immediately as the ducal couple entered the chamber. It was followed by a breathless hush as their eyes fell on the ethereal vision in ivory. Someone whispered, "It's one of the Beauties!" The murmurs spread in a wave. "Hamilton has taken one of the Gorgeous Gunnings for his duchess!" People on the outer edge of the crowd, standing against the tapestried walls, climbed on chairs so they could get a better look.

King George entered and saw only his courtiers' backs. Loudly clearing his throat brought on a paroxysm of coughing that effectively reclaimed everyone's attention. The crowd quickly shuffled into a semicircle about the monarch, and he began a slow progression. He stopped before Hamilton, his eyes bulging out of his head when he saw who the duke was escorting.

"The lady graces our Court with her beauty."

"Your Majesty, my duchess and I are honored."

"Eh? What?" The king, glancing at the ermine cape over Hamilton's arm, realized its significance. Elizabeth went down into a deep curtsy before him, and his bulbous eyes became transfixed on the twin curves of creamy flesh displayed so enticingly for his pleasure. His anger at the marriage receded as he took her hand and kissed it. "Her Grace will always be a welcome addition to our Court." He fondled her fingers for a full minute before he raised her. "I claim the first dance, Hamilton."

"Elizabeth! I cannot believe you married James without telling me." Charlie, with her husband, Will, in tow, had rushed across the ballroom the moment the king relinquished her friend.

Beth looked into Charlie's eyes, trying to communicate her deep aversion. "I refused him, but my parents accepted. They gave me no choice!"

"Your parents made a grand marriage for you, Elizabeth," Will acknowledged before his wife said something inappropriate.

"My lady marchioness," Hamilton drawled as he joined them. "Will, it's good to see you. I hope marriage gives you as much satisfaction as it does me. Our small circle of friends will all have wives when George weds at Easter. All except John, of course, unless there is truth in the rumor that he eloped to Scotland."

"No truth whatsoever," Will said grimly. "Did you not hear that Henry Campbell was killed in action on the Continent?"

Elizabeth gasped. A loud buzzing began in her ears; she went icy cold then hot. The floor seemed to rise up and hit her in the face. She fanned herself frantically to keep from fainting.

"Young Henry? That's tragic news." He searched his wife's face. "Are you all right, my dear? Did you know the young man?"

"I met him in Ireland." *Mother lied to me! John did not go to Scotland to get married. Oh, John, my love, how will you bear your brother's death?* She had an overwhelming desire to find him and comfort him. The rest of the evening was a blur to her. People continually offered congratulations to the newlyweds. She danced, she conversed, and later she recalled that at one point the duke ordered, "Smile. You are the Duchess of Hamilton."

At midnight, the duke took her home in the carriage. "I wager you are the most beautiful duchess to ever grace the king's Court. I was the envy of every man who saw you on my arm." When they arrived home the majordomo descended the steps of Hamilton House, opened the carriage door, and helped her to alight. The duke remained seated. "Good night, Elizabeth." The coach departed with Hamilton inside.

Relief swept over her. She was exhausted from being on display and smiling for hours, but at least she knew she would be free of his dominant presence until tomorrow. He had only come to her bed twice since the night they were married, but the paralyzing fear that he would come each night never left her.

It seemed to take an eon for Kate Agnew to remove her jewels, wig, makeup, and gown, and ready her for bed. The woman hovered over her like a spider and reported every word she uttered. When she was finally alone Elizabeth walked over to the mirror and stared at herself. *Smile. You are the Duchess of Hamilton.* Tears welled in her eyes and slowly spilled down her cheeks.

Two days later, John Campbell arrived in London. He spent the afternoon catching up on business matters and dictating correspondence to his secretary, Robert Hay, and he thought about seeing Elizabeth with growing excitement. He was almost tempted to call on her at Great Marlborough Street, then thought better of it. He would much rather see her alone than in the presence of her parents. They would learn of his intentions soon enough if Beth agreed to let him court her. Instead, he made his way to Burlington Gardens.

Charlotte stood on tiptoe to kiss him. "John, we are so sorry about Henry. He was so full of life. It doesn't seem possible."

Will embraced him. "We are glad we knew him and will never forget the good times we shared."

"Thank you." John took Charlie's hands. "Look at you! You are absolutely blooming. I take it you highly recommend marriage."

Charlie's hand caressed her midsection. "My waist has totally disappeared. I shall look like a little barrel before long."

"You exude such happiness it makes me envious. To that end, Charlie, could you invite Elizabeth tomorrow so I can see her?"

Her face froze into an unhappy mask. "That would be impossible."

John looked from Charlie to Will. "What is it?"

"Hamilton made Elizabeth his duchess last week."

John looked at them as if he did not comprehend their words.

"Elizabeth is married to Hamilton," Charlie said quietly.

He stood staring at them for a full minute before he broke his silence. "I'll kill him!"

Chapter Twenty-One

*E*lizabeth's parents and sister now occupied the north wing of Hamilton House on Grosvenor Place. The move from Great Marlborough Street had been a simple matter of transferring their clothing and personal items, since they owned no furniture.

Maria, grass-green with envy that her sister outranked her, sat watching Elizabeth being fitted for yet another costly gown. "You may have a grand title and a magnificent mansion, but you won't have the one great advantage that marriage will bring me. You won't be free of mother's domination!"

Elizabeth's lashes lowered, concealing the thoughts and emotions that raged within. The first week she had been dispirited because she thought she had traded one gaoler for another, but when her mother moved into Hamilton House she felt despair. It hadn't taken her long to learn that Bridget reported every move she made to Hamilton. Now she had two people who intended to control her life.

"Elizabeth, your dancing master is here." Bridget swept into her daughter's suite with authority. "You can be fitted for the gown later. Maria, you too could benefit from the lessons."

Elizabeth protested. "I never have a moment to myself. If I'm not being fitted for a dress or shoes, I have a music or dancing lesson, and tomorrow I must start sitting for my portrait. I have enough clothes, and I already know how to dance."

"It is a privilege and an honor to have your portrait painted.

You are the *Duchess of Hamilton*! You can never have enough clothes, and your husband wishes you to dance perfectly. You know the social invitations have been pouring in because every hostess in London wishes to have a good look at you. Hamilton lavishes you with love and gifts, yet you seem indifferent. If you are not careful, the duke will start to regret this marriage. He is a wealthy and powerful man, Elizabeth. If you do not please him, he could make life hell for you, to say nothing of what he could do to your father and I. You should be ashamed of yourself!"

Elizabeth thought of the gambling debts and knew with certainty the threat of Fleet Prison had been real. "I'm sorry, Mother. I will try to please him." *Nothing short of perfection will please him.* "I will try to be a perfect duchess."

Maria preened. "George is besotted with me. Once we are married, it will be *he* who must please *me*."

"Most beautiful women know how to make a husband their slave through sexual favors. Your sister seems to be devoid of the sensual skills that come naturally to you and I, Maria. But I'm sure your husband will teach you all you need to know, Elizabeth. Try not to be cold. Remember that Hamilton owns your body."

He owns my body because you sold it to him! Elizabeth veiled her eyes and made a vow that she would never complain about her situation again. The last thing she wanted was pity. Her mother and her sister thought her the most fortunate woman alive because she had not only a grand title but enjoyed every material comfort that great wealth could provide. Elizabeth swore that she would allow no one to ever suspect that she was desperately unhappy.

You enjoy acting, so here is your chance to play the role of beautiful, pampered wife. Smile. You are the Duchess of Hamilton. "Come, Maria, we mustn't keep the dancing master waiting."

John Campbell, garbed in impeccable black evening attire, entered White's accompanied by his best friend, William Cavendish. He nodded curtly to George Coventry and Richard Boyle, who were playing faro. He was not surprised to see them and surmised that Will had alerted them that there would be trouble tonight. He sat down to play baccarat and noted with grim amusement that Will stuck closer than his shadow.

When James Hamilton arrived, he accepted the glass of whiskey proffered by a porter then came straight to the baccarat table, as John knew he would. The rivals greeted each other in a civil manner. George and Richard left the faro game and approached the baccarat table, closing ranks. Hamilton tossed back half the whiskey and set the glass down.

"Sorry to hear about Henry. My condolences to Argyll. How is your father holding up?"

"Amazingly well, under the circumstances."

"Reckless young fools, squandering their lives in vainglory."

Campbell's eyes glittered with dark fury. He picked up the glass and threw the whiskey into Hamilton's face. "You impugn my brother's honor, calling him a vainglorious fool! Captain Campbell had great courage, while you are too cowardly to wear a uniform. I challenge you, Hamilton. Choose your weapons."

Every man present knew the duel was about Elizabeth and had nothing to do with Henry.

Hamilton, taken off guard, wiped the stinging liquor from his eyes. He knew Campbell, who was taller with a longer reach, was formidable with a rapier. "Sabres," he said decisively. He turned to Coventry. "Will you act as second?"

Coventry accepted. It was taken for granted that Cavendish would act as second for Campbell. The men conferred and agreed upon Green Park at dawn. "I'll arrange for a surgeon," Boyle said.

"He'll need the services of an undertaker, not a surgeon," Campbell muttered through bared teeth.

After Hamilton departed with Coventry at his heels, Will said, "He chose sabres because of your reputation with a rapier and because he's heavier than you, but I wonder if he realizes your experience with a battle sabre?"

"No matter the weapon, he's a dead man."

"As your second it's my duty to ask you to reconsider, but I can see that's rather futile." Will checked his watch. "It's barely eleven. I'll be at Half-Moon Street by four o'clock."

Coventry walked briskly beside Hamilton to his carriage.

"James, it is in your best interests to cry off. Christ, did you see John's face? He looked like a feral wolf!"

"Ask Campbell to reconsider. I meant no dishonor to Henry."

"It isn't about Henry."

"I know that, damn you, George!"

"You saw him. I don't dare approach him with such a suggestion. I shall come for you at four o'clock. Have your weapon ready."

Hamilton surprised his coachman when he told him to drive to Grosvenor Place. He'd never taken the duke home at eleven since he had been in his employ. "Don't unharness the horses."

Morton too was startled. He took the duke's cloak and poured him a double whiskey. He wasn't yet drunk, but he didn't look well.

"I'll be with the duchess. See that we are not disturbed. If anyone comes, have them wait." He picked up the decanter and took it with him. Hamilton was not afraid. He was terrified. The duke entered his wife's suite and walked into her bedchamber without knocking. He saw the fleeting look of panic on her face before she could disguise it. This usually gave him a heady feeling of control, but not tonight. His control was in danger of slipping away. *You still control her,* he sternly reminded himself.

Elizabeth, who had been about to undress for bed, was gripped by fear when Hamilton walked in. They had attended a musical evening given by the new Prime Minister and his wife the Duke and Duchess of Newcastle, which was over by ten o'clock. Hamilton had dropped her at home then gone his own way, and she thought she was free of him for the night. When he dismissed Kate Agnew, her knees turned to water, and she sank down into a chair before the fire. She watched him pour and drink a glass of whiskey before he spoke.

"Did you know that I came into my dukedom at eighteen because my father was killed in a duel?"

"No, Your Grace, I had no idea."

"He fought Lord Charles Mohun. They killed each other . . . both of them died on the field. *The Field of Honor,*" he emphasized bitterly. "There is no honor in dying!" He poured another glass and held it up so the light from the fire reflected through it. "I have an overwhelming revulsion toward duels, Elizabeth."

"That is understandable . . . your aversion is to be expected."

He withdrew his gaze from the amber liquor and looked into her eyes. "What I didn't expect was to be challenged by John Campbell."

Her hand flew to her heart in a protective gesture. "Challenged to a duel, Your Grace?" She felt the blood drain from her face. *Dear God, I am to blame for this . . . they are fighting over me!*

"I want you to go to Half-Moon Street and ask him to cry off."

Her hand moved up to her throat. "I cannot go to him." *John must hate me! The minute he left London, you forced my parents to marry me to you. I cannot face him!*

"You can and you will." He drew close and loomed over her. He set down the glass and took firm possession of her hand. "This duel is about you, Elizabeth. I stole the prize from under his nose. Now he is mad with jealousy that you are my wife."

"But I am married to *you* . . . there is no need for *jealousy*!"

"There is every need. One of the reasons I made you my duchess was because Campbell desired you. Now that I own you, his desire will have doubled. You don't know much about men, Elizabeth, and that's the way I want it. The sheer pleasure in possessing an object of rare beauty is that other men will covet it."

I am not an object! You do not own me—you will never own the least part of me! "I cannot go to him, Your Grace."

"You must. I am deathly superstitious! Have you never heard that history always has a way of repeating itself? We are to fight with sabres. If there is a duel, we will kill each other."

Elizabeth felt her hand being squeezed cruelly. His spatulate fingers tightened on hers, crushing the delicate bones.

"Remember the night your father was wounded, Elizabeth? Surely, you wouldn't wish him to have another unfortunate accident?"

She thought of the night her father arrived home covered with blood and shivered as she remembered that Hamilton had been with him. "I will go. I will try."

He released her, and she rubbed her fingers to ease the throbbing pain. She saw the light of victory in his eyes. "The carriage is ready and waiting. He will be able to refuse you nothing."

Inside the coach Elizabeth began to tremble. The thought of seeing John filled her with panic. She loved him so much, and her heart ached that she was another man's wife. Somehow she must stop this duel. If John was killed, she would not want to live. If he was wounded, the blame would be hers. What would she say? What would he say to her? She suddenly remembered his military button that she had sewn into the lining of her cloak. As her fingers found it they stopped trembling. *It will be all right. John will make everything all right.* She relived what it felt like to have his powerful arms about her. It lent her strength. It filled her with courage. He would do what she asked because he loved her.

In Half-Moon Street the servant who opened the door looked startled, but the sight of John at the top of the stairs with a sabre in his hand propelled her up the steps.

"Elizabeth! What the devil are you doing here?" He led the way into the room where they had dined so intimately before the fire.

"John, I came to stop you from doing this thing."

He set down his weapon, removed her cloak, and stood looking down at her. He had thought of her as his. The next time he saw her he had fully intended to ask her to marry him. Now all his plans for the future had been snatched away. He felt as if he had taken a sabre thrust to the heart. John had never seen a woman more elegantly gowned in his life. She was a vision in pale lavender with a collar of amethysts blazing at her throat above half-exposed breasts. Her glorious hair had been styled by a *coiffeuse* and her *maquillage* was flawless. She looked a duchess down to her fingertips. His jaw clenched. "Did Hamilton send you?"

"Yes. His father was killed in a duel, and he is superstitious that history will repeat itself."

"He is right! History will repeat itself. I have every intention of killing him."

"John, you must not! You must cry off. Please!"

He could not believe what he was hearing. She was actually

pleading with him. Pleading on behalf of *Hamilton*! "Cry off?" His eyes hardened and swept her from head to foot with contempt. "I see. 'Tis obvious you enjoy being a duchess. I must do nothing to rob you of being the wife of the Duke of Hamilton."

"That's not true! I was forced to marry him. How can you say such cruel things to me?"

His eyes were hard, angry, and unforgiving. "You are the one who inflicted cruelty, Elizabeth. The minute my back was turned, you sold yourself to the highest bidder. What a bloody fool I was. I should have known the Gorgeous Gunnings stepped out of an Irish bog and came to London to secure their fortune. 'Tis clear you had only one purpose in mind: to seek out a nobleman with wealth and title and trap him into marriage. Seems I've had a miraculous escape!"

She was wounded by his hateful accusation, and her hurt quickly turned to anger. "And 'tis clear to me that *you* had only one purpose in mind: From the moment you saw me step out of that Irish bog you intended to seduce me." *And you succeeded. Damn you to hellfire!*

"Who seduced whom?" he asked with irony. "You are a born actress, Elizabeth, playing the role of beautiful innocent to perfection, while setting your sights on the wealth and power of Argyll. You wasted little time! When I didn't offer marriage you immediately moved to the next powerful man. Straight from my bed to Hamilton's. The Gunning sisters are the most flagrant pair of fortune hunters to ever set foot in London and gull Society."

She flew at him with passion, raking her perfectly polished nails down his dark, arrogant face. Her breasts rose and fell with her agitation. *My God, all men are created vile!*

He captured her wrists in his ironlike grip, forcing her hands from his face. "Beneath that gentle *façade* you hide the temper of an Irish wildcat," he said with contempt.

Her uncivilized behavior shocked her. This man had the ability to provoke her to madness. When he loosened his powerful fingers she withdrew her hands and lifted her chin with regal disdain. "It seems, Lord Sundridge, that we have both had a miraculous escape."

Elizabeth picked up her cloak. On the outside she appeared

serene, but inside she was in a total panic. Her midnight visit had gone wrong from the moment she arrived with her heart in her mouth. She had said all the wrong things, and they had savaged each other with accusations. He still intended to fight—to kill, or be killed. She made one last desperate attempt. "You are acting like a barbarian. Dueling on the so-called 'Field of Honor' has nothing to do with honor and everything to do with arrogant male pride."

John Campbell stood motionless for a long time after Elizabeth left. Finally, reluctantly, he admitted that she had skewered him with the truth. He had challenged Hamilton because his pride had been mauled. His arrogant, male pride. He had not offered Elizabeth marriage, he had offered her *carte blanche*. Regrettably, he had only himself to blame that she had accepted an honorable offer and become another man's wife. If he killed James Hamilton in a duel, he would disgrace the name of Argyll. Worse than that, he would bring scandal down upon Elizabeth. A need to protect her rose up in him, and it was greater than his thirst for vengeance. She had begged him to cry off. It was the only thing she had ever asked of him, and he could refuse her nothing.

Elizabeth dreaded returning to Grosvenor Place. She pictured herself jumping from the carriage and fleeing into the night, rather than facing Hamilton. Where could she go? The house in Great Marlborough Street was no longer leased to the Gunnings. She could take refuge with her friend Charlie, but come morning she would have to return to her husband, or embroil her friends in her desperate situation. She had sworn that she would allow no one to ever suspect she was desperately unhappy; besides that, Charlie was going into her fifth month, and Elizabeth refused to upset her. She gathered her courage as the carriage stopped at Grosvenor Place.

Hamilton awaited her in the vaulted reception hall. "Well?"

As she swept past him into the salon, all she could smell was whiskey. He reeked of it. She turned to face him, veiling her eyes so he would not see the contempt. "I saw Sundridge and asked him to cry off, but I am afraid my wishes had little influence."

"You dare return without dissuading him? The most beautiful woman in London, and you did not use your feminine wiles on him?" Hamilton's face was purple with fear and anger.

"I'm sorry." *Sorry I am married to a drunken coward who is not man enough to fight his own battles. Sorry I ever left Ireland and came to this accursed city. Sorry I am the Duchess of Hamilton!*

He lifted his arm in fury and backhanded her across her face. It was as if the night exploded. She saw stars and felt the searing pain in her cheekbone. Slowly, she got up from her knees and raised her lashes so that he could see her disgust. "Perhaps when Joshua Reynolds comes to paint my portrait tomorrow, he can leave out the bruises on my face. If you destroy my beauty, men will not envy you—they will pity you."

At four o'clock William Cavendish arrived in Half-Moon Street. "As second it is my responsibility to examine the weapon. May I have your sabre, John?"

"No need for that, Will. I have decided to cry off. Sorry to stick you with the distasteful job of calling on Hamilton and informing him that your best friend is a coward."

"Coward? You don't have a cowardly bone in your body, John. You are a total stranger to fear, and everyone knows it. It takes a great deal of courage to cry off. I expect you are doing it for Elizabeth's sake."

My God, am I so transparent? "It's after four. Better make haste to Grosvenor Place before Hamilton leaves for Green Park."

"He won't be that eager. He'll hang on till the last possible minute, hoping against hope that you will let him off."

Alone in her chamber, Elizabeth bathed her face with cold water, hoping it would take down the swelling. She did not want the humiliation of anyone in Hamilton House learning that her husband had struck her. She may live in a hell, but she vowed it would be a private hell. Presently, she heard a carriage stop outside and went to the window. She saw William Cavendish leave the coach and come to the front door. She was surprised that Will was involved in this, then realized he must be acting as second. How reckless and selfish men were to indulge in killing games. She stayed at the window waiting to see

Hamilton leave. Perhaps it would be for the last time. Yet, much as she loathed him, it was wicked to wish death upon him. Especially by John Campbell's hand.

To her amazement and relief William Cavendish departed without Hamilton. Did this mean there would be no duel? She realized that Will had brought a message from John—he had done exactly as she asked and cried off! Her heart did not fill with joy. Instead, she felt infinitely sad. It meant that in spite of the angry accusations he had flung at her, he still had feelings for her. *Ne obliviscaris. No, no. Forget me, John. Forget me.*

A short time later, she stiffened as she heard a low knock at the chamber door. There was no one she wished to speak with, not mother, nor sister, nor ladies' maid. She moved to the door. "Yes?" she asked guardedly.

"It's Morton, Your Grace."

She hesitated then opened the door a crack. Morton's voice was so low that she had to strain to hear the words.

"He's unconscious. Tomorrow, he won't remember much."

Her heart lifted with a ray of hope. Someone in the house wished her well. "Thank you, Morton," she whispered gratefully.

The next morning Elizabeth applied some of the white-lead face paint, which her sister constantly used, to conceal the purple bruise that marred her cheekbone. When Sir Joshua Reynolds arrived, her morning was taken up by selecting the most favorable setting for her portrait. Then she posed for the artist for more than an hour before he was satisfied that her hands were in the right position, her head was tilted at the proper angle, and her smile was just right.

It was the hour of noon before Hamilton made his appearance. He was in high spirits and acted as if last night had never happened. He set down the box he was carrying and opened the lid. "I want my duchess to wear this special robe I have had made. It falls straight from the shoulder and forms a train. It is decorated with ermine tails to show her ducal rank."

"What a delightful touch, Your Grace," Reynolds said politely.

Elizabeth repressed her shudders as Hamilton held out the sleeveless robe while she slipped her arms into it. He was playing the devoted husband, besotted by his beautiful wife. *Morton may be right. When he drinks himself unconscious, perhaps he remembers little.* She tucked the information away for future use.

Chapter Twenty-Two

*T*he Easter wedding of Maria Gunning was undoubtedly the Society event of the year. The big draw for the *ton* was that it was to be hosted by the Duke and Duchess of Hamilton at Grosvenor Place. Since their nuptials had been kept secret and held at a wedding chapel, Society had been cheated of the spectacle and made up for it by flocking to Hamilton House for the sister's wedding.

The mansion overflowed with urns of white lilies, roses, and baby's breath, chosen by Elizabeth. Hamilton had allowed her *carte blanche* with the flowers to make up for refusing to allow her to wear the pink maid of honor gown that Maria had chosen. He insisted that his duchess wear the Douglas colors of blue and white. Elizabeth was privately delighted, though she pretended great disappointment over the pink dress. She was learning to let Hamilton *think* he controlled her. It took more courage than she thought she possessed, but she'd had years of experience in handling a dominant person and did it with skillful subtlety.

For once, Bridget was forced to take a back seat, since Maria made sure she was the star attraction at her own wedding, and Hamilton made certain that Elizabeth was the hostess of the social event. After the vows had been exchanged, the Duke and Duchess of Hamilton headed the reception line, followed by George and Maria, the Earl and Countess of Coventry, to welcome their illustrious guests. King George did not attend private weddings, but his heir, the Prince of Wales, along with his mother, Princess Augustus, attended, as did the Duke of Cumberland. Behind them came the Prime Minister and his wife, then Horace Walpole, London's greatest gossip.

Elizabeth welcomed Will and kissed Charlie on the cheek. It was now evident to all that Lady Charlotte was with child, and she made no effort to conceal the pregnancy. "I'm so pleased you are well, and I cannot help but envy you," Elizabeth whispered.

Will's father, the Duke of Devonshire, accompanied the young couple, but his duchess was still at Chatsworth in Derbyshire, stubbornly refusing to acknowledge her daughter-in-law or her expected grandchild. He thumped Hamilton on the back, eyed Elizabeth's middle, and asked bluntly, "Not breeding yet?"

Elizabeth blushed. *I was sick this morning . . . perhaps I am!*

"My bride was virgin. Unlike others we did not jump the gun."

Elizabeth's blush deepened at the cruel remark her husband directed at Charlie. She was deeply grateful that her friend had not overheard as she welcomed Charlie's parents, the Earl and Countess of Burlington. Suddenly, she became aware of something in the air. For a moment it was indefinable, then she realized that John Campbell had arrived. Abject fear rose up in her at what the two men would do. Only days ago they had been ready to kill each other. She was astounded when the men spoke with civility as if nothing were amiss between them.

Elizabeth felt cold as ice, then inexplicably hot as fire as she lowered her lashes and held out her hand to him. The cruel words they had exchanged danced silently upon the air.

John drank in the vision before him. He had been determined not to attend Coventry's wedding since it was being held at Hamilton House, but some perverse craving had compelled him. He knew full well it would be tortuous to see her at Hamilton's side, but he could not help himself. When he took her hand and lifted it to his lips, she raised her lashes and looked into his eyes. Not by word or sign did anything pass between them, but both felt the invisible golden thread that bound them one to the other.

Once all their guests passed down the reception line, Hamilton led Elizabeth to the ballroom, which had not been used since his parents had held a ball there more than a dozen years before. The musicians, sitting upon a raised dais at one end of the long room, began to play as the host brought the hostess to the dais. When he raised his hands an expectant silence fell over the guests. "I have had a special piece of music composed in honor of my bride. We would be honored if you would choose your partners and promenade to 'The Duchess of Hamilton's Fancy.'"

It was completely unexpected to Elizabeth. She stood speechless with a self-conscious blush upon her cheeks, trying to look pleased but secretly wanting to sink through the floor as couples paraded past her, starting with Maria and George. Her husband murmured, "You are the highest ranking lady in this room, with the exception of the princess. Your sister is a countess." Next came Charlie and Will. "Charlotte is a marchioness. Ah, here are the Cavendish sisters. Rachel is Countess Orford, and Cat will become lowly Baroness Duncannon. Even wealthy Dorothy Boyle is merely a countess. I've raised you to the pinnacle of Society, Elizabeth."

Her hand was enclosed in his. She felt his fingers squeeze hers and feared he would crush them if her response was not appropriate. "You honor me, Your Grace," she said low. *You honor me as a possession, an object of beauty to be displayed. You dishonor me as a woman! My role is to decorate your arm and make men envy you.*

When the piece of music was finished, the ballroom rang with applause. He smiled proudly down at her. "Now go forth and be a perfect hostess to our guests."

Only when she moved away from him was she able to take a deep breath. Shrewdly, she made a point of seeking out Horace Walpole for special attention. He often made witty references to the inappropriate things Maria said, and Elizabeth wanted to engage him in intelligent conversation so that he would know she had more to offer than a pretty face. He danced elegantly, and she pretended reluctance to change partners when the Prince of Wales approached her. By genuinely listening to the things young George let drop she learned that he had become enamored of the fifteen-year-old daughter of the Duke of Richmond. "Next time we entertain, I shall invite her." With that promise she won George's undying affection.

Elizabeth danced with each and every male guest, including the new bridegroom. "Maria is the luckiest lady in London to have your devotion, George."

"I'm taking her to Paris for our honeymoon. I hope she enjoys the sights."

Poor, dear George—it will be one long shopping spree. She kissed his cheek and said with genuine affection, "I am so glad my sister married you, my lord."

Coventry unwittingly returned her to her husband's side after their dance, but Elizabeth had perfected a serene smile that hid her emotions from everyone.

Hamilton interrupted a conversation between the king's son, Cumberland, and John Campbell. "I know how much Elizabeth loves to dance. Could I ask you to partner her, John, since I seldom dance myself?" He felt a surge of power as he dangled his beautiful wife before his rival.

"It would be my pleasure, James."

Elizabeth placed her hand in Campbell's without demur, and he led her into the dance. She felt as if the very air crackled and sparked between them. *You devil! What in hellfire are you doing here?* "Welcome to Hamilton House, Lord Sundridge."

You tempt me to madness! His dark eyes devoured her. "Thank you. May I say that you dance superbly, Your Grace."

She smiled her acknowledgment of his compliment. "My dancing master had a devil of a time. When I came out of the Irish bog, all I could manage was a clog dance."

John's eyes danced with sardonic amusement. "From actress to duchess in a few short months. You are to be congratulated."

"Such compliments will turn my head, you smooth-tongued knave."

The moment she said it she blushed furiously. She had no doubt her words had evoked how he had made love to her with his mouth. Desperately, she changed the subject. "For an uncouth, uncivilized Highlander your dancing skills are remarkable."

"Second only to my skills at seduction." *Curse you, Elizabeth, I want to make love to you right here in public!*

"That is doubtless the result of much practice."

"Nightly practice." Now it was his words that conjured pictures in their heated imaginations. The ache that had begun in his groin reached all the way to his heart. His arms throbbed to lift her and carry her off into the night. Then the throbbing spread to other vulnerable parts of his body.

As Elizabeth swayed and turned, the rhythm of the music insinuated itself inside her, filling her with a longing to be held in John's arms forever. The physical need to have him touch her was sweet torture, but the emotional need was far deeper. Her desire to belong to him, and him alone, was an overwhelming agony.

When the music stopped, their eyes and their hands clung possessively for half a dozen heartbeats. John could not bear to return her to Hamilton, so he enfolded her hand in his and took her over to her friend Charlie, who was watching the dancers from a comfortable chair at the side of the ballroom.

Charlie saw the haunted look in Elizabeth's eyes and said something outrageous to break the spell. "Will you allow me to sit in your presence, now that you outrank me?"

John kissed Charlie's hand. "She outranks us both."

Elizabeth's laughter rang out, though her throat was choking with unshed tears.

The dancing lasted until dawn, when Maria finally decided she was tired of the role of blushing bride. A gallant Coventry carried her to their carriage that would take them to the ship sailing on the morning tide to France. Elizabeth stood dutifully at her husband's side until their last guest departed. Hamilton reeked of brandy, and she noted with distaste that he was completely unsteady as he attempted to climb the stairs.

It was six o'clock before she fell into bed exhausted. In three short hours Kate Agnew awoke her when the portrait painter arrived. She stood posing, stifling yawns, until the hour of noon when Hamilton invariably came on the scene. When he did not come, she asked Kate to see that Sir Joshua Reynolds was served lunch, then she went in search of Morton, the duke's valet.

"He is indisposed, Your Grace. Dr. Bower is with him, but their raised voices indicate an altercation," Morton confided.

Elizabeth felt torn. It was her duty to see her husband if he was ailing, but fear of him held her at bay. With great daring she decided to go down to the entrance hall and speak with the doctor before he departed. Instinctively she believed she would get more from him than she would from Hamilton.

It seemed a long wait, but eventually she saw the medical man descend the stairs. "Dr. Bower? I am Elizabeth Douglas."

He looked at her keenly to see if talk of her beauty was exaggerated. Concluding that it was not, he decided to warn the duchess. "Your husband is a stubborn man, Your Grace. He has a liver condition that is exacerbated by imbibing too much liquor. My advice to you is to keep the decanters under lock and key, and to tread softly. He is all liverish spleen at the moment and ready to savage anyone who dares to point out the truth."

"I'm so sorry that he is a difficult patient, Dr. Bower."

"Don't apologize for him, my dear. The bills for my services always compensate me for his boorish behavior."

After lunch, Elizabeth posed for three more hours, hoping the portrait would soon be finished. When Reynolds told her it should be completed by the end of the week, she felt relieved. Lack of sleep had sapped her energy and when he left she removed the cape and gown and intended to lie down. Before she could do so, however, Bridget swept into her private suite with an armful of newspapers.

"The wedding was written up in all the society pages. It was beyond question *the* social event of the season! Every paper speaks of Maria's beauty and describes every detail of her gown. Most of them were extremely generous to you too, Elizabeth, praising your success as a hostess, but of course flattery is to be expected for the wife of a duke. That inveterate gossip, Horace Walpole, lays it on a bit too thick; he goes on and on about you: 'In the past the image of a duchess has always been dumpy, dowdy, and dull. The Duchess of Hamilton has changed all this with her exquisite face and form, which are incomparable. Her wit, intelligence, and charm earn her the right to truly be called Her Grace.' "

"That's nice," Elizabeth said absently, thinking she would be able to retire early because Hamilton was under the weather.

"All you can do is yawn! I'm sorry if the newspapers bore you, Miss Ingratitude, but you have me to thank for all this, you know!"

"*Ne obliviscaris,* I do not forget," she said softly.

Bridget was mollified. She did not hear the quiet threat in Elizabeth's voice. "The morning post brought four invitations, and you received another half dozen this afternoon. They are pouring in in reciprocation for the wedding of course. I have a new gown for Countess Orford's entertainment tonight. What will you wear?"

"I'm not going. I've decided to go to bed early."

"Are you unwell? Perhaps you're with child already!"

Could it be possible? Her spirits soared; a child to love would bring her a chance for happiness. *But who would be the father?* She immediately dismissed the terrifying question. "No, Mother, I am not with child."

"Hamilton may want an heir, but not this soon, I warrant. He enjoys having you on his arm, showing off your beautiful face and form. 'Tis the sole reason he married you. He won't be best pleased if you turn fat and frumpy within a month of your wedding."

Elizabeth's spirits fell. *It would be best if I'm not with child!* The last thing she wanted was to incur Hamilton's wrath.

"I saw the look of disgust on his face when he saw Charlotte Cavendish flaunting her pregnancy like a fat little sow."

"Charlie looks beautiful! Don't be hateful." It was one of the few times she had dared to speak sharply to her mother. She bit her lip, knowing Bridget would find a way to retaliate, but she didn't care. She would defend Charlotte with her last breath.

Bridget went straight to Kate Agnew with the information that Elizabeth was refusing to go to the Orfords' entertainment being held at Devonshire House. Then Kate told Hamilton. Within the hour he strode into her rooms with a smug-faced

Kate at his heels. He looked slightly jaundiced but ready to do battle with a disobedient wife. He eyed the silk robe she had slipped over her petticoat. "Why haven't you begun to dress?"

"I thought I would go to bed early, Your Grace. I'm tired."

"Tired? You are only seventeen, how can you possibly be tired?"

I'm tired of being a duchess. She licked dry lips. "I danced until dawn then stood posing for my portrait for seven hours."

"Such hardships," he mocked. "Get dressed immediately."

Kate went to the wardrobe, took out a sapphire blue gown with a white scalloped underskirt, then brought a corset.

Elizabeth did not remove her robe. "When I learned you were ill, I assumed we wouldn't be going to the Orfords' tonight."

"Ill? Have you been spying on me?" The yellow tinge of his skin turned a mottled red; he took a threatening step toward her.

"Spying? No! When the doctor came to see you—"

"Who the devil told you about the doctor?" He swung around and his accusing eyes fell on Kate. "Get out!" He was in a blazing temper now. "Lying and gossiping servants—I won't have it! And I won't have a wife who stands there and defies my wishes!" He reached out one powerful hand and tore the silk robe from her.

Elizabeth crossed her arms over her body in a defensive gesture, but he grabbed her and picked up the corset from the bed where Kate had dropped it. He pulled it over her head, then yanked it about her midsection and tugged cruelly on the laces.

She cried out in pain as her breasts were trapped and squeezed inside the corset. She pushed the boned garment down beneath her breasts with trembling fingers. "You are hurting me," she gasped.

"Take a deep breath, damn you!"

Elizabeth drew in her breath. He pulled the laces so tightly she screamed. Then she heard his grunt of satisfaction.

"Now finish dressing. Don't make me hurt you again."

At Devonshire House Elizabeth pinned a smile to her face and pretended she was enjoying herself. Under Hamilton's watchful eye, it was difficult to have a private word with Charlie, but finally she managed it. "After dancing until dawn, all I wanted to do was go to bed and sleep."

"Me too," Charlie admitted, "but Rachel is my sister-in-law now, and since she and Orford were entertaining at Devonshire House, I could hardly send my regrets. Because of my condition I've suddenly become so lethargic. I want to sleep for a month!"

Lethargic exactly describes the way I feel. "What other symptoms do you have, Charlie?"

"My breasts are tender and extremely sensitive, but they're also larger—and Will finds them very attractive."

Elizabeth smiled but winced inwardly. Her breasts were sore, but surely that was because Hamilton had been so rough with her?

"Do you suspect you might be having a baby, Elizabeth?"

"No, no," she denied quickly, but secretly she believed she was indeed with child, and hope and fear were at war in her heart.

For the first two hours of the ball she hoped that John Campbell would not attend, but as midnight approached she began to long for the sight of him. She wanted to look into his eyes, hear his deep voice. She ached for his touch, if only in the dance.

John Campbell too had been at war with himself. He knew he should avoid Devonshire House tonight, but as the hour advanced Elizabeth drew him like a lodestone. Even after he arrived he had no intentions of dancing with her, but the golden thread that bound them drew them inexorably toward each other.

As the music swirled about them, his eyes fell on the sapphires glittering at her throat. "Hamilton indulges your love of jewels."

Your beauty needs no jewels to enhance it, Elizabeth.

"How very fortunate I am that he enjoys flaunting his wealth." *They mean nothing to me.*

He wanted to snatch Hamilton's jewels from her throat and scatter them across the ballroom floor. "He enjoys flaunting you, Elizabeth. 'Tis the reason he married you."

Her laugh was brittle. "I'm not naive enough to suppose he married me for love, or my elegant manors."

The corner of his mouth lifted. "No, you have the manners of an Irish wildcat, though you keep your claws sheathed." *Sheath me.*

He longed to thread his fingers into her glorious golden hair and draw her mouth to his. His body ached to make love to her. What a bloody fool he had been. He should have made her his wife when he had the chance. Now all he had were regrets.

Suddenly she couldn't breathe. His closeness made her dizzy and she was afraid she might faint. She gasped for air.

"Are you all right?" His deep voice was intense.

She gave him a slumberous glance. *I want you to pick me up and carry me home. I want you to undress me, lift me into bed, and hold me close against your heart.* "For a moment I thought you had stolen my senses, then I remembered my tight corset."

His eyes lowered to her lush breasts that swelled from her low-cut gown. He was mad with jealousy that another had marital rights to touch her beautiful body and make love to her every night. His jaw clenched. *Cock-teasing little bitch.*

At four in the morning Hamilton decided to leave. He and old Devonshire had engaged in an unspoken drinking contest as they played cards. It finally ended when the duke fell asleep in his cups with a snore. Only then did Hamilton take Elizabeth home.

She found Emma waiting in her chamber. "Where is Kate Agnew?"

"Hamilton gave her the sack and asked me to be your maid."

"Oh, thank God, Emma! The woman has watched me like a spider every moment since I arrived in this house."

Emma removed Elizabeth's jewels and gown. When she unlaced her corset, the young duchess staggered. "That damn thing was far too tight. You are dead on your feet, child. Into bed with you."

Within minutes Elizabeth slipped into blissful sleep. Soon she tumbled headlong into a vivid dream:

*She was dancing and all she wore was a long strand of
jewels wound about her neck, her waist, and her hips.
John lifted the huge blood-red ruby that nestled atop the
golden curls between her legs and slowly began to un-
wind the string of glittering diamonds that was attached
to it. Laughing, she spun faster and faster, giddy with the
teasing, tempting, taunting game they played. She was
naked save for the jewels about her neck, and John held
the other end as if she were an animal on a leash. She
growled seductively and unsheathed her claws. He
laughed at her antics. "I always fancied an Irish wildcat
in my bed." She crouched, then sprang upon him, nip-
ping his throat with her sharp teeth. "It will take more
than a Barbarian Highlander to tame me!"*

*He licked his lips. "I have a secret weapon . . .
remember?"*

*She gazed at his mouth, mesmerized, and remem-
bered how he had used it to make love to her the first
time. "I will never forget. Ne Obliviscaris, John," she
purred.*

Chapter Twenty-Three

*T*he moment Elizabeth lifted her head from her pillow she was engulfed by nausea. She reached for the chamber pot and spewed up her heart. It instantly confirmed her suspicion that she was with child. Her emotions were hopelessly mixed. Her heart rejoiced, yet she dreaded Hamilton's reaction. Fear made her resolve to keep her secret as long as she could, for more than one reason.

It was impossible to hide it from Emma, but they had an unspoken pact to keep the news to themselves. Elizabeth longed to tell her father, but she seldom saw him these days. Now that she was a wife they no longer had any private, precious moments together. She suspected that her mother had guessed her secret, for each night she made sure she was present when her daughter dressed for the evening. Bridget relentlessly tightened her corset, making sure Elizabeth's waist measured no more than seventeen narrow inches. And just as relentlessly, Emma surreptitiously loosened the corset strings to accommodate the Duchess of Hamilton's expanding waist.

Elizabeth came to hate the social whirl that demanded two full hours of dressing each and every night. The duke's demand for perfection of her gown, makeup, and jewels amounted to an obsession, and she grew to loathe her position as Duchess of Hamilton. She began to dread the parties where she was expected to dance until dawn, where she was forced to mask her unhappiness, hide her exhaustion, and conceal her pregnancy.

Elizabeth began to dislike herself as well. The life she led was shallow, self-absorbed, and meaningless. After she was painted by Reynolds, the duke insisted that she sit for portraits by Francis Cotes, by Jean-Etienne Liotard, who had just done a portrait of Princess Augusta, and by Michael Dahl, who had painted the king.

Dislike was too mild a word to describe what Elizabeth felt toward her mother. One evening when Bridget was particularly brutal, tightening her corset strings to reduce her thickening waist, Elizabeth rebelled. "You don't give a damn if you injure my child, so long as I look slim and ornamental on Hamilton's arm!"

"So, it is true! You are breeding! You are nothing but a sly, secretive little bitch to keep such news from your mother! Does Hamilton know about the child?"

"Not yet, Mother. I'd like to tell him in my own good time, but there's little hope of that when you report everything to him."

"You are an unnatural daughter. I thank God for Maria who shows me love and gratitude for making her Countess of Coventry. I have missed her dreadfully, but she is finally returned after six weeks in France, and I cannot wait to see her tonight at Strawberry Hill."

Elizabeth closed her eyes and offered up a silent prayer that she would not vomit on the carriage ride to Horace Walpole's pretentious neo-Gothic castle in Twickenham. The only good thing about tonight was the fact that John Campbell was not likely to make the journey to Twickenham since he had scant patience for the likes of the effeminate gossip Walpole. Feeling guilty over the way she had spoken to her mother, Elizabeth apologized. "I'm sorry I kept the baby a secret, but I felt sure that you had already guessed. And I too am looking forward to seeing Maria."

As always, Hamilton came to inspect her appearance before they departed. "Your gown is all wrong for tonight." His eyes narrowed as they swept over Bridget and Emma. "Who chose it?"

"I did, Your Grace," Elizabeth lied to protect Emma.

"We are going to a castle. I want you to look like a medieval queen." He strode to the double wardrobe and flung open its doors. He pulled out a purple velvet gown whose sleeves were slashed to show their primrose satin lining. "This is also an opportune evening to wear a coronet—I've bought you enough of them."

"May I wear my new wig, Your Grace?" Elizabeth pleaded.

"Absolutely not! Your own golden tresses will attract every eye when adorned by your amethyst and diamond crown."

Elizabeth almost forgot to feign a look of disappointment. He was easy to manipulate, but she disliked herself for doing it.

Because they were late leaving, the coachman whipped up the horses, and the carriage swayed alarmingly. Elizabeth managed not to disgrace herself only because Emma had given her a dry biscuit and a few sips of wine to settle her stomach before she left. It was the only thing she had been able to keep down all day.

When they arrived at Strawberry Hill, Maria, Countess of Coventry, was already holding court, telling anyone who would listen how much she hated Paris and loathed its inhabitants. "It was filled with foreigners who refused to speak English!"

Horace Walpole blinked with disbelief. "My dearest lady, they were speaking French because you were in France."

"I found them most discourteous. Moreover, Coventry jibberjabbered to them in their own tongue until I was ready to scream!"

"And as punishment you no doubt sent him to Coventry?"

Walpole's witticism went over her head. "No, we came back to London with all speed. We have a new house in Berkeley Square."

Elizabeth kissed Maria's cheek. "It's good to have you home."

"Why are you wearing a crown?" Maria demanded peevishly.

"Because Elizabeth is queen of my castle." Walpole made it quite plain which sister he preferred.

Maria, who had been pointedly ignoring George, suddenly turned to him. "I don't have a crown."

"Elizabeth is entitled to wear a ducal coronet, my dear."

"And I am not! I should never have settled for a mere earl."

Elizabeth stood on tiptoe to kiss George and whispered, "She doesn't mean it, my lord."

George looked grim. "Unfortunately, she does."

Hamilton slapped his friend on the back. "Some of us are more fortunate in our wives than others, George. Let us go and sample Walpole's whiskey while I educate you on how to control a woman."

The thought that Maria and George did not have a happy marriage made Elizabeth feel sick in the pit of her stomach. She took her sister's hand. "Would you like to talk, Maria?"

"No, I should like to dance! I warrant I will have a dozen Lords of the Realm panting after me in five minutes flat!"

The last thing Elizabeth felt like was dancing, but it was obligatory. The Duke of Hamilton insisted his wife dance with every male who invited her. She knew that he enjoyed their looking, longing, and lusting. When men desired her, he felt triumphant that he was the one who owned the tantalizing prize.

By the time Elizabeth danced three times in succession, her energy became sapped along with her breath. When a Scottish reel was announced, she determined to sit it out because she realized her clothes were far too tight and constricting about her middle.

Then Walpole held up his limp-wristed hands. "This reel is in honor of my favorite lady at Court. The name of the new dance is 'Elizabeth Hamilton's Rant'! I cannot wait to partner her."

Her inner voice warned: *You cannot offend Horace Walpole. Smile. You are the Duchess of Hamilton.* By the time the rousing, lively reel was over, Elizabeth was staggering on her feet. She tried to take deep breaths but could only manage shallow ones. "Please excuse me, Horace. I must powder my nose." On knees turned to water, she headed from the great hall, and to her utter dismay came face-to-face with John Campbell.

He had vowed not to come tonight, had even sent his regrets to Walpole. Yet here he was, unable to deny himself the chance to see her and touch her. When he saw her, he cursed himself for a bloody fool. He was a military man with a will of iron, but his resolve melted like snow in summer when it came to Elizabeth. She stood beneath a circle of medieval torches that turned her hair to pure-spun gold, crowned by glittering jewels. His hot glance licked over her like a candle flame. His formal bow mocked her.

"Ah, the Queen of Diamonds."

"The Knave of Hearts! Alas, your bid wasn't high enough." Her retaliation was quick and cruel. Her breasts rose and fell with her agitation and lack of breath.

His eyes lowered deliberately. "Such a lush display. Your pair certainly trumps my cards."

"I doubt that, Sundridge. The best I can hope for is a draw."

"*Touché.* Your tongue is sharp, Wildcat."

"You think your tongue is not a formidable weapon?"

"Let's see." He took her hand, turned it over, and placed a sensual kiss in her palm. Then he licked it.

A wave of desire almost drowned her. Blood rushed from her head to her heart, and she fought desperately for breath. Her violet eyes were huge in a face pale as a ghost. Her careful *façade* vanished. "John," she gasped, her hand reaching in supplication.

He saw her lashes sweep to her cheeks, saw her body go limp. He caught her before she hit the floor and lifted her in his arms. "Sweetheart." He gazed down at the delicate features, noticed the shadows beneath her eyes, and was gripped by a desperate need to protect her. When he realized that it was not a momentary faint, that she was completely unconscious, fear knotted his gut. He looked around at the gaping spectators and knew he had no choice but to find Hamilton. Holding her against his heart, he forced himself to put one foot in front of the other and take her to her husband. It was the hardest thing he had ever done in his life.

Campbell knew where to find Hamilton; he was as addicted to gaming as he was to liquor. He did not take Elizabeth into the smoke-filled room, but stood at the entrance holding his delicate burden. Hamilton saw immediately and strode to the door. Their hard eyes met for long stormy minutes, while Campbell fought the urge to kill. The veneer of civilization was dangerously thin over the savage Highlander at this moment. It took every ounce of discipline he had ever learned to surrender Elizabeth into her husband's keeping. "I hope she is precious to you, James." Implicit was the threat that she had *better* be precious.

Hamilton smiled with triumph. It was obvious to them both that she had quickened with child. "John, she is my treasure."

*   *   *

Though Elizabeth hadn't thought it possible, the Duke of Hamilton stepped up the pace of their social engagements. When they were not being entertained at St. James's Palace or the great houses such as Leicester, Burlington, and Devonshire, they were hosting parties at Hamilton House. Often before a gala affair, they attended a play or were seen at the opera.

Elizabeth felt her vitality draining away with each function she attended. More and more, exhaustion overwhelmed her. She had no appetite and lost weight everywhere except her expanding belly. Her stamina was considerably diminished, yet Hamilton would not excuse her from socializing, for now he was not simply showing off his wife's extraordinary beauty but flaunting her pregnancy and advertising his virility.

She dragged herself listlessly through the Season, from ball to party to reception. Though outwardly serene, on the inside she was terrified that if her social pace continued, she would do her baby irreparable harm. Moreover, she no longer encountered John Campbell. At first she felt relief, but far too quickly her relief changed to longing, and her heartache became almost unbearable.

John Campbell was determined to cut the golden cord that bound him to Elizabeth. Seeing her lovely face, hearing her voice, kissing her hand, touching her in the dance while her fragrance intoxicated his senses, then watching her leave with Hamilton was an agony he could do without. With an iron determination he swore an oath that he would stop torturing himself and Elizabeth.

His regiment was called back to active duty, and he devoted his time to the soldiers he had recruited in Scotland, turning them into His Majesty's 98th Argyllshire Highlanders. They had traveled from Glasgow to London in March, but for all the training Argyll had provided, they still seemed like raw recruits compared to the disciplined and experienced veterans of war he presently commanded in the 3rd Highland Regiment of Foot Guards.

"Charlie, you are absolutely blooming with health!" Elizabeth kissed her friend and picked up Dandy for a quick cuddle.

Burlington Gardens, the home of Charlotte and Will, was one of the few places Hamilton allowed Elizabeth to visit alone.

"I wish I could say the same for you, Beth." Charlie scanned her face anxiously. "Are you still having morning sickness?"

"Every day, I'm afraid. But honestly, I don't mind that. It's the lethargy I find hard to cope with, and I often feel ill. I think I could go to bed and stay there for the rest of my life. At Leicester House last night, it wasn't just a matter of hiding my yawns behind my fan—I actually fell asleep and awoke to find Princess Augusta waving her smelling salts under my nose."

"Come and put your feet up, Beth, and I shall do the same. I'm as big as a pig full of figs! I feel well enough, but it really is time for me to withdraw from Society until after the happy event."

"July will be here before we know it. Are you afraid, Charlie?"

"No . . . yes! I'm so ignorant about childbirth. What about you?"

"I have a lot of questions that I cannot bring myself to ask my mother. I thought perhaps it might be easier to ask *your* mother."

"Excellent idea! After lunch we'll both go over and ask her."

Jane served them their lunch on trays, so they would not have to move from their comfortable couches before the fire. It was the first time in months that Elizabeth felt completely relaxed, and for once she kept down some light broth, followed by *blancmange.*

They decided to walk over to Burlington House so they could enjoy the fragrant May blossoms on the trees. "Father's gone to Rutland to see that all is in readiness for me at Uppingham Manor. It's the most beautiful countryside. The River Welland runs through our property—you would love it. Oh, I wish you would come with me, Beth. London's air is so unhealthy in the summer."

Elizabeth thought longingly of Uppingham, but knew it would be impossible. Hamilton would never allow her to leave London.

"I shall get Will to suggest it to James. He indulges you so. I'm sure he will insist you come to the country for your health."

When they got to Burlington House, Dandy ran in with tail wagging madly before the majordomo could answer the door.

"It's only me," Charlie said. "We've come to see Mother."

The man looked nonplussed. He opened his mouth to speak, then closed it, not sure how one handled these complicated situations.

The terrier ran upstairs, intent on rooting out Dorothy, and they heard a little scream. "Dandy has surprised her!"

Presently, as Dorothy Boyle made her elegant way down the stairs, she wasn't the only one to be surprised. Elizabeth stared in amazement. "Father . . . what are you doing here?" The moment the question left her lips, she blushed hotly. It was perfectly obvious what Jack Gunning was doing here, upstairs with the Countess of Burlington, while the earl was away in Rutland. *No wonder I never see you these days, Father.* Elizabeth felt betrayed. She remembered the words he had used to persuade her on that fateful Valentine's night: *Do this for me, Elizabeth, and you won't ever regret it.* Well, she had regretted it every moment of her life since. He had married her to a duke then considered his duty done. When she had needed her father's love, support, and advice the most, he had abandoned her and gone about his own selfish affairs. *Affair,* she corrected herself. *There isn't a man breathing whom a woman can trust!* "Oh, of course, I forgot you were looking for a riding mare," Elizabeth said succinctly.

Dorothy Boyle raised an appreciative eyebrow. The Duchess of Hamilton's wit carried a sting. "Jack, our daughters are going to make grandparents of us. We should climb into the saddle often, while we can still mount and ride."

Elizabeth noted with satisfaction that her father had the decency to flush.

When Jack Gunning departed, Charlie kissed her mother. "We need answers to some rather delicate questions. Elizabeth feels shy about broaching the subject with her own mother."

Dorothy held up her hand. "Say no more. I know which delicate subject you refer to. Come out on the terrace and I will enlighten you both." Once she made them comfortable with cushions and footstools she began to advise them about pregnancy and sex. "When your swollen belly makes frontal sex impossible, there are a dozen other ways to go about the thing, so don't despair, darlings."

"A dozen? Will and I have only found two! I'm rather fortunate that he's so much taller than I. It's a simple matter for him to wrap his long body about mine and enter me from behind, and then of course I sit on him in a chair—I suppose we're not too inventive."

Elizabeth sat very still, her face a complete mask.

"Your tummy's already too large for strenuous contortions, Charlie. You'll soon have to keep Will happy by fellating him."

"Fellating?"

"You know . . . Frenching. Men love to be Frenched. A lot prefer it to intercourse, and some don't even care if the mouth is female!"

Elizabeth said faintly, "Actually the questions I had were about childbirth." She didn't fully comprehend what Dorothy was talking about, but she knew it was something overtly prurient.

Dorothy laughed. "Of course, darling. I should have known Hamilton's wife wouldn't need sexual advice. His experience is legendary. I warrant many a brothel would have gone bankrupt without his business over the last decade."

Elizabeth asked quickly, "How long does childbirth take?"

"Once labor begins, a first child usually takes about twelve hours. I had Charlotte in record time, only three or four hours, but of course she wasn't my first." Dorothy immediately realized her careless words evoked the spectre of infant mortality. "It's best not to dwell on thoughts of labor. Ignorance is bliss."

"Indeed," Elizabeth agreed ruefully. *I for one was in blissful ignorance of many things before our visit today.*

"Just make sure you get lots of rest, fresh air, and pampering during the months before your confinement, and all will be well."

"I want Elizabeth to come to Uppingham with me. I'm going to get Will to suggest it to James."

By the time she got home, Elizabeth felt acutely ill. With determination she set aside thoughts of her father's dalliance along with that of her husband, but she could not banish thoughts of how easily she could harm the baby she was carrying. She searched her brain for a way to stop the duke from forcing her to keep up the reckless social pace. Fear for her child was suddenly greater than her fear of Hamilton. She vowed she would outwit him.

"I think you are fevered," Emma said, feeling Elizabeth's brow.

"Yes, I know. The same time each day I get this shivery feeling and I know it can't go on. Emma, I've thought of a way to shock Hamilton to his senses, but I'll need your help. It involves something extremely personal and I'm embarrassed to ask you."

"Ask away, child. I'll do anything for you."

Elizabeth's cheeks turned bright pink. "Next time you menstruate, will you wear one of my silk petticoats and try to get as much blood on it as you can? If we can convince him I'm in danger of losing the baby, he will have to summon Dr. Bower."

A week later the pair of conspirators set the stage, then Emma frantically summoned Hamilton who was with Morton, his valet, dressing for an evening at the Prime Minister's home. James strode past Emma to Elizabeth's apartment and threw open the door to her bedchamber. He found his wife abed with a frightened look on her pale face. One of her silk petticoats, covered with dark red blood, lay across the foot of the four-poster.

A breathless Emma caught up with him. "I found her on the floor, Your Grace, and put her straight to bed. I don't think she's lost the child . . . yet. But perhaps we should get the doctor."

An hour later, Bower took in the scene and demanded privacy for his examination. He had to order Hamilton from the room. The doctor pulled down the covers and placed his hand on the small mound. "Are you experiencing pain, Your Grace?"

"Not now," Elizabeth answered truthfully. "But when my corset was tightened I had pain." She cast him a beseeching look. "If I miss the Prime Minister's ball, the duke will be furious with me."

Bower had heard enough. He left Elizabeth and summoned Hamilton for a private word. "Let me be blunt. If your duchess continues to dance the night away in a tight corset, she will miscarry. She will lose the precious Hamilton heir she is no doubt carrying. The choice is yours, of course, as will be the full blame. She needs complete bed rest for the next twenty-four hours. Then she must leave London for the country. Your wife requires peace and quiet, good food, fresh air, and plenty of rest and relaxation."

When Bower left, Hamilton returned to his wife's bedside. "How would you like to spend the next two months with Lady Charlotte? Will is sending her to Uppingham Manor in Rutland, and I believe a rest in the country is just what you need, Elizabeth."

"I shall do whatever you think best, Your Grace."

Chapter Twenty-Four

"I think my labor has begun!" Charlie dropped her fork and clutched Elizabeth's hands. The pair was enjoying an early breakfast of scones with fresh strawberries and clotted cream.

"I'll get your mother . . . sit absolutely still." Beth knew that Dorothy Boyle kept late hours even here in the country and never arose before eleven. Will had been with them at Uppingham for the past fortnight but had ridden up to Chatsworth, approximately fifty miles north, to inform his truculent mother that shortly she would become a grandmother and to try to bridge the gulf.

Dorothy immediately dispatched messengers to Charlie's husband in Derbyshire, her father in London, and her midwife in Rutland. Then she spent a quarter of an hour with Charlie berating the Duchess of Devonshire. "My daughter's child should rightfully be born at Chatsworth. Someday, Charlie, you will be the Duchess of Devonshire, and when you are, I shall personally see that the bloody dowager duchess is turfed out of Chatsworth on her bony arse!"

Charlie's face contorted as a labor pain distended her belly.

"I cannot bear to witness my child's agony. Promise you will stay with her, Elizabeth. You have such a serene nature."

But that's just a pretense. Inside I am in emotional turmoil!

"Of course I shall stay with her. Charlie is more dear to me than a sister." It was the last day of June, and the baby had not been due to arrive until mid-July. "Perhaps your labor's started early because we were racketing about in the pony cart yesterday."

"It isn't early, Beth. Will and I were intimate from the start."

Elizabeth felt her panic rise up inside her. *John and I were intimate before I married Hamilton. What on earth shall I do if my baby arrives early?* She forced the frightening thoughts away as the midwife arrived. The woman put Charlie to bed, then took herself off to the kitchens for some tea and scones. For the next six hours Elizabeth read to her friend, massaged her back, sponged her face, and did her utmost to keep both Charlie's panic and her own at bay. The midwife finally took over, and shortly thereafter delivered Charlotte of a son and heir, destined to become the Fifth Duke of Devonshire. He was the image of his handsome blond father.

Baby Cavendish had two nursemaids and a wet nurse from the hour of his birth. His mother had the usual ten-day lying-in period. Will, arriving the day after his son was born, went straight to Charlie's bedside with kisses, gifts, and a promise.

"I'm sorry I wasn't here, darling, but the baptism will take place in Chatsworth's chapel, as is right and proper. I hope and pray you are well enough to travel by the end of July."

Elizabeth, unsure of what Hamilton would expect of her, consulted with Emma. Should she travel with Will and Charlie to Derbyshire, or would her husband expect her to return to London? She had regained both health and happiness in the country and dreaded returning to Society. And the all-controlling Hamilton.

Will Cavendish gave her the answers she needed. "I've issued all our friends invitations to the christening. Father is even traveling from London with the Earl of Burlington, and James will either meet us here or go straight through to Chatsworth. I hope George and Maria will come too. It will be like old times!"

Elizabeth knew that if Maria had any say, and of course she had *all* the say in her marriage, she would insist that the Earl of Coventry take her to Chatsworth, the Palace of the Peaks. An invitation to the heir's christening would be the envy of the *ton*.

By the third week in July, Charlie was outdoors with Elizabeth playing shuttlecock, and Beth discovered that exercise greatly increased her energy. At the end of the month Charlie and Will's respective fathers arrived, and the aging Duke of Devonshire proudly led the large entourage north to Chatsworth.

The new grandmother, the Duchess of Devonshire, was noticeably absent, but everyone seemed more relieved than offended. Will gave Charlie and Elizabeth the grand tour of England's premier stately home, which would be his when he came into his dukedom. Elizabeth loved the cascade and fountains, while Charlie was more excited that the grand mansion had its own skittle grounds and immediately demanded that Will teach them how to play the game.

Though Elizabeth was in her fifth month of pregnancy, she had gained less than a stone. The small mound of her tummy was easily disguised by the clever alteration of her gowns by Dorothy Boyle's sewing women, and her movements were not yet ungainly in any way. Both the country air and her pregnancy had given her an inner glow, and her golden hair was more luxuriant than it had ever been before.

There was a full moon on the second night, and after dinner Elizabeth strolled in the water garden enjoying to the full her last hours of solitude before her husband arrived. She drank in the beauty of the cascading water, which the moon etched in silver.

"Ill met by moonlight, proud Titania."

Elizabeth whirled around thinking she had imagined the voice that set her heart thudding and her pulse racing erratically.

"John Campbell, what are you doing here?" she asked breathlessly.

"I am to be one of the godfathers."

"Charlie never told me." Her voice held an accusing note, as if they had conspired against her.

"I wasn't sure I could come. Then conveniently the king asked me to recruit more Highlanders. I'm on my way to Argyll." He closed the distance between them and stared enthralled at the lovely vision before him. "You are absolutely blooming. Thank God Hamilton had the good sense to send you from London."

Elizabeth was thankful that for once they were not at each other's throats. Perhaps the night and the beautiful setting allowed them to share their inner thoughts without savaging each other. "I have so loved being in the countryside. I dread the thought of going back to London," she whispered.

"I predict you won't be going back to London for some time."

"What do you mean?"

"If I know James, he will want his heir born at his ancestral home in Scotland. The Duke of Hamilton is laird of clan Douglas."

"God help me, I'm so ignorant!"

"Innocent," he corrected, reaching out with his fingertips to trace where the moonlight silvered her cheek. "You will love Scotland, Elizabeth." *If only I could be the one to show it to you.* "It will touch your heart and soul."

She shivered involuntarily. *You touch my heart and soul.* "John, we mustn't be alone like this together."

He cupped her cheek then withdrew his hand. "I know, sweetheart. I shall keep a discreet distance from you, if only for my sanity. The moment baby William is baptized I shall leave for Inveraray."

He had ridden hell for leather to make sure he would see her before Hamilton arrived. These few precious moments together would have to last them for a long time. He started to dip his head but stopped. *If I kiss her, we are both undone.* "Good night, Elizabeth—sweet dreams."

He doesn't suspect that my child could be his, and neither must I. All pregnant women have ridiculous fancies!

It was not until the following afternoon when Hamilton arrived that Elizabeth realized they would be sharing a bedroom at Chatsworth. Panic knotted her belly as she sketched him a curtsy. "I hope you had a pleasant journey, Your Grace."

He raised her, placed his hand beneath her chin, and kissed her full upon the mouth before everyone. "I still enjoy seeing you blush, Elizabeth, but I shall restrain myself until we are alone."

She blanched at his words as the warm blood drained from her cheeks. She did not dare look in John Campbell's direction.

Later that night Elizabeth retired along with the other females, leaving the men to their cards and their whiskey. She undressed and got into bed but found sleep impossible. Nervous anticipation of what would transpire once Hamilton joined her in their chamber kept her on edge. As the minutes dragged into hours her graphic imagination painted pictures that filled her with dread. Though she tried to banish them, Dorothy Boyle's words insinuated themselves into her head: *When your swollen belly makes frontal sex impossible, there are a dozen other ways to go about the thing.*

Elizabeth's imagination could only conjure the two that Charlie had described—entering her from behind, and sitting on him in a chair. Both were more than enough to put the fear of the devil in her. She remembered the word *fellate,* which was associated with the mouth. She shuddered and hoped Hamilton would never demand it.

By three o'clock in the morning, Elizabeth was a quivering mass of jelly. When she saw the doorknob turn, she went rigid with apprehension and wished she had blown out the candles.

Shock and surprise registered on her face as Morton entered her bedchamber, half carrying Hamilton, who was legless from drink. The duke waved his arms wildly, mumbled something incoherent, then sank unconscious into a chair.

Elizabeth sprang from the bed and rushed to his side. "He's unconscious. Does he need a doctor, Morton?"

"No, Your Grace, three o'clock in the morning is the duke's regular time to pass out." He proceeded to remove Hamilton's shoes and hose, then demonstrated amazing dexterity in taking off the rest of his master's attire.

"Does this happen every night?"

Morton nodded. "The exception is if he gets a gastric attack. He stops for one night, then he's right back at it. He's addicted."

The valet opened the duke's luggage and extracted a nightshirt. "I usually drop him into bed stark naked, but the sight would offend you, Your Grace." Without ceremony he picked up Hamilton's limp body and hauled him onto the bed. "Drunken swine," he muttered.

Once they were alone Elizabeth watched her husband warily for the next half hour. When he didn't move a muscle, she cautiously crept into the wide bed and lay still. When he began to snore she felt she would be safe so long as she could hear him. As her body began to relax, she finally closed her eyes. *Drunken swine!*

Elizabeth felt a hand touch her shoulder, and her eyes flew

open to find John Campbell bending over her. A cautionary finger touched his lips, warning her to be silent. When she nodded her understanding, he swept back the covers and lifted her from the bed. When her arms slipped around his neck, his arms tightened, and as he carried her from the room, holding her high against his heart, she realized that he was naked.

Only when they gained the privacy of his chamber did he dip his dark head and take possession of her lips. Her pulse raced wildly at his recklessness, and she surrendered her mouth willingly, eagerly. He set her down on his bed and slid the silken night rail from her body. Then he knelt behind her, swept aside the golden curls that cascaded down her back, and touched his lips to the nape of her neck. As his hot mouth trailed kisses down the curve of her back, she shuddered uncontrollably. She felt his hands cup her breasts, and heat leaped between them.

He pushed her down gently and curved his long body against her back, nuzzling her neck with his lips, whispering love words that told her what he was about to do. Desire swept through her body like flames of wildfire burning out of control. She felt his erection nudge her bottom cheeks then slide between her legs from behind. She longed for him to bury his hard length inside her, craved to feel his powerful strokes that would make her lose control of her senses. She closed her eyes and moaned softly as her need for him overwhelmed her.

When she lifted her lashes, Elizabeth was disoriented. For a moment she did not know where she was or who she was with. When she saw Hamilton lying beside her, the reality was like a blow to her solar plexus. The delicious interlude with John had been only a dream. Her heart and her body mourned his loss. Unable to bear her husband's proximity a moment longer, she slipped from the bed and put on the clothes Emma had laid out for her. Quietly, she made her way outside into the lush gardens to greet the dawn.

Later that day, baby William was baptized in the alabaster font of Chatworth's chapel whose ceilings had been painted by Laguerre. Elizabeth, who had been asked to be his godmother before she learned that John Campbell was to be his godfather, tried to compose her face and her emotions. She did it by fo-

cusing on the beautiful child and prayed that he would have a
healthy and happy life.

At the christening celebration the food and wine were so
plentiful there was enough left over to feed the village of
Baslow, and the Devonshires welcomed their rustic neighbors
to Chatsworth's lawns so they could pay homage to the baby
princeling.

John Campbell stayed only long enough to sample the christening cake then said his farewells. James Hamilton made certain that he and Elizabeth were close by when John emerged
from the stables mounted on Demon. "We too are on our way
to Scotland. It is high time that the Duchess of Hamilton actually visited Hamilton."

John was right. I am going to Scotland! The prospect delighted her, and not simply because it would prevent her from
returning to London. She genuinely wanted to see the beautiful
Scottish countryside with its mountains and lochs.

"You could call it our delayed honeymoon trip. Feel free to
come and use the hunting lodge any time you fancy, John,"
Hamilton said magnanimously. His father had built Chatelherault Hunting Lodge on the vast Hamilton lands south of Glasgow. "Mi casa, su casa," he said, deliberately placing a
possessive arm about his wife to demonstrate his ownership.

John kept his eyes from Elizabeth. "Thank you, James. I am
tempted to take you up on your generous offer sometime."

"Good-bye, Lord Sundridge." Elizabeth was seething inside
at the way Hamilton dangled her along with his hunting lodge
before John. He was in his element when his friends coveted his
possessions. "I assumed we would be returning to London,
Your Grace." She imbued her voice with reluctance that he was
taking her to Scotland, thankful that her acting lessons now
stood her in good stead.

Elizabeth gazed through the window, entranced as the black
berline traveling coach with the ducal crest of an oak tree on its
doors rumbled across the border into Scotland. She and Emma
had the carriage to themselves because the duke preferred to
travel astride his bay gelding, Acorn, and had sent Morton
ahead to arrange their accommodation.

"Scotland is lovelier than I ever imagined. Look yonder—

some of the mountains are purple with heather, and their peaks are hidden by the clouds. I've never seen such breathtaking vistas. I believe these brilliant green ferns that blanket the hills turn russet in autumn and are called bracken."

"It's beautiful now, but I've heard the winters are fierce." Emma much preferred the stone buildings of London to the craggy rocks that towered in every direction.

Elizabeth, however, could breathe deeply again, and though she felt like a bird in a cage, she knew this was a place where her spirit could fly free if it was ever given the opportunity.

In the late afternoon a great pink sandstone castle with twelve turrets came into view. The medieval fortress stood high, centered in a saucer of wooded hills, and it dominated the surrounding landscape. The gatehouse guard waved them through, and the coach stopped in a central courtyard with a square tower at each corner.

As grooms rushed from the stables to tend the horses and servants came to carry their luggage, Hamilton handed Elizabeth from the coach. "This is Drumlanrig Castle. The land was granted to the Douglases in the fourteenth century by Robert the Bruce."

"It is magnificent, Your Grace." Elizabeth's thoughts took wing. Until this moment she'd had no notion of the vast Douglas wealth and landholdings. Her husband led her into Drumlanrig and introduced her to the Douglas clan who occupied the castle, in every capacity from kin to keepers, stewards, and inside servants.

"It is my great pleasure to present my wife, Elizabeth Douglas, Duchess of Hamilton. I know you will serve her well."

She knew that her title gave her prestige among the *ton* but, for the first time, she began to realize how exalted the rank of Duchess of Hamilton was in the Scottish noble hierarchy. And as the Douglas clan paid their homage, Elizabeth felt overwhelmed.

They rested for a day then resumed their journey, stopping at another castle where even the town was called Douglas. After dinner, when Elizabeth went into the library hoping to find a map that would indicate just how much of Scotland belonged to Hamilton, she found the duke speaking with the castle steward.

"Forgive me, Your Grace, I was looking for information about Castle Douglas."

"This is Douglas Castle, not Castle Douglas. That infamous stronghold is forty miles south, near the open sea of the Solway. Come, let me show you." His face was filled with arrogant pride as he unfolded a huge map and spread it out across the desk.

Her curiosity overcame her reticence, and her glance followed his spatulate finger as it moved across the ancient territories. "The names are confusing to outsiders, but now that you carry my heir, Elizabeth, you are hardly an outsider." He laughed as she blushed.

"We are going to Hamilton. Do you own yet another castle?"

"I own many, but in Hamilton my castle Cadzow has all the amenities of a manor house. It is not a bleak pile of stone."

"Cadzow! Isn't that the ancient name for Glasgow?"

He nodded. "You are as educated as you are beautiful, my dear. I also possess a lovely castle near Edinburgh called Lennoxlove, but the landholding is small, only two thousand acres of cattle."

That night, as she lay abed, she thought about how Hamilton led a useless life that consisted of socializing, drinking, and gaming. As head of the Douglas clan and Duke of Hamilton he possessed untold wealth, which was all funneled to London to support his dissolute lifestyle. Her hand caressed the child beneath her heart. *If you are a boy, you will be the next Duke of Hamilton. I promise you I will do my utmost to teach you to be a responsible man. I shall never allow you to waste your life and your wealth the way your father has done.* Elizabeth sighed deeply. In her heart she secretly longed for a daughter. *And if you are a girl, I shall try to teach you to be courageous and not allow men to bully you and make you afraid, as I have done.*

Two days later, they arrived at their final destination, Cadzow Castle in Hamilton, ten miles from Glasgow. To Elizabeth's amazement she learned that Hamilton owned most of those ten miles. She lost her heart to Cadzow as soon as she saw it. She loved everything about it, from the mellowed stone to the breath-stopping views from the upper windows of the pretty lawns and gardens that swathed the ancient manor in brilliant flowers. A great deal of work had been done on the chambers, turning it into a small palace, and the River Clyde ran close by, adding to its enchantment.

The stables were vast and housed some of the animals from the home farm such as oxen, Border ponies, and donkeys. There were no cats about because the mews above the stable housed hunting birds but she did spy a black-and-white Border collie and fully intended to make friends with it. She had always wanted a dog but had been forbidden such a pet by both her mother and her husband.

Beyond the cultivated gardens and meadows of the home farm stretched forests and fells that must teem with wild creatures such as deer, wolves, and even a lynx or two. Elizabeth, who was at heart a child of nature, couldn't wait to explore her new surroundings and test their boundaries.

Elizabeth and Emma hardly had time to unpack before the duke was planning a great party. "I want Glasgow Society to meet the Duchess of Hamilton while you are still in possession of your great beauty. It won't be long before you are ungainly and unfit to be seen in fashionable company."

Elizabeth lowered her lashes to mask the hurt his words caused, while inwardly cursing herself for allowing anything he said to even touch her. "Your Grace must choose something for me to wear." The exquisite sarcasm went completely over his head.

"We have a renowned artist in our clan. I shall arrange for Gavin Douglas to paint your portrait. I hope Emma packed your ermine-trimmed cape. Oh, and speaking of fur, I've decided to have a sable cloak made for your birthday. It gets bitter cold in Scotland. The ships from Russia that anchor in the Clyde at the Glasgow docks carry the most luxurious pelts. I shall take you aboard so you may select your own."

The thought of choosing dead furry creatures made her queasy. She had such a love of animals that wearing fur was distasteful to her. "You are too kind, Your Grace." *Posing for yet another portrait and selecting sable pelts for a cape—what else could an eighteen-year-old desire for her birthday?*

"By the way, did I mention that I have sent for your mother?"

Elizabeth repressed a shudder. *That makes everything bloody perfect! I might as well be in London. I shall have to pose for my portrait all day until I am ready to drop, then dance all night with the Scottish* ton. *To top it off, Mother will be here to spy on my every move and report it.* "How do you think of these things?" she asked sweetly. *Smile. You are the Duchess of Hamilton!*

Chapter Twenty-Five

*E*lizabeth, gowned in the Douglas colors of blue and white with sapphires blazing at her throat, stood beside Hamilton and graciously welcomed their guests who had traveled from Glasgow. The curve of her breasts swelling from the low-cut gown, with help from the glittering jewels, drew attention from the small mound of her belly. The duke had allowed her to wear her own golden hair, which also drew the eyes of both male and female alike.

"Tom Calder, at yer service." The flame-haired man in his mid-thirties bowed formally. "May I partner ye in the reel, Yer Grace?"

"I should be delighted, Mr. Calder." Elizabeth couldn't recall if this was the mayor, the provost, or chief magistrate of the burgh, but hoped the man in the kilt would not trample her feet.

"Do ye appreciate bagpipes an' Scottish music, Yer Grace?"

"Oh, yes. I consider it a great compliment to have reels and rants named in my honor, though to dance them takes much stamina."

"Yer a braw lass!" her partner beamed.

When the reel was over he drew her aside. "I ha' no doubt yer husband can refuse ye naught, so I'm solicitin' yer help."

You are wasting your breath—I have no influence with Hamilton. "It is the duke who wields the power, not the duchess, I'm afraid."

"I ha' ma doubts about that! Yer exquisite beauty must make

him putty in yer hands. I'm provost of the Glasgow Zoological Society, and I'm hopin' tae persuade Hamilton tae donate some land."

Elizabeth recoiled. "Zoo? I don't approve of putting animals in cages, sir!" *Oh, Lord, I've made an enemy with my sharp tongue.*

"No, no, lass . . . I mean, Yer Grace. We don't put them in cages. We've created a wildlife preserve where animals are free tae roam about in a natural environment. It prevents extinction from o'erzealous huntsmen an' protects creatures fer future generations. Scotland has many unique species. That's why we need more acres."

Elizabeth's face lit up. "That is such a splendid concept!" A frown marred her brow. "You must know that the duke's father built Chatelherault Hunting Lodge here on the Hamilton estate. My husband is an avid hunter, I'm afraid."

"Any Scot worth his salt is an avid hunter, lass, but huntin' an' preservation are no' mutually exclusive, do ye' ken?"

"Yes, I do understand and wholly approve. The question is *will my husband?* You will have to broach the subject yourself, I'm afraid, but I promise to lend whatever influence I have to persuade him to give you some land, Mr. Calder."

The provost squeezed her hands gratefully and walked a direct path to the Duke of Hamilton. Presently, she watched other men join them. Their expressions were dour, yet all held glasses of Scotch whiskey that the servants continually replenished, and she hoped the liquor would put him in a receptive mood.

Later, when Hamilton placed a proprietary hand on her arm and led her toward Lord and Lady Erskine, she gathered her courage and spoke up. Urging him to deny the land just might push him in the opposite direction. "I was approached by a man of unmitigated gall who actually expected you to give him land for an animal preserve. I told him it was out of the question. Hamilton land must be passed on to our children, not given away!"

His raised eyebrow mocked her. "Now that I've gotten my mare with foal, she is trying to take the bit between her teeth!" His next words showed her exactly who held the reins. "I've decided to give the Zoological Society a couple hundred acres.

The Douglas clan owns so much land it will never be missed. Try not to be so openly avaricious, my dear."

As the hour advanced and the liquor flowed, the atmosphere grew wild, and the crowd became uninhibited. The music increased in volume and tempo, as did the shouting, laughter, and cursing. Many of their guests decided to stay overnight rather than make the journey back to Glasgow, so it didn't matter how much they imbibed.

Elizabeth took the opportunity to retire about three in the morning when other ladies went to bed and left their men to their whiskey.

Because they had guests, Elizabeth arose early and went downstairs. The dining room was deserted, and breakfast food sat on serving tables in sterling silver chafing dishes. She selected scones and honey for herself then made up a tray of more hearty fare for Emma. On her way upstairs she encountered Morton. "Will His Grace be down shortly?"

Morton shook his head and lifted his hand to his mouth to mime a drinking motion. "He blacked out completely . . . awoke in a bad way, with a bit of memory loss again."

She felt guilty satisfaction that Hamilton was suffering for his overindulgence. "If he has forgotten, please remind him that some of our guests stayed overnight. But if he is unfit to leave his chamber, assure him that I will see to them."

Over the course of the next two hours, their overnight guests departed. Few of them took breakfast, but all assured her that they had enjoyed their visit immensely and looked forward to entertaining her in Glasgow. With her serene smile in place, Elizabeth thanked them graciously. Then a small curl of excitement spiraled inside her. With the guests gone and Hamilton indisposed, she intended to visit the animals in the stable. Before she made good her escape, however, she encountered Morton.

"His Grace wishes to see you, ma'am."

Resentment immediately replaced her excitement. "He has a knack for spoiling every pleasure. Do you know what he wants, Morton?"

"He wants you to fill in some of the blanks, I expect."

She followed the valet, feeling decidedly uncharitable toward her husband. When she saw the drink in his shaking hand, she felt disgust and lowered her lashes lest he read her thoughts.

"Hair of the dog for my hangover." He took a long swig. "I vaguely recall us having a slight altercation last night, Elizabeth, over a few acres of land. Would you refresh my memory?"

Her thoughts darted about like quicksilver, then she raised her lashes and looked into his bloodshot eyes. "You donated land to the Glasgow Zoological Society for an animal preserve."

"Ah, now I remember. Was it one hundred acres or two?"

"You were right to be generous over my selfish objections, Your Grace. You made them a gift of two thousand acres."

"Two thousand!" he roared as the whiskey in the glass sloshed over his hand. "You must be mistaken!" He glanced quickly at Morton, seeking help from any quarter.

"You mentioned it as soon as you retired from the party, Your Grace. I distinctly recall you saying you would never miss two thousand acres of Douglas land," the conspirator confirmed.

Hamilton swung back to face his wife and saw her serene smile.

"Your name will go down in the history books, Your Grace. Until now Hamilton's claim to fame in these parts has always been Chatelherault Hunting Lodge. Now, thanks to you, it will be Cadzow's animal preserve. Your generosity humbles me, Your Grace." Her success made her feel so giddy she was tempted to take a bow. "You must be hungry. Would you like some ham and eggs, or a few lamb kidneys perhaps?" As his skin turned a bilious yellow before her eyes, she savored sweet revenge.

Elizabeth immediately wrote a note to Tom Calder, confirming the Duke of Hamilton's generous gift of two thousand acres of land: *When you thank him, it would be prudent to let my husband believe the idea was his, and best for me if you burned this letter.* She gave the note to Morton, the only Hamilton servant she could trust.

Within a couple of days the duke recovered and took Elizabeth into Glasgow, not to show her the city but to show his duchess off to its leading citizens. In the late afternoon they boarded a Russian trading vessel anchored in the Clyde to buy sable pelts for her birthday cloak. Elizabeth carried a scented ball containing dried flowers, herbs, and spices to ward off the offensive stench of fish, animal pelts, and bear grease that the Russian sailors rubbed on their skin. Before she left the ship, however, she saw something that offended her far more. A small cage held two bear cubs that were completely white. The Russian captain informed her they were polar bears, something she had never known existed.

"Are they for sale?" she asked, keeping her fingers crossed.

"Indeed, Your Excellency. We keep them alive so they will grow and their skins increase in value until we find a buyer."

"If you want white fur, Elizabeth, arctic fox is far prettier," Hamilton informed her.

"No, no, Your Grace, I don't want them for their skins. I want you to buy them for your zoological preserve. How many people have ever seen white bears? They would cause a sensation!"

Hamilton pinched his nostrils. "The damn things stink!"

"That's because they've been kept in a small cage." When he moved away, Elizabeth clutched his arm. "Please, James, please?"

He looked into her pleading violet eyes and realized it was the first time she had ever called him James, or touched him of her own volition. In that moment he felt omnipotent as a god who had the power to bestow favors, or not, on a mere whim.

"I think not," he drawled and took delight in the anguished look on her beautiful face. He stood looking at her for long drawn-out minutes then exercised his power once more. "Why not? It is your eighteenth birthday, after all." He watched as joy suffused her delicate features.

"I thank you with all my heart," Elizabeth whispered.

The control he exercised over her emotions made him feel extremely masculine. He decided to send her back to Cadzow and stay in Glasgow tonight. He needed the services of a whore. Badly.

As it turned out, Hamilton's absence from Cadzow stretched from one night to one week. The parsimonious city had few gaming hells, but its trulls were more plentiful than fleas on a pack of hunting hounds and because of cutthroat competition were inventive, compliant, and grossly debauched in carnal sins of the flesh.

Elizabeth again corresponded with Tom Calder, telling him of the polar bear cubs and asking him for a special pen to accommodate their needs. She breathed easier with every day of Hamilton's absence. The head gardener built a dog run for the bear cubs, and when they arrived, she laughed at his pungent swear words. She even organized his young helpers to fish in the nearby river to supply the bears with food. She visited the mews each day and made friends with the falconer and his tethered birds of prey, vowing to remove their hoods if and when the opportunity presented itself.

She spent untold hours in the stables, brushing a sure-footed Border pony that took her fancy and petting the donkeys. These were a smaller breed than other donkeys, and their soft wooly coats made them look and feel fluffy as a child's toy. Whenever she was outdoors, her constant companion was the Border collie. When she learned that the black-and-white female had no name, she searched her mind for something appropriate. She thought of a chessboard and its pieces then christened the dog Queenie.

"Good God, you look like a ragamuffin!" Bridget made no attempt to hide her outrage when she arrived to find her daughter the duchess wearing a loose smock. "And keep that dog away from me."

Elizabeth placed a restraining hand on Queenie and immediately fell into the old submissive habit of excusing her appearance. "I was in the stillroom helping to make potpourri and scented candles. I hope you had a pleasant journey, Mother."

"I most certainly did not! I was uprooted from my London home, family, and friends and jolted over hundreds of miles to watch over your welfare, only to find you looking and acting like a scullery maid. You have no dignity! No sense of your station, Elizabeth! No wonder Hamilton sent for me. I can see these Scottish servants need taking in hand too. Where's Emma? Where is His Grace?"

"He is in Glasgow . . . on business, I believe."

"Funny bloody business, like all men, I warrant."

She suspects Father! She's angry she had to leave him in London where he cannot be trusted, and I'll get the brunt of that anger. She shooed Queenie back toward the stillroom, intent on soothing and appeasing the tyrant. "Come, you need a little pampering after such an arduous journey. I've chosen a lovely bedchamber for you with glorious views. Have a rest and I'll bring you some sherry and shortbread, then I'll get Emma to prepare a bath for you."

Upstairs they found Emma already unpacking Bridget's luggage. The maid had no illusions about how demanding Elizabeth's mother could be. She bobbed a curtsy. "Welcome to Cadzow Castle, ma'am."

Bridget sniffed and looked from the high window. "Hyde Park is my idea of a glorious view, not this godforsaken wilderness. It's worse than Ireland! Though I will admit this castle is far more luxurious than Castlecoote."

"I loved Castlecoote," Elizabeth said wistfully.

"You look like you never left! Go and change immediately. I brought you up to be a lady and, at great sacrifice to myself, arranged your marriage to a Duke of the Realm. You pay me back by dressing like a tinker's brat. Moreover, you do it deliberately!"

Elizabeth went to do her mother's bidding. *I might be a duchess in the eyes of the world, but when Mother confronts me I am reduced to a submissive child. How I wish I had the courage to defy her!*

The following day Hamilton returned and summoned Elizabeth and Bridget to the library. "Now that your mother is at Cadzow I have no qualms about returning to London for the opening of Parliament. Of course I'll return late October in time for the happy event."

Elizabeth's spirit soared. *I shall have all September and October to enjoy Scotland without him!*

He turned to Bridget. "I leave the welfare of the duchess and my unborn heir in your capable hands, madam."

"Be assured I shall send a written report weekly, Your Grace."

Elizabeth smiled serenely. *Emma and I will burn your bloody reports!*

"There is one thing that disturbs me, Your Grace. I've seen

a mangy dog hanging about. It could jump up on Elizabeth and harm your unborn child."

Elizabeth seethed. *You bitch! You know that Queenie brings me pleasure and are intent on depriving me of her.* "The matter has been taken care of, James. I ordered one of the gamekeepers to shoot it." The facile lie sprang to her lips with ease. She had beaten her mother at her own game, and for once her conscience did not even prick her.

"I shall have to leave before your birthday, my dear, so we shall celebrate it early in Glasgow with a grand birthday dinner. I shall present you with your sable cape, then I'll announce my gift of the polar bears to the wildlife sanctuary . . . *in your name.*"

"Your generosity humbles me, Your Grace." This time Elizabeth spoke from the heart. Such a gift meant more to her than all the furs or jewels in Christendom.

At her birthday celebration in Glasgow, Elizabeth introduced her mother to as many people as possible. She had lent Bridget her sapphires to go with the royal blue gown that contrasted so vividly with her red hair. Her intent was completely selfish; she hoped her mother would prefer Glasgow to Cadzow Castle and encouraged her to make friends with Lady Erskine, a woman of her own age.

Tom Calder sought Elizabeth for the next reel, and she accepted because she wanted to talk with him. "I was right, lassie, His Grace is putty in yer hands. How can I thank ye fer wheedlin' two thousand acres from a Hamilton? No mean feat!"

"You can thank me by creating a special place in your preserve for a pair of white polar bear cubs."

"Can ye talk him intae importing a pair from the Arctic?"

"He already bought them from a Russian trading ship in the Clyde. The duke will be announcing it to great fanfare." Her mischievous smile turned serious. "Tom, do you think Scotland might be too warm for polar bears?"

Calder threw back his head and laughed. " 'Tis clear ye've never spent a winter here, lassie. 'Twill freeze yer very bones! I'll make sure the wee bears ha' a big pond. It'll be covered wi' ice eight months outa twelve!"

"The duke must return to England for the opening of Parliament. After he's gone you mustn't be a stranger. Please bring your plans for the wildlife preserve to Cadzow. I'm dying to see them." As the overture to the next reel began she spied her chance to get out of it. "Oh, Tom, allow me to introduce my mother, the Honorable Bridget Gunning. She adores Scottish reels. Mother, this is Tom Calder." She winked. "You know what they say about redheads."

Two days later, as Elizabeth stood waving a dutiful and subdued good-bye to her husband, on the inside her wicked juices were bubbling. She couldn't wait to get out of her whalebone corset and petticoats and into a soft lambswool dress. She would take Queenie to the river for a swim while she fished for a trout. Then they would go for a long walk and take a look at Chatelherault, the infamous hunting lodge that the last Duke of Hamilton had built.

She spoke to Queenie as she would to any friend. "For the next two months I intend to be happy every single moment. Perhaps tomorrow I'll ride my favorite pony, and one day soon I'll get the falconer to let us fly a hunting bird. What's that you say? Will Mother let me? I spent a dozen years in the Irish countryside, keeping out of her way and learning to be a master of deceit."

Queenie's tongue lolled out as she laughed up at her new friend.

Chatelherault turned out to be a rustic palace with every comfort. A cleaning staff went there weekly to dust the furniture and polish the gleaming wooden floors and paneled walls. In spite of the fact that the place was seldom used, it was always kept in readiness for the duke or his guests. Elizabeth often accompanied the servants and as autumn arrived she enjoyed seeing the squirrels gather nuts and watching the leaves turn brilliant red and gold before they fell to blanket the forest floor.

Everyone at Cadzow soon learned to love Elizabeth, from the servants to the stewards and gamekeepers. When the weather turned cold she spent a lot of time in the castle kitchens learning how to cook and bake, knowing it was a place that her mother avoided. Elizabeth and Emma began to fashion baby garments and welcomed the Cadzow maids who joined their sewing circle.

As the babe inside her became more active, she talked to it continually. Her face was full, her breasts lush, though she hadn't gained a great deal of weight. She carried the child high and delighted in the maids' predictions about what such a sign signified. She wrote letters to her sister and her friend Charlie. Maria never replied, but of course Lady Charlotte did.

Dearest Elizabeth:

It was lovely to receive your letter and learn how much you are enjoying your stay in Scotland. I am so happy that you regained your strength and that you now bloom with health. Baby William is fat as a little piglet. The time goes so quickly. I can't believe he will soon be four months old. In no time at all, you will be a mother too, and I know you will enjoy it as much as I do.

I have a shameful secret, and you are the only one I dare tell. Will and I are having another baby! It happened in July, and though others will be shocked that I'm breeding again so soon, Will and I are very happy about it.

Here in London, all the talk is of war. French hostilities in America and India have flared up again, and Will says war between England and France cannot be avoided. You and I are lucky that our husbands chose politics rather than the military.

I wish I could be with you when you have your baby. I shall never forget the comfort you brought me when I had baby William. My second is due in April, so as soon as the Christmas festivities are over, I shall withdraw to Uppingham. It would be wonderful if you stopped for a visit on your journey back from Scotland so I could see you and your new baby.

Fondest love,
Charlie

Though Elizabeth was surprised that Charlie was already carrying another child, she was not shocked. Charlie and Will had such a happy marriage, and it was expected that a dynastic family such as the Devonshires would produce a large number of children.

That night as she reread the letter, the words about war filled her with dread, and she could not get the picture of John in his uniform out of her head. He had said that he might be tempted to come to Chatelherault, but in her heart she felt that he never would. Both of them knew it would be too painful, forever longing for what might have been. When they met she had needed someone to love, and she had lost her heart. But soon she would have her baby and Elizabeth felt certain she would never be lonely again.

An impulse compelled her to find her old cloak in the wardrobe. She cut the brass button from the lining and decided to put it away in a drawer. She vowed to put away her memories of John too; it was far safer to stop thinking of him. But when she fell asleep, Elizabeth had the token of John's love clutched firmly in her hand. That night, as usual, John Campbell haunted her dreams.

Chapter Twenty-Six

"The Douglases have more royal blood and more right to rule as Kings of Great Britain than that upstart German George Hanover!"

The Duke of Hamilton arrived at Cadzow Castle on October 31 still livid from an insult the king had delivered at his monthly levee. When James had hinted that he'd like a royal appointment, King George had asked if the Douglas clan had Jacobite leanings. Hamilton ordered his duchess and her mother to the library, where he spread fading genealogy charts across his desk to prove his point.

"Anne, daughter of King James the Third, married James Douglas, the first Lord Hamilton. King James the Fourth had a natural daughter who married the next James Douglas. Not only that—the king's widowed queen, Mary Tudor, married Archibald Douglas, another Hamilton noble." His thick finger jabbed at the chart as he documented his royal blood. "The Hanovers were never kings until they usurped Britain's throne—they were nothing but *electors*!"

The duke's arrival ruined Elizabeth's tranquility and destroyed her peace of mind. She knew better than to point out that his ravings were treasonous and instead tried to calm him. "We must be thankful that King George never comes to Scotland, Your Grace."

"He doesn't need to! He has nobles like me to represent him. How dare he sneer down his German nose at the leading Lowland clan? As Duke of Hamilton I am Hereditary Keeper of Holyrood Palace!"

To mollify him, Bridget added, "You are also Duke of Brandon and Marquis of Clydesdale. Perhaps the king is envious of your ancient titles, Your Grace, and I warrant he is secretly jealous that you married Elizabeth and took her from his Court."

"Death and damnation, you are right, madam! He's been a peevish old swine since I informed him I was anticipating an heir." He swept Elizabeth with a speculative look from head to toe, as if assessing her pregnancy to make sure she had nearly another month to go.

Elizabeth suddenly went icy cold. Only this morning she had felt her baby move about as if it were doing a somersault, and now she seemed to be carrying it much lower. If her child was born today, Hamilton might suspect she had conceived before their marriage. She resolutely pushed the thought away, telling herself that such a thing was not possible.

"Start packing. Pack everything. We are going to Edinburgh!" Hamilton smiled with smug satisfaction. "The heir to the dukedom of Hamilton will be born at the Royal Palace of Holyrood."

Elizabeth felt a rising panic. She was happy at Cadzow Castle; she knew the staff and felt at ease with them. The thought of a journey to Edinburgh frightened her. Fear of the unknown engulfed her. "Your Grace, I would like to have my baby at Cadzow."

He dismissed her words and banged his fist on the desk. "It is in my heir's best interest to be born at Holyrood, as is his due. It will also send a clear message to the king regarding the power of Douglas. 'Tis only forty miles away, and an Edinburgh midwife is just as competent as one from Glasgow, I warrant."

Bridget, ever a glutton for status, was not about to argue with the powerful Hamilton. "There is no need to fret, Elizabeth. You have at least three weeks to go yet—plenty of time to get you settled in. Come, we have much packing to do."

The mother-to-be struggled to her feet. To Elizabeth it was like a recurring nightmare, where other people always decided her fate. A woman facing childbirth for the first time had little enough control, but what little she had was being swept away. She placed protective hands on her kicking child and spoke to it silently. *All will be well. I won't let anything or anyone harm you, little one*. To her amazed relief, the baby quietened.

As the carriage rumbled along, Elizabeth appreciated the sable cloak for the first time. Bridget and Emma both had fur lap rugs tucked about their legs, yet still the three women were far from warm. When they spoke, their breath was visible in the cold air. Hamilton had ridden ahead with his valet, his secretary, and one of his stewards, ostensibly to make arrangements for the arrival of his duchess and their expected child, but Elizabeth knew he refused to be confined in a coach with three females.

When the carriage jolted over a particularly rough patch, Emma saw the strained look on Elizabeth's face and asked, "Are you feeling all right, my dear?"

Elizabeth hesitated. A nagging pain had begun in her back, but when she glanced at her mother's stony countenance, it clearly conveyed that she had better not be in labor. "I'm fine, Emma."

An hour later, just as dusk began to descend, the coach drove through the iron gates and swung to a stop in Holyrood's courtyard. A gaggle of servants stepped from the main entrance and formed a line to welcome the Duchess of Hamilton. Emma opened the carriage door, stepped out, and held up her hands to assist Elizabeth, who climbed stiffly down the step. "Straight to bed with you. I hope they have roaring fires to thaw us out."

"My legs are cramping . . . I need to walk a little, Emma."

Bridget stepped from the coach ready to do battle with the servants of the royal household. "I take it you have prepared the Queen's suite of rooms for Her Grace, the Duchess of Hamilton." It was not a question but an assumption. She no longer played a role; her regal demeanor had become an integral part of her.

As Elizabeth walked slowly through the luxuriously appointed chambers she found the atmosphere strangely oppressive. She tried to dismiss the feeling: *I'm being fanciful because I would rather be at Cadzow.* She put her hand to her back as another spasm of pain took her breath then slowly eased away. She denied to herself that she was in labor. *Labor pains would be in my belly!* An inner voice answered her: *You'd better find your rooms and Emma, just in case!* She turned to find a palace maid who had been following her at a respectful distance.

The maid bobbed a curtsy. "I'll show ye the way, Yer Grace."

When they reached the suite of rooms that had been prepared, Elizabeth found the atmosphere even more foreboding, though the sitting room was large and a cheery fire had been lit. She entered the bedchamber and saw Emma already unpacking her things. "I have a recurring pain in my back, but it's far too early for labor, don't you think?" she asked apprehensively.

"Oh, my love, I've never had a child. Let's put you into bed and I'll get your mother."

"No, no, Emma! I'm sure if I lie down the pain will go away." Moving slowly and with great care, she undressed and slipped into the bed, but her mind was racing, her thoughts chasing each other in circles. *If you admit the truth, you want your baby's father to be John Campbell.* She answered the inner voice: *No! No! That is a wicked thing to say. My child is Hamilton's! If he is a boy, he will be heir to the Dukedom of Hamilton. There must never, ever be the slightest doubt about his paternity. There must never be even a hint of scandal connected with my name.* Suddenly her abdomen went rigid, and she was gripped with a heavy pain that tore a cry from her throat. When it eased away, she threw Emma a look of apology. "I'm sorry . . . I'll try to be quiet."

"Elizabeth, you must let me get your mother. We don't want any harm to come to this child."

Elizabeth bit her lip, knowing she had no choice. Her baby's welfare was paramount, so she gave Emma permission.

The minute Emma told Bridget about Elizabeth's pain, her mother sought out Hamilton. She found him ensconced in the state apartments. "We need a midwife without delay, Your Grace. The coach ride has brought on early labor!"

"Damn and blast that coach driver! He always sets a reckless pace. If aught happens to this child, I'll have him hanged! I have already summoned the royal physician. He will no doubt know of a competent midwife." Hamilton turned to his secretary. "Go and see what's keeping the man." He turned back to Bridget. "I gave orders to have the royal nursery refurbished, but they'd better start work tonight." He spoke to Morton, "Summon the steward and the housekeeper."

Bridget did not want her competence called into question. "I made arrangements for a nursemaid and a wet nurse at Cadzow, Your Grace, but that won't help us here in Edinburgh."

"Have no fear. All will be taken care of, madam. Make sure that Elizabeth is comfortable and gets whatever she needs. Inform me immediately of any developments."

"I shall, Your Grace, but keep in mind that the birth of a first child can be a lengthy process. She will be in labor most of the night, and the child likely won't be born until tomorrow."

"The length of her labor matters not, madam, so long as she has a safe delivery and my child is unharmed."

Bridget returned to Elizabeth's rooms and confronted a uniformed maidservant. "I asked that my daughter be put in the queen's suite of rooms, but I have just learned that the state apartments are the ones used by the royals."

"These rooms belonged tae Queen Mary, madam."

Bridget frowned. "Surely you don't mean Mary, Queen of Scots?"

"The very same, madam. That most ancient and sacred chamber in Holyrood Palace is where Queen Mary gave birth tae King James."

"Very well. I suppose it will have to do. See that a fire has been lit in my bedchamber, and see that we get some food. We are like to starve to death in this *sacred* place!"

Elizabeth, who had heard the exchange between her mother and the maid, shivered as if a goose had walked over her grave. She slid from the curtained bed and walked in her night rail to the fire.

Mary's life was tragic. She imprinted her sadness on these rooms.

Emma, seeing her shiver, wrapped her sable cloak about her shoulders. "Keep this around you while I look for a warm bedrobe."

"My pain has moved to the front. I don't fancy any food, Emma, but I would like some watered wine, if I may."

When two maidservants arrived with trays of food, Bridget took hers to her bedchamber, which was a few doors away down a corridor. Emma diluted a goblet of wine with a little water and brought it to Elizabeth at the fireplace. "This should warm you and take the edge off."

Elizabeth took a sip then spoke to the serving women. "Show me where Rizzio was murdered."

The two women exchanged a speaking look that told her there was no need to explain that Rizzio was Queen Mary's Italian secretary, stabbed to death before her eyes on the order of her husband, Darnley. The maids beckoned her, and she followed them into the adjoining sitting room. The women pointed to a stain on the floorboards.

As Elizabeth gazed down she did not know if this could possibly be a bloodstain from two centuries past, but the evil deed had somehow left its indelible imprint upon Mary's private chambers. She felt the sinister memories and the ghosts they left behind.

"Thank you," she murmured sadly. "Could you bring more wine, please?" Her hand went to her belly, and she knew the baby's head had moved to the birth canal. She sent up a fervent prayer: *Please don't punish my baby for the sins I have committed.*

By ten o'clock the doctor had arrived and examined her. Bridget emerged from her room to consult with him. "My daughter has gone into early labor from a rough carriage ride. I advised His Grace that it would be dangerous to undergo a journey this late in her confinement, but he insisted that his heir be born at Holyrood."

"The Douglas is a law unto himself, madam," he said dourly. "How far apart are her pains?"

Bridget consulted Emma then replied, "Her pains seem to come on an hourly basis, doctor. Do you foresee any difficulties?"

"Too soon to tell. The midwife is on her way, but I don't expect the child will be delivered before morning."

Bridget was about to take the news to the duke when the midwife arrived. She examined the young duchess and agreed with the doctor. He advised the woman to have a trundle bed set up for herself, just in case the patient went into hard labor during the night. Then he took a bottle of laudanum from his bag and set it on a bedside table. "In my experience, duchesses refuse to suffer like mere mortals. If she starts to scream, dose her before her caterwaul alarms the duke." The doctor then informed Bridget that he would relay the news to the Duke of Hamilton himself.

By midnight Elizabeth was exhausted by her efforts to remain silent when the heavy pain gripped her body, and between contractions she closed her eyes and tried to doze. She was aroused from light slumber by a voice.

"Elizabeth!"

She opened her eyes, thinking it was Emma, but her faithful maid was asleep in her chair. Then she saw a woman standing at the foot of the curtained bed who, inexplicably, looked like Queen Mary.

"Never let any learn your secret!" she whispered urgently. "Guard it with your life, as I guarded mine. Promise!"

"I promise," Elizabeth breathed. As the vision faded, her body was suddenly racked with a strong persistent pain. Her low cry awoke Emma, who jumped up from the chair and took her hand.

"I'll stay with you, my lamb. You are so brave."

As the spasm eased, Elizabeth laughed. "I'm not brave, Emma. I'm frightened as a little rabbit . . . I'm afraid of Hamilton . . . afraid of Mother . . . afraid for my baby . . . oh, Lord, I hope it's a girl!"

"Don't wish that. He expects a son and heir, not a daughter!"

Elizabeth's eyes widened as another pain, greater than the one she'd had a few minutes ago, sank its vicious fangs into her and would not let go. She heard a scream and realized it was her own.

The midwife arose from her trundle bed and, a minute later when Bridget appeared on the scene, confirmed to her that Elizabeth had gone into hard labor. "Make note, her water broke at two o'clock."

Emma, with the help of a maid, changed the bedsheets, then she poured water into a basin and sponged Elizabeth's face and neck, which were drenched with perspiration.

For the next two hours the mother-to-be writhed with an agony that gripped her every few minutes. She panted, she laughed, she cried, and she cursed. At four o'clock when the baby's head crowned, her screams began in earnest. She reached up and tore down a thick cord that held back the bed-curtains, then she wrapped it about her fists as she obeyed the women's orders to push, wishing she had not stubbornly refused the laudanum.

Suddenly she was convulsed with an unendurable paroxysm of pain, blessedly followed by a gushing feeling of release that made her lose consciousness. When she opened her eyes, she obediently gulped down a spoonful of laudanum her mother proffered.

"My baby—"

"Your baby's delivered, Elizabeth. The midwife is cleansing it."

"Please, let me see!"

The midwife came back to the bed carrying a bundle swathed in a flannel blanket. When she looked at Elizabeth, she thrust the child at Bridget and spoke to Emma. "She's bleeding . . . get some pillows . . . prop her feet higher than her head."

Elizabeth felt herself leaving them, as if she were dissolving as the ghost of Queen Mary had done earlier. "No . . . wait!" As she opened her mouth, the midwife thrust in a spoonful of laudanum.

"I already dosed her!" Bridget cried.

"No harm done. She needs complete rest so the bleedin' will stop. There, she's already asleep. What's the time? Five o'clock? I think it would be prudent tae wait an hour before we rouse the duke from his bed."

Elizabeth heard the bedchamber door crash open, and a cold finger of premonition touched her. Hamilton strode to the bed—his mottled skin told her that his anger was high. He needed to vent his spleen, and she was his target. *He suspects that the baby is not his!* She struggled to speak, but her lips felt numb and she could not form words.

"I brought you to Holyrood Palace so that my son and heir could be born here in his rightful place, and what do you give me in return? A girl—a useless female like yourself! Even that wretched Charlotte Boyle gave her husband a son. I'll be a bloody laughingstock! All Edinburgh is waiting to celebrate, and all you can produce is a daughter. Well, if you know what's good for you, you'll keep the brat away from me. As soon as you're fit to travel, we'll go back to London and try all over again."

Elizabeth closed her eyes in utter defeat and humiliation. *I want to die . . . why didn't you let me die?* Her eyes flew open as she heard the door bang again, and she realized he was gone. She felt so ill, so tired, so hopeless. All she wanted was sleep. The atmosphere at Holyrood was so oppressive she longed to escape from it. Wearily, she thought of London and saw her future stretching before her, one unhappy day after another, and knew she would sell her soul to escape from Hamilton. Her eyelids were so heavy they began to close, then she saw the bottle of laudanum beside her bed. Here was her answer. She reached for the bottle, feeling euphoria wash over her. Hamilton would never bully her again.

"Stop!"

Elizabeth jumped, and the bottle slipped from her fingers to the floor. Her eyes widened at the regal vision at the foot of the bed. "What do you want?" she asked listlessly.

"I want to give you courage! Don't let them do this to you, Elizabeth. Fight them! Fight them as I did!"

"It's easy for you . . . you are a queen."

"You are a duchess! And a mother! You have a child who needs you to be strong and courageous. Fight them, Elizabeth."

The vision dissolved, and she struggled to sit up.

Emma came in from the adjoining room and hurried to the bed. "You're awake at last. Heaven be praised! You've slept through a day and a night. Are you feeling better, my lamb?"

"Where's my baby?"

"In the nursery with your mother and a battery of nursemaids." When Elizabeth threw back the covers, Emma said, "Oh, the doctor said you mustn't get up. He's been to see you three times, though I doubt you remember."

"No, I don't recall seeing the doctor. All I remember is Hamilton's visit. His cruel words devastated me, Emma."

"The duke hasn't been to see you, my lamb. You must have been dreaming. They gave you laudanum to make you sleep."

"I wasn't dreaming . . . Hamilton was as real as Mary—" Elizabeth realized what she had just said and shook her head, bewildered.

"Mary?" Emma looked at her with concerned eyes.

"The Queen of Scots. She must have been a vision. She came to give me courage and, by God, not before time. If they try to keep my baby from me, they won't find a rabbit—they'll find a wildcat!"

Elizabeth touched her breast, ripe with milk. "My baby needs to be fed." She swung her feet to the carpet and into her slippers.

"Don't fret. Your baby has a wet nurse, two nursemaids, and your mother. Let me change your night rail—that one is blood-stained."

"Hurry." Elizabeth stood impatiently while Emma brought the white nigh trail. She stripped off the old one and donned the clean one then hurried through the door.

Emma scurried after her, setting the sable cape onto her shoulders. "You could start to bleed again."

"I don't care!"

Elizabeth found the nursery a few doors from her mother's bedchamber. She swept in like an avenging angel.

"Why aren't you in bed?" Bridget demanded.

"Because I choose otherwise." Elizabeth met her mother's challenging look with one of her own. "I have come for my baby."

Bridget spread her arms to block her way. "It is feeding time. Go back to bed this instant!"

Elizabeth drew herself up to her full height and lifted a regal chin. "I am Her Grace, Duchess of Hamilton. Step aside, madam, or I shall shove you on your arse."

Bridget's mouth gaped open, but she dropped her arms.

Elizabeth took the child from the wet nurse. "Thank you for feeding my baby, but your services are no longer required."

All the women stared after the regal figure of the duchess, draped in sable, as she departed cradling her newborn child. All knew that titled ladies did not feed their own babies.

Elizabeth returned to her chamber, climbed into bed, and gazed down at the tiny miracle she had produced. The baby screwed up its face, ready to cry, and she quickly lifted her breast from the nigh trail and popped a nipple into the bright pink mouth. A look of ecstasy came into the child's eyes as it began to suckle. Elizabeth laughed with delight. "She is so beautiful!"

"She is a *he*." Emma bent to pick up the cloak from the floor.

"I had a boy?" Elizabeth asked uncertainly. Then she looked down into the brown eyes and watched, entranced, as dark-fringed lashes lowered in contentment. "I have a son!" she whispered.

Chapter Twenty-Seven

*A*s Elizabeth lay in bed with her sleeping son in her arms, she felt empowered. She had finally found the courage to challenge her mother's authority and, to her amazement, Bridget had acquiesced. John Campbell's words floated to her from the past when she'd once asked him what it was like to fight in a war: *When you go into battle your greatest foe is not the enemy—it is fear. But if you face your fear and challenge it, it invariably surrenders, and you emerge victorious.* Elizabeth knew this was what she had done with her mother. She vowed to never let her gain the upper hand again. She reflected about her vision of Mary. The Scottish queen had prevented her from seeking eternal sleep, thank God. This wasn't a time to sleep. It was a time to awaken . . . to wake up and live! *Mary made me promise to guard my secret with my life, but that was a manifestation of my own fear.* Elizabeth's thoughts drifted to Hamilton. Her nightmare about his rejection of her child also had been brought on by her own deep-seated fear. She wondered what his real reaction had been when he learned he had a son and heir. Elizabeth didn't have long to wait to find out.

"There he is, there's my little prince!" Hamilton actually swaggered across the bedchamber. "I went to the nursery and found a gaggle of hissing geese accusing you of kidnapping my son!"

"They are the kidnappers! They snatched him away so quickly I didn't know if I'd had a girl or a boy."

Hamilton grinned fatuously down at her. "There was never any question that I'd have a *son*. I'm very pleased with you, Elizabeth. Let's have a good look at him." He pulled the blanket away and began to undo the tapes on the baby's flannel gown.

"No!" Elizabeth snatched her child from him. *You must not see him naked!* "It's winter—he'll catch cold."

Bridget, who had followed the duke into the chamber, said, "There's a roaring fire. Of course he won't catch cold."

Elizabeth fixed her with a cool glance. "You are intruding. My husband and I would like a private visit with our baby son."

"Your Grace," Bridget murmured stiffly then retreated.

Hamilton chuckled. "You are fierce as a lynx with her kit. Let me have my son . . . I won't hurt him." He took the baby in the crook of his arm and rocked him gently. "He's very dark."

"I believe his hair will be auburn, like yours." *You think no such thing,* her inner voice accused.

"Most likely. 'Tis plain he won't have your golden curls." He lifted up the long folds of the nightgown to view the child's limbs and private parts. "He's a lusty male, all right!" When the baby started to cry, he handed him back to his mother.

Elizabeth cradled her son against her heart and made soothing noises that quietened him almost instantly.

Hamilton gazed down at the lovely woman in the bed. The pristine white night rail and halo of golden hair gave her a gentle, Madonna-like quality that made him feel blessed by the gods. He sought to indulge her. "You deserve something special for the priceless gift you have given me. What do you desire, Elizabeth? Diamonds? Emeralds?"

She raised her eyes from her child. "I desire that his cradle be brought to my chamber. I desire to be at Cadzow Castle in Hamilton. Holyrood has a dark, foreboding atmosphere."

"Aye, well, it has a dark history," he admitted. "Holy Rood Abbey lies in ruins, so he can't be baptized here. I've been up on the rock at Edinburgh Castle celebrating my son's birth with the provost. We could have him baptized up there. I could send word to John Campbell that we want him to be godfather."

"No!" She stared at Hamilton aghast. *Does he suspect? Is he playing cat and mouse with me?* "The Highlands are a hundred miles away, and Christmas is coming. He'll want to be with his family."

Hamilton nodded. "Why have a Campbell when we can have a Douglas for godfather? As soon as you're strong enough, we'll go back to Cadzow and have him baptized on New Year's Day."

Elizabeth felt overwhelmed with relief. Not only was he proudly possessive of the child; he was taking them back to the castle she loved. She kissed her baby's brow and said in gratitude, "I think he should have your name . . . James George Douglas." *If he has your name, there can be no question that he is your son.* Her inner voice taunted, *You're not being generous, Elizabeth—you're being expedient. Shut up!* she warned her inner voice.

"I still intend to gift my duchess with jewels."

She looked into his pouched eyes and saw the whites were permanently yellowed from his excessive drinking bouts. She realized that though she had overcome her timidity and stood up to her mother, it would take a great deal more courage to overcome her fear of Hamilton. She also feared herself: One day her resentment and anger might flare and explode so violently she could be consumed by the conflagration. She reined in her emotions and vowed to take one small step at a time. "Then I would ask that you buy me some turquoise . . . I've always fancied the blue-green stones. They are an ancient symbol of protection and good luck."

"If turquoise pleases you, so be it."

She lowered her lashes. Today, because he was exultant over the birth of a son, he had conceded to all her wishes. She silently vowed that this would not be the last time.

The next day when the nursery was moved into Elizabeth's suite of rooms, Bridget's resentment at having her authority usurped knew no bounds. She refused to speak to her daughter but filled Emma's ears with bitter recriminations about her sacrificing London's festivities to spend Christmas in dreary Scotland for her daughter's lying-in. Her thanklessness added insult to injury!

"You shouldn't be out of bed. It's only been three days since you gave birth. Even Lady Charlotte stayed abed ten days."

Elizabeth smiled at Emma from the rocking chair as she fed baby James. "You are beginning to sound like Mother."

"Heaven forbid! Your mother's catalogue of grievances grows longer by the hour."

"She's homesick for London, and I know she misses Maria. The blame for a quiet Christmas is mine. The duke can take himself off to Edinburgh Castle to be feted and congratulated, but Mother is stuck here, with only herself for company. She'll be no happier when we return to Cadzow, but I know I shall."

On the twentieth of December, James Douglas kept his word and took Elizabeth and his son back to Hamilton, with a strict warning to the coach driver to exercise caution on the icy roads. At Cadzow the entire household celebrated the arrival of his son and heir, and the maids vied with one another to serve the new mother and child. Hamilton appointed two Douglas cousins to stand godfather to his heir, and the baby was baptized James George Douglas in the castle chapel on New Year's Day, followed by a great celebration.

When the duke sobered up on the third day of January, his secretary opened his business mail and handed Hamilton his personal letters from London. One from George Coventry caught the duke's attention. "Poor George hasn't gotten his mare in foal yet. Wonder if I should do the job for him?"

His secretary, used to Hamilton's coarse remarks, laughed on cue.

James suddenly stopped laughing as he read the second part of the letter.

Rumor has it that the old Duke of Devonshire will
resign his appointment as Lord Steward of the Royal
Household. On the journey back from his grandson's
christening at Chatsworth he came down with
pneumonia and has never regained his health. Since this
particular appointment is not heritable, I can only
imagine the arse-kissing that will go on at the king's
next levee. Despite the fact that our friend Will

Cavendish deserves to take over from his father, the
appointment will be up for grabs.

"Will Cavendish doesn't deserve any such thing! He has had
far too many honors handed to him on a silver platter."

"I beg your pardon, Your Grace?"

"Prepare a report on Holyrood Palace. Make sure it shows
my administration as Hereditary Keeper in the best possible
light."

James took a piece of parchment stamped with his ducal
crest and dipped a quill into the inkwell on his desk. He proceeded to write a letter to King George, announcing the birth of
his son and informing him that he had named his heir after His
Royal Highness. He sent a special greeting from his duchess,
Elizabeth, hinting how much she missed Court. He also mentioned that he had left his head steward at the king's official residence in the capital to make sure that the palace was run
efficiently and economically, without waste. He made no mention of Devonshire's Lord Stewardship in the letter but asked
for an appointment with the king upon his return. "Send this
posthaste, along with your report. Then start packing for London," he ordered his secretary.

A short time later he spoke to Morton, his valet, and told him
to pack his things for London. Then he had a word with the
Douglas steward in charge of the inside staff. He promoted him
to land steward and told him to employ a new household steward.

Before Morton began to pack, he sought out the duchess.
"Your Grace, I thought you might like to know that the duke
has ordered me to pack for London."

Elizabeth's heart flew into her mouth at the news. "Thank
you, Morton. I appreciate your confidence." The last thing in
the world she wanted was to return to London. Apart from the
fact that such a long journey in winter might be harmful to her
baby, she loved Cadzow and the beautiful wild country that surrounded it. She found Emma upstairs, rocking her sleeping
son's cradle, and confided her fears.

"Surely he won't expect you to accompany him? But just in
case, why don't you get into bed and I'll tell him you are feeling overtired and that you need to rest more?"

Elizabeth felt both relieved and worried. "Emma, if he ever learns that we are conspirators, he will dismiss you on the spot."

Emma winked. "I could always go back to the stage."

"Do you miss it?" Elizabeth asked anxiously.

"Miss lining up every day of my life with a score of other starving actresses and getting passed over nine times out of ten?"

"I'm glad you don't miss it. I confess that I've often yearned to be an actress rather than a duchess the past year."

Emma helped her into a night rail and turned back the bed-covers. "Look at it this way—you get to be both."

"What in the name of Christ do you think you are doing?" Hamilton stopped dead as he stared at his duchess propped up against the pillows in the carved bed, holding his son in her arms.

Elizabeth went icy cold and drew her baby closer, shrinking down into the covers as if they would provide protection.

"When your mother informed me *you* were breast-feeding him, I thought the woman was deranged, but now I see with my own eyes that you are behaving like a peasant girl. I arranged for a wet nurse. Where is she?" he demanded.

"In Edinburgh. I don't need her services," Elizabeth said low. *I should have known Mother would take her revenge. I've been feeding him for weeks; it's a wonder she didn't tell him sooner.*

"This is preposterous! You are the Duchess of Hamilton, not some little drab in a slum! By Christ, I said you were like a lynx with her kit, and it's true—you are behaving like an animal."

"I want to feed my own baby," she said quietly, trying to control the rage that was building inside her.

"You may *not,* for the simple reason that it will ruin the shape and size of your perfect breasts. The London Season starts in the spring, and when it does I want you beside me with your famous beauty unimpaired."

Elizabeth, don't lash out at him now. You are at a disadvantage, and he is leaving soon. Deal with this swine from a position of strength, not weakness. Wait . . . wait . . . all things come at their appointed time.

"I've given Bridget orders to employ a wet nurse today. This is the last time you will feed him. Is that understood?"

"I understand, Your Grace." *I understand that you need to be in control and that Mother has the same sick affliction.*

"That's better. I must return to London. I have an appointment with the king. 'Tis no wonder you are not well enough to return home with me—the child has sapped all your strength. Get your health back, Elizabeth. I want you in London by spring. Baby James needs a brother."

She repressed a shudder. *I never want you in my bed again!*

Within half an hour of Hamilton's departure, Elizabeth jumped out of bed and got dressed. Five minutes later she was singing and tickling baby Jamie who lay on the big bed, kicking with delight. She danced across to the windows and dragged back the curtains to let in the pale winter sunshine. "Emma, I'm so hungry I could eat a horse . . . saddle an' all."

"I don't know about horse, but perhaps we could arrange to have *donkey* put on the menu," Emma teased.

"Oh, the dear little donkeys! I haven't seen them for weeks. When Jamie has his nap, I'm off to the stables for a visit." She picked up her baby and kissed his nose. "Let's go to the kitchen."

As she descended the stairs she saw her mother. Bridget was talking to a plump young woman with dark hair and rosy cheeks.

"Elizabeth, this is Nan Douglas, the wet nurse His Grace asked me to arrange for." She set her shoulders, ready for a fight.

"Thank you, Mother. How will I ever manage without you?" Elizabeth asked sweetly. The implication that she would be without her soon was not lost on Bridget.

"Nan, are you a cousin of the duke's?"

Nan shook her head. "Nothing so fancy. There's hundreds of Douglases hereabouts, Yer Grace."

"No, please don't curtsy to me. Would you like to come to the kitchen with us and have something to eat, Nan?"

Inside the vast kitchen, Elizabeth sat down at a scrubbed table and motioned for Emma and Nan to sit. "Nell, I'm ravenous," she told the head cook. "The delicious smell is making my mouth water."

"That's mutton an' barley broth." The cook beamed, ladling out a bowlful for each female then cutting up a fresh-baked loaf.

"Do you have a baby, Nan?" Elizabeth asked between spoonfuls.

"Aye, my mam is mindin' her. I'm tryin' tae wean her, so I should have lots of milk fer the wee lordling."

"No need for that, Nan. I have my own milk. I don't need a wet nurse, but I am looking for a good nursemaid. You can keep your baby with you if you like. I have Jamie's cradle in my own chamber right now, because I can't bear to part with him, but I'm going to turn the adjoining room into a nursery."

Cook poured two beakers of milk for the new mothers. "I've got the kettle on fer yer tea, Miss Emma."

"Do ye really mean I can keep my bairn wi' me, Yer Grace?"

"Of course. It's cruel to keep a mother from her child. When you've finished eating, go and get her and bring her upstairs. It's nap time." She gazed down lovingly. "He's already asleep."

A short time later, Elizabeth put on fur-lined walking boots, a warm hood and cape, and walked to the stables, humming happily.

She knew she had three glorious hours to herself before Jamie would need feeding again and planned to enjoy the invigorating outdoors. "Queenie!" she cried with joy as a black-and-white streak rushed across the courtyard. "I've missed you so. We'll go for a long walk after I've said hello to the donkeys."

Inside, her eyes widened with delight. "You have a baby too!"

She scratched the donkeys' ears and peered down at the woolly little bundle suckling its mother. "When did the baby arrive?" she asked a stableman.

"Christmas, ma'am. A right surprise fer all of us. Winter's an odd time fer foalin', but donkeys is strange beasties at best."

She rubbed the baby's head. "You're a sweet beastie. Your fluffy coat is soft as thistledown . . . I'll call you Thistle."

She spoke to the mother donkey. "I will bring my baby to see your baby one day soon." She pictured a little boy with black curls sitting on the back of a donkey. "They will be great friends."

After Elizabeth talked with the ponies, she and Queenie went for a walk. There was a light covering of snow on the ground, and along the riverbank she saw the distinctive prints left behind by deer, lynx, and otter. They followed the deer tracks back into the woods where rabbits and game birds scattered as Queenie flushed them from their snowy evergreen cover.

When she returned to the castle her companion trotted beside her like a faithful friend and she decided to let the dog come inside. Queenie walked warily, ears pricked, sniffing the unfamiliar objects that lay in her path, yet trusting enough not to cower. Elizabeth was not surprised when she heard her mother's shout of outrage.

"Who the devil let that dirty dog in here? Get it out, quick!"

Elizabeth stepped through the archway into the chamber where Bridget and Queenie stood transfixed. Both had raised hackles.

"*This* bitch stays, so long as she minds her manners."

"Are you calling me a *bitch*?" Bridget challenged.

"I am indeed." Elizabeth pushed off her hood and shook out her hair. "You have intimidated me all my life, Mother, but at last I have lost my fear of you. Like Queenie here, I will be wary, but I will never cower again. I would caution you too to mind your manners, for in the Duke of Hamilton's absence, I am the authority here at Cadzow."

Bridget immediately backed down and capitulated. "I'm glad you found your backbone."

Elizabeth threw back her head and laughed. At Bridget. At herself. At the irony of how simple it had been.

The next day, the Douglas steward who had been promoted introduced her to the new inside steward. Mr. Burke proved to be a quiet, competent head servant who ran the household smooth as clockwork. Elizabeth was wary of him because he often appeared silently out of nowhere, and she wondered if he had been hired to spy on her. When she mentioned it to Emma, her maid said, "Oh, I don't think so, Elizabeth. It wasn't the duke who employed him—it was the Douglas steward. The housemaids are all mad for him, and he's even charmed your mother."

"What about you, Emma? Do you like him?"

"Well, I must admit the attractive devil of a man plays hell with my imagination!"

As one day folded into another, Elizabeth had never felt happier in her life, and she began to glow with health. January was bitter cold, though only light snow covered the hard frozen ground. The entire household predicted that the weather would deteriorate in February but told her that the worst month in Scotland was usually March.

The snowstorms and blizzards held off, allowing Elizabeth to walk each day, and sometimes, if there was no wind, she carried Jamie across to the stables to show him the animals. "This is Thistle, your very own pet donkey." She knew her baby was too young to understand, but she wanted him to learn the smells and sounds of animals so he would get used to them.

Some days she ventured out on her favorite pony, with Queenie at their heels, and sometimes she flew a hawk from the mews. Often she visited the hunting lodge and stood gazing in awe at its pristine, isolated setting where the only human footprints were her own.

Almost every day of February brought a fall of snow, but still no massive storm. During the last week of the month, Elizabeth began to think about spring. She wished the winter could last forever, wrapping her and Cadzow in its safe cocoon, but she was realistic enough to know that wishes would not make it so. Too soon her idyll would be over, and she would have to go back to London. She knew she would have no choice and that one day Hamilton would return to get her. She prayed for heavy snow to keep him away, but finally, reluctantly, at the end of February she decided it was time to start weaning Jamie.

Chapter Twenty-Eight

*O*n the first day of March, Elizabeth had a visitor. Tom Calder's carriage arrived at Cadzow, and Mr. Burke invited the coach driver into the castle kitchen to warm himself with food and a seat by the fire. He then ushered Calder into the library for his visit with the Duchess of Hamilton.

"I thought I'd come before a March blizzard makes the roads impassable, but I had no idea the duke had returned to London. I was eager to show him the layout plans I've designed for the two thousand acres he so generously donated."

"My husband will most likely return by the end of the month, Tom. I believe he had urgent business with the king. Actually, he considers this more my project than his." *It's only a small lie. I am the one who considers it my project.*

Tom Calder spread the plans across the desk. "Much of the preserve will be left in its natural state, but part of it will be accessible tae the public by means of nature trails. Most Scots are avid hikers, so I've incorporated some steep hills that'll ha' tae be climbed. Rustic benches will be provided at the summits where folk can sit an' look out o'er some breathtakin' vistas." He pointed to a spot along the trail shaded in blue. "Yer polar bears' pen is an acre wi' a natural spring that forms a pond. We've stocked it wi' fish an' built them a wee cave fer shelter."

"These are wonderful plans, Tom." Her finger traced the lettering at the top of the parchment. "Why have you called it Hamilton Park? I think it should be named Calder Park. It was all your idea, and you are the one who will carry it through to completion. You have done the lion's share of the work, and you should receive the credit."

He was so flattered he was speechless for a moment. "The committee thought it prudent tae name it after Hamilton."

"I shall write to the committee and suggest Calder Park. *Once it's a fait accompli, Hamilton will hardly embarrass himself by insisting it be called after him.* "You will stay for lunch, Tom?"

Elizabeth excused herself and found her mother. "I believe I can persuade Mr. Calder to give you a ride to Glasgow when he returns. It isn't London, but after Cadzow's isolation I warrant it will be a welcome respite to visit the shops and theaters."

Bridget jumped at the chance, as Elizabeth had anticipated.

"I'm heartily sick and tired of being buried alive in the country."

Elizabeth hid her smile. *Bless you for your visit, Mr. Calder. Let us hope that tomorrow brings snow up to the eaves!*

During the next fortnight, Elizabeth did not get her wish, but her days were happily focused on Jamie, getting him used to taking nourishment from a bottle. Taking advice from the women of Clan Douglas who lived at Cadzow, she made a mixture of milk, barley water, and honey that her son drank greedily. He was a happy, roly-poly baby with fat pink cheeks, who seemed to thrive on the attention lavished on him by all the females in the household.

By the end of the fortnight, her milk had decreased. She surveyed her breasts in the mirror. *'Tis untrue that feeding a baby ruins a woman's figure. Mine look exactly the same as before . . . none will ever know my secret.*

Mid-March arrived with suddenly lowered skies, and everyone predicted that the annual March storms were about to descend with a vengeance. Mr. Burke even said he could smell the approaching blizzard. Servants brought in extra wood for the fires, and the shutters were closed across the windows before the household retired for the evening. During the night it began to snow and the wind picked up, but when Elizabeth arose and went downstairs to let Queenie out, she concluded that the brunt of the blizzard had missed them. "Don't you go far. I heard wolves howling in the night." She went upstairs to give Jamie his morning bottle then turned him over to Nan in the nursery while she went for her walk.

Elizabeth pulled on her fur-lined boots and donned her sable cape with its warm hood rather than the wool cloak she usually wore to visit the stables. She called Queenie, but the dog did not come. She called again and waited, then she heard some sharp barks coming from the direction of the stables and decided to investigate. Though a path had been cleared from the castle to the outbuildings and stables earlier, the blowing snow was rapidly obscuring it.

When she got closer to the stables she could see Queenie jumping about in agitation, then she heard the braying of a donkey between the dog's barks. She found the stable door open just wide enough for the female donkey to get her head through. Apparently the latch was broken, and a stableman had rolled a small boulder against it to keep it closed—but unfortunately not closed tight enough. Her heart jumped into her throat as she realized a predator might have gotten inside.

Elizabeth's hands stuck to the icy boulder, peeling off bits of skin as she moved it aside, and she regretted leaving off her gloves. When she opened the door to go inside, Queenie immediately herded the donkey back to her box stall. It was dim inside so Elizabeth called out to see if anyone was there. When she received no answer she lit a lamp and cautiously searched the large building to see if a predator had slunk inside for a quick meal.

She returned to the box stall and gasped aloud when she saw that the baby donkey was missing. She raised her lantern to search for Thistle, but her sinking heart told her that the little donkey's mother had been trying to follow her baby outside.

She was furious at the stablemen's carelessness and annoyed that the stables were deserted. Then she acknowledged that anyone with any sense would be inside near a warm fire on such a dreadful day.

She blew out the lantern and headed for the door. "Come, Queenie. We must find Thistle!" This time she used her boots to roll the boulder against the door, making sure it was shut tight.

When she turned around, the sight that met hers eyes was

hard to believe. The thick snow was blowing sideways, obliterating not only the castle but even the closer outbuildings. Any
tracks the little donkey had made were long gone, along with
her own prints, but Queenie loped across the snowdrifts as if
she was tracking an animal, so Elizabeth pulled her hood closer
against the biting wind and took a calculated risk, trusting the
dog's instincts.

She walked with her head down against the blowing winds
and thick, wet flakes that clung to her fur cape, turning her into
a snow-woman. Each time Queenie became invisible, she
called her name and the dog returned to her. It was slow going
because the drifts seemed to be getting deeper by the minute. At
first she thought she knew which direction she was heading, but
when she stopped and tried to pinpoint her location, it was impossible. The entire world had turned white.

As she struggled along, she heard ear-splitting cracks from
the towering Douglas firs and realized that some of the frozen
tree limbs were breaking off as they became weighted with
heavy snow. At length Elizabeth knew she must give up her
search. Common sense told her that she must turn about and try
to find her way back through her own tracks, which were
quickly being erased.

"Queenie! Queenie! Come, girl. We must go home!"

This time the dog refused to return. Though Elizabeth could
not see her through the blinding blizzard, she heard her exited
barks, as if she had found something. Again, Elizabeth weighed
the odds and decided to trust the Border collie's instincts. By
the time she slowly plowed her way through the drifts to where
Queenie was going berserk, she felt exhausted and lay down on
the snow to catch her breath. She was freezing cold, but her
lungs were afire.

After a minute's rest she crawled on hands and knees beneath the tree where Queenie was frenziedly digging. She
looked down into the hole and saw Thistle's huge soft brown
eyes, fringed with long ice-caked lashes, staring up at her in
stark terror. Elizabeth knew if she didn't free him, the little donkey would be eaten by wolves, dead or alive. Frantically, she
began scooping away handfuls of snow with fingers that were
blood raw.

A crack as sharp as a gunshot made Elizabeth stop digging

and look upward. To her horror she saw a huge limb, packed with heavy snow, come hurtling down upon her. Then everything went dark. Her world instantly turned from blinding white to obliterating black.

John Campbell awoke, threw back the thick eiderdown, swung his long legs from the bed, and padded naked to the window. When he saw that visibility was nonexistent, he gave a low grunt of satisfaction that his Highlander instincts about the approaching blizzard had been right on the mark.

He thought about the recruits he'd sent to London. *If they managed to avoid bad weather, they should have arrived by now.* Then he thought of the confidential letter he'd received in Glasgow from the Duke of Cumberland asking that he bring any and all Scottish recruits without delay, as the king was on the brink of declaring war. *My first duty was to let my father know that war with France was imminent.* Campbell had dispatched his Highland recruits with his officers then ridden back to Argyll with the pressing news. He'd left Inveraray almost immediately, hoping to catch up with his men, but just south of Glasgow the ominous pewter clouds moving in from the Atlantic had told him a March blizzard was inevitable.

Since it was late afternoon and the light was fast disappearing, he'd known he must seek refuge. He'd thought of Cadzow Castle but dismissed it immediately. Seeing Elizabeth was dangerous. He'd never be able to control himself, especially if Hamilton was absent. Then he remembered Chatelherault Hunting Lodge and knew he'd solved his dilemma.

He strode from the bedchamber he was occupying to the lounge, which boasted comfortable, masculine furniture and a huge granite hearth. He built up the dying fire, thankful he'd had the foresight to chop wood before the blizzard hit. Then he dressed and put on his fur-lined doublet so he could beard the storm and tend his horse, Demon, the lone occupant of the stables.

When he opened the front door, the wind almost tore it from his grip. He fought to close it then lowered his head and struggled through the deep snow to the stables, which were attached to the lodge. There was plenty of oats and hay and even horse blankets.

"Sorry you have to wear a blanket of Douglas plaid, old man, but you know the sailors' addage: Any port in a storm."

Demon whickered in reply.

John waited until a bucket of snow melted, then gave the horse a drink. "Think I'll steal a few oats. Porridge will keep my guts from growling if there's no other food about." He rubbed Demon's nose. "Looks like we're stuck here for at least the next twenty-four hours."

Outside, before he returned to the lodge, he trudged through the snow to the edge of the trees where he'd set a couple of snares. The first was empty, but he'd caught a coney with the second. Back inside he removed his doublet but kept on his boots as he made his way to the kitchen to look for food. He found dried peas, lentils, and barley in a cupboard, alongside some flour and yeast. On the spot he decided to spit and roast the rabbit legs and make stew with the rest of it. He'd also bake some flat bread. John unsheathed his knife and began to skin and gut the rabbit.

He had just set an iron cauldron on the fire to simmer the ingredients for his stew when he heard scratching at the front door. Curious, he strode over and stood listening. When he heard what sounded like a dog's whine, he opened the door.

"Hello, where the devil did you come from? Smart girl! You smelled the chimney smoke and knew there was someone here." When the Border collie bounded inside, he quickly shut the door. John was puzzled that the dog did not make itself at home but, instead, began barking and bounded back to the closed door. "Leaving so soon, lass? We're having rabbit stew for dinner."

The dog stared into his eyes and barked insistently, communicating her message the only way she could.

It was obvious to John that the Border collie wanted to take him out into the storm to show him something or someone the dog had left behind but refused to abandon. He shrugged into his coat. "Okay, lass, show me what's so bloody important." He pulled the lodge door tight against the wind and followed the dog, who was now out of sight. He caught a glimpse of her as she circled back then battled his way through the blizzard again. Defeat was not in Campbell's nature. When she reached the tall firs, he cautioned himself about forest wolves and cursed because he'd left his knife behind in the kitchen. Then he saw the downed limb and, by the way the dog was acting, knew there was something or someone beneath it.

At first he saw nothing. The eight-foot limb's evergreen branches were encased in thick ice and snow, and it took all his strength to lift it and throw it aside. When he saw the body, he realized it was a woman. The dark sable fur was white with snow, and he pulled aside the hood to see if she was alive. "Mother of God!" Elizabeth's eyes were closed, her lashes encrusted with snowflakes. Then, weak with relief, he saw that her shallow breaths were visible in the freezing air.

The dog tried to distract him, barking and digging frantically. John took a second glance and saw the head of a small coltlike creature whose body was buried in the deep snowdrift. "First things first," he muttered as he knelt down and lifted Elizabeth into his arms. With his precious burden clutched tightly, he struggled to stand, then slowly, resolutely, battling to put one foot in front of the other, he fought his way through the blizzard to the haven of the lodge.

John laid Elizabeth down before the fire. He removed the sodden fur then ran to the bedchamber for an eiderdown. He covered her ice-cold body and tried to revive her by patting her cheeks and calling her name. She opened her eyes, gave him a ghost of a smile, then closed them. The dog was driving him mad with her distracted barking. He knew what the collie wanted, but the dilemma almost tore him in half. "All right, damn you!" He ran to the kitchen for his knife. The animal in the snow was wolf bait, so he might need a weapon; if it was injured, he would put it out of its misery.

The dog struggled alongside him, clearly near exhaustion herself. The collie pinpointed the spot, then John, down on his knees, dug the snow away from the small animal with his bare hands. Deeper in the woods he glimpsed a dark shadow slinking through the trees. The thought of Elizabeth at the mercy of wolves knotted his gut and almost froze his heart. As he lifted the wooly creature it gave a pathetic little bray and he realized it was a baby donkey. When he saw no sign of blood, he hoisted it up in his arms and staggered to his feet. It took grim determination to carry it through the deep snow and biting wind back to the lodge.

Without ceremony he deposited the donkey on the floor by the hearth, and the dog dropped down beside it, tongue lolling out, panting as if she was ready to expire from shortness of breath. Immediately they ceased to exist for John as he flung off his coat and boots and turned his full attention upon Elizabeth. Her eyes were still closed and her body limp, though she was breathing evenly.

The fur cape had prevented her clothing from becoming soaked, but her garments were damp and cold. He removed her boots and found her small feet icy. As he took off her gown he noticed her hands. "Judas, your hands are raw . . . perhaps even frostbitten!" He hurried to the bedchamber and from his saddlebags took a small pot of ointment, made from alkanet and hops grown on his Kent estate. He removed her petticoat and tore it into strips. Then he coated her hands with the healing ointment and bandaged them.

Without opening her eyes, Elizabeth began to murmur. The only word he could understand was *thistle*. He assumed she was telling him what had taken the skin from her fingers. "Why the devil would you be picking thistles? They have few medicinal properties." He peeled off her damp stockings and vigorously rubbed her icy feet to restore their circulation. Then he lifted the eiderdown from her and removed her busk and drawers. Her icy skin was as pale as alabaster. As he gazed down at her naked form he could hardly believe that less than four months ago she had given birth. She had the same lovely, delicate, tantalizing figure as before.

"Whiskey! Any place Hamilton owns must have liquor." He glanced about and saw a carved oak cabinet against the wall. He hurried over and found it well stocked with Scotch whiskey. He took a flacon back to the fire and knelt beside her inert body.

John took a quick swallow then trickled some on her belly, thighs, and breasts. With long, smooth strokes he rubbed warmth back into her icy-cold flesh. He tried to rid his mind of lustful thoughts as his powerful hands circled her breasts and belly, massaging in a steady rhythm. Then he rolled her over and, after pouring some of the fiery liquor on her back and buttocks, set to work stroking firmly down her back and down her long, slim legs.

Soon he could tell by the feel of her skin that her body temperature was returning to normal. He propped her up with one muscled arm about her back and lifted the whiskey to her lips. She gasped and coughed as a few sips went down, and she opened her eyes.

She smiled sleepily. "Not real . . . just a dream." Before the whisper left her lips, her heavy eyelids descended.

John picked up Elizabeth and the eiderdown and carried her to the bed he had slept in. He tucked her in, tenderly brushing back the tousled curls from her brow. "Just a dream. Go back to sleep."

With difficulty he forced himself to leave her side and went back into the other room. His amused glance swept over the odd pair of animals stretched out side by side, sound asleep. He stirred the rabbit stew, poured in some whiskey, and covered it with an iron lid. He removed the pot from the direct heat, set it on the hearth where it would slowly simmer, then banked the fire with logs.

John removed his own wet garments and set them by the hearth to dry. He shook out Elizabeth's wool gown, hung it over a chair along with her hose and drawers and moved the chair closer to the fire.

Naked, he stretched his arms wide, then rubbed his aching shoulder muscles. "Thank God, I don't have to carry many donkeys."

He was tired, but he felt joy in the very blood that was singing through his veins. Despite the threat of war, despite the blizzard, he admitted that there was nowhere on earth he would rather be than snowed in with his beloved at Chatelherault Hunting Lodge.

Elizabeth drew him like a lodestone, and he saw no reason on earth to resist her magnetic pull. He padded into the bedchamber and stood gazing down at her for long drawn-out moments. He felt as if they were still attached by an invisible golden thread that had never been severed. No matter how many separations they endured, the power of their attraction for each other was so compelling that he believed their lives would touch again and again. Why else had the Fates delivered her up to him? Finally, he drew back the covers and slipped in beside her.

John lay against her back, one arm across her waist, her head tucked beneath his chin. He felt her sigh of contentment. In spite of the fact that she was another man's wife, lying in bed together with his body curved about hers felt *right*. She was his woman. Always had been. Always would be.

Chapter Twenty-Nine

"Oh, my God! John Campbell, you have kidnapped me!" Elizabeth sat up in the bed, her violet eyes wide. "You have bound my hands so I cannot fight you. And you are *naked*!" she accused with alarm.

He gazed at her, bemused. "Beth, I *rescued* you. I *tended* your hurt hands. And you too are *naked*," he teased lightly, immensely relieved that she was awake and feeling feisty. "I found you in the blizzard, knocked unconscious by a fallen tree limb. It's a miracle that you didn't freeze to death." His words suddenly turned harsh. "I should take my belt to you, you reckless little bitch—risking your life over a donkey!"

She drew up the eiderdown as if it would protect her from him. "I remember now. Thistle got out of the stable, and I feared wolves would eat him. Queenie and I found him buried beneath the snow."

"I take it Queenie is the Border collie and Thistle is the donkey?" The fallen bedcover had revealed much of her high-thrusting breasts, and he found it difficult to reprimand her.

"You found them?" Her eyes shone with hope.

"Queenie found *me* and insisted I follow her. I brought you to Chatelherault first, then went back for the bloody donkey. I left them both in there, asleep by the fire."

"Chatelherault is where we are? How long have I . . . have we . . ."

"Been sleeping together?" He grinned. "About two hours."

"How dare you dishonor Hamilton hospitality, sir? Get out of my bed immediately! And get that lecherous grin off your face."

He threw back the cover and, naked, stepped from the bed. "The first order I can obey. The second is impossible." His grin widened. He held up his hand, "No, Your Grace, I insist no thanks are necessary. I enjoy carrying damsels and donkeys about. But of the trio, the bitch in the other room has the most intelligence."

Her eyes flashed their warning. "Bring me my gown."

"It's woolen. It will still be soggy."

"Then bring me my petticoat!" she ordered imperiously.

"Sorry, Duchess. You don't have a petticoat. I used it to bandage your hands."

Elizabeth held up her hands helplessly, trying to muster her defiance, and burst into angry tears. "Don't call me Duchess! You must know how much I hate, loathe, and detest being a duchess."

He was beside her in two strides and gathered her into his arms. "Don't cry, Beth." He raised her face and wiped her tears away with gentle fingertips. "You'll feel better once you have some food inside you, I promise."

She pulled away and nodded, angry with herself for weeping.

In a very short time, John returned with a big bowl. He indicated her bandages. "I'll have to feed you. I gave Queenie her own bowl, but we'll share."

"It smells wonderful. I'm so hungry! Oh, what about Thistle?"

"I gave the donkey oats I brought from the stable for porridge." He lifted the spoon to her lips and took delight in watching her.

"Mmm, I haven't tasted rabbit stew since I left Ireland."

The word *Ireland* evoked memories for both of them. Each wished they could turn back the clock to that carefree, unfettered time.

Elizabeth blushed. Sitting here naked, sharing warm food, was far too intimate, especially with the attractive devil's dark eyes devouring her. She watched his hands as he fed her. They were beautiful, sensual, disturbing. Her memory caught the thread of something they had done to her earlier. It eluded her for a moment, then she remembered the feel of those hands, massaging her from head to foot, front and back, above and below. His hands coupled with his nakedness were too wickedly tempting. She opened her mouth for the last spoonful but lowered her lashes. "Aren't you cold?" she asked pointedly.

"You know I'm not . . . this close you can feel my fire, Elizabeth." He ran his finger round the empty bowl and raised it to her lips.

She could not resist licking it, though she knew it was provocative. Her blush deepened. If she were truthful, she'd admit she could resist nothing about him. "Please, get my undergarments. I want to come out by the fire. I want to see the animals."

John returned with her busk and drawers, but when she donned them she suddenly realized how inappropriate they were. She tossed back her hair with a defiant little gesture and walked with the haughty pride of a duchess wearing an elaborate ball gown.

Her pretension vanished the moment she saw the dog. "Queenie! Careful, don't knock me over. Yes, Queenie, I love you too." When the dog's tail swished against her bare legs, she laughed with delight and scratched the collie's ears, one white, the other black.

John left her to enjoy the animals while he repaired to the kitchen. He returned with the rabbit legs spitted for roasting and a pan of kneaded dough. He was wearing a sackcloth apron tied about his middle, but when he bent to put the flat bread on the fire to bake, she saw his exposed bare buttocks and laughed merrily.

"You think your drawers don't make you a figure of fun?" he asked in mock offense. "Here"—he placed a long iron spit in her bandaged hand—"make yourself useful."

As they sat side by side, roasting meat over the fire like boon companions, Elizabeth mourned what might have been, and her honesty bubbled to the surface. "I wish I'd said yes when you asked me to come and live with you at Sundridge. You were right, John. I'm not suited to being a titled lady of the *ton*. I prefer the country to London . . . detest Court functions . . . loathe being a duchess."

"Regrets are a waste of time, love. Pretend you are not the Duchess of Hamilton. You are a born actress—you can be Elizabeth, or Titania, or my lady in gray—" His fingers stroked her cheek.

"No, John. I am married to another man. I am not yours."

"Shall I show you that you are?" He took the spit from her and set it on the hearth beside his. He knelt before her and cupped her face in his hands, gazing down at her reverently, intensely, possessively. His lips touched hers. "Mine now and forevermore."

Elizabeth sighed, and her mouth clung to his. The kisses were gentle at first but gradually turned fierce. "Your kisses are like snowflakes—no two are alike." Just for this moment she had decided to be Elizabeth, Titania, *and* his lady in gray. It wasn't real, it was only pretend, and what did it hurt? She felt his lips trail kisses along her cheekbone and her throat. His warm breath on her skin sent delicious shivers all the way down to her lush breasts and sensitive nipples.

John removed his apron then unfastened the busk and lifted her naked breasts to his lips. He ran his tongue across one pink crest and heard her moan deep in her throat. "You taste like whiskey," he whispered huskily. His dark eyes held hers, and he saw her response to him flare up like a flame. Her eyes told him she knew that he had marked her as his; it was impossible to hide it from him. With possessive hands he removed her drawers and gazed at her with adoration. The fireshine turned her hair to red-gilt, her pale flesh to golden honey. She was truly an achingly beautiful woman to be cherished. He gently pushed her down on the thick rug, captured her wrists, and lifted her arms above her head as he moved his body over hers. "Wrap your legs high about my back."

She remembered how she loved his weight and his fullness inside her and yielded eagerly, arching up to meet his downward plunge. Until he was inside her, she'd had no idea how much she wanted him, or how long she had hungered to have him make love to her again. She wanted the feel of him, the smell of him, the taste of him to engulf her senses. She kissed his throat then licked it, and as he began to thrust, she bit him in a little sensual frenzy. The first time there had been pain mingled with the pleasure; now there was no pain whatsoever, only deeply thrilling enjoyment.

Her sheath felt like hot silk as she tightened passionately around his shaft, joining him in the tantalizing rhythm that was so achingly perfect. He yearned to watch her shiver and shudder as he brought her to climax, so he unleashed some of the fierce desire that had been goading him for months. She arched up with a cry and tightened on him, sending fire snaking through his loins. He felt the pulsebeat in his cock, felt his seed start, and, coming to his senses with a low groan, withdrew before he spent. He took his weight from her but held her close and rolled until they lay together on their sides.

She buried her face against his chest, and as he feathered kisses along her brow into her hair, she could hear the strong, steady thunder of his heart. As they lay embraced, she felt replete, happy, and cherished. Joy sang in her blood; love almost melted her very bones.

When at last they could bear to separate, John wiped his pearly ejaculate from them with the sackcloth apron. "I've never felt this way before. Beth, you consume me, waking or sleeping. Promise me you will never, ever regret loving me!"

Don't ask for promises I may not be able to keep, John. She smiled into his eyes and offered her lips for his kiss. As she became aware of her surroundings, she reached for her undergarments and saw him double up with laughter. "What?"

"Her Highness has eaten our bloody rabbit legs while we were otherwise engaged!" He couldn't stop laughing. "She slaked her appetite while we were doing the same."

Elizabeth was relieved that he was in no mood to punish Queenie, and she joined in his laughter. Then she saw that Thistle had peed on the expensive Oriental carpet and it too struck her as being funny. *So much for Hamilton's priceless possessions!*

"I should take the donkey to the stables. There's plenty of hay for him there. My horse will keep him company."

"Thistle is just a baby . . . his mother is still suckling him."

Elizabeth immediately thought of her own baby and knew she must get back to the castle. "I must go back to Cadzow, John."

"That's impossible tonight."

"I have to get back to my child. I've been gone all day."

He took her hand and almost dragged her to the door, then he flung it open and allowed her to both see and feel the blizzard. "You cannot leave tonight . . . perhaps tomorrow."

"I'd rather go tonight," she said stubbornly.

"The decision is mine, Elizabeth," he said quietly.

"Why should it be yours?" she challenged.

"Because I am the man, you the woman."

She lowered her lashes to mask her resentment, but she did not dare defy his towering male authority. *Even naked— especially naked—he is every inch the dominant military major!*

"We'll have to eat what's left of the rabbit stew and some hot bread. I have to feed and water Demon. I'll take Thistle to the stable and bed him down in some straw. I set some snares— perhaps I'll be lucky again. Can you warm up our food while I'm gone, or do your hands hurt too much?"

"I can manage." *I'll have to postpone leaving until he sleeps.*

John quickly pulled on his clothes and picked up the donkey. When she opened the door for him, he bade her close it tightly after him. Though the stable was only a hundred yards distance from the living quarters of the lodge, he had to struggle against the biting wind and ice pellets. He kept close to the stone walls of the building, realizing that out in the open the blizzard would defeat even the strongest of men.

When John reached the stable he made a bed of straw for the little donkey and piled the stall with hay. Baby or no, it would soon learn to feed itself. He talked to Demon as he fed him, then filled buckets with snow and brought them inside where they would melt for drinking water. When he checked the snares, he found wolf tracks and blood and knew they had carried off whatever he had caught. With a ripe curse he went back into the stable for oats—they'd have to make do with porridge for breakfast.

While he was gone Elizabeth spoke to Queenie. "He never even offered to help me get back to the castle. He has a soldier's courage and strength, to say nothing of a horse. Surely he could at least *try* to get me back to my baby!"

Queenie gave a defiant bark.

"You are supposed to be my friend. Why are you on his side?"

Her bandages impeded her dexterity and, frustrated, she removed the one from her left hand. The raw patches stung, and she found that she couldn't touch the heated iron pot without pain, so she left her right hand bandaged. She felt her woolen dress, found it was dry and quickly pulled it over her head before John returned.

When he came in, he took the oats to the kitchen then filled a couple of large iron kettles with snow so that they would have water. He filled a bowl for Queenie. "Here, girl. No doubt the rabbit legs made you thirsty." He eyed Elizabeth as he removed his boots and jacket and hid a smile as he began to take off his breeches. "Your clothes might be dry, but mine are soaked again." He had sent his baggage to England with his men, and though he did have a dry change of clothes in his saddlebags, he had more sense than to let Elizabeth know.

Once again they shared a bowl and he fed her with the spoon, although he did allow her to hold her own bread. He watched her dip it in the gravy and relish the taste of it in her mouth. "You enthrall me, Beth. You are the only lady of my acquaintance who would not turn up her nose and disdain to eat rabbit."

"That's because I am not a lady," she said lightly.

"No," he agreed, "you are more *woman* than any female I know." He arose and filled two small goblets with whiskey, brought them back to the fire, then put one in her hand.

Spurred by his praise, she confided, "I'm not afraid of my mother any longer. I finally took my courage in my hands and asserted myself. She didn't exactly collapse like tissue paper, but she did defer to my authority." She began to sip the whiskey.

"I'm glad you are no longer afraid. What about Hamilton?"

She lowered her lashes. She had vowed to tell no one about her unhappiness. She'd told John she hated being a duchess, but she could not tell him how much she hated Hamilton. There was already too much dangerous rivalry between the pair of Scots.

Her masked eyes gave him his answer. He knew what

Hamilton was; how could she not be afraid of him? Concern for her knotted his gut. "You regret marrying him."

"Sometimes," she admitted, "but the one thing I can never regret is having my son, Jamie. Nor do I regret that he will be the Duke of Hamilton some day. Being a mother fills me with happiness."

"As it should, my beauty." He drained his goblet and stretched his arms over his head in a subtle hint that it was time for bed.

She glimpsed the black mole in his armpit and turned her head away quickly, denying the evidence that was never far from her private thoughts. It was too frightening for her to contemplate. She heard him put logs on the fire, banking it for the night. Butterflies fluttered in her belly. He was about to carry her to the other chamber and sleep with her in the big bed. "John . . . no."

"Elizabeth, yes!" He swooped upon her from behind, lifted her high, and carried her to the bed. Her ear brushed against his chest. "Can you hear the wild hammer of my heart?"

She met his dark eyes with a shy smile as he undressed her for bed. His long-starved passion flared high again as he gazed down at her exquisite beauty. When he put her in bed and slipped in beside her, she cast aside all her reserve. *This man is worth any risk!* For a whole hour they lost themselves in the bliss of slow, melting kisses. Then, with his mouth pressed against the sensitive skin of her breast, he whispered love words that told her how she made him feel and what he was going to do to her in his loveplay.

John Campbell intoxicated her. He was far more potent than the whiskey. Finally, their arousal was so intense that he mounted her and took them on a ride they would never forget. A scream gathered in her throat, and her nails dug into the powerful muscles of his shoulders. This time there was no holding back, and they climaxed together then held absolutely still to savor every last shudder of their primal mating.

After the loving he held her possessively, and they drifted to the edge of sleep. Elizabeth drowsed as she waited for his breathing to tell her he was fast in the arms of Morpheus. Though she felt boneless, she softly edged away from his body and slipped from the warm bed. She gathered her scattered clothes and dressed in the other chamber by the fire. Noiselessly, she put on her boots and sable cape then bade Queenie to be quiet as she silently opened the door and slipped outside. The impact of the icy blizzard almost felled her. She clung to the stone wall doggedly and began to make her way toward the stable.

She had gone less than fifty yards when the door of Chatelherault was flung open. She heard it crash against the wall and saw the yellow lamplight illuminate the snow, then she heard Queenie's barks over the howl of the wind. She crouched against the wall hoping to escape discovery, but it was in vain. A naked John Campbell swooped down upon her and caught her in his talons. He had the look of a raptor who had just captured its prey. She stared into the hard, dark face, rigid with anger. Ungently, he dragged her back and shoved her through the door.

She stood pretending defiance. "I would be a poor mother if . . ."

"Not another bloody word." His voice was like the crack of a whip as he strode to the fire to warm his freezing flesh.

Her wet fur slid from her shoulders and lay where it fell.

"You actually intended to steal my horse. If Queenie hadn't barked, you could both have died. There is a hungry wolf pack out there. You'd be a poor mother if your deliberate recklessness got you killed! Take off those wet clothes and get to bed."

Elizabeth obeyed him without demur. She had been in the wrong; she had known it the moment she went outside. In a few minutes he came into the room and climbed into bed. He enfolded her in his arms so that what body heat they had left mingled to warm them.

His towering anger at her disappeared as quickly as it had arrived and was replaced by apprehension. He was going off to war and after tonight could not be there for her. Nor could he protect her from Hamilton, because she was the other man's wife. He stroked her hair and spoke softly. "Beth, I've had word that the king will shortly declare war. I'll be sent to France, and I'm filled with disquiet."

She stiffened. "Dear God, no wonder you are worried!"

"I'm not worried about *me*!"

She gazed up at him. "That's what frightens me, John." Her arms tightened about him. "Just don't die. Don't you dare die!"

He tucked her head beneath his chin. "Get some rest. Tomorrow might be a trying day."

They awoke late and realized that some time in the night the fierce wind had dropped. They both went to the kitchen and laughed at the domestic picture they made, cooking porridge then trying to eat it without benefit of cream or sugar. They shared it with the dog to get rid of it and couldn't stop laughing at the woebegone face she made while eating it, as if she were being punished.

John took Queenie and was gone an hour seeing to the animals in the stable. When he returned, he removed his doublet and the dog shook herself. "The temperature must be rising. The snow is turning to rain. It won't take long before it will all be slush. Much as I hate to part with you, my love, I think I will be able to get you back to Cadzow Castle today."

"My God, John, I mustn't be seen with you. The servants report everything to Hamilton. It's only two miles distance."

He refrained from arguing with her, and they went to the kitchen to tidy it, then they went into the bedchamber to change the linen and remake the bed. She suddenly looked sad and serious, and he wanted to make her laugh. He launched himself across the freshly made bed and pulled her down into his arms. They rolled about like children, laughing and playing as if they hadn't a care. Neither of them heard the front door open and someone enter.

Elizabeth suddenly glanced up and froze. "Mr. Burke."

"Your Grace, thank God you took shelter at the hunting lodge. It was our only hope." He quickly stepped from the room so they could compose themselves.

Elizabeth's face was white with shock, and she began to tremble. "I am disgraced," she whispered. "The scandal will be horrendous."

"Mr. Burke is my man, Beth. I sent him to watch over you."

She stared at him in disbelief, then a wave of relief washed over her turning her knees to wet linen.

John stuffed the soiled sheets under the bed. "I'll have him take care of these." He winked when she blushed scarlet.

When she emerged from the bedroom, shyly following John, Mr. Burke said, "I'm sorry to be derelict in my duty, my lord. I'm afraid I did a poor job of watching over her."

John grinned. "She's a willful little bitch, Mr. Burke. Almost got away from me in the night. I shall leave her in your capable hands. Er . . . there's also a baby donkey in the stables that will need your assistance."

When they stepped outside the sun emerged, producing a rainbow.

John kissed her hand. "It touches the earth in just two places . . . where you are, and where I am. *Ne obliviscaris,* Beth."

Chapter Thirty

"God and Mr. Burke be praised!" Emma cried when she saw Elizabeth.

Bridget, who had returned from Glasgow that morning, voiced her disapproval. "I knew one day that your obsession with animals would get you into trouble!"

"I am truly sorry for the worry I caused everyone. Please forgive me. I promise to be more cautious from now on."

The entire household of Cadzow rejoiced that Elizabeth had safely returned. Mr. Burke was regarded as a hero for battling his way to the hunting lodge the moment the blizzard lessened and rescuing the young duchess.

Elizabeth took Jamie from Nan's arms and hugged him hungrily. "I thank you with all my heart for looking after him."

Nan laughed. "I had a dozen hands tae help me, ma'am."

Elizabeth cooed to her baby. "I warrant Thistle's mother feels just the way I do today." She thought of the wolves and silently thanked John Campbell for saving the little donkey's life.

After the brief thaw the temperature plummeted again, and all the slush froze hard, keeping everyone close to the castle. By the end of March, however, the ice and snow began to disappear, and on the third day of April, Hamilton's big, black, berline traveling coach arrived at Cadzow.

Elizabeth was alerted immediately by Mr. Burke, and her heart flew up into her throat. She hid her disappointment, gathered her courage, and dutifully went to greet her husband. Relief engulfed her when she learned from Hamilton's coachman that the duke was not with him. He handed her a letter, and she rewarded him with a grateful smile and bade him ask the cook for a good hot meal. She waited until she was in her own chamber before she read it.

> My Dearest Elizabeth:
> A journey to Scotland is impossible for me at this time. I have therefore instructed my coachman to take you to Uppingham, Rutland, where I shall meet you.
> I have business with Will Cavendish and know you will enjoy a visit with Lady Charlotte, who has just presented her husband with a daughter. I cannot wait to show off our son to them.
> Do not delay your departure. The nobility is already returning to London for the Season and we must make plans for our ball.
> Your devoted husband,
> James, Duke of Hamilton

Elizabeth wondered if this was calculation on Hamilton's part. If it was, he had certainly chosen a good inducement to pry her from Scotland. She eagerly looked forward to visiting Charlie.

The next day she received a letter from Charlotte telling her about her baby, whom they'd named Dorothy after her grandmother. Charlie urged her to stop for a visit on her way back from Scotland, and Elizabeth told Emma and Bridget to start packing.

"Nan, I wish I could take you to London with me, but I imagine your husband would object to leaving Scotland."

Nan flushed. "I dinna have a husband, Yer Grace. 'Tis a most shameful thing . . . but I thought ye knew. I'm most sorry, ma'am."

Elizabeth touched her hand. "Oh, Nan, it doesn't matter to me. Would you like to come and be Jamie's nursemaid?"

"I would, but I canna leave ma own bairn, Yer Grace."

"Nan, as if I would ask a mother to leave her child! Your

baby girl is already a part of my household. Go and pack at once."

In two days the baggage compartment of the carriage was filled and a number of trunks were strapped onto the roof. Elizabeth bade good-bye to Queenie, knowing the dog would be unhappy to leave Cadzow. The berline traveling coach comfortably held the four females and two babies, but there was no room to spare. Elizabeth was astonished at the last minute to see Mr. Burke climb up beside the driver. When she saw that Emma was pleasantly flustered, she smiled a secret smile. *You are a devious devil, John Campbell.*

"You've only just had your baby. Are you sure you should be up and about, Charlie?" Elizabeth carried her son into the manor, eager to show him off to her dear friend and her mother, Dorothy.

"I refuse to stay abed ten days, especially when the weather is so springlike. Oh, your son is so darkly beautiful, and he's almost as big as baby William! No wonder James boasts about him."

Elizabeth paled. "James is here already?"

"Yes, he arrived yesterday. He's closeted in the library with Will. Why don't you go along and surprise him?"

"No, no! I won't disturb him when he's talking business."

"Come to the nursery, then, and I'll show you both my children."

"Run along," Dorothy Boyle said, linking her arm through Bridget's. "I have months of gossip to impart to your poor mother who has been buried alive in Scotland all winter."

How can Charlie's mother be so two-faced? After having an affair with my father, she pretends to be my mother's friend. Elizabeth guiltily dragged her thoughts from the scandalous situation; her own behavior did not bear scrutiny. "This is Jamie's nursemaid, Nan, who you can see has her own baby girl. She generously agreed to come with me from Cadzow."

"The more, the merrier," Charlie said, laughing. "We have cradles aplenty, which is a good thing. At the rate Will and I are breeding, we shall fill them all!"

Elizabeth stayed in the haven of the nursery hoping to postpone the reunion with her husband. Eventually Hamilton sought her out.

"There's my little prince!" He held out his arms and she reluctantly relinquished her baby son.

"Elizabeth, my dearest, you are blooming." As he bent to kiss her, his pouched eyes roamed over her figure, openly assessing it. "I trust you had an uneventful journey?"

"Yes, J . . . James, Mr. Burke smoothed our way at every stop."

His brow lowered. "Burke traveled with you?" He handed Jamie back to her and left the nursery.

Hamilton needs to be in control. He will dismiss Mr. Burke because he overstepped his authority, and it will be my fault! After a minute she gained courage to follow the duke and found him with the steward. She overheard Mr. Burke say, "The roads in the Borders were still slick with ice. The safety of the Duchess of Hamilton and your son was my first priority, Your Grace. I also took the liberty of bringing you a case of fine Scotch whiskey."

Hamilton's brow cleared immediately. "Very good, Burke. I'm glad to know you are a man who takes his duties seriously."

Dinner was a grand affair, as were most meals in a Devonshire household. Elizabeth, however, had lost her appetite contemplating the approaching night. Not only would she have to share a chamber with her husband but also a bed. Her emotions were in turmoil. As well as being filled with dread, she was consumed by guilt.

Will and James carried on a running conversation, as did Dorothy and Bridget. Elizabeth failed to notice that Charlie hardly spoke.

When the meal was finally finished, Charlie laid her napkin on the table. "Would you all excuse me? I have such a headache."

Oh, Lord, Charlie is pretending a headache so that the duke and I can retire early. She's playing Cupid . . . I could strangle her!

James got to his feet, moved behind Elizabeth, and put his hands on her shoulders. "I shall take you upstairs, my dear. You must be ready for bed after your journey."

"I . . . I must look in on the nursery."

He smiled indulgently. "We shall both look in on the nursery."

In the huge room they found two nursemaids and four cradles. The duke looked in each until he found his own son, then he lifted his little heir and held him at arm's length, admiring him.

He truly loves the baby, Elizabeth thought. *That's because he thinks Jamie is made in his own image,* her inner voice answered. She pushed away her guilt and dropped a kiss on her son's dark head. She turned to Nan. "I'm used to him being in the next room. Please come and get me if he starts to fuss."

Hamilton handed his child to Nan then placed a firm hand at the small of Elizabeth's back. "I shall take you up now."

Her steps lagged, and she was filled with dread as they climbed the elegant staircase to their assigned bedchamber.

As soon as he closed the door, James said, "Undress for me."

She could hardly breathe as rebellion flared up in her. She knew she could not bear to comply if he demanded his marital rights. A small part of her wanted a knock-down, drag-out fight. Yet she dreaded a loud, angry confrontation in their friends' home. She bought time by sitting down before the mirror to brush her hair. She saw his reflection coming toward her, and she stiffened.

His spatulate fingers closed over hers and he removed the brush from her hand. "Elizabeth, I want you to undress for me. Now!"

She stared at him, frozen with indecision. *Yield or fight?*

"Damn you, I haven't got all night! I still have important business to discuss with Cavendish. Get your clothes off. I want to have a close look at your figure."

She experienced immediate relief that his goal was not sexual, yet she was outraged. The bastard wanted her to strip so he could assess the damage that having a child had done to her body. *Yield or fight?* She weighed the advantages of refusing with the disadvantages of a stinking row and chose to yield— this time. The rebellion was coming, it was as inevitable as a Greek tragedy, but she wanted to be in her own territory when the appointed time came.

Fearing that if she did it slowly, it might tempt and arouse him, she stood and removed her clothes in a matter-of-fact manner.

When she was naked, he slowly circled her, observing her from every angle. Then he drew close and examined her minutely, missing no finest detail of her breasts, belly, or thighs. Elizabeth felt like a racing filly being assayed for flaws at a Tattersall's horse sale, but she refused to blush or lower her lashes.

"You are almost perfect. Perhaps a little more lush, but that could increase your admirers. Since bearing a child did no visual damage, I think I can go about the business of siring another son."

Over my dead body!

After he left, Elizabeth went to bed, but it took her a long time to fall asleep. *When he looked at my body, I was lucky he could not see where it had been or what it had been doing.* Guilty feelings surfaced, but again she tried her best to bury them. She must have finally slept, because she awakened with a jolt when the chamber door opened and she heard voices.

Hamilton, supported by Morton, his valet, entered. It was clear to Elizabeth that the duke was legless from drink. She arose, slipped on a bedrobe and approached them. "Can you manage him?"

"Always do, Your Grace. I'll soon have him abed. He'd still be drinking if Cavendish hadn't been summoned to his sick wife."

"Lady Charlotte? I'd better see if there's anything I can do."

When Elizabeth arrived in her friend's bedchamber, she found a disturbing scene. Charlie was vomiting into a chamber pot held by Jane, her ladies' maid. Will hovered over his wife, obviously racked with worry. Dorothy Boyle declared, "I shall send for the doctor, though I doubt the wretched man will come before morning."

Charlie saw Elizabeth and held out her hand. "My head is still pounding," she gasped out between retches.

Oh, my God. I thought her headache was pretended. Elizabeth reached for her hand and was immediately alarmed. Charlie was feverishly hot. Beth felt her friend's forehead. "She's burning hot . . . I'll get some cool water to bathe her."

"I'll get it," Will said quickly. "You stay with her."

In an amazingly short time Will was back with bowl and flannel cloth. He handed them to Beth. "I'll get her a clean night rail."

Jane removed Charlie's soiled night rail, and Elizabeth sponged her with the tepid water. The sick girl didn't seem any cooler, but she was at least fresher. They helped her up so that they could put fresh linen on the bed.

"My back aches too," Charlie said wearily.

"Darling, I think you got up too soon after the baby." Will's voice revealed his extreme concern. "The doctor will give you something for fever."

Elizabeth saw that Charlie was now a dull red, so she bathed her face once more. When Jane gave her mistress a sip of cool water and it came back up, Beth said, "Barley water is best for nausea."

"I'll get cook to make some." Will hurried from the chamber.

Dorothy Boyle returned. "I dispatched a footman for the doctor and gave him a note stressing how ill she is."

They all did their best for the patient until the doctor arrived at dawn. When he examined her, he prescribed a fever powder but looked grave. He asked Will to step outside for privacy.

When Will came back into the chamber his face was ashen. "The doctor said he will be back in a few hours."

"Is that all he said?" Dorothy demanded.

Will gestured for Dorothy and Elizabeth to come away from the bed and Charlie's hearing. "He said the midwife who delivered our baby died of smallpox yesterday. There are other suspected cases in the village. But he cannot confirm Charlie has caught it."

"Dear God Almighty!" Dorothy crossed herself.

"As a precaution he advised me to get the children away from Rutland." He looked at Elizabeth. "You must take your son away."

The blood drained from Elizabeth's face as she and Will went back to the bed. Charlie's eyes were now closed, and she was murmuring incoherently. A lump came into Beth's throat as she watched Will tenderly stroke Charlie's fevered brow.

"I won't leave her," Will whispered. "Dorothy must take the children to London."

Elizabeth said softly, "I will get Nan to start packing Jamie's things." *I must get Mother and Emma out of here. James too.* She found Nan in the nursery feeding her baby daughter. Elizabeth did not approach her son's cradle. "Lady Charlotte is sick, and the doctor says there is something going around the village. I want you to pack up quickly and be ready to leave for London. I must awaken Mother and the others. We are going to need two carriages." When she knocked on Emma's door she found her already up and dressed. "Charlie is ill and it could very well be contagious. Please awaken Mother and help her pack. Nan is getting the babies ready to leave. Perhaps you could also get word to Mr. Burke?"

Elizabeth encountered Morton in the upstairs hall. "Come with me, Morton. We have to rouse His Grace."

They entered the bedchamber together and found James Hamilton still snoring. Morton shook him and repeated the process until the duke opened heavily pouched eyes and began to curse.

"James, I'm sorry to disturb you, but Lady Charlotte has come down with an ailment that could be contagious and the doctor has advised that we all leave for London immediately. I've told Jamie's nurse to pack everything."

Hamilton blinked his bloodshot eyes. "Contagious?"

"He thinks it might be chicken pox," Elizabeth lied. "Children are extremely susceptible to the infection."

Hamilton threw off the covers. "Pack my things, Morton!"

Within the hour three traveling coaches, piled with luggage, stood ready in the courtyard. Two Cavendish nursemaids, each holding a child, sat in the first waiting for Jane to help the Countess of Burlington. Dorothy was leaving under protest. "As soon as the children are safe in London, I shall return to my daughter!" Morton helped Nan put the two babies into one of the Hamilton coaches. The duke placed his hand under Elizabeth's elbow, urging her inside, his temper and nerves in tatters.

"I'll wait for Mother. You know how long it takes her to pack. Mr. Burke will take good care of us. Please get Jamie out of here quickly, James. Emma will help me hurry Mother along." She knew that her husband would call the doctor as soon as he arrived home to have both himself and his heir examined.

"Your mother is an officious bitch. If she isn't down in ten minutes you are to leave without her. Do you understand?"

"Yes, yes, just go! I shall see you in London, Your Grace."

Morton climbed up beside the coach driver just as Bridget and Emma emerged into the courtyard. Elizabeth waved goodbye as the first two coaches drove off, then she joined Mr. Burke who had just loaded some trunks. He helped the two women into the luggage-laden carriage and took Elizabeth's arm.

"I'm staying, Mr. Burke."

"That would not be wise, Your Grace. They suspect smallpox."

"Yes, I know. That's why I must stay with her."

"*Smallpox?*" Bridget shrieked. "Elizabeth, either get in or stay, but make up your mind. We must tarry no longer!"

When Mr. Burke raised his eyebrows, Elizabeth shook her head.

"Someone will have my neck for this," he predicted grimly. He closed the coach door and climbed up beside the driver.

Elizabeth returned to the master bedchamber. "They've gone, Will. We can devote all our attention to Charlie now."

"You should have gone with them, but I thank you with all my heart for staying. You are truly a devoted friend, Elizabeth."

By the time the doctor returned in the late afternoon, Charlie's fever had begun to subside, but a rash of tiny red spots had appeared on her face. "Keep her cool and comfortable. Just as a precaution I advise you to keep the rest of the household away from this room. I shall come again in the morning."

Will brought a feather mattress from another chamber so that he and Elizabeth could take turns resting if they got the chance. Charlie spoke for the first time in hours after she had been bathed, and Beth withdrew a distance so Will could speak with his wife.

"You have a rash, darling. I think it may be measles."

"Keep the children away from me," Charlie whispered.

"Of course, but I can't keep Beth away. She refuses to leave."

"She is the sister I never had. I'll soon be well again." Exhausted from speaking, Charlie closed her eyes.

By morning, the red rash had spread to Charlotte's body, and by evening, spots appeared on her arms and legs. Will convinced himself that it was indeed the measles, but the doctor looked at Elizabeth and shook his head.

By the third day the spots turned to blisters that looked watery; by nightfall they became puss-filled pustules. Charlie's fever returned, and she became delirious. Will no longer deluded himself. "I cannot bear to see her suffer." Yet he sat beside his wife, hour after hour, holding her hand and telling her how much he loved her.

Beth was afraid to wash her; burst pustules would leave ugly, disfiguring scars. Around midnight of the fourth day, Charlie became lucid. She smiled sweetly. "I love you both so much." She sighed deeply, closed her eyes, and stopped breathing.

Will looked at Elizabeth, despair and disbelief written all over his face. The choking lump in Beth's throat made it impossible for her to speak. She walked quietly back to her own room and vomited into the chamber pot. *This is how Charlie's illness started.* Her inner voice said calmly, *You are not ill—you are grief stricken.*

Elizabeth, with leaden heart, waited patiently for Will to emerge from the bedchamber. Tears streamed from his deep blue eyes down his cheeks. He held up a tiny tapestry purse that held her favorite comb. "This is all I have of her."

Elizabeth placed her hand on his arm in a comforting gesture, though she knew it was futile at the moment. "No, Will. You have her children."

Her words made him sob. He hurried on, seeking to be alone.

Elizabeth informed the household staff that Lady Charlotte had passed away. Then she straightened her spine, filled a porcelain bowl with warm water, and went to say good-bye to her dearest friend.

She washed Charlie and, as she dressed her in a white night rail, sadly realized that her friend's small body was already stiffening.

"It's not fair, Charlie. You were supposed to become the next

Duchess of Devonshire." After a few quiet moments, she went to the dressing table and picked up a pair of nail scissors, then she cut a dark curl of Charlie's hair.

Elizabeth found Will in the library, staring into space, looking more lost than any man ever deserved. "Here's a love token for you, Will. It's a part of her you may keep forever."

He held the dark curl reverently. Then seemed to come out of his trance and began thinking of the ordeals ahead. "It will be a private funeral. Dear God, how am I to comfort Dorothy when she arrives? She lost two children before Charlie, you know."

"We'll tell her together."

"James will run mad when he learns you have deliberately exposed yourself to smallpox. You must return to your family immediately."

"Yes, I know, Will. I shall leave after Dorothy gets here."

Chapter Thirty-One

*E*lizabeth put her feet up on the seat of the coach that Hamilton had sent. The driver had been instructed to use force if necessary to bring the duchess back to London immediately. She had asked the doctor if she might be carrying the contagion home to her child, but he had assured her that if she hadn't come down with smallpox by now, the incubation period had passed.

Elizabeth, physically exhausted and emotionally bereft, curled up beneath the carriage rug and tried to sleep. She found it difficult because her conscience was riding her relentlessly. Her sorrow mingled with her guilt until they became inextricably bound together. She somehow felt that because she had broken God's law, Charlie's death was her punishment. She told herself she was being ridiculous; the tragic loss was to Charlie's husband and children. Surely God would not punish them for a sin she had committed? Shakespeare's condemning words about Lady Macbeth ran through her mind: *Not all the perfumes of Arabia will sweeten the stench of her name and of her adulterous relationship.* Elizabeth pressed her face against the squabs and the floodgates opened. Fate was such a cruel bitch, to deprive Lady Charlotte of becoming a duchess when she was so suited to the rank, yet had bestowed the position of duchess upon Elizabeth Gunning, when she hated and detested it.

Once she had cried herself out, Elizabeth did fall asleep. When she awoke her sorrow came rushing back, but she saw that the coach had reached London and knew she would have more trouble to face. She felt sad and weary beyond belief. All she wanted was to see her baby son, take a bath, and go to bed. The last thing she wanted was a confrontation with Hamilton.

She climbed from the coach on shaky legs and went up the steps of the Grosvenor Place house. Servants rushed out for her luggage and the majordomo announced His Grace awaited her in the library.

"You are a sly, manipulative little bitch! You led me to believe you would accompany your mother in the coach behind mine. That was a deliberate lie, and I demand an explanation!" Needing to assert his control, the duke sat behind his massive mahogany desk, knowing it added to his intimidating authority.

Elizabeth met his eyes. "Charlie is dead."

"Dead?" Shocked, he rose to his feet, staring hard to see if this was some ploy. "What did she die from?"

"Smallpox."

"*Smallpox?*" He recoiled so violently that his chair crashed over. "Christ Almighty, you knowingly stayed with her, recklessly exposing yourself to a deadly contagion? Are you insane, madam? I could have you committed to the madhouse for such behavior!"

"She was my dearest friend."

"Some friend, to expose you to smallpox!" He felt sweat beading on his forehead and reached for his handkerchief to wipe it off. "Now you have thoughtlessly brought it home to me and to my son!"

"The doctor assured me the incubation period was over," Elizabeth replied wearily.

"Do you not have enough sense to realize that you risked dying? Or worse, having your beauty destroyed by disfiguring pockmarks?"

"The loss of a wife's beauty is indeed greater than the loss of a wife, but try telling that to your friend, William Cavendish."

"How dare you be insolent to me, you defiant little baggage?" He took threatening steps toward her then thought better of having contact with her just yet. "I forbid you to see Jamie for the next week. We must be certain that you do not contaminate him." He looked at her with distaste. "You look abominable! Have you forgotten you are the Duchess of Hamilton? I advise you to spend your days restoring your delicate beauty in time for the Season."

"I am in mourning, Your Grace. May I retire?"

He waved a dismissive hand. "Get out of my sight."

After his wife left the library, James sat down, rested his elbows on the desk, and steepled his fingers. *Will in mourning might give me the advantage.* James had lobbied the king for old Devonshire's post of Lord Steward of the Royal Household but suspected the king would bestow it upon Devonshire's son, William. Now, with Cavendish in deep mourning and old Devonshire tottering to the grave, it put a different complexion on matters. *I stand a damn good chance of this appointment, if I press my advantage. Surely it should follow, as night follows day, that since I am Hereditary Keeper of Holyrood, I should qualify for the post of Lord Steward of the Royal Household.*

Elizabeth encountered Bridget hovering at the top of the stairs. "Mother, will you come to my room and bring Emma and Nan? Ask Nan to leave Jamie in the nursery," she added reluctantly.

When the three women entered her chamber, they found a dejected Elizabeth sitting on her bed. "How are the babies, Nan? I pray they show no signs of fever or rashes?"

"The bairns are both thriving, ma'am."

Elizabeth nodded her gratitude. "My friend Lady Charlotte has died of smallpox. Her husband and her mother are grief stricken."

"I am offended that Dorothy Boyle didn't see fit to tell me!"

"Dorothy didn't learn her daughter was gone until she returned to Uppingham. She is devastated. Charlie was her sole surviving child. She and the earl doted on their daughter. I don't know the details, but the funeral will be private. We must arrange to send flowers. White roses and snowdrops, I think. I shall write letters of condolence, of course."

"You look ready to drop," Emma said, turning down the bed.

"I'd like a bath first, please. Nan, I am aching to hold Jamie, but my husband, and I too, think it best that I keep my distance for a few days. The doctor said the incubation period had passed, but it's better to be safe than sorry."

Two days' rest was all Elizabeth needed to restore her looks and vitality. Her emotions were another thing entirely. She knew instinctively that her sadness would not lift until she had mourned Charlie. There would always be a tender place in her heart for the girl who had befriended her without reserve. She had just finished writing a letter to the Earl and Countess of Burlington when she heard a tap on her door. Curious, she called, "Come in."

Jack Gunning entered and closed the door quietly. "Beth, I am so sorry for your loss. I know how much Charlie meant to you."

Beth brushed away a tear. "I talk to her every day," she said brightly. "An odd Irish thing to do, I suppose."

"Elizabeth, there's been a gulf between us since you wed Hamilton. I'm sorry if this marriage brought you unhappiness, but at the time I couldn't go against your mother."

"You found enough courage since then to be unfaithful."

"I'm so sorry you found Dorothy and I together."

"I can't condemn you. Let him without sin cast the first stone."

Jack's blue eyes widened as the implication of her words sank in. He did not ask who the man was; he didn't need to. "From your mother's complaints I gather that you too have gained courage."

Elizabeth smiled. "She was a paper tiger. The moment I stood up to her, she crumpled. My fear of her vanished into thin air."

"I rejoice that you are no longer that timid seventeen-year-old girl. In little more than a year you have become a woman in her own right. Baby James is a credit to you, my beauty."

"He's my entire world. Let's go and visit him!" *I'll wait no longer to hold my son. Who the devil will tell Hamilton anyway? Certainly not Nan, Emma, Morton, nor Mr. Burke. Even Mother knows which side her bread is buttered on.* Elizabeth kissed her father's cheek. "I've missed our time together. How about giving me a fencing lesson tomorrow?"

*   *   *

Elizabeth was mildly surprised when the duke was home in time for dinner. He spent little time at Grosvenor Place. She donned one of her plainer dinner gowns and joined him in the dining room.

"Good evening, Your Grace. My appetite is improving daily."

He ignored the small talk and frowned. "Why are you in gray?"

"It . . . it's a mourning color."

"We are not in mourning." He poured himself a whiskey.

"*I* am mourning," she asserted.

"Then do it privately." He changed the subject immediately. "I'm joining you for dinner so we can discuss plans for our ball. Ours was the most successful of the Season last year. This year, I want ours to be the *first*. Since they're all the rage, I've decided it shall be a masquerade."

Elizabeth could not believe what she was hearing. "When our good friend is bereaved, I think a ball would be in bad taste."

"I am the Duke of Hamilton. Nothing I do is in bad taste." His tone forbade contradiction. "The *costumier* will be here tomorrow. I would like to see you gowned as the Queen of Scots."

Elizabeth could not repress a shudder as the vision she had seen at Holyrood Palace came full-blown into her mind. *I cannot!* Her inner voice contradicted, *You mean you will not!*

"You may show off Jamie to our guests. Perhaps we can have a small golden crown made for him so he can be King James Stuart?"

Surely he is jesting? "Jamie is to represent King James, the child, while you no doubt will be King James, the man?" Her sarcasm was exquisite, but inside she was quailing.

"Brilliant idea! Beauty and brains in a wife is a rare combination. Something Coventry will never enjoy."

Elizabeth's chin went up. "Maria is my sister, Your Grace."

"Difficult to believe. She has neither mind nor morals."

She stood up defiantly. "I'll have no part of this *charade!*"

"Sit down." He drained his whiskey. "I have the means to make you obey my every whim, madam."

Suddenly Elizabeth found it difficult to breathe. Surely the swine wouldn't use her baby to control her? She slowly sat down.

That night in bed, she could not sleep until she devised a plan for the ball that would appease him yet give her the freedom of choice she was finding so difficult to live without.

When the *costumier* arrived the following day, Elizabeth stood patiently while the woman measured her for the Mary, Queen of Scots costume and took her advice on which neckruff would be most flattering. When all was decided, Elizabeth held out a pair of ruby earrings. "I need another costume made for the ball, but I insist upon secrecy. It is to be a special surprise for my husband. If I can count on your discretion, these will be yours."

"Your Grace, I understand completely. Many ladies wish their costumes to be a surprise. You may rely upon me to keep mum."

"Excellent! I would like to disguise myself as a male. Black satin formal knee breeches and coat, with perhaps a gray waistcoat. I want a subdued look, nothing flashy. I'll need a black tie-wig and black shoes, of course."

"I shall have all ready for your first fitting within the week."

"Thank you. On that day the rubies will be yours."

When the woman left, Elizabeth made her way toward the nursery.

She had decided to spend every possible hour that she could with Jamie. God alone knew when Hamilton would take it into his perverse head to separate her from her child. On her way past the dining room she saw Mr. Burke cleaning silver. She had taken to avoiding him because he kindled her guilt. Today, however, she was so worried that John Campbell might show up in disguise at their ball that she decided she must speak with him.

"Mr. Burke, I suppose you are aware that the duke insists that we hold the first ball of the Season at Grosvenor Place, even though I am in mourning?"

"Yes, Your Grace. A masquerade ball, I believe."

She hesitated then plunged in. "We have a mutual acquaintance who must not take advantage and attend in disguise."

"That would be impossible, Your Grace. Our mutual acquaintance has been posted to France."

Elizabeth drew in a swift breath. *War will be declared any day! Surely if England is at war the Season will be greatly curtailed?* "Thank you, Mr. Burke." *Don't die, John. Just don't die!*

That evening, once she had tucked Jamie into his cradle, she went along to her parents' wing, ostensibly for the fencing lesson, but more for an opportunity to talk with her father. "Have you heard anything about war being declared?" she asked anxiously.

"Actual fighting has been going on for more than a year between the English and French in India and America. It's inevitable that war will soon be declared and fought in Europe, my beauty."

"Do you know *when* we will be at war?"

"If Newcastle wasn't such a dithering old woman, he would have declared war already. Last night at White's I heard that Minorca in the Mediterranean had been captured by the French fleet."

"Minorca is an English possession?"

"Aye. In spite of Newcastle, the king will act tomorrow or next day—his electorate of Hanover has been overrun by the French army."

"That will effectively put a stop to all the balls and parties."

Jack threw back his head and laughed at his daughter's naivete. "The number of galas will double and will be twice as spectacular. The Court will put on a magnificent show to prove England's superiority and royal ascendancy over the French, even if our army suffers calamity . . . especially if our army suffers calamity."

Elizabeth's hand flew to her throat. "We must not lose!"

Her father handed her a sword and winked. "Better get on with the lesson so you can defend yourself when the Frenchies come."

The following day Elizabeth took Jamie to show him off to her sister. "Maria, you have red spots on your face! My God, have you been feeling unwell?"

"Stop worrying! I shan't die like your silly friend, Charlie."

Maria looked smug. "As a matter of fact I have had bouts of morning sickness lately. I believe I'm with child."

"That's wonderful, Maria, but what about the spots?" Elizabeth could hardly breathe for anxiety.

"It's not very polite of you to mention them, Beth. Every once in awhile I get face eruptions. I don't know the cause, but the cure is simple enough. I simply cover them with *maquillage.*"

"Do you mean the white lead paste? Perhaps that's the cause!"

"What nonsense. You always did have quaint notions. The palest shade of pink paste has been named Maria in my honor. You'll see, it will be all the rage when the Season begins."

"I've brought your invitation to our masquerade ball. I think it totally inappropriate for us to entertain so soon after Charlie's death, but James is bent on opening the Season."

"Tsk, tsk, Elizabeth, I've never heard you criticize your duke before. You never did know how to handle him." Maria touched her hair. "I think I shall attend your ball as Lady Godiva. Rather appropriate since I'm Countess of Coventry, and it will give the *ton* something to gossip about. I hope you are inviting Prince George."

"I can't imagine James *not* inviting royalty. Why do you ask?"

Her sister gave her an arch look. "I wish to add him to my list of conquests. I've had a viscount, an earl, a marquis, and a duke. In the great hierarchy, a prince is next in line for my favors, and George is the only prince I know."

Maria's fabrications are preposterous. I suppose that's what comes of being taught to act stage roles from the age of two. It becomes difficult to tell fantasy from reality. Elizabeth's inner voice mocked: *Don't use that excuse for your own infidelity. You knew exactly what you were doing!*

Beth dropped a guilty kiss on her son's head. "I must be going. Jamie is getting restless. I brought him to see his aunt Maria, but she has hardly glanced at him," she said lightly.

Maria waved a dismissive hand. "Babies are all the same."

"Until you have your own." Elizabeth didn't take offense. "Good-bye. Give my love to George. I haven't seen him in months."

"I shall give him *your* love. He will never have *mine*."

Beth shook her head. Maria was Maria; she would never change.

War was declared against France two days before the Duke and Duchess of Hamilton's masquerade ball, guaranteeing its success. London's nobility was in a mood to celebrate.

On the night of the ball, Elizabeth donned her Mary, Queen of Scots costume with Emma's help then told her to go downstairs to enjoy the party. Beth went along to the nursery to have a word with Nan. "I shall bring him back upstairs at the first opportunity, and we'll put him to bed. It's wicked to put a baby on display and parade him about like a trophy." As she dressed him in his elaborately embroidered christening robe, Jamie gurgled and pulled on a curl of her red wig.

James entered the nursery, resplendent in his King James Stuart costume. His critical eye fell upon Elizabeth, and he ordered her to turn around so he could view her from all angles. When he found no fault, he placed his hand on his sword and bowed, waiting for Elizabeth to curtsy.

Beth grit her teeth. It was anathema for her to abase herself and bow down to him. She knew he did it to show that he controlled her. She wanted to fly at him and scratch out his eyes, but the thought of him taking Jamie from her made her mask her temper. She sank into a low curtsy and waited for the "king" to raise her.

Hamilton opened the box he'd brought with him. "I had this ermine cape made for baby James and this gold circlet, of course."

Elizabeth was seething. Her hands actually trembled as she put the ridiculous costume on her baby. "Ready, Your Majesty!"

The royal trio became the center of attention before they even got to the ballroom. Their guests, all wearing elaborate disguises, gushed over the little lordling, who seemed to thrive on the attention. He began to crow, and everyone except Elizabeth dissolved in laughter. *Smile. You are the Duchess of Hamilton.*

The liveried servants circulated with silver trays of drinks, and everyone began to drink toasts to the Royal Family. Elizabeth knew that once Hamilton had consumed enough liquor he would lose interest in her and hopefully their son, Jamie.

It seemed that everyone in London had decided to attend the first entertainment of the Season. Not only was there a crush of people in the ballroom, but the rest of the spacious rooms were beginning to fill up too. When Maria arrived wearing the flesh-colored, skin-tight gown and the long blond wig that brushed her thighs, she caused a sensation. Elizabeth watched her husband join the throng that followed Maria to the ballroom and spied her chance to leave. She took Jamie upstairs and handed him over to Nan.

In her own chamber she carefully removed the elaborate Mary, Queen of Scots costume, neck-ruff, and red wig and put them out of sight in the wardrobe. Then she wiped her face clean of cosmetics. She put on white hose and a white shirt and tied the stock in a simple style. She donned the gray waistcoat and black satin suit then slipped her feet into black shoes. She took the black tie-wig over to the mirror and carefully covered her own golden hair, making sure no tendrils escaped. Finally, she fastened on the smallsword she had used for years when fencing with her father.

Elizabeth was both surprised and pleased at the reflection of the sober young man who stared back at her from the looking glass. Not only was Beth fulfilling Charlie's fantasy, but she was finally dressed in mourning for her friend. *Charlie, this is for you.*

She descended the stairs quickly and mingled with the crowd. Her heart was hammering at the daring thing she was attempting, but as she walked about unobtrusively, none took much notice of her, and her pulsebeat settled down to almost normal. She bowed to Newcastle, the Prime Minister, and thought he would have made a better woman than a swashbuckling seafarer.

Some of their guests' disguises were very good, and Elizabeth could not guess their identities, but there was no mistaking Prince George in a Hussar's uniform. She decided that if the prince was close, Maria would not be far. She turned around and came face to face with Lady Godiva. Beth bowed gallantly, and spoke in a deep voice. "Who could this be in such a spectacular costume? I'm sure I know you."

"In the biblical sense, no doubt," said a sardonic voice behind her. Elizabeth stiffened. The voice belonged to her husband.

As Maria swept past her to take Prince George's arm, Beth turned to Hamilton. "I beg your pardon?" she said coldly.

"No apology necessary." He lifted his glass in mocking salute. "She's a whore—both Lady Godiva and the female portraying her."

Elizabeth was incensed. She wanted to draw her sword and run him through. "You are an uncouth swine, sir! No gentleman would impugn a lady's honor by repeating such vile gossip."

"Not gossip, m'boy. I speak from personal experience. The Beauty has spread her legs more than once for me lately. Now she's set on fucking a prince. Sorry, you don't stand a chance."

As the sneering Hamilton walked away, Elizabeth stared after him. Blood rushed to her cheeks and pounded at her temples.

Chapter Thirty-Two

*I*t's a filthy lie!

But Elizabeth's mind flew back to what Maria had said: *I've had a viscount, an earl, a marquis, and a duke.* She had thought these were preposterous fabrications, but now she realized that the duke Maria was boasting about being intimate with was Hamilton! She stalked from the ballroom intent on confronting him. Her intense glance swept each room as she hunted for him. Then suddenly she saw him enter the library with a tall, thin man who looked like Coventry. *Poor George, cuckolded by his closest friend!*

When she reached the library door, she was arrested by raised voices. Hamilton and Coventry were having a terrible row. Because her anger was so hot, she did not hesitate to listen.

"Goddamn it, you'd better stay away from her!" Coventry shouted.

"Once I bagged her, my interest ceased," Hamilton declared.

"It all began with that bloody wager we made to see which of us would be first to bed one of the Gorgeous Gunnings. When you found out I asked Maria to marry me at Easter, you had to wed Elizabeth in a secret ceremony at Valentine's, just to beat me."

"You lost the wager, George. All's fair in love and war!"

"Love? The only one you ever loved was your egomaniacal self!"

"Love is your problem, you poor deluded fool. Love has turned you into a green-eyed monster—a laughable poltroon!"

"You degenerate lecher! Not satisfied with one sister, you had to have both! Even that doesn't slake your depraved appetite. You've just gotten some poor little drab with child."

"Lily Clegg's a whore, as is your beauteous Maria! Do not mention my duchess, Elizabeth, in the same breath as her sister!"

"I am a bloody fool," Coventry said bitterly. "I've always known what you were, yet persisted in the friendship. Well, it's over!"

Elizabeth was stunned at the revelations. She reeled away from the library door in shock, blood-red fury almost blinding her. She rushed upstairs to the sanctuary of her own chamber to gather the pieces of her shattered illusions together and decide what to do.

As her breathing became calmer, her brain began to function more clearly. She knew beyond a shadow of a doubt that the confrontation with Hamilton was imminent. Her outrage was finally greater than her fear. Using her child to blackmail her and keep her in abject fear added fuel to the fiery fury that raged within. *All things come at their appointed time. Tonight is the night!*

She went to Hamilton's bedchamber and found Morton. The valet looked at her blankly. "It's me . . . Elizabeth."

His eyes widened in recognition. "I would never have guessed!"

"I need your help. I want you to summon Hamilton . . . tell him he's needed upstairs. Once he enters my chamber, I want you to stand guard outside and see that none enters, not even you."

Elizabeth returned to her room and began to pace impatiently. She could not wait to stand up to the bully. Yet inside, deep at her core, serene calm reigned.

Quarter of an hour passed before Hamilton entered the room. He came to an abrupt stop. "Who the devil are you?" he demanded.

"Lily Clegg's brother, come to avenge her!" Elizabeth drew her sword from its scabbard.

"Morton! Morton! Get in here!"

"He's not coming. It's just you and me." She touched her blade to her nose. "*En garde,* Your Grace."

Hamilton turned purple with rage as he reached for his sword.

"I'll kill you!" he vowed.

Elizabeth smiled. "I, who am about to die, salute you."

Hamilton lunged furiously. He was taller, broader, with greater strength and longer reach, but his opponent was quicker. The youthful figure in black sidestepped and parried every thrust. "'Tis rumored you are fated to die in a duel, as your father did."

The words stirred the duke's superstition, as they were meant to. She saw fear erase some of the anger on his face, as the lethal blades flashed in the lamplight. He began to sweat profusely, and she was enjoying this supreme challenge. She had no fear. It was as if this were only a staged duel and she acting out a role, as her sword arm extended and retracted, parried and thrust, building to the climax of the play.

Hamilton was breathing heavily, as she had him on the defensive. As always, he had been drinking, and his agility was sadly impaired. His lunges were becoming wildly desperate, and he bellowed for help.

Elizabeth reached up, snatched off her wig, and tossed it aside. Her golden hair tumbled down about her shoulders in all its glory. She reveled in his gasp of surprise. Then she delivered the *coup de grâce*, deliberately catching the tip of his sword in the intricate basket design of her rapier's hand guard and with a swift twist of the wrist she sent it sailing across the chamber.

Hamilton fell back on the carpet in disbelief, and swift as an arrow the point of her blade flew against his throat. She pressed slightly forward and felt bloodlust as his eyes bulged with fear. "I am the one who is in control now, James."

For a full minute she looked directly into his pouched eyes, allowing him to fully comprehend his precarious position. "From this moment on, our marriage will be in name only." She saw some of the fear leave his face as he realized she would not kill him. She pressed the sharp tip into his throat, pricking him. "From now on we'll have a new partnership. I am a generous woman. In public I will still be your devoted Duchess of Hamilton. In private I will make the decisions regarding my own life." She paused. "If you violate the rules I am laying down, I will create such a scandal it will ruin you in the eyes of the king, the Court, and Society at large." She paused again. "Do we understand each other?"

Hamilton immediately nodded his understanding.

She hovered over him, not nearly finished. Sweat trickled down his face. "*This* is for using my baby to control me." Quick as lightning she dropped the point of the sword to his shoulder and thrust it home. As his scream of pain rent the air, she gave him back the words he'd used on their wedding night. "I *did* hurt you." Her voice held a note of satisfaction. "There should be pain when a man's body is penetrated. Don't hold back your cries."

She sheathed her sword and opened the chamber door. "Morton, I believe His Grace needs a whiskey and the services of his doctor." Elizabeth returned to the party. Wearing her own hair immediately gave away her identity. She proceeded to the ballroom and asked the musicians to stop playing for a moment. Then she held up her hands for silence. "I hope my male attire will not shock your sensibilities. My dearest friend, Lady Charlotte, Marchioness of Hartington, devised this costume for me, and I wear it tonight to honor her memory." After a moment's silence, everyone applauded. "Now that I have revealed my identity, I think it only fair that those who so desire may remove their masks."

Elizabeth sought out her father and asked him to dance.

"You are very daring tonight, my beauty. You look as though you have a secret that is making you look radiant."

"I do, Father. Tonight I became a woman in my own right." She kissed his cheek. "Why don't you open up a gaming room? I'm sure most of the gentlemen present prefer gambling to dancing."

"I thought Hamilton would open one. Where is he?"

"Changing his costume. King James Stuart didn't suit him. If you start a card game, I'm sure it will lure him downstairs."

Before midnight, the subdued host did return to his guests. Saving face meant everything to this man of shallow values. Before she allowed him to escape to the card room, Elizabeth lifted a glass of champagne from a silver tray, took his hand, and pulled him into the ballroom. She held up her hand for silence. "I should like to propose a toast to London's most gracious host and most indulgent husband. Ladies and gentlemen, the Duke of Hamilton!"

The applause was thunderous. The *ton* had grown used to his haggard looks. The duke nodded his head in acknowledgment. His bandaged wound prevented him from bowing.

Beth spied her mother talking with Peg Woffington. "Ladies, you both look spectacular tonight. Have you seen Lady Godiva?"

"Just as Maria was enjoying herself with Prince George, Coventry insisted that they leave. He's so possessive of her!"

"I warrant he disapproved of her naked lady costume," Peg said.

It's just as well Maria has left. I mustn't hold her responsible for Hamilton's sins.

At one o'clock the musicians struck up a rousing march then played a medley of military music to celebrate England being at war. At two o'clock, while there were guests still able to stand, Elizabeth handed out the prizes for costumes. She pretended difficulty in declaring a grand prize winner then announced, "I shall take the bull by the horns and give it to the magnificent matador. Why, Horace Walpole, I swear I had no notion that was you in the red satin cape." Elizabeth smiled and handed him the silver trophy. *Horace will declare the Hamilton ball an unqualified success. All things considered, I have to agree!*

By three o'clock the guests began to leave. By four, Hamilton was the only one who remained in the gaming room. He lay with his head on the table, surrounded by playing cards and empty glasses. Elizabeth encountered Morton, who had come down to retrieve him. "I shall summon Mr. Burke to help you. Be gentle. Luck wasn't with him tonight—he suffered quite a few losses."

The next day, Hamilton was quite ill and once again Dr. Bower had to be summoned. When he was leaving, Elizabeth waylaid him. "He isn't in any danger, is he doctor?" she asked guiltily.

"Not from the pinprick he received. His drinking, however, is another matter. He has jaundice again. Yellow as a Chinaman! I gave him something to stop the vomiting, but one of these days he could hemorrhage from the stomach, and it will be all over."

Hamilton did not leave his chamber for three days. Finally he recovered and Morton helped him don full Court dress so he could attend the king's levee. An hour after he left Grosvenor Place, a footman brought a message from William Cavendish telling them that his father, the Duke of Devonshire, had passed away.

Elizabeth immediately sat down and wrote a letter of condolence. She would have gone to see Will but knew he would be on his way to Chatsworth. She sent one of their own footmen with a note for Hamilton to St. James's Palace, though he would likely hear about old Devonshire at the levee.

An hour later, the footman returned and informed her that he had missed Hamilton. Apparently the duke had been at the levee but departed in haste. James Douglas did not return to Grosvenor Place. A week went by and still the Duke of Hamilton had not returned home. Elizabeth spoke with her father and asked him to make some discreet enquiries. Jack learned of places where Hamilton had been but was unsuccessful in locating him.

Finally, Elizabeth went to her sister's and asked George Coventry if he knew anything.

"I don't know *where* he has disappeared to, but I have a good idea *why*. The king passed him over for the post he sought. The moment His Majesty got word that Devonshire had died, he made Will, the new Duke of Devonshire, Lord Steward of the Royal Household."

"Oh, Lord, he will be ready to kill!"

"The blow to his pride must be staggering." Coventry didn't sound displeased. "I'll try to find out where he is, Elizabeth, but other than White's we don't frequent the same places. Have you spoken with his driver?"

"His coachman is also missing. Thank you, George."

Two days later a note was delivered to Grosvenor Place:

His Nibs is at Dirty Gert's, Hanging Sword Alley, Whitefriars. Kindly come and remove him from the premises.

Elizabeth showed the note to Morton and Mr. Burke, who left immediately in a carriage without the Hamilton crest on its door.

The man they carried in the back door of Grosvenor Place bore no resemblance to a Duke of the Realm. He was unshaven and unkempt. His soiled garments stank of urine, vomit, and gin. Hamilton was also extremely ill.

"I am sorry your task is so distasteful, gentlemen, but if you will bathe him and put him to bed, I will send for Dr. Bower."

Elizabeth stayed in the room while Bower examined her husband. When he was finished, he did not take her aside but spoke to both, even though he was not sure that Hamilton would comprehend. "The foremost vice of the nobility is drink. His Grace has acute alcohol poisoning. More than a dozen years of abuse has permanently damaged his liver, hence the repeated bouts of jaundice. He must be weaned from whiskey. If he keeps on, he will be dead in weeks. If he totally abstains, he may recover to some degree, but I believe a slow, downhill decline is inevitable." Bower cleared his throat. "Make sure his will is in order."

"I shall make it my business to see that he abstains, doctor."

"Deprivation will cause tremors, anxiety, and terrifying hallucinations. Nursing him won't be easy, Your Grace."

When the doctor departed, Elizabeth repeated his words to Morton and Mr. Burke. "Get rid of all the spirits in the house. Someone must be with him night and day. Are you willing to help me?"

The first few weeks were a nightmare. Hamilton displayed all the symptoms Dr. Bower had described and more. He had profuse sweating bouts, after which he needed bathing and the bedlinen needed changing. His hands trembled, and he was afraid of everyone and everything including food. He had vivid hallucinations of strange animals and insects that attacked him or crawled all over him, making him scream and rave and sob.

Elizabeth, Morton, and Mr. Burke took turns nursing him day and night. The doctor came on a regular basis to monitor him, but it was a whole month before there was the slightest improvement. When the duke finally stopped raving, the servants lifted him into a chair for a few hours each day, but he was withdrawn and morose.

Bridget learned from Dorothy Boyle that Will Cavendish, the new Duke of Devonshire, was back from burying his father in Derbyshire. When she told Elizabeth, she visited Will at Burlington Gardens.

Dandy greeted her with exuberance. She picked him up and scratched under his chin. "I'm so sorry for your loss, Will, so soon after Charlie. How are you coping? How are the children?"

"The children are the only joy in my life. It breaks my heart that they'll never know their mother. Everywhere I look in this house, each room, every object reminds me of her and of my loss. I feel guilty that I am alive, while she is dead."

"Will, you must have no guilt. Charlie wouldn't want that."

"The king has offered me the viceroyship of Ireland, and I've decided to take it, Elizabeth. I shall take the children with me. There are too many poignant memories here at Burlington Gardens."

"I think a sojourn in Ireland is a splendid idea. Work is an antidote to grief." She hesitated then decided to confide in him. "James has been very ill. The doctor says he mustn't drink again."

"Shall I visit him before I leave, or would that embarrass him?"

"Better not, Will. I should get back, but may I see the children before I leave?"

"Yes, come. We'll take them into the garden. Beth, would you like to have Dandy? He mopes about all day without Charlie."

"Oh, Will, thank you. You know I've always loved him."

"And he adores you. Thank you, Beth."

During the next few months Elizabeth did not accept any social engagements. She spent all of her time at Grosvenor Place, dedicating herself to the care of her son, Jamie, and her ailing husband. The first brought her immense joy, the second helped assuage some of the guilt she felt.

Hamilton made only a partial recovery. Physically, he was debilitated, aged beyond his years and suffering from chronic gastritis that made it difficult to keep food in his stomach. He also developed a permanent tremor in his hands and shuffled when he attempted to walk. Mentally, his memory was badly impaired. Out of frustration his secretary and his stewards turned to Elizabeth in matters of business.

It was James himself who asked Elizabeth to summon his solicitor regarding his last will and testament. His primary concern was for his son and heir. He wanted everything to be right and tight legally for Jamie to inherit not only his titles but his property in both England and Scotland. He was well aware that his demise would likely come while his heir was still a minor, and the decision of a guardian had to be dealt with. Since he could not abide the thought of either William Cavendish or George Coventry having a finger in the pie, he chose Elizabeth, Duchess of Hamilton, to be his son's legal guardian.

Beth was extremely grateful to James for his decision regarding her son, though it added to her feelings of guilt. She sat with her husband hour after hour, reading to him from newspapers such as the *Political Register.* She also played cards with him and often persuaded her father to join in their games of chance. James seemed most animated when she brought Jamie to visit. The first word she taught her baby was *dada*; it brought a tear to Hamilton's eye, but it was a tear of joy. Jamie learned to take his first steps at his father's knee, and Elizabeth made sure that the pair spent part of each day together.

"Elizabeth, why are you kind to me, when I was often a swine?"

The question startled her. She gave him a half-truth. "You *were* totally controlling, James, but you were always extremely generous with gowns and jewels, and you provided me and mine with all the comforts of life. I had little until you married me." *The real reason I am kind to you is because I don't want a guilty conscience when you are gone. Guilt is worse than fear, really. It eats at your soul. Fear can be overcome more easily than guilt.*

Chapter Thirty-Three

E lizabeth spent the day quietly at home. She didn't realize that it was her nineteenth birthday until evening after she had tucked Jamie into bed. As she left the nursery she met her father.

"Happy birthday, my beauty." He handed her a horoscope scroll.

"I had completely forgotten! Thank you, Father."

"I haven't forgotten. Your horoscope predicts you will see many changes in the coming year and that a secret wish will come true. I'd like to make your wish come true, Beth."

"That would be impossible," she said wistfully.

At the end of October, Elizabeth stood at the window watching the last leaves fall. The wind swept them across the lawn in spirals. *Where did the summer go? Autumn is half over. I can't believe Jamie is nearly one year old! Christmas will be upon us shortly and then Maria's baby.* She had barely finished the thought when a message was delivered from the Earl of Coventry. She ordered a carriage be made ready and ran upstairs to find Bridget.

"Mother, Maria has suffered a miscarriage. We must go at once."

Elizabeth left Jamie in the capable hands of Nan and Emma, and Hamilton in the care of Morton and Mr. Burke, explaining that she would likely be away all night.

Maria's appearance deeply shocked her. Her sister lay in bed, so pale and thin Beth hardly recognized her. Bridget immediately burst into tears. George, haggard and distraught, hovered about looking helpless. Elizabeth knew she would have three patients on her hands if she didn't distract them. "Mother, go and speak with the cook. Instruct her how to make barley water, and I think Maria would benefit from some broth."

She took George aside. "Did she see the baby?"

He shook his head. "The midwife took care of . . . er . . . everything."

"Good! I want you to get Maria a doctor, George."

"I'll go and fetch him." George was desperate to be of use.

When Beth was alone with Maria, she bathed her brow, then took her hand. "Are you in pain? No, don't try to talk. It makes you cough." *Dear God, I don't like that cough. She looks consumptive.*

Within the hour George was back with his doctor. Elizabeth had a private word with him and voiced her fears, then she steered George downstairs into the drawing room and poured him a brandy.

"What's happening with the war? I'm cut off from the world these days and know the newspapers often get it wrong."

George seemed glad to be distracted from his personal worries for a few minutes. "All our losses are being laid at Newcastle's door. He is only able to stay on as Prime Minister because he has just appointed William Pitt the Minister of War. Pitt is to have supreme direction of the war and of foreign affairs. Thank God! John Campbell and Argyll have always supported Pitt's views that we should send the Dutch and German forces packing and utilize Britain's own armies. Pitt can be a despot, but that's what's needed to win wars, not a dithering old woman like Newcastle."

"Have you heard from John?" She held her breath.

"Yes, he has been promoted to colonel. He must have iron guts." George had an ear cocked for the doctor. "Here he comes."

"Lady Coventry needs to convalesce in a warm climate. She needs rest and nourishing food to recover from the miscarriage, but she also needs fresh air and sunshine to cure her cough. England's climate is too damp and cold in the wintertime. I've

given her a sleeping draught and left a tonic with her mother. I
think she would benefit from a full-bodied port wine too."

"I shall take her to Italy when she's well enough to travel.
When do you think she will be strong enough, Doctor?"

"A week to ten days bed rest should be sufficient. Italy is a
good choice . . . food, wine, and sunshine are the best medi-
cine."

When he left, George said to Beth, "You have your hands
full with James, but do you think Bridget will agree to come
with us?"

"I'm sure she would, George. Go up and ask her."

At midnight, Elizabeth persuaded her mother to sleep for a
few hours, so that Bridget could take over when she herself returned to Grosvenor Place. George refused to leave Maria's
bedside, and during the night while she slept, Beth and her
brother-in-law passed the long hours by talking about Court,
politics, and war. Then she packed her sister's lovely clothes for
her coming sojourn to Italy. After breakfast she kissed Maria
and returned home.

Elizabeth had been up all night and knew she needed to go
to bed for a few hours. First she went to her husband's suite and
found he was still sleeping. She and Morton left his chamber together. "If he asks for me when he wakens, tell him I'll come
after lunch."

She didn't open her eyes until three o'clock and chastised
herself. She penned a note inquiring about Maria and gave it to
a footman, then she went straight to the duke's rooms. She was
surprised to find him still asleep. She put her hand on his shoulder and gave him a gentle shake. When he did not rouse, she became worried. "James, can you hear me? James?" Her hands
lost their gentleness as she turned him over and shook him
harder.

She bent close to make sure he was breathing, and as he ex-
haled a miasma of whiskey fumes assaulted her nostrils. She
stepped back in surprise. *He's not dead. He's dead drunk!*

"Morton, Morton, where are you?" She opened the door angrily.

He came up the staircase. "What's amiss, Your Grace?"

"Hamilton is not asleep. He is unconscious from drink!"

Morton followed her into the bedchamber, and when he

tried to rouse his master, found it impossible. "Go and get Dr. Bower."

Elizabeth was furious. *When Morton returns, I shall have it out with him!* Then another thought occurred: *What if it wasn't Morton but Mr. Burke? Someone supplied the whiskey. Someone who knew he would consume it if it were made available!*

When Bower arrived he examined Hamilton and turned to Elizabeth. "Your husband is in a coma, I'm afraid. A coma induced by alcohol. He may or may not come out of it. There is little I can do, Your Grace. We will just have to wait and see. I shall come tomorrow."

Hamilton's condition remained unchanged for a week. When Bridget returned to Grosvenor Place to pack for Florence, Italy, she brought the good news that Maria was immensely improved. Elizabeth minimized Hamilton's deteriorated health to her mother, reasoning that Bridget had enough to worry about.

The day after the Coventrys set sail, James Douglas, Duke of Hamilton, drew his last breath. He died without regaining consciousness, and it threw Elizabeth's emotions into turmoil. Anger and guilt were inextricably coiled together. She had known for some time that Hamilton's years were numbered, but she had wanted him to die of natural causes so that she would be free of guilt for hating him. That night she told herself over and over that she wasn't the one who had provided the whiskey, but she believed in her heart that she was indirectly responsible because she'd stayed away overnight.

Needing to vent her anger, she called Morton and Mr. Burke into the library. "Which one of you did it?" she demanded.

Both men met her accusing stare with silence.

"Such commendable male loyalty makes me want to spew! Since neither of you is willing to condemn the other, I am terminating your employment. Your services are no longer needed!"

She left them standing there and slammed the library door. She swept past Emma and Nan, throwing them a look that warned they had better walk on eggshells around the Duchess of Hamilton. She retreated into her own bedchamber and firmly closed the door. She stood at the window, gazing into the darkness with unseeing eyes.

An hour had ticked away when she heard a tap on her door.

She wondered who would dare disturb her solitude. She strode to the door, threw it open, and found her father standing there.

"May I come in, Beth?"

"Of course." She walked to the middle of the room then turned.

Jack Gunning touched a finger to the horoscope scroll on her bedside table. "You will see many changes in the coming year."

And a secret wish will come true. I'd like to make your wish come true, Beth. "It was you!" She searched his face. "Why?"

"I should have prevented the marriage. I could have saved you from unhappiness. It was my duty as your father to do so. Hamilton was responsible for his own ill health. You overcame your fear but went from obeisance to martyrdom. It's over, Beth."

"No, it's *not* over! I'm covered with guilt. I hated him, I loathed being a duchess, and now I'm glad! Oh, God, not glad that he's dead, but glad that I am no longer married to him— glad that I no longer have a husband! Does that make any sense?"

"It makes perfect sense, my beauty. Get some rest," Jack advised. "You'll need stamina to get through the next few days."

She nodded. "Would you summon Morton and Mr. Burke?"

After her father departed, the two men came to her door.

"Come in, gentlemen." She lifted her chin and looked at them. "I want to humbly beg your pardon. There will always be a place in my home for you. I need loyal people around me."

The next month was torturous for Elizabeth. She got through the funeral, which was attended by the king and all members of the Court, but not without feeling like a hypocrite regarding her mourning. She felt no grief, so instead she secretly mourned for her friend Charlie, for whose loss she experienced real sorrow.

Ironically, he had never allowed her to own a black gown, so she had taken the white dress in which she'd been forced to marry him and could never bear to wear afterward and dyed it black for the burial. She felt the small act of revenge was justified, and it put a symbolic end to her unhappy marriage.

For weeks after the funeral she received condolence visits from every prominent family in Society, as well as solemn visits from all members of the government and those who had sat with Hamilton in the House. She learned that her title as the widow of a duke was Lady Elizabeth Hamilton and that Society expected her mourning period of one year to be strictly formal.

Deaths come in threes. Elizabeth, brought up in Ireland, could not rid herself of superstition. *The first to die was Charlie, the second James. Who will be the third? God forbid it be Maria!* After she said prayers for her sister, her thoughts always turned to John Campbell who was fighting on the front lines in the war. She quickly revised her counting and told herself firmly that the first death had been her grandfather in St. Ives. *Don't die, John. Don't you dare die!*

She did not miss the entertainments where she had been on display as the beauteous Duchess of Hamilton. Nor did she miss the frantic Christmas balls and parties where everyone tried to outdo one another. She was also extremely relieved that she was not invited to attend the New Year functions at Court where perfection had always been expected in her clothes, looks, and demeanor. Elizabeth longed to escape to Scotland, but since the harsh winter weather dictated that she must wait until spring, she spent the time with Hamilton secretaries and solicitors, making sure that her son's title and properties inherited from James Douglas were legally transferred. Jamie was now Seventh Duke of Hamilton, Fifth Duke of Brandon, and the Marquis of Clydesdale.

Spring finally arrived, and while the *ton* rushed back to London to prepare for the all-important Season that officially began on May Day, Elizabeth packed up her entire household for the journey to Cadzow Castle, at Hamilton in the Scottish Borders.

Elizabeth knew that Nan was every bit as happy as she that they had returned to Cadzow; they shared the feeling of coming home. When members of the Hamilton clan offered condolences, she thanked them politely and reminded them that her son was now the Duke of Hamilton and they could best serve by giving him the allegiance and fierce loyalty they had shown his father.

"Queenie! Oh, how I missed you. Come, take us to see the

donkeys. Later, when I take you into the castle, you must promise not to savage my little dog, Dandy."

As the Border collie jumped up to lick Elizabeth's face, the dog was careful not to scratch the child she was holding. Queenie danced round in circles, barking her joy at the reunion.

"Thistle! I can't believe you are grown big as your mother." She set her eighteen-month-old son on his feet. "Jamie, this is Thistle, your very own donkey. Be gentle."

"Donkey!" he squealed, stroking its long, wooly coat. Their noses were on a level, and when Thistle licked him, Jamie laughed with delight. Before Beth and her son left the stables, both of them disheveled and a little dirty, she felt her heart fill with joy. She took a deep appreciative breath as if the miasma of the stables were the elixir of life. She realized that it was freedom that brought her happiness, and she reveled in it. Never again would she allow anyone to control her life. She vowed that no one would ever again make decisions for her. *Freedom is the most precious thing on earth. I shall never risk losing it again.*

Spring gave way to long summer days and before the autumn arrived, Elizabeth had taught her son how to swim in the river and to sit on a docile pony while she held its leading rein. Jamie played with Nan's little girl and the other children of Cadzow. Whenever the bairns wandered off too far, Queenie's instincts kicked in, and she rounded them up and herded them back as if they were sheep gone astray. Queenie allowed Dandy to rule the roost inside the castle but outside was strictly her territory, and she rounded up the little terrier along with the children.

Elizabeth grew to love Scotland as much as Ireland. She was unbelievably happy here and shuddered whenever she thought of London. The tight corsets, extravagant gowns, and hideous wigs were things of the past for her. She now donned simple dresses or smocks and wore her hair loose about her shoulders. When she laughed, she was free to throw back her head, open her mouth, and let her mirth bubble forth from her throat—a far cry from the serene, false smile she had perfected for Court functions. She had accepted only one invitation, to the upcoming formal opening of what was now known as the Calderpark Wildlife Preserve. She would cut the ribbon in the afternoon and attend the evening gala in Glasgow. Her days were filled with things she enjoyed teaching her child. They swam, fished, picked flowers, sang, went for pony rides, made themselves at home in the vast kitchens, talked to the animals in the stable, and walked their dogs.

George and Maria had returned from Italy in midsummer and, according to a letter she received from Bridget, Maria seemed to have recovered her health. Elizabeth contemplated returning to London before the harsh winter set in, but kept pushing the thought away because she could not bear to leave her Scottish haven.

"I'm twenty today!" Elizabeth swept back the drapes of her bedchamber window and saw that it would be a glorious September day, where the sun shone brilliantly in a last burst of exuberance before its warmth was extinguished by the approaching winter.

Jamie, with Emma on his heels, ran to his mother. "Happy bird day, Mamma!" He laughed with glee as she scooped him up for a kiss.

"The birds are indeed happy today," she said, laughing. "See?" She pointed through the window. "They're eating the rowan berries."

"Come . . . blow candles!" Jamie urged.

Emma rolled her eyes.

Elizabeth set his feet to the carpet. "I think the cake and candles were supposed to be a secret, m'lad. That's for tonight."

He ran to Emma, grabbed the small parcel she held, and thrust it at his mother. "Present . . . open it."

With surprised delight Elizabeth opened the package. "Why, thank you, Jamie. It's exactly what I wanted!" She held the little wooden duck in the palm of her hand. It was a toy that Mr. Burke had carved for him. "After breakfast we'll let him swim in the pond." Burke, whom she had appointed head steward at Cadzow, had made them a carp pond where Elizabeth had planted bulrushes and yellow king cups from the river.

"It's a good thing you're wearing green. The grass stains won't show." Emma didn't really approve of the simple cotton dresses she wore. In her opinion, a duchess should dress like a duchess.

Elizabeth hid her smile. "Oh, please, let me romp about, Emma. It's my birthday!"

"Ha! As if you didn't romp about every day of your life, and as if you give a fiddler's fart what anyone thinks."

Jamie climbed on the bed and jumped up and down. "Fart . . . fart."

"Hush! That's a bad word, Jamie!" Emma chastised.

"No, it isn't, Emma." She climbed on the bed with Jamie. "Let's all shout it. One, two, three: fart . . . fart!" Mother and son rolled on the bed, and Dandy, deciding to join in the fun, jumped up with them, while Emma rolled her eyes heavenward and gave up trying for any semblance of decorum.

Later that morning, Elizabeth and Jamie, their arms filled with wooden boats, ducks, turtles, and a carved loch serpent, descended upon the fishpond for water games. "If you allow your monster to eat my duck, I shall be devastated," she said dramatically.

"You'll be tated," he threatened, his dark eyes glittering with mischief. He plopped his bum on the grass and pulled off his shoes and stockings, clearly showing his intent to wade.

With an exaggerated sigh of resignation, Elizabeth took off her shoes, removed her stockings and garters, then tucked up her skirts. Intent on the serious business of eluding the terrifying loch monster, Elizabeth was soaked to the waist within half an hour.

"Happy birthday, Beth."

The deep masculine voice sent a shiver slithering down her spine. She turned in disbelief, then a smile of purest joy transformed her radiant face. "John!" She waded from the pond and ran into his waiting arms. "John. I don't believe it!"

He picked her up and swung her round. "Believe it."

Her heart thudded wildly as his powerful arms enfolded her. His intoxicating male scent made her dizzy. She lifted her mouth and received the kiss of life for which she'd never stopped hungering.

Suddenly, they were jarred as something barreled into John's thigh. Her eyes flew open in time to see a black-browed Jamie.

"*My mamma!*" he shouted possessively, and he determinedly squeezed between their bodies to separate them.

"Jamie, sweetheart, it's all right." All at once she was terrified and knew that it wasn't all right. Her son looked too much like the man he had attacked. "John is my friend."

Campbell knelt down so he was on a level with the child. "Hello, Jamie. My name is John." He held out his hand.

"No!" Jamie spat into his proffered palm.

Elizabeth was momentarily aghast, but then her nerves made her burst into laughter. Jamie's mouth turned up at the corners, and he joined in his mother's mirth.

"Your protector is so earnest, so gallant—a little Spawn of Satan who needs his arse tanned."

"Yes, I know," Elizabeth said with great pride.

The air was filled with barks as two dogs came running across the lawn. Both had recognized John from afar, but Queenie soon loped past Dandy to greet him with lolling tongue and wagging tail.

Elizabeth was glad of the distraction. She saw Emma watching them and spoke urgently to Jamie. "You have to get dry clothes on for lunch. Go to Emma." When he looked reluctant she bribed him.

"We'll blow out the candles."

Jamie nodded excitedly and ran to the castle.

John watched him go. "He's a fine boy. I envy you your son."

She changed the subject. "George told me you are now a colonel. How are you able to be here? Is the war over?"

"No such luck," he said ruefully. "As a colonel, I no longer lead men into battle as I did when I was a major. I work behind the scenes . . . I administrate, among other things."

She stood on tiptoe and kissed him swiftly. "Thank you for not getting yourself killed, John."

Possessive arms went around her and refused to release her. "I cannot stay here at Cadzow tonight—it would compromise you. I'll go to Chatelherault. Will you come to me there?"

"You know I will. This is such a wonderful birthday present."

He kissed her nose. "You have no idea, my beauty."

"I'll come when I can. We are having a small celebration here. Oh, John, I have so much to tell you."

Reluctantly, he released her. He watched her pick up her

son's shoes and stockings and bent to retrieve hers. He lifted her pretty garters to his lips then stuffed them into his pocket. "I'll keep these until I can put them on you."

She blushed profusely and realized she hadn't blushed since the last time she'd seen him. It had been at Chatelherault. As she hurried after Jamie, her pulsebeat was so rapid she could feel it in her throat, and her heart whispered his name over and over. How on earth would she be able to wait until they could be alone together? She knew time would slow down in an agony of torment. Nighttime was hours away. *How will I endure them?*

Chapter Thirty-Four

*J*ohn stood in the lingering twilight waiting for the first glimpse of his beloved. When she finally arrived astride her Border pony, he lifted her from the saddle and squeezed her tightly before setting her feet to the ground. "I thought you'd never come."

She gazed up at him with loving eyes. "You are the moon, and I am the tide. You knew I would come. You draw me irresistibly."

He took the reins, then handclasped they led the pony to the stables. John removed the saddle and harness and put the pony in a box stall with plenty of hay, next to one he'd given Demon. His eager arms gathered her close as if he could not bear any distance between their bodies. Then his mouth came down on hers in a kiss that almost devoured her. "God, you smell of autumn roses and sunshine and woman."

"Mmm, and you smell of leather, horses, and hay." She lifted her mouth for another kiss.

"The smell of hay is from the loft. It's very tempting—would you like to go up there?" He waggled his eyebrows suggestively.

She brushed against his hard length, glanced at the ladder, and whispered breathlessly, "I don't think we could make it that far."

With a whoop he swept her up into his arms, snatched another quick kiss, then began to run. He didn't stop until they were inside the hunting lodge. He kicked the door shut with a booted foot. He did not put her down but moved toward the bedroom.

She lifted her arms from around his neck and threaded her fingers into his black, wavy hair. It was longer than fashion dictated and she realized he'd come straight from the war where there was little time for haircuts. "You're uncivilized."

"Guilty as charged."

She glanced at the bed. "And you expect me to be uncivilized."

"Oh, God, yes!" He squeezed her bum cheeks.

She turned in his arms, wrapped her legs about him, and bit him on the neck. "Like an Irish wildcat?"

"Like an Irish wildcat in heat." He knelt on the bed and lowered their bodies, still entwined, onto the soft eiderdown. He gazed into her eyes. "Beth, I've thought about you or dreamed of you every night since we were here last—a lifetime ago."

"I didn't dare think about you. The longing inside me was an unbearable agony. And now you're here—real—not a dream."

They started to undress each other, laughing exultantly at the tangle they got into; when they were naked, their amusement vanished, replaced by the reeling urgency of scalding passion that had been denied too long. His hungry mouth moved from her lips down to her lush breasts, soft belly, and hot cleft between her legs. Her mouth too was ravenous as she traced her tongue down his rib cage and brushed her lips against his muscled thigh.

"Dear God, Beth, don't put your mouth anywhere near the ravening beast, or I'll spend." He took her firmly by the shoulders, forcing her to lie still, then straddled her hips.

She stilled for a moment, though her breasts rose and fell as she gasped for breath, then she arched against him, inviting him to plunder the hidden treasure she would never yield to another. She had never felt less like a lady, or more like a woman, in her life. Only he could arouse such flagrant desire . . . only he could inflame her passions . . . only he could put out the fire that threatened to consume her. She surrendered without regret or reservation.

With each hot, driving thrust he relished every shiver, every shudder, every hungry moan, every scream of excitement. Then his own groans and exultant shouts rent the air as he exploded, and his love and passion poured over her like molten lava.

He collapsed his weight upon her and they lay suspended in another time and place, a dark erotic cave where they alone dwelled and the world receded, leaving them in a cocoon of contentment.

With her lips against his throat, Elizabeth whispered, "John, that was perfect. This time there will be no guilt."

"Guilt?" John sounded as if the emotion were alien to him.

"Last time I was covered with guilt. After the storm, Hamilton sent for me and said he would meet me at Uppingham. I knew Charlie had smallpox the day after I arrived. I sent baby James home with his father and promised to follow. I didn't, of course. I stayed with Will to nurse her. When she died I thought I was being punished for committing adultery with you."

His arms enfolded her, wanting to protect her. "You showed great courage. Guilt is destructive. I hope you banished it forever."

Her lips brushed his cheek. "I finally realized Charlie's death had nothing to do with my sins. But I didn't banish it forever. It came rushing back when Hamilton died. I feared a third death . . . yours . . . would be my punishment."

"I shall die on the upstroke—" He stopped. It was an old joke.

"Beth, I'm so sorry about Charlie. I had no idea you were with her when she died. I know that Will almost went mad with grief." He hesitated. "Why did you feel guilt over Hamilton's death, love?"

"Because I hated him—because I was glad that he died." She hesitated. This was no fit subject for lovers. If she was not careful, guilt would again sink its relentless fangs into her.

"It had naught to do with you. James drank himself to death. Plain and simple. We all knew it was inevitable. That's one of the reasons why I was so incensed when you married him."

She raised her eyes to his. "When I learned that my mother had accepted Hamilton's offer, I came to Half-Moon Street to tell you I would come and live with you in Kent. You had left for Argyll because your brother had been killed. But everyone told me you had gone to marry Mary Montagu."

"You should never have believed them, Beth. You had all of

my heart. I came back from Argyll realizing that life was too short to live without happiness. I returned, intent on asking you to be my wife, but you were already wed. How sinfully ironic."

"Sinful?"

"Sinful to have wasted so many years apart." He leered down at her with dark, smoldering eyes. "Now I shall have to make up for lost time." He covered her soft lips with his in a melting kiss that rendered them boneless. It was a prelude to the slow lovemaking he intended to draw out for hours. After the hot, impatient sexual encounter in which they had indulged, he was now ready to teach her what making love was all about.

Afterwards, at last replete, they drifted into sleep, their arms and legs still entwined. At dawn they stirred in their warm nest, and Elizabeth brushed her lips against his heart. "I didn't even ask why you are here."

"I'm on my way to Argyll to recruit again. This time we are in need of sailors for the British navy. It will be good to see my father. He doesn't have the robust health he once enjoyed."

Beth's arms tightened about him to comfort him, and they drowsed away another delicious hour until the sunlight woke them. She sat up in bed and stretched luxuriantly. "I must go home and so must you, my love. I regret that our time together has been so short."

"We won't be apart for long. Your year of mourning is almost up. As soon as I get to Inveraray I'll prepare them for our wedding. The only question that remains is *when* you'll marry me."

She threw back the covers, slid from the bed and turned to face him. "I will never marry you, John."

He sat up like a shot. "What the hell are you talking about?"

"I hated marriage and loathed being a duchess. I don't want us to be husband and wife. I want us to be lovers."

"That's out of the question. You are a duchess—you cannot carry on a flagrant affair! You would be ostracized, your name dragged through the mud. You have no idea what vultures the nobility are."

"Oh, I think I do." She pulled on her petticoat. "Elizabeth Gunning wasn't good enough to be the wife of Argyll, but the Duchess of Hamilton is imminently suitable. Because I was wed to that swine, James Douglas, and he bestowed his noble title upon me, I am now eligible to become your wife."

"That's rubbish!" He threw back the covers and jumped from the bed, naked. "I want you to be my wife because I love you!"

She surveyed his powerful body from head to heel. "Dark, dominant, and dangerous . . . delicious in a lover. Anathema in a husband. I shall *never* marry, *never* put myself under a man's control again. Please understand, John. I am free. I will never under any circumstances squander my precious freedom."

He strode round the bed and grabbed her by the shoulders. "You willful little bitch!" He began to shake some sense into her.

"If you shake me till my teeth rattle and your balls dance up and down, you won't change my mind. Rather you will reinforce my horror of husbands."

His teeth ground together, and his jaw clenched into a lump of iron. "I love you. I thought you loved me."

"John, I adore you. And I know you worship me. That's why I won't risk ruining our love with marriage."

"You are the most maddening creature who ever drew breath."

"You forgot beautiful . . . the most maddening, beautiful creature." She threw back her head, and her laughter came rolling out.

He flung himself away from her and began to throw on his clothes. "Get dressed. I'm taking you home. Perhaps Emma can talk some sense into your stubborn head."

"No! I'm perfectly capable of riding home myself." She suddenly didn't want him to see Jamie. She fastened the buttons on her gown then defiantly tossed her disheveled hair over her shoulders. "Go to Argyll, John Campbell. Or go to hell!"

"Not another bloody word, madam." His dark eyes glittered dangerously, and she did not dare flaunt his command.

Elizabeth, astride her Border pony, could not pull ahead of Demon. Campbell kept pace with her, ignoring her icy disdain and the obvious displeasure at his company that she exuded. The hour was early, and she fervently hoped that Jamie would still be asleep.

When they arrived at the castle, he turned their mounts over

to a groom. Elizabeth could not argue, for that meant she would
have to break her silence—and this she stubbornly refused to
do. He followed her inside, totally indifferent to her rigid back.
The only person abroad was Mr. Burke, who acknowledged a
speaking look from Campbell by immediately withdrawing.

John strode to the bottom of the stairs and bellowed,
"Emma!"

Elizabeth's heart sank. Even if Jamie had been asleep, the
thundering male voice would have awakened him.

Emma appeared immediately. As she descended the stairs,
her keen glance assessed the agitated pair who had just arrived.

"She refuses to marry me!"

Emma continued down the stairs, her eyes focused on Elizabeth.

"She spent the night in my bed, refusing me nothing, then
threw my proposal back in my face." He could not conceal his
outrage.

Elizabeth gasped at the intimate secret he had revealed.

"What? You think Emma doesn't know we spent the night
together making passionate love? You think she doesn't know
we slept together that weekend we disappeared from Chiswick?
Emma might be discretion itself, but she doesn't wear bloody
blinkers!"

"Mamma, Mamma!" Jamie came running down the stairs
only half dressed, with Nan on his heels carrying his shirt.

Beth's heart jumped into her throat. She broke her furious silence. "Don't run! You'll fall!"

The toddler stumbled three steps from the bottom and went
sprawling. The joy of seeing his mother was greater than his
hurt, and he held up his arms to her.

"Now, see what you've done!" She rushed to her son and
lifted him against her heart.

John Campbell stood quietly with a stunned look on his
face.

Elizabeth's heart contracted.

"I clearly see what *you* have done." He turned to Emma.
"When is Jamie's birthday?"

Emma hesitated then replied, "The first of November, your
lordship."

"I thought he was a New Year's baby?"

"That's when he was christened," Emma said quietly.

Campbell firmly took the child from Elizabeth's arms and handed him to Nan, then he looked at Emma. "Leave us."

When she was absolutely sure the women were out of earshot, Elizabeth bared her teeth like a vixen defending its kit. "A black mole means nothing! Thousands of people have them! His father was James Douglas, Duke of Hamilton. My son is the rightful Seventh Duke of Hamilton. Don't you dare to question it!"

"He is *my* son, the rightful heir to Argyll."

"You are mistaken!" she said vehemently.

"If he was born on the first of November he was conceived the night of Charlie's masquerade party, when I took you to Half-Moon Street."

"You are mistaken!" she insisted again. "My baby was born prematurely after a rough carriage ride. On All Hallows Eve, Hamilton insisted his heir be born at Holyrood Palace. My labor began, and I gave birth the next morning. You are not his father!"

"Stop lying to yourself. I *asked* you to marry me earlier— now I am *demanding* that you do so. I intend to be a father to my own son, Elizabeth, even if you deny my paternity with your last breath."

She dug in her heels, lifted her stubborn chin, and defied him. "I will never marry you, John Campbell. I hate you!"

He leashed the violence he was feeling with an iron control and bowed stiffly. "If that's your last word, madam, I bid you good-bye."

Elizabeth spent the entire day with Jamie. They took the dogs into the woods and gathered brilliantly colored leaves and acorns, laughing when the squirrels scampered up the trees to chatter their displeasure with twitching tails. Her gaiety was forced, but her relief was very real. Though John had discovered her secret and was angry as a bear with a sore arse because he could not bludgeon her into marriage, he had left. *It's over. I cannot deny that I love him, but I love my child more. Jamie will always come first.*

At dinner that night, she allowed her son to stay up late. She stuck candles into the piece of birthday cake that was left and

let him blow them out. Only when he began to yawn his head
off did she put him to bed and kiss him good night.

In her own bedchamber she sat down at her desk while
Emma lit her lamps and closed her drapes. "If you have something to say, then say it," she challenged the faithful servant.

Emma gave her a level look. "You are twenty years old, a
woman grown, who knows right from wrong. You don't need
my advice."

Elizabeth slept badly for the next two nights, but gradually
her apprehension left her. Her sexual cravings, however, were
not as easy to banish. She picked up the invitation to the gala in
Glasgow and thought of Tom Calder. He was an attractive Scot,
without doubt, and more than half in love with her. Suddenly
she began to laugh at the absurdity of Tom Calder assuaging her
needs.

Elizabeth packed her mauve evening gown in tissue and
chose amethyst jewels to go with it. She was glad that mauve
was an acceptable mourning color, for strictly speaking her first
year as a widow was not quite over.

Emma handed her the high-heeled dancing slippers. "Are
you sure you won't need me in Glasgow tonight?"

"I'm not sure at all, but I much prefer you stay with Jamie.
I'll tell the coachman to have the carriage ready at dawn tomorrow. I promise to be home in time for breakfast."

"What have you decided to wear for the ribbon-cutting ceremony?"

"The gray velvet afternoon dress with the fox collar. I have
a matching hat somewhere. I saw it a moment ago."

"Uh-oh, I just saw Jamie in a gray hat. Where are you, Milado?" Emma rescued the chapeau but had to clean off the raspberry jam His Grace had smeared on the fur.

Mr. Burke knocked on the door. "The carriage is ready,
ma'am."

"Oh, I'm not even dressed. Do give the coachman my
apologies, Mr. Burke, and tell him I'll be down shortly." She
handed him her luggage.

She dressed quickly then went down on her knees, unmind-
ful of her velvet, to hug Jamie. "Do exactly as Emma tells you,

and I'll bring you a present. Good-bye darling. I'll see you at breakfast."

The September afternoon was glorious as Lady Elizabeth Hamilton cut the green ribbon to mark the official opening of Calderpark Wildlife Preserve. It had been open to the public all summer, but today was the official ceremony, complete with Glasgow's dignitaries. Tom Calder, whom the park had been named after, beamed down at Elizabeth. "Would ye like a tour, Yer Grace?"

"I'd love to see the polar bears, Tom, but I'll wait until I return in the spring for the full tour. By then my son will be old enough to hike with me to view all the animals."

As she prepared to leave the park, happy that her polar bears were growing and flourishing, she noticed a man selling kites at the gate. They were fashioned after birds of prey—eagles, falcons, seahawks—and she knew she'd found her present for Jamie.

That night at the gala Elizabeth danced every quadrille and schottische, every reel, rant, and Highland fling, reveling in the knowledge that she had selected her own gown and chosen to wear her own hair rather than a powdered wig. She responded freely to the gentlemen who flirted—and there were many, both single and married.

She didn't fall into bed until three o'clock in the morning but was up again at five for the journey back to Cadzow. She curled up in the corner of the coach with closed eyes for the ten-mile drive.

When the carriage pulled into the courtyard, she felt quite pleased with herself. At such an early hour, Jamie would still be abed. Clutching the kite, she slipped through the castle's front door and smugly noted that not even the servants were yet abroad.

She tiptoed quietly into Jamie's bedchamber and was surprised to find his bed empty. *Oh, Lord, I hope the little devil hasn't taken total advantage of poor Emma.* She went into her own chamber to set down her parcel and remove her cloak, then she went along to Emma's room expecting to find Jamie sharing her bed. She found only Queenie, who looked at her mournfully; not even Dandy was about.

"I can't believe they've gone for a walk and left you be-

hind." Elizabeth rubbed the dog's head. "And I can't believe
that son of mine got Emma up at such an ungodly hour!" She
looked at Queenie. "I'd better let you out before you pee on
the carpets. Come on, girl. Won't they be surprised when they
come back and find I'm here for breakfast before they are!"

When she arrived in the kitchen she told the cook that she
was starving. "Where's Mr. Burke this fine morning?"

"He left yesterday wi' t'others, Yer Grace."

"What others?"

"Miss Emma an' the wee duke."

"My son, Jamie?"

"Aye, didna Nan tell ye?"

Elizabeth's brows drew together in consternation. She was
getting nowhere with cook, so she hurried from the kitchen and
went upstairs in search of Nan. The nursemaid was just leaving
her room, but when she saw the duchess, she ducked back inside.

Beth immediately followed her. "Nan, what on earth is
going on? I can't find anyone, and cook said you'd tell me
where they are."

"They're gone." Nan looked stricken.

For the first time icy-cold fingers clutched Beth's heart and
began to squeeze. "Gone where? With whom?" she demanded.

"Emma and Mr. Burke went off wi' the bairn in the carriage."

Elizabeth's throat went dry. "Whose carriage?"

"Colonel Campbell's carriage." Nan slipped an envelope
from her pocket and wordlessly offered it to Elizabeth.

She snatched it from Nan's fingers, tore it open, and blinked
in utter disbelief at the words that met her eyes:

> Elizabeth:
> I have taken my son to Inveraray. He is in safe
> hands, so there is no need for alarm. I look forward to
> seeing you. We all eagerly await your arrival.
> John Campbell

"You whoreson!" Elizabeth screamed. "Do not look forward
to seeing me, John Campbell. It will be a battle to the death!"

The coachman came upstairs with her luggage, and she met

him on the landing. "Don't put the carriage away. We are going to Argyll." She went into her bedchamber to prepare for her journey. Elizabeth chose her clothes very carefully for her encounter.

She selected gowns in dark powerful colors that would lend her authority and packed her most precious and regal jewels with which she would adorn herself. She took her sable cape from the wardrobe then reached up to the top shelf and took down the sword that her father had first taught her to wield when she was twelve.

"No need for alarm? Think again, Lord Bloody Sundridge!"

Chapter Thirty-Five

*I*t took two full days of travel to get to Inveraray, even though the coach set out at four in the morning on the second day. She bade her driver stop at an inn at the tip of Loch Fyne, less than five miles from Inveraray, where she took a room for a couple of hours so that she could change into an elegant gown and pin her hair in the latest fashion.

The late sunset was turning the sky a spectacular crimson and fuschia as her driver pulled into the castle courtyard. Elizabeth, swathed in sable, stepped from the carriage and came face-to-face with John Campbell, who had been awaiting her for two hours.

He grinned. "What took you so long?"

She had never been as incensed in her life. "You arrogant swine!" Her rage almost blinded her. She reached up, grabbed the coachman's whip, and lashed out at him with passion.

It caught him about the thighs, and he quickly gripped the thin leather thong and jerked the handle from her hands. "I see you are playacting again. What role is this? Molly Mallone, fishwife?"

"Where is Jamie?" she demanded, her temper sizzling.

"He's in bed at this hour, of course." He let the whip slide from his fingers. "Allow me to offer the hospitality of Argyll. Surely we can settle our differences in a civilized manner?"

"Civilized? You are a Highland Barbarian!"

"Follow me, Your Grace." His voice was smooth as black velvet.

The last thing she wanted to do was obey him, but she knew she had no choice but follow him into the huge fortress that was Inveraray. The turreted castle dwarfed Cadzow, but Elizabeth felt confident that it could never be furnished as elegantly. As they entered the Great Hall she realized she was wrong. It was magnificent. Her glance swept the hall, noting the silken banners, the noble devices on the crests and shields displayed around the craggy stone walls. Below the emblems were weapons, and she marveled at their size and number. Her eyes came to rest on a strikingly attractive lady with graying hair who stood tall before the gigantic fireplace.

"It gives me great pleasure to introduce my mother, the Duchess of Argyll. Mother, may I present the Duchess of Hamilton?"

"Welcome to Inveraray, Your Grace." Her serene smile was genuine.

"Thank you," Elizabeth said regally then stiffened as she felt her sable cape being lifted from her shoulders.

John's mother looked at the exquisite female before her, gowned in purple velvet so dark it looked black, her throat ablaze with diamonds, and her glorious hair pinned in golden loops about her beautiful face. "Judas! Now I understand why I could not tempt John with Mary Montagu." She nodded to Elizabeth. "I shall retire and surrender the field to the younger generation."

When they were alone, Elizabeth's eyes glittered their challenge. She was not afraid of John Campbell or any other force that threatened her child. She would defy him with her last breath. She would fight him to the death and never count the cost.

"Elizabeth, will you sup with me?" he asked pleasantly. "I did not dine yet. I chose to wait for you."

Her outrage did not diminish. "I cannot think of food until I have seen with my own eyes that my child is safe."

"Of course you may see him. My son's safety is paramount."

She bristled. "He is *not* your son—"

He held up his hand. "Yes, yes, you've made your position

clear. Can we declare a truce and discuss this calmly over supper?"

"Truce, my eye! You are a bloody colonel, trained to win a battle at any cost, or by any devious means!"

"Surely a battle isn't necessary. A skirmish, perhaps?" he said lightly. "Come, I'll let you see Jamie."

"A tactic designed to soften me!" She blushed at the sensual image her choice of words evoked.

He raised amused brows. "Damned if I do, damned if I don't."

"Yes, you are!" She refused the arm he offered. "Lead on."

Damn, I keep using the wrong words! He will certainly lead me on if I give him half the chance. She followed him through the castle until they came to a set of stone steps that led up into one of the turrets. As she ascended beside him, she lifted her skirts so she would not trip over her hem and lose her regal dignity.

He pressed down the latch on a studded oaken door and allowed it to swing silently open, then he put his finger to his lips.

Elizabeth stepped inside but stopped halfway to the bed when she saw how peacefully her child slept. Beside him on the pillow lay his favorite bedtime toy, a stuffed donkey made in the image of Thistle. Her face softened as she looked at him, admitting to herself for the first time that Jamie was made in the image of John Campbell. She saw that a lamp burned low. The door to an adjoining chamber opened, and Emma came through it carrying another lamp.

"Are you all right, Emma?" Elizabeth whispered urgently.

"We're perfectly safe," Emma murmured her assurance.

Elizabeth nodded and walked quietly back to John Campbell who awaited her at the bedchamber door. She followed him up another spiral staircase to chambers above and, when she stepped into the first room, realized this turret was his. The sitting room was furnished luxuriously, yet every item was masculine in the extreme. The Georgian table, chairs, and bookcases were dark polished mahogany, the rugs were olive-green Aubusson, and a maroon leather sofa and chairs sat before the fire. The chandelier was Venetian crystal, and the paintings on the walls were old masters. *His taste is impecca-*

*ble because it has been bred into him by his mother, Duchess of
Argyll. She is a true noble lady, something I can never be.*

Alone with her adversary at last, Elizabeth swept around to
face him. She dug her heels into the Aubusson rug, lifted her
chin, and set her hands on her hips. Before she could fire her
first sally, Mr. Burke came in carrying a food-laden tray, which
he set on the table. "Well, well, it seems I am outflanked and
outnumbered. Mr. Burke, I trusted you, but you turned out to be
a snake in the grass."

"Forgive me, Your Grace. My loyalties are hopelessly di-
vided."

Her eyes told him that she did *not* forgive him. She waited
pointedly until he departed before resuming her attack on
Campbell. "Because you have the power and wealth of Argyll
behind you, you think you can order the universe and it will
kowtow to you!"

"If you marry me, the power and wealth of Argyll can be
yours."

"I have no interest in such things!" she stated emphatically.

"Little liar," he murmured. "You stand before me reveling in
the wealth and power of the Duchess of Hamilton. You are
aware of how magnificent you look. You know I cannot resist
you."

"Flattery won't work . . . I can certainly resist *you*."

"I'm hoping you won't be able to resist the food. Come.
Sit." He held a chair for her and watched as she lost the battle
with hunger. Before he took his seat across from her, he poured
them wine. " 'Where there is no wine there is no love,' " he
quoted.

"I can go further back than Euripides." She smugly displayed her knowledge of the arts. "*In vino veritas*."

"Pliny. In wine there is truth." He lifted his goblet. "Then
acknowledge this truth, Elizabeth: Jamie is my son."

"James George Douglas is the Seventh Duke of Hamilton,
Fifth Duke of Brandon, and Marquis of Clydesdale. *Know this
truth:* As his mother and guardian it's my duty to see that these
noble titles are not taken from him." She quaffed deeply to
punctuate her words.

"There is absolutely no need for that, Beth. If you marry me,

I am prepared to keep my mouth shut about Jamie's paternity. I will sire another son to become heir of Argyll."

He thinks to cut my legs out from under me, promising to let Jamie retain the Dukedom of Hamilton. He does not yet realize I refuse to marry another noble husband and give up my freedom. She set her goblet down. "I do not want another son."

"I do!" he vowed. He lifted a silver cover to reveal a pair of game birds. "I'll never forget the blissful look on your face when you first tasted partridge."

She sniffed indifferently. "My gorge rises at noble excesses."

He nodded knowingly. "I should have ordered rabbit."

"Go to hellfire!" *You know too well my likes and dislikes.* As he served the food and poured more wine, her eyes lingered on his hands. His long, tapered fingers contrasted with Hamilton's blunt, spatulate ones. Though Campbell's hands were strong and powerful, she knew them capable of tenderness and of arousing her passion. She quickly raised her eyes, and her glance came to rest and linger on his mouth. This time it was more difficult to drag her attention away. *The wine is heating my blood. I must eat something.*

He too seemed to have difficulty keeping his eyes from her.

"Must you stare? Can't you restrain yourself?" she demanded.

"I am restraining myself more than you'll ever know. I want to take you by the shoulders and shake you until the jeweled pins drop from your hair and it falls over my hands in silken splendor. I want to disrobe you, sweep the food to the floor, and lay you back on this table. I want to touch, taste, and feast upon you."

She recoiled. "You think a ravening beast appeals to me?"

"The last time we were together, it did."

"That's because I thought of you as my lover, not my husband!"

"I intend to be both."

"The road to hell is paved with honorable intentions," she mocked, licking her fingers.

"Christ, let me do that."

"Now *you're* doing the playacting, pretending that everything I do arouses you, while what you're really trying to do is

disarm me and bend me to your will. But I have learned that between a man and a woman it is always about domination and
submission."

"You play the game well." His eyes showed their admiration.

"John, please understand. I am *not* playing games."

"Neither am I, Beth. I am deadly serious. You need a husband, whether you realize it or not, and Jamie needs a father, no
matter his paternity. His land, castles, and wealth need to be
managed by a noble hand, a strong hand. There's none so powerful as Argyll." He stood, moved around the table, and reached
for her.

"Don't touch me! Keep your powerful, *ig-noble* hands from
me!"

"As you will. But I ask that you honor our truce, Elizabeth.
Tonight I am asking you to marry me. Tomorrow morning I
want you to ride out with me over Argyll. Then you may give
your answer."

She wanted to shout *No!* but held onto her temper and nodded her assent. He led her back downstairs and showed her to a
chamber not far removed from her son's. When she went inside
and closed the door, Dandy was sitting on the bed as if he
awaited her.

As she lay in bed with the little dog curled against her, she
felt emotionally drained. Unused to two goblets of wine, she
soon succumbed to temptation when sleep beckoned.

Elizabeth awoke early. She retrieved a bedrobe from her
trunk and slipped along to awaken Jamie, with Dandy at her
heels.

"Mamma!" He stood on the bed and wrapped his arms about
her.

She reached beneath the bed for the chamber pot. "Pee pee."

"Uh-oh." He pointed as Dandy cocked his leg up the bed-
post.

"Bad boy!" she scolded the dog. "Come, we'll take him outside."

On the main floor of the castle they found a door that led
outside. As Elizabeth opened it, a tall, craggy-faced man filled
the door frame. She instinctively knew it was Argyll.

"Dandy peed," Jamie informed him.

Beth wanted to sink through the flagstones.

Argyll's dark eyes glittered. "This is Mother, no doot?"

"*My* mamma!" He placed a possessive hand on her bedrobe and pulled her away from the elderly man.

"I beg your pardon, Your Grace." She lowered her lashes.

"Ye need never beg tae get what ye want from a mon. Tho' I suspect ye already know that, Lady Elizabeth."

She blushed against her will. *Another John Campbell . . . another silver-tongued devil!* She stepped aside to let him pass and watched him limp away with an awkward gait. After Dandy made his deposit, they returned upstairs to find Emma unpacking. "No need to unpack my things, Emma. We will not be staying."

"Bath!" Jamie shouted with glee.

"Yes, go get your ship. You can have a bath," Emma agreed. "The bathing room is huge . . . tub's big enough for both of you, Mamma."

"I've agreed to ride out with Campbell. I must dress, Emma. If I keep him waiting, I shall be at a disadvantage."

Wearing the jade-green habit that Charlie had given her so long ago, Elizabeth rode sidesaddle beside Campbell. Morning mist hung over the purple peaks of the Grampian Mountains. The vistas were breathtaking. The crystal air smelled of bracken and heather.

"Argyll land stretches as far as the eye can see, north, south, east, or west, far beyond the Grampians. If you ride west until you come to the sea, beyond that is Morven and the Isle of Mull. If you ride south to the bottom of Loch Fyne, you will see the great Isle of Kintyre. Those are the places I must go to recruit. The men of our isles are natural born and bred sailors."

The vastness of Argyll was magnificent, impressive, but for Elizabeth it was also overwhelming. In the not-too-distant future, John would be Duke of Argyll, lord of all they surveyed. His wife would be Duchess of Argyll, and she knew she could never live up to the standards set by past and present duchesses. Nor did she have the least ambition to do so. *I even hate riding sidesaddle!* "I encountered your father this morning. He was limping badly."

"An old war wound that never bothered him when he was

younger—but now he's permanently crippled. It hasn't affected his eye for the ladies, however." John grinned. "He said you were feminine enough to quicken an old mon, then amended it to *even a dead mon.*"

"Why do men always bring sex into it?" she bristled.

He tried to hide his amusement. "Human nature. You are playacting anger, when in truth you are flattered. Human nature."

"You have an answer for everything!"

"Not quite, Beth. I don't have the answer to the question I asked you last night." His face was intense. "Will you marry me?"

I want him to love me, and I think he does, but if I were his wife, we would both eventually be miserable. I cannot be molded into something I am not. It would be a joyless existence. She reined in and met his eyes. "John, my answer is no."

She saw surprise written on his face. It quickly turned to anger as he narrowed his dark, glittering eyes. "I did not want to issue an ultimatum. I didn't want it to come to this, but you leave me no choice. I will not allow you to deprive me of my son. If you agree to marry me, our son will remain Duke of Hamilton and none will ever know that he was not James Douglas's legitimate heir." His powerful hands tightened on the reins. "If you refuse to marry me, I shall take Jamie from you, reveal to the world that he is my son, make him my heir, and he will be deprived of the Hamilton title and holdings."

It was Elizabeth's turn to feel surprise. "You would truly deprive him of his Hamilton title and holdings?"

"Not I, Beth. *You* would deprive him. The choice is yours."

A curl of fear spiraled inside her. It mingled with her fury. She was shrewd enough to contain her anger so she could think clearly and weigh the advantages and disadvantages for herself and her son. If she pit herself against the power of Argyll, she would lose. *I thought he loved me!* Her sense of loss was staggering.

Without a word, she set her heels to the sleek mount he'd provided and rode, as fast as the restrictive saddle allowed, back to Inveraray. The need to escape was overwhelming.

John Campbell let her take the lead. She had much to consider. He remained silent. He had presented his position and felt confident she was intelligent enough to do what was expedient. When they arrived at the stables he wisely did not try to lift her from the saddle. He'd not give her the chance to scorn his offer.

She could feel his eyes boring into her stiff back as she walked from the stables. He remained behind to see to the horses, even though there were many grooms about. She went directly up to the bedchamber she had been assigned, closed the door, then gave vent to her frustration by removing a riding boot and hurling it against a mirror. It bounced off the polished silver surface without doing the least damage, and she didn't know whether to laugh or cry. Ruefully, she realized that was as much effect as she'd have if she pit herself against Argyll; she wouldn't even leave a dent.

Once more, she slowly went over her catalogue of reasons why she did not want to marry, with their attendant disadvantages. The list was compelling. A knock distracted her, and when she answered the door, she found a maidservant had brought her lunch. Then Jamie arrived, accompanied by Emma, who had their lunch on a tray.

Elizabeth pushed her silent dilemma from her conscious thoughts—although it remained just below the surface—as she enjoyed the sojourn with her little boy. "What have you been up to this morning?"

"Tacking," he replied happily, his mouth filled with cheese.

"He means tracking. Mr. Burke was showing him animal tracks. Milado has taken quite a shine to the man."

"Jamie isn't the only one," she said pointedly. "I'm sorry, Emma. I have no call to chastise you. It was two dominant men against one woman. I'm grateful you stayed with him."

After lunch, Elizabeth knew she must get back to making her decision. Doubtless, it was the most important of her life. "Why don't you go with Emma and have a nap?"

"No!" He grabbed his mother's hand. "Come out an' play."

Elizabeth was torn. Jamie could always persuade her. *He's just like his father.* "It's all right, Emma. We'll go outside. Jamie, let me wipe your mouth." He wriggled as she rubbed away his milk mustache, then they descended to Inveraray's courtyard.

He immediately spotted John Campbell, sitting on a bench in the pale sunshine, cleaning his weapons. Jamie loosened his mother's hand and ran toward the dark man. She almost stopped him but thought better of it. What surer test than to observe the Scot's reaction to, and treatment of, her child? And vice versa.

Campbell sheathed the sword he'd sharpened. "Hello, Jamie." He saw that the weapon was a magnet for the small fingers. "It's dangerous. It can hurt you, so be careful."

Jamie took hold of the scabbard and tried to draw out the blade.

"Like this." John revealed the trick to it, resheathed the sword, and handed it back.

Jamie's chubby fingers imitated the maneuver exactly, and he laughed as he successfully drew out the blade. He touched the tip of his finger to the sharp edge and cut himself. "Ooh!"

Elizabeth's heart jumped into her mouth.

John immediately cut his own finger. "Like this." He lifted the digit to his mouth and sucked off the blood. Jamie copied.

I don't need a husband, but perhaps Jamie needs a father. As she watched them, making sure she stayed a short distance away, she began to review the advantages of the marriage he offered. Her glance lingered on the black hair, the strong jaw, and the broad shoulders of the man talking with her son. She knew one thing beyond a doubt: She would never love another man save him. Her mind moved on to the advantages to her son. They were myriad.

Surely it is my duty as a mother to put my child before myself? I am honor-bound to do what is best for Jamie. If I allow John to become his father, James George will be the undisputed Duke of Hamilton. She shivered. John was a military man. The country was fighting a war with France. What if he was killed? And the amazing answer came back to her: *If Jamie were our only son, perhaps he'd be heir to the Dukedom of Argyll, as well as Duke of Hamilton.*

Surely the small sacrifice of marrying the man she loved would be in Jamie's best interest? He would also have a mother and father who adored him. As Elizabeth closed the gap between them, her eyes softened, and the corners of her mouth lifted.

John looked up expectantly, ready for her surrender.

As she met his gaze she realized that he was using her child to control her. Exactly as Hamilton had done. She snatched Jamie away from him. "Go to hellfire, John Campbell! I'll be *double damned* if I'll ever allow myself to become a *double duchess!*"

She picked her son up and stalked back inside the castle, ignoring his protests. She found Emma mending a torn sleeve on one of Jamie's shirts. "Pack your things. We are leaving immediately." She opened a bureau drawer, pulled out her son's garments, and put them in his trunk. She left Emma to gather his toys and went to her bedchamber to do her own packing.

When it was complete she sought out Mr. Burke. "Please tell my driver to ready our coach. We are packed and ready to leave."

"His lordship sent your carriage to the coachmakers for repair."

"It needed no repair. Where is my driver?" she demanded.

"I would tell you his whereabouts if I knew, Your Grace."

Furious and beside herself with frustration, Elizabeth herded Emma, Jamie, and Dandy into her chamber, turned the key in the lock, and propped her sword against the door frame. It was too late to do anything today, but if her coach and driver were not in evidence in the morning, she would go directly to the powerful Duke of Argyll.

Chapter Thirty-Six

*J*ohn Campbell lay in bed, his arms folded behind his head. He cursed himself for the clumsy way he'd handled the situation. He sat up, thumped his pillow for the tenth time, then threw himself down in a futile attempt to make himself comfortable. He was a man who would not accept defeat, even when it stared him in the face.

His blood was high, as it was in battle; his mood was fierce and dangerous. He flung off the covers and set his feet to the rug, determined to go down to Elizabeth's bedchamber and force her to his will. She was the most infuriating, stubborn female he'd ever encountered. She was deliberately taunting him to resort to violence and, by God, he'd make her yield to him if it was the last thing he did. He'd make love to her until she was writhing and frenzied and moaning in submission. He would demand her unconditional surrender.

Why do men always bring sex into it? He heard her words clearly, as if she had just uttered them. He stood up and thrust his fingers through his black hair in utter frustration. He could easily seduce her physically so that she would willingly, eagerly yield her body to him, but John knew he wanted more than that. He wanted, nay, *needed* her to surrender her heart and her soul to him.

He paced his chamber like a caged lion. It made absolutely no sense to him that she refused to be his wife. They had ached to be together for years, and now that the impediment of her

husband had been removed, nothing on earth stood in the way
of their marriage. They already shared a son, and John wanted
to be the father of her future children. The damnedest part was
he knew she loved him.

He poured a dram of whiskey and sat down on the bed to
drink it. As he stared down into the amber liquor the fumes met
his nose. The smell reminded him of the late Duke of Hamilton.
He set the glass down untouched as realization dawned: *Elizabeth isn't rejecting me, she is rejecting marriage to a nobleman.
The mere thought of becoming a duchess for the second time
terrifies her!*

He had always known what Hamilton was. It was the reason
he'd never dared allow himself to picture her with James. He
forced himself to do it now. Beth had been such a delightful
free spirit when they first met. He contrasted that with the
serene *façade* of the Duchess of Hamilton. She had been like a
puppet, a perfect doll James kept at his side as if she were an
ornament. *I knew she feared her mother. Why didn't I see that
her fear of Hamilton almost paralyzed her?*

John ground his teeth in anguish at the abject fear Beth must
have felt when she learned that she was carrying his child. *For
her own survival she had to pretend her baby was her husband's. She did a convincing job; James swaggered with pride
over Jamie.* He went to the window and threw the casement
wide. *Hamilton thrived on control. Once Beth had a child,
James had the perfect means to control her every move.* He
smashed his fist on the stone sill. *Christ Almighty, I tried to use
Jamie to control her! To use a child as a pawn is uncon-
scionable.* An inner voice mocked: *And she had the guts to defy
you.* John laughed at his own folly.

Elizabeth was awakened by a knock. When she slipped from
the big bed where they'd all slept, Jamie and Emma also
roused.

"It's Mr. Burke. I've brought you breakfast."

"Leave it outside the door," she instructed warily.

"I also have a message, ma'am. Your coach and driver are
ready at your convenience in the courtyard."

She opened the door. "Mr. Burke, do I have your word that

this is not a trick? That I am free to leave and take my son with me?"

"You have my word, Your Grace."

With hot food in their bellies and their warmest garments on their backs, the trio descended the turret stairs, followed by Dandy and servants carrying their trunks. Elizabeth felt relief when she saw her waiting coach but stiffened when she saw John Campbell.

He walked toward them across the courtyard. "Beth, I humbly apologize." He handed her a letter.

She took it then deliberately let it flutter to the flagstones before she stepped up into the carriage. She did not see Jamie scoop it up before Emma lifted him into her waiting arms, but she was aghast when her son waved and shouted, "Bye-bye, Daddy!"

"He is *not*—" Elizabeth pressed her lips together and set Jamie on the leather seat beside the dog, then she tucked the dark blue-and-green Campbell plaid about him. She cast Emma an accusing glance.

"I never told him. He's just wishful thinking."

As the driver released the brake, Elizabeth turned her head away from John Campbell and looked in the opposite direction. She held her breath, still half expecting him to prevent their leaving.

At Strone the carriage stopped so they could enjoy the lunch that had been packed for them in a big basket. The coachman watered the horses and sat down on the grass to eat his food. Elizabeth allowed Jamie and Dandy to have a good run while she picked a purple sprig of Highland heather, then they piled back into the coach for the long journey ahead. As the carriage swayed, she absently lifted the heather to her nose. *This is too easy!*

In the afternoon the sky became overcast. Though the wind kept the rain off, evening would close in early. She entertained Jamie with a game of animal-spotting. Sheep and cattle were too numerous to count but they saw many deer, a few foxes, and, when they neared water, saw playful otters. As if she had a warning premonition, Beth occasionally glanced back along the road. The third time she looked she saw something in the distance that could possibly be a rider. The hair on the nape of her neck began to prickle, but she told herself to stop being fanciful.

Emma dozed and finally Jamie's eyelids closed. When the road curved, Elizabeth again took the opportunity to look back. This time there was no mistaking the darkly cloaked rider mounted on a black horse. She cursed beneath her breath: *I knew it was too easy. Damn you to hellfire, John Campbell!* She glanced back at ten-minute intervals, glad that the rider did not seem to be gaining on them. Just before the afternoon light left the sky, a drizzling rain started to fall.

The driver stopped to have a word with her. "The town of Arrochar lies about five miles ahead. There's a good inn, Your Grace. Would you like to stop for the night?"

"No, no . . . I'd rather go on. And could you pick up the pace a little? I don't expect to get all the way to Dunbarton tonight, but perhaps we could get to Luss on Loch Lomond?"

Dusk fell, making it impossible for Elizabeth to see if the rider still followed, but she felt his presence in her bones. She hoped the rain would make him take shelter at Arrochar or at least slow him down. After two hours Jamie awoke. "Have to pee."

"Can't you hold it a little while longer?"

"No!"

She opened the picnic basket and took out a cup. Emma opened her eyes and shifted about to get more comfortable.

"I peed in the cup, Emma!" Jamie informed her.

"I hope your mother doesn't expect me to do the same."

"I'm sorry. We're going to stop at the town of Luss—it can't be much farther." She bit her lip. "I think he's following us."

When they arrived at the inn, someone came out for their luggage while their driver saw to his horses. Elizabeth paid for three rooms, hoping they were the last ones available. When she went upstairs she made sure that the keys actually locked the doors.

Elizabeth ordered supper for Emma and Jamie, then she washed her face and brushed her hair. After their food came, she handed Emma the room key. "Lock the door after me and don't open it to anyone while I'm gone." She went down to the common room and ordered some mulled wine, then she waited for him. *I know him too well—cold rain and darkness won't deter him.* By the time she had finished the wine, her blood was warm and her temper hot. She was ready, nay, she was *eager* for the coming confrontation!

It took only a half hour for the traveler to arrive. As the innkeeper went out to the yard to welcome the man and direct his hostler to tend his stallion, Elizabeth went rigid with tension.

The tall, dark Scot stepped through the inn door and swept off his rain-soaked cape. As his hand brushed back the wet black hair from his face, Elizabeth stood transfixed. *It isn't him!*

The man gave her a long, appreciative look then nodded.

She was at a complete loss. The disappointment she felt was staggering. *What the devil is the matter with me? I should be immensely relieved!* She told herself she was disappointed because she'd been deprived of a fight, but her innate honesty asserted itself. *Admit the truth: You were secretly flattered at the thought of Campbell following you to beg you to change your mind.* Elizabeth sat for awhile, as if she were still waiting. The rain stopped, and some of the townspeople arrived for their weekly get-together. She was lost in thought and didn't notice the curious stares she received. When a piper began a lively skirl and people began to laugh, she came out of her reverie and retreated upstairs.

Emma unlocked the door. "Well?" she asked expectantly.

"It . . . it wasn't him." Elizabeth sounded forlorn.

"Then your worries are over." Emma sounded sardonic.

"Oh, Jamie, you mustn't let Dandy have paper—he'll chew it up and choke." She bent down and took away the envelope that the pair were using to play tug-of-war. She saw her name, *Beth,* written on it. She opened it and saw that it was from John. Her legs weak as she sat down to read the letter.

Elizabeth:

When I asked you to be my wife, I did not wish to marry the Duchess of Hamilton. I wanted Elizabeth Gunning, the Titania who first stole my heart. Rather than a beautiful ornament, I wanted a woman who would be an equal partner in my life. The quality I most admire is courage. I am happy you have acquired it in abundance.

I am confident you also have the intelligence and
integrity to look after your son's interests, so I
relinquish any claim to him. You have earned the right
to direct your own life and make your own decisions.
Though disconsolate that I am not included in your
future, I understand and will respect your decision. I am
returning the love token you gave me, so you will
believe that I set you free.

John Campbell

Beth quickly tore open the envelope and the bright curl he
had cut from her hair fell into her hand. As she looked down at
it, a lump came into her throat. The letter had a postscript:

P.S. If you or your son ever need my help in any way,
send me the brass button from my uniform.

The curl reminded her of the one she had cut from Charlotte's hair to give to William. Beth realized that she was still
wearing the jade-green habit that had once belonged to her dear
friend. Her eyes flooded with tears. "Oh, Charlie, you and Will
were so much in love, and your time together was so short."
Beth was completely undone. She glanced up at Emma and realized she had spoken aloud.

Emma searched Elizabeth's face and saw the teardrops
sparkling on her eyelashes. When she smiled, Emma's heart
filled with joy.

"I shall leave you alone with your thoughts. The piping and
laughter below are irresistible. I think I'll join the revelers."

A short time later, when Emma had struck up a conversation
with the Scots in the common room and enjoyed a few glasses
of wine, she decided to satisfy their avid curiosity about her
mistress. It seemed that everyone wanted to know who she was,
and where she was going. "She is Elizabeth, Duchess of Hamilton, on her way to marry the future Duke of Argyll," Emma
confided importantly.

Early the next morning, the inn yard was filled with curious
spectators. As Elizabeth climbed into her carriage and turned to
take Jamie from Emma's arms, the people cheered. As the

coach drove north, the townspeople of Luss stood on the road, waving as she passed. "Emma, why are all these people here?"

"One thing's certain: Your mother hasn't paid this lot!"

"But who are they, and why are they cheering me?"

"They are your audience, of course, and they are applauding your brilliant decision to marry a Highland Scot."

It was long after dark when the coach pulled into Inveraray Castle's courtyard. Emma was weary from travel, and Jamie was sound asleep on the seat. Elizabeth, however, was breathless with nervous anticipation as the carriage pulled to a stop. She opened the door hesitantly and tentatively set her foot down on the iron step.

Suddenly, powerful arms enfolded her and lifted her high. John had been waiting for hours and had given up hope. "Sweetheart, I swear I'll never take you for granted again!"

"Oh, John, hold me close."

He set her feet to the ground and held her captive against his heart. He bent his head and brushed his lips against her hair. "Beth, thank God you came . . . I couldn't live without you."

She heard the steady thud of his heart beneath her ear and knew she had at last come home, where she had always belonged.

Emma closed her eyes, happy, relieved, but too tired to move.

Elizabeth lifted her head from his chest. "Help me with Jamie."

John moved into the carriage and, wrapping the Campbell plaid closely about his son, picked up the child with tender, loving hands, revealing how much he cherished the bairn. "Would you like me to come back and carry you, Emma?" he murmured.

"I can manage, my lord. Though I wouldn't say no to Mr. Burke!"

With Elizabeth at his side, John carried Jamie into his own turret where the child had slept before. He watched Beth undress their son and tuck him into bed, bemused that he never even opened his eyes. He turned the lamp low and held out his hand.

Elizabeth placed her hand in his, and they ascended the

stairs to John's chambers. He led her to the leather couch before the fire and removed her cloak. Then he knelt down to take off her boots.

"I took Jamie, knowing you would follow. I never meant to keep him . . . that doesn't make it right, though. I thought I was showing you my strength, but instead I was revealing my weakness."

"I want us always to be your weakness," Elizabeth said honestly.

"While I'm down here I'm going to ask you again to marry me, but I want you to know what you're getting yourself into. Tomorrow, on the afternoon tide I have to set sail for Kintyre to recruit sailors, after that I sail to Mull, Morven, and Tyrie. I'll be gone a month, and I'm asking you to come with me. The fishing villages are barren, windswept places even in summer. Now that it's late in the season the weather may get fierce and bitter. The villagers' homes are humble, their lives often bleak. I want you to come with me, Beth, because you know what it's like to go hungry. You know what it's like to have only a smock to wear. They will feel your empathy and know you are not looking down your nose at them."

"Of course I will come with you."

He held up a warning hand to show he wasn't finished. "As well as being a professional soldier, I am also heir to Argyll. As sure as night follows day, you will become a double duchess, and there will be many times when you will have to attend Court in silks and jewels. You will have to divide your time between London and Scotland. There are times when we will have to entertain lavishly, but there also will be precious, private times we can share to laugh and love and make more babies. Will you marry me? Tonight?"

"Yes. Yes, I will!"

He kissed her fingers. "Come, I'd like to inform my parents."

Elizabeth gasped. "Oh, must I? Can't you do it alone?"

His voice softened. "You sound afraid."

"I am," she whispered.

He pulled her to her feet and slipped a possessive arm about her. "I love to watch you display your courage."

She took a deep breath and accompanied him to the master turret. It felt like the longest walk she'd ever taken.

Mary Campbell opened the chamber door to admit the couple who were so obviously in love. The Duke of Argyll sat before the fire with his crippled leg propped before him. The look on both their faces was eager and expectant.

"I have asked Elizabeth to marry me, and she has accepted."

"Congratulations, John. This is marvelous news!" Mary's face beamed with genuine happiness.

"Come, lass, let's ha' a look at ye," Argyll demanded.

With John's hand at the small of her back, Elizabeth approached Argyll. She felt shy and unbelievably young.

Argyll looked his fill then nodded. "I think ye've met yer match, Campbell." He winked at his daughter-to-be.

"We're getting married tonight in the chapel."

His mother's face showed her objection. "No, no, you must have a proper wedding. A formal wedding before the whole clan!"

John firmly shook his head. "Even if Beth were willing to wait, I'm not. We'll say our vows tonight and sail tomorrow."

Mary looked at Elizabeth. "Argyll men are so bloody dominant."

Elizabeth smiled. *He's putty in my hands.*

John ushered her through the door then turned back for a word with his mother. "I'll try to talk her into a formal wedding when we get back. I'm an Argyll male: When domination fails, our powers of persuasion are formidable. It just takes a little time with willful females." He kissed his mother's cheek and winked at his father. "I'd wait forever, but my bride is insatiable!"

Burning incense masked the damp smell of the chapel, and tall, tapered candles cast their flickering glow over the couple who stood before the altar exchanging their sacred marriage vows. Elizabeth, in amethyst velvet, carried purple heather. John, wearing his Campbell kilt, held his bride's hand tightly and solemnly gave her his pledge.

"Elizabeth, wilt thou have this mon tae thy wedded husband, tae live together after God's ordinance in the holy estate of matrimony? Wilt thou obey him, and serve him, love, honor, and keep him, in sickness and in health; and, forsaking all other, keep thee only untae him, so long as ye both shall live?"

John felt her hand tremble and knew how much courage it took for Elizabeth to put the control of her life into a man's hands.

"I will." Her clear voice showed no hesitation.

"Who giveth this woman tae be married tae this mon?"

When Mr. Burke stepped forward, she gave him a tremulous smile.

"I, John, take thee, Elizabeth, to my wedded wife, to have and to hold from this day forward, for better for worse, for richer for poorer, in sickness and in health, to love and to cherish, till death us do part, according to God's holy ordinance; and thereto I give thee my troth."

Elizabeth was surprised when the wide gold band he slipped on her finger fit her exactly. *How long has he had this ring?*

John looked into her eyes. "With this ring I thee wed, with my body I thee honor, and with all my worldly goods I thee endow."

When they were pronounced husband and wife, Emma surreptitiously wiped away a tear at the obvious love they gave each other.

Their lips clung briefly in a chaste kiss, and as they turned from the altar, Elizabeth saw that the Duke and Duchess of Argyll stood at the back of the chapel to watch the ceremony. As the newlyweds reached John's parents, Mary enfolded her new daughter in her arms. "When you sail tomorrow, will you entrust Jamie to me?"

"Yes, but he can be an imp of Satan," his mother warned.

The duchess smiled. "Rather like my own son when he was a boy."

Argyll winked. "Come, Grandma, ye should be abed at this hour."

Handclasped, the bridal couple quickened their pace as they left the chapel and made their way to their own turret. They glanced in at Jamie and laughed when they saw he hadn't moved since they'd put him to bed two hours ago.

John swept Beth into his arms and carried her up the stone turret stairs. "I've loved you forever, Elizabeth Campbell."

"That's Lady Sundridge, if you don't mind." She bit his ear.

He grinned down at her. "I don't mind. Never before has a *duchess* stepped down so gracefully to the rank of *lady*."

"I'll never really be a lady," she whispered seductively.

"I'll hold you to that promise, my *Irish wildcat!*" He carried her across the threshold and set her feet to the carpet, intending to kiss her, but she gleefully darted away from him across the sitting room toward the bedchamber. "I need a head start."

He stalked her slowly, savoring the moment. When he entered his chamber she was standing in the middle of his bed unbuttoning her gown. "Damnation, I want the pleasure of undressing you!"

She came down into his waiting arms in a flurry of petticoats. As she yielded her mouth to his, her hands slipped beneath his kilt and cupped his bare buttocks. "Highland savage!" she teased.

He groaned his pleasure against her lips, thanking the gods that this exquisitely beautiful woman, who had laughter and passion in abundance, was his at last. "You've given me a merry chase and no doubt will continue to do so, but I wouldn't want you any other way." John undressed her slowly, savoring the moment, yet when they were at last naked, neither of them could control the fierce desire they'd held in check for what felt like forever.

The second loving was drawn out as the groom paid homage to his bride's beauty. "I love the feel of your hair. It slides like golden silk through my fingers and cascades down upon my chest." His lips glided from the nape of her neck, down the curve of her back, then pressed kisses on her bottom cheeks. He changed her position from prone to supine and, starting at her toes, moved up her legs and thighs, tasting every inch of her luscious flesh.

Her response was more generous than in his wildest dreams. *Lord God, how she makes me quiver!* "I long to draw out my lovemaking all night, but our passion is far too hot for such control." When they spent together it was achingly perfect.

They lay replete in each other's arms and whispered about their future. "Your parents know Jamie is your son."

"They're not blind, sweetheart."

"Do you think they resent him being the Duke of Hamilton?"

He kissed her brow. "Of course not, love. The Douglas-Hamilton clan is renowned for its fierce strength and dauntless courage. I will teach Jamie its glorious history, and together we'll make sure he grows up to be a worthy leader of his Border clans."

"I've never left him for more than a night before."

"It will be difficult for both of you, but he's going to have to learn to share you. He'll be safe here. The young devil already has Mr. Burke eating out of his hand, and by the time we return he'll have my parents' heartstrings wrapped around his fingers."

She brushed her cheek against his heart. "I know he'll be safe." Elizabeth herself had never felt safer in her life, and it wasn't entirely because of Argyll's wealth and power. She was secure in John Campbell's unconditional love. He had put her wishes before what he wanted for himself. Because of his deep and abiding love, he had offered to set her free. Beth smiled her secret smile. *My heart will never be free of him.*

Early the next morning, when John opened his eyes and saw her beside him in the bed, his heart overflowed with happiness, and his spirits were high. He leaned over to kiss her and offered a tempting suggestion. "While we're still in Argyll, why don't we try for another son?"

She pushed him back onto his own pillow and came over him in the dominant position, her eyes glittering with mischief. She raised his arms above his head and kissed the black birthmark in his armpit. "What will you do if he doesn't have the mark of Argyll?"

"Beat you to a jelly, of course."

"Ye'll need a stout stick fer that. D'ye have one, laddie?"

John raised his head to look down at his jutting arousal, then he erupted in a roar of laughter. While he had slept, Elizabeth had been busy with her black beauty patches. She had stuck one next to a flat nipple, one beside his navel, and one above his cock. As he watched her lick her lips, he shook his head and surrendered. "Madam, I am undone!"

Author's Note

Elizabeth Gunning outlived her sister, Maria, by thirty years. Maria died in 1760 of consumption. Her health had been impaired by the use of white lead face paint.

William Cavendish, Duke of Devonshire, returned from Ireland and became Prime Minister of England, with William Pitt as his Minister of War.

Elizabeth became the Duchess of Argyll upon the old duke's death, and John Campbell, her husband, rose to the rank of general in His Majesty's forces before the Seven Year War with France ended. After their marriage they had two sons and two daughters.

King George II died in 1760, and when George III came to the throne, Elizabeth was chosen to accompany the king's bride, Princess Charlotte, to England. Elizabeth was then appointed a lady of the bedchamber to England's new queen.